THE MOONRISE OF WOLVES

INFINITE ARTIFACTS TRILOGY

KAITLIN R MARESCA

THE MOONRISE OF WOLVES

Book Cover Design by Mariska Maas

Editing by Eden Northover & Megan Harris

Interior Formatting by Brittany Wilson

ISBN-13 (paperback): 979-8-9903902-0-1

ISBN-13 (eBook): 979-8-9903902-2-5

To anyone who has sought books in exchange for friendships—you are seen.

XX

Chapter 1

Change was inevitable, and dreams were easy until they came true. My fingernails dug into my palms at this constant reminder, the pain a welcome distraction. I heaved large, controlled breaths until I no longer felt trapped in my own skin. As the realization sunk in, I leaped from where I stood, squealing.

Dear Maris,

Congratulations! You have been accepted to Johns Hopkins University—a place where...

I had not expected this today. I applied back in November, and it's now halfway through March. My mind whirled as I reread the first sentence. After years of late nights bent over books, wondering if it would be worth it, it finally amounted to something. I was going to go to college. I was finally leaving. Squealing again, I grinned like a fool before the sizzling high faded, plonking onto the hardened mattress.

This was the only home I knew: Crescent Falls, New York. Yet the pull my soul felt to leave this town was a heavy weight to carry; after all, my friends, family, and all that was familiar to me were here. My older brother Luka, too, and aside from my own uncertainties, he was why I waited two years after graduating from community college to pursue a bachelor's degree. Growing up, we only had each other, and Luka leaned on me more heavily than he realized. The thought of leaving him made me afraid.

Metal screeched as the garage door creaked open. Sitting up on Derek's hard bed, I fiddled with the frills on one of his pillows. He asked me to meet him at his place with no context as to why, which meant he could want a triage of things. I had not expected to receive my acceptance letter today, but I was glad I was here when I did. Derek was the only person who knew I applied; it only felt right to tell him the news.

Derek ducked under the half-open garage door with an ear-splitting grin, clutching large paper bags to his body. Catching my gaze, he raised his eyebrows, slight amusement glinting in his pine-green eyes.

"Maris," he chirped. "You seem—"

"Depressed, confused, nursing an ever-present headache that is my life?"

Derek chuckled as he fully entered his small studio apartment, shutting the garage door behind him. "Studio apartment" was a generous way of putting it. In truth, Derek lived in a two-bedroom house with two other roommates and pulled the short straw when it came to their living arrangements. The person before him up and left rather quickly, leaving only a strange collection of daggers behind, but Derek never complained about living cooped up in the garage. He moved in four years ago, having nowhere else to go, and at eighteen, he made the most of it. All he needed was a couch and a TV for his video games, but I eventually convinced him he needed a bed if he ever expected to get laid. We even managed to squeeze in a desk and coffee table, too, and despite the cramped interior, this place always felt like a part of me.

Derek set his bags down on the coffee table and began rifling through them. "Lucky for you, I have just the cure for all of those things," Derek said, walking toward me with a tall clear cup that rattled with ice.

I tossed the pillow aside and sat up straighter. "Coffee?"

Derek grinned as he handed it to me. "One oat milk latte with blonde espresso and an extra shot." He wrinkled his nose as I took a long sip.

"Hey, don't knock it till you try it."

"Where would I be if I wasn't judging your coffee choices?" He smirked.

Derek was like the spare piece of my soul, having lingered too long in darkness before finally finding the light. We met five years ago when Derek was hired as a new waiter at my brother's bar. Derek simply showed up one day with his purple-tipped hair, looking for work, yet his initial shyness was like throwing him to the wolves. The other employees, Rico and Renetta, were employed at the bar before Luka even owned it, and they didn't take well to strangers or newbies. While they were never unkind, they weren't welcoming either. So, I took him under my wing until he eventually became the guy who could make me laugh with only a look.

Barely any traces remained of the lanky boy I met five years ago. Derek grew out his color-streaked hair to his natural white-blond, spiking it up where it was longer on the top. His frame had filled out to accommodate the layers of muscles packed on at the gym, and his once loose-fitting clothes now hugged his frame. In many ways, he still reminded me of the shy anxious boy I met five years ago.

Turning away, Derek practically bounced toward the other bags on the table.

"Are you okay?" I asked, getting up and following him.

"That's always up for interpretation," he grumbled, continuing his digging.

I laughed, sitting beside him on the dingy red couch that reeked of old cigarettes and cheap booze. Derek promised to reupholster it, but that was three years ago. The idea was lost along with his many other unfinished projects. His littered desk was proof of that—a graveyard of hobbies scattered with thousand-pieced puzzles, yarn, sewing needles, and a half-painted canvas with various jars of paint.

He pulled out a bundled-up newspaper and flattened the worn pages across the table. I leaned forward, trailing my fingers across the pages—old and musty, like dried oil.

"What are these?" I asked, leaning back and sipping my coffee.

I pushed my college acceptance letter to the back of my mind. Whatever this was, Derek desperately wanted to speak about it. He leaned back and braced his hands on his knees.

"Okay. I know I was going to give it a break, but I couldn't resist." His hesitation told me all I needed to know.

"Derek," I groaned.

"I know, I know." He raised his hands in surrender. "These are a bunch of old newspapers from the town they last disappeared in. They might mention something useful."

The desperate whine in his voice won out.

Thirteen years ago, Derek's father took his older brother and left. Three years later, both were found dead. His father set ablaze the house they were found in, lighting himself on fire with his already dead child inside. The law ruled it a murder-suicide.

However, the reports had inconsistencies. The police claimed his brother had been dead for five days before the fire, while the autopsy stated two weeks. The stories of how they were found varied, too. Some reports claimed the neighbors called the police, while others said the police found the scene unexpectedly.

Derek was desperate to know the truth. His mom died from a heart attack when he was eighteen, meaning there was no one left to remember or talk about them anymore, and very soon after, he spiraled. Yet his discoveries, if you could call them that, had been coming less and less frequently.

"These papers are all from the town they were found in," Derek said animatedly, spreading the papers across the table. "We already know that the crime rate in the town and surrounding areas was next to nothing. So, you would think a murder-suicide would be a *huge* deal."

"Okay, I'm following," I said, watching him closely.

"Well, recently, I found a local newspaper that's super lowkey. I never thought to check the local sources because I focused only on the bigger news outlets. Silly mistake on my part because," Derek paused, flicking through the newspapers until finding the right page, "there's a local interview with someone stating to have seen them days before they disappeared."

Derek often referred to the tragedy as a disappearance; he rarely spoke like they were dead. I shuffled closer to him and painted on a smile, hoping this could bring him a step closer to the peace he desperately needed.

"That's great, Derek," I tried.

"This is my first solid lead, I think." He grinned.

"What does it say?"

Derek leaned over to skim the pages. "Not a whole lot. He says that he watched them move in and wasn't shocked to hear there was foul play involved. There are some mentions of him claiming to have watched my dad hit my brother, but that's total bullshit because my dad was never like that."

I scrunched my eyebrows together. "How is that a lead?"

"Oh, they mentioned the guy by name. Zayne Meyers, twenty-six of Fort Lauderdale, Florida," Derek added. "All I have to do is find him, and if I do, I want to contact him to see if he can recall more details."

I felt his light green gaze sense my hesitation before I spoke. "Derek, I don't think you should be contacting strangers."

"No, no—it'll be super safe!" he said, pulling his laptop out. "This is my first lead to some real answers."

"Your mom never mentioned it? Not even a hint of what happened to them?" I asked, and not for the first time.

"She never spoke a word about them. Not even on her deathbed."

With the bite in Derek's tone, I let the topic drop. Over the next few hours, I scrolled through my phone and occasionally pointed things out to Derek, all the while distracted by the life-changing information I possessed. I didn't know how to process my college acceptance, but I knew I had to tell him. Derek was the only one who knew I applied; it was only right that he knew first.

"I got in," I muttered.

Slouched over his computer, with his glasses falling down the bridge of his nose, Derek looked up with wide eyes. "You got in?"

I handed my phone to him, unable to stop the grin spreading across my face as Derek brought the screen closer, reading over the words at dazzling speed.

"Oh my god, you got in!" he exclaimed, jumping up.

I was barely able to stand before Derek pulled me fiercely to him. "I got in," I echoed, words muffled against his shoulder.

Derek's hand untangled from my hair as I stepped back, my grin faltering. "What is it?" he asked.

If it were anyone else, I may have hesitated in answering, but to him, I said, "I don't know what I'm going to do."

Derek nodded. "Because of Luka?"

I exhaled, thinking of my brother. "Yes. It should be an easy choice, but its *Luka*..."

"Luka wouldn't—ah, I can't even pretend like I mean it," Derek said. "I'd like to think Luka would understand after the initial shock wears off."

I laughed aloud at that. "You've met Luka, right?"

"He means well, you know that," Derek said. "He just comes off strong."

Derek and Luka were friends, too, because of their shared interest in keeping me safe. In their bubble of paranoia, they were a united front against unseen threats and foes, and while I mostly didn't mind, sometimes they were suffocating.

My phone buzzed, and a text from Luka lit the screen. "Speak of the devil," I muttered.

Derek pulled out the keys to his truck and raised his eyebrows in silent question.

"I ought to get going before it gets late and he *really* flips his lid," I said, grabbing my shoes. "I'm twenty-two and I already took two years off after my degree to save up. Luka must know this is coming, right?"

"I think this is a conversation you need to have with him." Derek opened the garage door, twirling his keys around his finger while waiting for me to leave.

"Yeah, I know. I just figured I would ask you since you're his friend, too."

Derek huffed a laugh. "It's hard to be friends with someone who puts the fear of god into you on a daily basis."

"He isn't *that* bad," I tried.

"Maybe not to his little baby sister."

Luka was complicated, but for valid reasons. Our mother passed away before I turned three, and then when I hit nine, our father left us. At age fifteen, Luka chose to raise me whilst battling through his traumas. He had a harshness to him, though I liked to think I mellowed him out to some degree, and while he never made me feel indebted for his sacrifices, he suffocated me with his overprotectiveness. Even attending a regular high school was a concern, and instead, he demanded homeschooling me, only conceding after I fought him tooth and nail on it.

Derek held open the door of his old beat-up truck, and I slid across the worn, brown leather. He pushed the keys into the ignition and twisted, the engine clicking on repeat.

"No, no, no. Don't do this to me, Rosie," he whined. Rosie was the name he gave his truck.

"Here we go again." I sighed. "Derek, I think you need to take this into a garage for real."

He scoffed. "It's not worth it to keep pouring money into her, but she'll come back. The cold weather's put her in a bad temper, that's all." He continued to twist the ignition, pumping his gas in the process, and after a minute, the engine roared to life.

"This truck is going to get us killed one day. I hope you know that."

My phone buzzed again. Luka. Rolling my eyes, I pressed answer, but the phone slipped from my grip as we hit a pothole. I groaned and reached under the seat.

"Hang on, Luka," I shouted, hoping he'd hear me through the receiver.

"Luka?" Derek asked, glancing over. "What are you doing?"

"Luka's on the phone, but I dropped—" I looked straight ahead. "Derek, look out!"

A large wolf stood in the middle of the road, lip curled and blood dripping from its jowls. I screamed as it rose to its full height, its dark fur glinting against the headlights as the truck hurtled at the beast. I locked eyes with the wolf, frozen by its piercing golden glare until it lunged away.

Derek cursed and flung the steering wheel to the left. The truck spun out of control, and I gripped the seat as Derek scrambled to realign the wheel. As he slammed down on the brakes, the seat belt jerked me to a stop.

We both sat in stunned silence.

"Are you okay?" Derek asked.

I swallowed the dryness in my throat and peeled my tongue from the roof of my mouth. "Yes, just—yes." After a moment, I asked, "What was that?"

"We almost hit a bear," said Derek, still shaken. He turned to look me in the eyes. "It was just a bear."

I replayed the events that unfolded moments ago: the creature on all fours, with big jowls and blood dripping from it. "A bear? No, that was a wolf. A *huge* wolf."

A half-smile played on his lips as he continued staring at me. "Wolf? Please. When was the last time this town had wolves?"

"No, I'm telling you. That was a wolf. It practically jumped right at us!"

"Bears are way more common around here, and you know it. You're the one who bought me the can of bear spray, remember?" Derek's nonchalant tone had me rolling my eyes. "What matters is we're both safe."

Logically, Derek was right. Wolf sightings were near impossible on this side of New York, but bears were more common. Maybe it was a bear. I'd only seen it for a millisecond before we almost crashed.

I nodded and reached to grab my phone. The call with Luka had disconnected, which meant he heard enough, hung up, and was likely halfway here.

We drove the rest of the journey in silence. Maybe Derek was right. It made sense for it to have been a bear. While it was not something to worry over, I couldn't shake the feeling in my gut.

Derek pulled into the driveway and slowly approached my house. Surrounded by huge, burly pine trees, you would never know a house lay beyond, almost two miles from the road. It was the only house for miles, but Luka relished the seclusion.

The house belonged to our mother, and after she died and Dad left, the property was left to Luka and me. Legally, Luka owned it, but we both contributed to the bills—another thing we fought over, with Luka refusing to take my money until he eventually conceded.

The two-story house came into view, illuminated by the floodlights surrounding the wraparound porch. They were bright enough to high-light every speck of dirt and dust on the dashboard as Derek pulled the car to the end of the driveway behind Luka's black Jeep. His expression was stark as he fumbled with his seat belt. He cursed and got out while I quickly unbuckled my seatbelt. The moment my feet hit the ground, Luka sprang into action.

Yeah. He knew Derek almost crashed the truck with me in it.

I halted my steps, and Derek skidded to a stop.

Luka moved swiftly, shrouded in the shadows, his nostrils flaring like a bull. His onyx hair was a mess, sticking out in all directions, and as he drew his shoulders back, he rose to full height, his hands balled into fists by his sides. Luka's dark sapphire eyes assessed me before flicking to Derek.

"Maris, get inside." Luka's voice held a note of chilling calm that frightened me more than his shouting.

"No," I argued. "It was only a bear in the road; it wasn't something Derek could have controlled."

Luka spun toward me. "I told you to go inside."

"And I told you *no*," I spat, crossing my arms over my chest.

"Maris, maybe—" Derek began, but Luka's growl cut him off.

"I'm only going to tell you this one more time. Get inside and lock the doors. I'm not in the mood to do this with you."

His eyes glazed over in an icy rage, his posture stiff and unyielding. I understood the accident could have ended much worse, but this reaction seemed extreme, even by Luka's standards. When I came home with bruised and bloodied knees from a fall on a run, his reaction was much milder.

"Luka, please," I begged. I held his gaze until he jerked his attention back to Derek.

"Maris." Authority rippled through his tone.

The argument was over. I stormed up the stone pathway, rallying a string of profanities, and rammed my foot into our old garden gnome. Jamming my key into the door, I quickly locked it behind me, setting my keys on the small crescent-shaped dish, and discarded my boots.

I padded into the living room and yanked open the curtains, but Luka and Derek had already vanished. I pulled the curtains back into place, flicking lights on as I passed. I plopped onto the leather couch and rested my feet on the wooden coffee table. The TV mounted over the fireplace hummed, and I clicked the volume up with the remote. A female news reporter stood in the center of Crescent Falls.

"A recent and deadly animal attack on Richard Jameson, a local business owner, has the town of Crescent Falls worried and on edge. At this time of year, events like this are unheard of in such a small borough of New York. It is unclear what kind of animal attacked Mr. Jameson in his own backyard, but local authorities wish to assure the public that everything is being managed and there is no need for concern. Coming up next: are unprecedented weather storms heading our way?"

"That's weird, isn't it?"

I nearly jumped out of my skin and whirled to see Luka. I hadn't heard him approach, ever the silent assailant. Leaning against the kitchen door frame, a small, crooked smile played on his face. His range of moods always baffled me.

"You scared the shit out of me!" I tossed a pillow at him, and he caught it casually, his movement a blur. Walking into the room, he chucked the pillow back at my head and slunk onto the recliner across from me.

"Haven't I taught you to be more vigilant about your surroundings?"

"Yeah, yeah," I grumbled, sinking further into the couch. "Where did Derek go?"

"I sent him on his way," Luka said. "He was lucky his reaction time was up to par and his brakes weren't shoddy."

"It wasn't his fault," I argued. "It could have happened to anyone."

"It didn't. It happened to you," Luka said, an edge to his voice. He cleared his throat and nodded toward the TV, eyebrows raised. "Since when have you watched the news? Don't you have like fifteen seasons of that medical drama to catch up on?"

"The TV was on when I came in," I replied. "I assumed you were watching it, keeping tabs on the local criminals. Though now I guess it's animals you need to be mindful of."

Luka narrowed his eyes at me. "I wouldn't worry too much about it. The news likes to hype up small things to make people more paranoid than they should be."

I snorted. "Are you talking about the news or yourself?"

He rolled his eyes, leaning back in the recliner. "Watch it."

Neither of us spoke for a while as I flicked through channels, Luka's earlier behavior eating away at my curiosity. Luka was a livewire and quick to judge, but this reaction was odd for him. Plus, I needed to tell him of my college acceptance letter. I made a fist, digging my fingernails into my palm.

"Are you working tomorrow?" Luka asked.

"Tomorrow is Saturday," I said absentmindedly. "Also, Renetta asked me to work a double, so I won't be home until late."

"Oh, *did* she?"

"You're the one who fired Sam, the first semi-decent waiter we've had in ages," I argued. "She asked me to cover."

I worked at the only bar in Crescent Falls; Luka had owned it since he was my age, overseeing the bar's needs but rarely stepping inside the building. While I didn't have to worry about the complexities of working with my brother, it was awkward when most of the staff grumbled about his disdain for them all. I had never witnessed it, but it wasn't hard to imagine.

"I think you should call in," Luka said.

I whipped my head to look at him. "Are you kidding me?"

"No," he said calmly as if his words made perfect sense. "Things have felt weird lately, and I don't want you out on your own. It doesn't feel safe."

"That's ridiculous, and you know it," I snapped. He started to reply, but I cut him off. "No, don't start. I understand your anxiety over me being in mortal peril, but there just comes a time when I have to draw the line." I gave him a pointed look. "Does this have anything to do with why you were angry earlier?"

Luka stayed silent, his expression unreadable. When he finally spoke, his words sounded calculated. "Look, you know how things were growing up. It wasn't easy. Because of that, your safety is my priority."

"Safe from what?" I protested. Anger rushed through me at his skill for evading questions. "What are you going to do when I leave for college?"

Luka stood, and I wished the words hadn't come out in anger. But had he expected me to live with him forever? He was the one who encouraged me to go to a community college; he was the one who helped me with my studies and talked me off a ledge when I wanted to drop out. This shouldn't come as a surprise.

"Luka, I don't want to be serving people my whole life," I said, standing, too. "I always planned to go back eventually."

He appeared somber when he answered. "I don't know. I didn't expect you to want to leave."

"You know it's not that simple." I shook my head. "It's not been an easy decision. I only got the confirmation today—"

"Confirmation?" He gave me a sidelong look.

I took a deep breath, wishing I could have done this differently. "I should have told you I was applying for schools but I was afraid of your reaction. I couldn't tell you unless it was actually happening, and then today, I got into Johns Hopkins University to continue my education to become a nurse."

Any reply Luka might have said seemed to deflate from him. Resting his hands behind his head, he peered up at the tall, vaulted ceilings. When he spoke again, his words were clipped. "I can't protect you out there. The world is a dangerous place, filled with more monstrous people than not."

"What do you mean by that?" I pressed. When his silence was my answer, I shook my head. "Luka, I know there are bad people in the world, and I don't know what made you fear it, but I can't let fear consume me like you do."

"I only want to protect you," Luka snapped. "That's all I want!"

"I appreciate that; believe me, I do. But you can't scare me into not going."

We held each other's stare as silence built the tension. Luka's gaze was unyielding, but I could see part of him wanted to tell me the truth of what he was so afraid of. Yet his silence—his need to protect and save me—always won out.

"Fine," he said. "Do what you want."

With that, he rose to his feet, and the slam of the front door echoed through the house.

Chapter 2

I writhed beneath the thick blanket, my limbs tangling around the sheets. A sheen of sweat trickled over my body as vivid images plagued my half-conscious mind. Everything spun out of control, and I barely grasped to reality as the golden eyes of a wolf seared into me in all its terrifying glory. Its bloodied jowls dripped as it stalked closer, and when I opened my mouth to scream, no sound came. As the beast rose on its haunches, a silent scream clawed out of me. I turned to run, then the world turned black.

I shot up, gasping and clutching the blanket to my chest. My hands trembled as I tried steadying my breath, tethering myself back to reality. Night terrors had plagued me since I was ten. Luka got me into the habit of taking melatonin before bed or drinking a hot cup of tea to manage it. Nightmares were his territory, too, which I always chalked up to our unusual shared upbringing. A dead mother and an absent father isn't exactly normal.

Last night, however, I went straight to bed, too furious with Luka to stick to my usual routine. Yet that nightmare hit a little too close to home, considering the beast that ran into the road. Closing my eyes, I counted backward from ten.

It was a bear.

With one last staggering breath, I felt anchored again. I fell back against my pillows and reached for my phone. It was seven-thirty in the morning. With a groan, I sat up and stretched, the gilded morning light glowing through the thin curtains. Yet as I recalled my conversation with Luka last night, I contemplated crawling back under the covers.

I made myself get up. I lingered in the shower until the water ran cold and took the time to comb every tangle in my hair before braiding it back. I crossed to the dresser and rifled through my clothes, my gaze snagging on the small silver frame on my bedside table. The only picture I had of my family.

In the picture, we stand outside the house: Father, Mother, Luka, and me. Luka was eight years old, and I was two. I had no memories of my mother, aside from bits and pieces Luka told me. The picture was old and faded, but Luka said I resembled her: the same brown hair and blue eyes, even the same stubborn attitude. Yet it was strange to look at the photo, knowing the people in it were strangers.

My father's uncanny likeness to Luka unsettled me, and growing up, I had never noticed the resemblance; it was overshadowed by my father's reign of terror. My earliest childhood memory was Luka clutching me tight against a wall, stroking my hair to shield me from our father's rage. I sobbed, watching my brother take the beating intended for me. All my memories were like that. Luka always protected me.

There was no denying the resemblance, though, despite Luka trying not to be or act like him. If there was one thing Luka and I agreed upon, it was our hatred toward our father. Luka even went as far as legally changing our last name from Danika to Bakar, scrubbing any affiliation to our father away.

Coffee aroma drifted through the vents, and I dressed quickly to head downstairs. Knocking myself against the marble kitchen counters, I cursed. A brewing pot of coffee sat on the stove and dishes filled the sink. Luka was awake. Given the early hour, he was probably outside jogging or practicing yoga.

I slid the back porch door open, but it jolted, refusing to budge. I had forgotten about the new security measure Luka installed: a heavy metal pole wedged against the door. It was adequate but unnecessary against the three deadbolts and coded-keypad—his own invention. I yanked it up and walked out into the chilly morning air.

"'I'm still getting used to that pole being there." I squinted at Luka, the sun in full-blaze.

"It's just a precaution," he replied. "In case you're ever home alone and anyone tries to pull some shady shit. Have you gone on your run yet?"

I ran five miles around the property every morning on a path Luka marked for me. Over the years, I'd become quite fast, and most impor-tantly, I enjoyed it. It had become second nature to me now.

"Not yet," I answered.

"Join me first then," he said. "Yoga is good for you."

I walked to where my yoga mat was stored in a gray plastic tub while soft, therapeutic melodies filled the porch from Luka's speakers. He sat cross-legged on a yoga mat, his arms bent and his index fingers touching his thumbs. Every morning, Luka came out and practiced yoga. It helped curb his anger and still his mind. He took up the practice around ten years ago, but I had no clue where he learned it, but whoever taught him taught him well. I've seen Luka balance upside down on only the tips of his fingers.

I settled beside Luka, who moved into downward dog. My flexibility was nothing like his. I only practiced yoga on days when I felt particularly tense, preferring running as an outlet to relieve my stress. Yet tension remained coiled in me after last night's fight. While Luka and I often butted heads, I feared he was adamant in his stance about me going away to college.

"Were you having a nightmare last night?" Luka asked.

"It's not that out of the ordinary." I positioned down on the mat, mirroring his position.

"I know," Luka said. "Do you want to talk about it?"

I huffed a breath and adjusted into a cross-legged position, leaning forward. "Isn't the point of yoga to relax your mind and body?" I asked. Met with silence, I knew it was not well received.

"Maris."

"I just had a nightmare about a wolf chasing me," I said distractedly. "Not that it matters. I wouldn't even call it a nightmare. It was just scary. If anything, it was left over adrenaline from the animal jumping in the road last night."

He paused before saying anything and drew his eyebrows together. I could see the wheels turning in his head. "If you're afraid, the likelihood of a wolf attacking you is pretty slim—they aren't native around here."

Which was why it made sense that it was a bear. Crescent Falls was a town shrouded in trees and beat-up back roads. This time of year, on the cusp of spring, it made sense creatures like bears would be spotted as they emerged from hibernation.

"I'm not afraid. It's a subconscious thing, I think," I said, assuming a neutral sitting position. "At least, I don't think I am."

"Well, it's good to remember they're only dreams," he said, standing. "C'mon. The coffee is probably ready."

Luka held out his hand to help me up, and I eagerly followed him into the kitchen, darting toward the coffeepot. I grabbed two mugs and poured fresh coffee into them, and behind me, I could hear Luka rummaging through the cabinets of pots and pans.

"Do you want eggs or pancakes?"

"Pancakes," I said automatically. It wasn't even a choice.

I peered inside the empty fridge and made a mental note to go shopping as I pulled out the creamers. I dumped two scoops of sugar into my mug and a splash of creamer, and for Luka, a scoop of collagen and almond milk. I handed him the steaming cup while gleefully sipping my own, letting the sweetness fill me with warmth. I slipped into a chair across the room.

"Maris?" Luka said as he placed down the whisk. I looked up. "I'm sorry I got upset with you last night."

I glanced down. I was never fond of blunt confrontations. I hated fighting with Luka. It felt wrong. Last night was a rarity. Besides, we only had each other, and we held onto that. "I'm sorry, too. I shouldn't have sprung it on you like that."

"We can both be kind of hotheaded." He grabbed the whisk and slowly turned it, scrunching his eyebrows together. "I don't know. It's hard for me to draw the lines between our lives."

"What do you mean?"

Luka shook his head, a slight tremor in his hands.

"The way we grew up was so opposite," he said at last. "The hardships I faced aren't something you had to endure, but it's something I worked to keep you from. As you've grown up, it's harder to keep you guarded, and that frustrates me at times."

"I get it," I said, voice low. Luka choosing to raise me meant he sacrificed his own youth, becoming a man overnight. I could not imagine being forced to make the choice that he did. "I really do."

Luka set down the bowl, a smile on his lips. "I never got to tell you congratulations. I've seen how hard you've worked for this, and I am unbelievably proud of all you have achieved." His words were nothing but sincere. "You are becoming the young woman I always hoped you would be."

Emotion swelled in my throat, and I stood from the chair and barreled into him. He stiffened in surprise before squeezing me back, and that was all the approval I needed.

The rest of the day moved on quietly. I spent most of the day devouring the internet, researching apartments, looking at classes, and assessing what textbooks I might need. Finally, I let myself feel excited about the next chapter in my life. Luka left to deal with things for work. Before I knew it, it was past noon. I got ready for my shift, sporting black leggings and a matching T-shirt with my name on it.

Cars flooded the parking lot when I arrived at work, and I groaned. A Saturday afternoon guaranteed a rush at the only bar in town. Thinking of the tips the next twelve hours would bring, I mustered the courage to step inside.

Once I started taking orders, I fell into the natural rhythm of work, moving around endless tables, scrawling across my notepad, and bringing various food and drinks to hunger-stricken customers. Around four, it started to settle, but the dinner rush would soon come. The bar was nearly empty, aside from a handful of stragglers sitting on the stools, clutching half-filled glasses. But if I knew Renetta, she had likely filled them with water.

"Hey, hon," Renetta said as I leaned against the sticky bar. "How's your brother been? I haven't seen him around in a while."

I shrugged. "You know Luka. He likes to keep busy."

Renetta stalked over with a damp rag and began wiping down the back of the bar. Her long gray ponytail swayed with each movement, and as she glanced over at me, sunlight poured from the window, casting a golden shadow over her features. Across her neck ran three thin scars—faint, but there.

"Tell him to drop by when he can," Renetta said. "There are things he needs to sign off on. New equipment and whatnot."

I nodded before slinking away to the back. I liked Renetta, but she was strange. Reserved. I'd known her for years; she even watched me when I was little when Luka had to work, yet after all these years, I could never put my finger on her quiet reserve.

I strayed to the back of the bar and sat in an empty booth for my break, and as a figure slunk across from me, I looked up to find Derek grinning from ear to ear. Even under the dim lighting, I could see his green eyes alight with excitement.

I gave him a quick once over. "You look far too pleased for someone just starting work."

Derek thrummed his fingers over the table. "I don't start for fifteen minutes," he said, heaving to catch his breath. "I'm early because I hate to be late, and I needed to see you."

I reached forward to grab his hands, holding him steady. "How much coffee have you had?"

"I stopped counting after six cups," he buzzed, reaching for his phone.

"It's your funeral." I laughed. "So, what did you do?"

"Why do you assume *I* did something?" He shot me a look of mock horror, pulling back to clutch a fist to his chest. After a knowing look, he conceded. "I may or may not have finagled my talents to scour the internet to my advantage."

"Derek," I groaned.

"Zayne Meyers." Derek lowered his voice, a slight grin spreading across his face. "'I found him."

Zayne Meyers... the name scratched at my memory. "The guy in the interview?" I asked, and Derek nodded. "What do you mean, you found him?"

"I mean, I *found* him." Hope glittered in his eyes as he flicked through his phone. "Look, I found an Instagram account, and I'm ninety-nine percent sure it's him."

I pursed my lips. I understood Derek wanted answers, but I couldn't escape the ringing alarm bells. He was chasing truths he wasn't ready to accept. His dad and brother were dead. If he finally got answers, what's to say he would accept them? Meeting strangers on the internet felt sketchy to me, but voicing my concerns would seem like an outright dismissal of his feelings.

Derek flipped his phone toward me, showing me the profile of a man named Zayne Meyers. His dark hair stuck up in obnoxious spikes, the youth in his face chased away by haunted brown eyes and thin, faint scars running along his cheekbones. I could not deny the chill of dread running through me.

"Derek, he does not look like the sort of guy you should mess with," I said, furrowing my brows. "Everything in this picture is a giant red flag, and besides, how can you know it's the same person?"

"I don't see it," Derek said, continuing to scroll through the feed. Each picture only intensified my unease. He zoomed in on one photo and pushed the phone toward me. "Here, look—the house in the background? That's the house that caught on fire."

The picture was old, the pixilation a dead giveaway. It must have been taken around twenty years ago, but in the background was the same house his father and brother were found. He was right. An undeniable link.

"Okay, but in the next picture, there are literally knives in the background. *Multiple.*" I stopped his scrolling and zoomed in. "You can't meet someone who proudly posts photos of their weapons."

"They're swords, actually, not knives," Derek grumbled.

"Well, in that case, by all means." I leaned back in my seat. "I won't tell you what to do, but try to be sensible."

"I'm being sensible!" Derek argued, setting his phone down. "Is my wanting answers so hard to understand?"

I turned from him, noticing a few wayward glances from the stragglers. Scanning the rest of the bar, still empty of patrons, I exhaled and faced Derek again, lowering my voice.

"No, of course not. But this all seems a little too easy," I said. "You have gone down this road before with little to no luck; you've just found a newspaper article about their deaths and happen to find who they interviewed the next day. Plus, he just so happens to have a public profile."

"What are you saying?"

Derek met my gaze, and I shrank back. Derek was rarely harsh, preferring to tease me to diffuse the tension, yet this topic brought out a different side to him. He could not be reasoned with. I sighed just as the doors opened and a pool of customers flooded in.

"I trust you, Derek, but you have a bit of a blind spot when it comes to this. Please—*please*—just think this through before you do anything rash." I begged, hoping he would understand this came from a place of concern.

Derek pulled his phone back and tucked it away, nodding slowly.

"Alright, I see your point," Derek loosed a held breath. "I won't do anything rash; I promise."

Before I responded, a deep voice drawled Derek's name. I glanced up at the chef, Rico, a broad-chested man who looked more bark than bite. Scars ran across every visible bit of his skin, and there was an edge to his dark eyes and the firm setting of his jaw. While Rico was always friendly with me, he wasn't with Derek. Derek stiffened and scurried out of the booth, and I managed to suppress an eye-roll at the male dominance crap.

The rest of the shift went by without much merit, so I was relieved when the night ended. My body ached. It was just past one in the morning. I crossed the room to set the alarm, my footsteps echoing. Stifling a yawn, Derek finished hauling chairs over tables while I punched in the ten-digit code Luka changed weekly. I flicked off the lights as we headed to the back door and shouldered it open, holding it for Derek, who shuffled through with large trash bags. Night air entwined around us, and I shivered, clicking the back-door lock into place.

"If I never have to work twelve hours in a bar again, it would be too soon," I said.

"You and me both," Derek grumbled. "I don't know what I'll do when you leave."

"You could always come with me," I said, striding behind Derek to the trash. "You are fated for better things than a waiter."

"I like it here," Derek said as we walked down the steps. "Besides, I could always be upgraded to a bartender."

I bumped into him lightly, laughing as we turned the corner. "You know that's not what I mean."

I could see my breath expel into wisps beneath the dim yellowed streetlights. The parking lot was deserted, aside from my car and Derek's truck at the opposite end. My shoes crunched under the gravel as we approached the battered dumpster. As I lifted the lid for Derek, I froze. A black motorcycle perched mere feet from us, and a boy leaned against it.

I squeaked and fell into Derek, who dropped the trash bags and pulled me behind him. The boy chuckled lowly, peeling away from the motorcycle to saunter slowly to us. Derek clutched my hand and took a step back.

Stopping his prowl, the boy rested against the streetlight, crossing his arms over the broadness of his chest. Despite the dim lighting, I could see a faint smile twisting his lips as he looked past Derek and surveyed me with predatory ease, his eyes a dark gold. I gulped as he stepped forward, coming to his full, towering height. It was an effort to keep my face neutral.

"What do you want?" Derek demanded, his voice a deep rasp.

This was not someone I recognized and, given Derek's stiff posture, this wasn't anyone he knew either. I slowly reached into my pocket to pull out my keys, uncapping the pepper spray Luka bought me for Christmas. At the time, I thought carrying pepper spray was obscene and dramatic. Boy, was it a comfort now. Carefully, I wedged the pepper spray in Derek's hand, and he took it.

Stepping forward, the stranger grabbed the two trash bags with one hand, his eyebrows raised and his gaze trained on Derek. When the boy turned his head, Derek lunged. I clutched my chest as the boy managed to toss the trash bags into the dumpster while dodging Derek's attack. The stranger elbowed him in the face, and a crack ripped through the night. Derek moaned. The boy turned toward me, his smile twisting into a snarl. He shook his head.

"Nice try," he said with a backward glance at Derek.

The boy moved between one blink and the next, and I recoiled as he stood inches from me. Further from the streetlamps, we stood in the shadows. I gulped. The boy shook his head, a low clicking noise emerging from his throat. His eyes did not venture over me but pierced into my core as he reached toward me.

Derek let out a low noise of protest, jumping up from the ground.

The boy threw up a hand, and in it, a long knife flashed. Pointed at Derek. My blood ran cold.

"Down, boy," the stranger purred, eyes still on me. "You are almost impressive—if the shoes you had to fill were not so big."

I squinted. That was odd to say to anyone, let alone a stranger. Derek's rumble of anger was his only response, and beneath the moonlight, Derek's hard stance wavered, battling with himself as to whether he should intervene. I stood, frozen to the spot. If I moved, I would only get in the way.

"Get away from her," Derek ground out. It was not a request.

"I've never been in the business of taking orders from—" the boy paused, glancing back at Derek. "Sloppy seconds."

Derek huffed and circled back toward me, but the boy did not stop him. Derek grabbed me, clutching my shoulders to pull me to him. I felt the tension in his grip as he lowered his hands to cling to my wrists.

"What do you want?" I asked as Derek's body trembled.

The boy gave a flat laugh. "You really don't want me to answer that, Maris."

"How do you know who I am?"

He sneered. "Don't flatter yourself by thinking you're special." He jerked his gaze to the name badge pinned to my chest. I held my breath.

"Get out," Derek said, stepping in front of me. "I'm not asking. It is in your best interest to leave. Now."

The boy's fist came down on the dumpster, the reverberating sound echoing through the night. "Might want to get that cleaned out. It's starting to smell like rotting eggs," he crooned.

Derek snarled and pushed past me, but the boy was a blur. I heard the clicking of keys then a rumble as the motorcycle roared to life. He skirted past us, too close for comfort, as his motorcycle buzzed out of the lot. Was I imagining things? Tired to the point of delirium?

Derek started to pull me forward to where my car was parked, ignoring my protests as he opened the driver's door.

I broke free of his grip and forced him to look at me. "What the hell was that?"

"I don't know," Derek said, running a hand through his hair. "I've never met him before. Look, why don't you just go home? It's late."

I balked at him. There was no denying some strange recognition existed between Derek and the stranger.

"What?" I asked. "I'm not an idiot, Derek. You might not have known him, but you felt threatened by him. Why?"

"Anyone with sense would be threatened by a random stranger lurking outside a bar at one o'clock in the morning!"

"It was different, and you know it."

Derek loosed a breath, staring up into the sky. "Let me take you home. We can get your car in the morning."

"What?" I rebuked. "I'm not leaving my car here. That has nothing to do with what happened. You're evading the question."

"If you let me take you home, I promise to talk about it tomorrow," Derek said.

"You know what, forget it. Just give me my keys. It's late and I want to go home," I held my hand out to Derek, who hesitantly handed them over. I barged past him toward my car. "I'm not dropping this, so either be ready to fess up or think of a really good lie."

We parted ways, and I still felt numbly on edge. Derek was across the lot in his truck, Rosie's engine coming to life as I locked the doors to my own car. He peeled out of the lot, his tires screeching against the asphalt. I sighed, setting my head back for a moment of serenity to sort through the events that had unfolded. Once a semblance of calm fell over me, I turned the car on.

It wouldn't. As I twisted the keys, the car clicked. I tried starting it again with the same results.

Okay. *Weird.* I bought this car last year, and I'd never had issues with it before. With clammy palms, I tried five more times before admitting defeat. I got out and lifted the hood, and smoke burst from beneath it. I sputtered and coughed and flapped my hands. Annoyed, I leaned against the side of the car and called Derek. When it went straight to voicemail, I cursed and dialed Luka. He answered on the third ring.

"Hey, where are you?" I asked, mustering enough steel to mask my panic.

"What's wrong?"

"My car won't start, and I'm stuck at the bar," I explained, starting to walk as I talked. "I opened the hood, and it looks like something exploded."

"Where's Derek?"

"He left," I said. I stopped my pacing where the woods began, my phone sweaty in my palm as I considered the following words. "Luka, there was a guy here that knew Derek and he was acting really strange. I don't know what Derek's got himself into, but the guy was making bizarre threats."

"Threats?" Luka's voice rose. "Maris, I'm on my way. Get inside until I get there."

A rustle in the woods caught my attention, and I stopped my pacing. I slowed my breathing and narrowed my gaze ahead. The trees were unmistakably moving, and within, a pair of glowing yellow eyes stared at me through the leaves. I didn't stifle my scream as a giant wolf flew from the bushes. Directly at me.

CHAPTER 3

I whirled and bolted with my fingers clamped around the pepper spray attached to my keys. My only defense? A weapon I swore to Luka I'd never need but now was grateful for. I ran toward the road and cursed, regretting not heading back into the bar. The air bit my face, its harshness like glass nipping skin. I rummaged for my phone but it was gone. It must have slipped from my grip when I ran. Exertion pumped through my lungs as I held my breath. The whisper of a scream lodged in my throat. I heard it behind me.

The wolf.

When the need for air finally overcame me, I slapped my hands against my knees and sucked in a deep, gasping breath, the only spare moment I could dare before running once again. Behind me was the parking lot, void of any life aside from my own. Pressing a hand to my mouth to muffle the sob, I stepped backward.

I was not crazy. I know what I saw. Didn't I? But I dreamed of this the previous night. Wolves were obviously on my mind. I was seeing things—I had to be. Luka's old fears were resurfacing and seeping into me. All his caution drilled into me as a kid was suddenly fresh in my mind; all the fear injected in me from his rough upbringing was forcing me to see things, too. It was late, and I was already spooked to begin with. Being jumpy and on edge made sense.

I turned to look ahead at the road when two strong hands clasped my shoulders. I screamed, looking up to find a man sneering down at me—an older man with a head of dark curls scattered with gray, sallow, pale skin, with eyes light enough to match. His twisted grin exposed yellowed teeth, and my stomach lurched.

"Little girlie, it's not safe to dwell in these parts alone." Voice rough like nails, he made a tutting noise and glared. "What shall I do with you?"

I brought my knee up hard against his groin, a move I could only chalk up to adrenaline. As the man cried out in more surprise than pain, his grip slackened enough for me to wiggle free. He yelled as I bolted toward my car, clutching my pepper spray for dear life. In hindsight, I should have used it, but I felt awkward using any weapon. I hoped Luka would be here soon.

A hand yanked at my ponytail, and I soared backward, screaming. Smacking into the asphalt face-first, he tossed me aside like a rag doll. Pain festered, numbed by shock, and before I could move, he spun me on my back and leaned over me, a feral fury in his eyes.

"I didn't think you would put up such a fight." Amusement flashed in his eyes, like a cat toying with its food. He stroked my face, and I cringed at the touch. "I certainly love a challenge."

"Leave me the hell alone," I growled, tasting warm blood in my mouth.

I whipped my hand up and squeezed the pepper spray into his face, remembering Luka's advice. *Even if it's not a direct hit, the smell alone will give you an advantage.* He was right. It was not a direct hit, but it was enough to throw him off guard.

Wailing, he shot out his hand to knock the pepper spray from my grip, sending my keys with it. The bar was close, and I sped my gait, my eyes beginning to blur and sting. I rubbed at them furiously, which only made it worse, but despite my unsteadiness, the bar was a dozen feet away.

Running up the stairs to the door, I nearly toppled into it as I scrambled in my pocket. My heart sank. I didn't have the keys. Frantically, I jiggled the doorknob and kicked at the steel door, and as I glanced back, the man stood only few feet away.

I cried out as he grabbed my ankle from beneath me. I flailed for the banister, but my fingers slipped as he yanked me, thrashing and clawing to the ground. His grip was iron as he dropped my ankle and grabbed my throat instead, a snarl ripping through my teeth.

The man gazed down on me with red-rimmed eyes, all amusement replaced by anger. His mouth was moving, but the words were a distant buzz. He gripped my shoulders, slamming me against the ground. Stars danced in my vision.

"I want you to remember this, bitch," he sneered.

Elongated fangs gleamed in the moonlight as the man's mouth opened wider. Long and lethal, they dripped with cunning desire as his razor-sharp fangs pierced my skin, sinking deep into my shoulder. I couldn't tell if I was screaming, but the blinding pain exploding over me was unlike anything I'd felt before. This felt charged—purposeful—with the intent to leave a mark. He ripped my flesh away into his jowls, my blood dripping from those teeth as his face split into a monstrous grin.

My head lulled to the side, eyes barely open enough to see headlights. A feeble smile tugged at me, despite my disheveled, beaten state. "You lose," I croaked.

He flew off me like a livewire, the feral look vanishing from his eyes, and replaced by scattered fear. I started to push myself up but fell back onto my elbows. Luka's Jeep screeched to a halt mere feet away. Desperate prayers spilled from the man's lips before he tore off like a bullet into the woods.

"Maris!" Luka yelled, out of his Jeep and to me in a matter of seconds.

Falling to his knees beside me, Luka scooped me into his arms. I couldn't focus, my eyes stinging, but I knew his face was a mask of steel. Gently, he laid me down into the backseat while his blue eyes searched me for damage. Bright anger blazed, his only hint of emotion. I moved my head, and dizziness clouded me, nausea roiling inside my stomach.

"He bit me." The words were a tangled whisper in my throat.

"It's just a scratch," Luka said, voice hitched. He reached into the console, rifling around before producing a small vial with a pinky liquid inside. "Here, drink this for the pain."

I didn't have the energy to question it. I took the open vial and brought it to my lips, wincing at the acidic taste as it burned down my throat, raw from screaming. My mouth was covered in blood. Luka tore off his shirt and pressed it against my wound. I winced, cursing. The wound was like tiny needle pinpricks, and I reached to touch it, glancing down at the faint lines etched into my neck. My head spun. I was definitely delusional.

Luka propped a finger under my chin and forced me to look at him, his eyes darting over every injury. His breath shook with rage, and I knew if it weren't for my injured state, he would have torn off after that man and do God knows what. But Luka would never leave me alone.

"We should call the police," I croaked.

"No," Luka said at once. "He got away. There's nothing to report."

"What if he comes back?" I whispered, my mind barely keeping up.

"He won't."

"There was a wolf. I don't know where it went."

Luka drew his shoulders back, turning to look to where the man ran off. He ran a hand along his jaw and down his neck before looking up at the sky and cursing. Shutting the passenger side door, he walked stiffly to the driver's seat.

"We're going home." The finality in his tone kept me silent.

As he drove away, I leaned my head against the cool window, eyes heavy.

"Hey, hey, you need to stay awake," Luka said, voice alert. "No falling asleep. You might have a concussion."

I knew the words were logical. Staying awake was pertinent. I made myself ask him, "Who was that?"

"I don't know," Luka admitted, his knuckles white where he gripped the steering wheel. "Are you okay?"

I took a deep breath and felt the full force of my nerves. Oddly, with each passing moment, I felt less at odds with my aching body, and where the man had bitten me was nothing but a dull throb. My hands still trembled, and my heart beat a mile a minute. My body felt sore, and I was frightened to see what I looked like on the outside.

"I—I'm okay, but I'm scared."

"I was terrified," he admitted, which was a feat for him. "All I heard was your scream, and then the phone died." He brought a hand to his mouth before slamming it against the wheel. "Where was Derek?"

"I told him to leave. He didn't know," I said. "It wasn't his fault."

Luka snarled his disagreement but spoke no more on the matter. We drove the rest of the way home in silence.

The following week came and went with little disturbance. Luka forbade me from working for two weeks so I could rest and heal. I knew when I went back to work, it would be different. Aside from Luka increasing security, he also ripped into the staff about what happened to me. Derek, I knew, took the heat of it. Luka made him cover all my shifts, meaning Derek worked doubles daily. When I did speak to Derek, I had to reassure him I was okay a dozen times. He was being too hard on himself and taking the blame as he often did.

The attack still stunned me, and processing it with a clear mind felt worse. I could still feel where the man's hand grabbed me, like an oily mark permanently stained on my skin. I tried to rationalize what had happened but to no avail. It was a senseless attack—a cheap shot of adrenaline. He bit me and wanted me to remember it. When I'd got home, I took one look at the bite and begged Luka to take me to the hospital. The marks were swollen red, surrounded by purple lines. It looked infected, but Luka insisted it was fine. I needed to rest, he'd said, but if it looked bad in the morning, we could go.

When the morning came, the bite could have been a cat scratch for how small it looked. Across my body, where I expected large welts were only faint bruises—barely even purple. Luka chalked up my initial worry to shock and adrenaline; I was lucky, he said. His nonchalance over the situation baffled me, but what could I say to him? *Please, Luka. Freak out and wreak havoc over this?* If he had any reaction, it might have made me feel the tiniest bit better, but his only comment was about getting me a new pepper spray.

I tried not to dwell on what happened, but what I saw—or thought I saw—haunted me.

Luka returned to look at my car and said it worked fine. He even drove it back home. Since then, it remained parked outside. That had me *really* feeling nuts, yet the smell of gas was fresh in my senses.

Something thwacked my head, and I jerked up from the couch. A small stuffed dog lay on the floor, and I grabbed it, throwing it back. "What the hell was that for?"

Derek caught it without glancing up from his computer. "You seemed to be in your head," he said, setting it down.

"I was," I admitted. "How did you know?"

"What?" Derek answered, eyes still fixed on the computer.

Luka, as paranoid as ever, sent Derek here to babysit me. Not that I minded Derek's company or blamed Luka for being extra cautious. I worried about Luka and whether he was keeping himself together. He turned all his emotions inward, yet all his fears unraveled that night at the thought of losing me—the realization he couldn't protect me. If anything had happened to me, Luka would be alone. To my knowledge, he never dated or socialized; he barely had friends. He'd always desperately clutched to me and the idea of keeping me safe.

I peeled myself from the leather couch and padded across the living room, warmth emanating from the low burning fire. Derek sat at the dining room table, elbows resting on the oak. I flicked on the chandelier and leaned over Derek, draping an arm over his shoulder. Squinting, I peered closely at the screen. Messages filled it.

"Derek, what is this?" I asked.

Derek pulled his focus to look at me, taking the glasses from his face, and rubbing at his eyes. "I've been in contact with Zayne," he admitted.

I took a moment to let the words settle. "Okay, and has anything come from that?"

"Kind of." Derek shrugged, fixing his gaze on the ceiling. "It's a little dodgy, honestly, but he agreed to meet me."

"Tell me you said no!" When he didn't answer, I shoved him from his spot in front of the computer. I read the screen and whirled to face him. "Really, Derek?"

"I know, I know," Derek groaned, holding his hands up. "It might sound stupid, but this feels like the right thing. I think this is what will give me answers."

"You're talking about meeting a stranger on the internet to discuss murder," I retorted. "Do you hear how that sounds?"

"I realize it's not practical—"

"Practical? It's suicidal! Should I remind you that I—your *best friend*—was just attacked by a total stranger? I didn't sign up for that!"

"Maris, I *need* these answers," Derek insisted. "I've needed answers since the moment they left. I can't ignore a lead when it's right in front of me."

"Lead for what, Derek? Did you forget that they died?" I cringed at the cruelty of my words. Derek flinched and stood, reaching into his pocket. "I'm sorry, that was mean."

Rummaging through his wallet with shaky fingers, Derek looked up at me, glaring as he tossed a photo down on the table. I glanced down at two young boys with the same tousle of light hair, green eyes, and matching joyous expressions. They could have been twins. Young Derek stood beside his older brother in front of an old truck—Rosie, I recognized. If it were his father's, it was no wonder he wouldn't get rid of it. The adults standing behind wore similar expressions, and it was clear where their children's beauty came from.

"This was taken two weeks before they disappeared." Derek's voice came out flat. "Two weeks before everything changed. This picture is the only proof I have that it was even real. Yes, I know they died, even if I don't act like it. But I need to understand this—understand what happened in those two weeks."

Derek's shoulders tensed, a wet sheen glinting in his eyes. He blinked it away, and behind the harshness of his stare, I saw the hope he clung to. I gulped.

I handed him back the photo, nodding. "I'm sorry I snapped at you."

"It's okay," he said. "I know I can be a bit much with this."

"No," I countered firmly. "You are never too much, Derek."

Derek loosed a long breath. "Thank you."

Never one for navigating overly sentimental moments, I suggested we eat, my stomach grumbling in approval. I cooked three frozen pizzas, knowing Derek would eat two and call it a "snack." Yet hours passed, and I felt myself nodding off as it neared midnight. I walked to the garage and opened the door. Luka wasn't back.

A knot twisted in my stomach, and I drew my shoulders back, prodding Derek awake from where he slept on the couch. He moved in a blur, half sputtering as he lurched toward me. I screamed as he forced me against the wall, a dagger poised against my throat.

Derek's green eyes widened as he realized what he was doing. He snapped out of it, dropping the dagger with a clash and jumping back. I gawked down at the long, thin silver blade. It had to be at least six inches long, and at the hilt, an emerald jewel gleamed.

"Oh my god," Derek rasped. "I'm sorry. I'm so sorry, Maris. Jesus, are you okay?"

"Where did you get that?" I asked slowly, pressing a hand to my throat. "And why the hell are you sleeping with that thing?"

Derek drew his gaze away from the blade and peered up at me, horror-struck. He moved his mouth, unable to speak, then traced his hand through his hair. "I don't know."

"Who the hell are you stabbing in your sleep?"

Derek picked up the dagger and crossed the room to place the blade into his bag. He hesitated, squirming like a worm on a hook, all the while avoiding my gaze.

"You could kill someone with that," I hissed.

"Strictly speaking, anything—when used the right way—could kill someone."

"Because that makes me feel so much better."

Derek paced and took a deep breath before saying, "I'm probably not ever going to use it, honestly."

"That still doesn't explain why you felt the need to buy it!" I said with growing irritation. Derek stayed silent, pinching the bridge of his nose with a scowl. "*Derek.*"

"Okay, okay," he threw his hands up in defeat. "I don't want to lie, but I can't tell you the truth."

"Did Luka give it to you?" I asked. Derek's silence was my confirmation. Shock registered first, making it hard to grasp the right words. "Why?"

"What happened to you rattled me. I—went to Luka and asked for it," Derek babbled. "With how he is, I knew he would have something."

Luka kept guns in the house, that much I knew, but he tucked them away somewhere safe. He drilled gun safety into me before he even brought them home. I never knew where he kept them and never wanted to know. Weapons were his forte. But a blade? Stabbing someone was close and personal—not a typical weapon of defense. The fact Luka would have that in his possession unsettled me.

My blood boiled. Luka didn't want to speak to me; he insisted I stay home and rest while he handed out knives to my friend instead. I felt like I was going crazy, my spiraling thoughts threatening to take over. I hated that he put me in a position to question him.

"Where is he?" I asked.

"What?" Derek watched me, confused.

"Where is he?" I asked again. "He isn't home. This isn't like him."

"Probably got stuck with something at work," Derek said, walking toward the window, his face turned from me. *Yes, wiggle around the truth some more, Derek.* "You know, it gets a little hairy on Friday nights. Extra security is always welcomed."

"If he was only at work, he would have said something." I insisted. "Hell, if he were only at work, you'd be there and not him. He'd always choose to be my first line of defense."

"Maybe—"

"—What about the other night?" I interrupted. "You don't think I noticed you weaseling your way out of an explanation then? When that stranger showed up to the bar right before I was attacked?"

"That was different," Derek said. "That was complicated, and it still is—"

"What's complicated? The truth or telling it?"

Our eyes locked for what felt like eternity. Anger swelled in me, even if it might have been displaced. But I could see it then—I knew it. Whatever the truth was, Derek would not tell me. The realization stung. I trusted Derek, but so did Luka.

"Get out," I said in forced calm. "Get out, Derek."

"What?"

"You always make excuses for him!" I said through gritted teeth. "I'm tired of hearing them. Get out."

"Are you comfortable here alone?" Derek asked. "I can call him and—"

Call him. He knew where Luka was. I shook my head and cut his next words off with a warning glare. Derek picked up his things and only glanced back once before leaving through the front door. I slammed it shut, bolting all the locks before sliding down the wall and putting my head in my hands.

Chapter 4

Sleep did not come after that. I lay in bed, fighting the invasive thoughts creeping into my head, and just as sleep held me in its claws, I realized I was completely alone. There was no Luka here to protect me. I'd always brushed aside Luka's fear, explaining it away as the overbearing older brother. I never considered looking past the surface, and I was beginning to wonder if there was something he needed to protect me from.

I could not imagine what that might be. I wasn't blind. I knew Luka had a side to him, one that flaunted his worst qualities—an undiluted rage he kept leashed. Years ago, his anger took over. It had only been a year or so since our dad left; Luka was still learning to navigate raising me, let alone himself. He picked fights and messed with the wrong crowd, coming home bruised and bloodied until Renetta finally got him on the straight and narrow.

Since then, he was good—perfect, even. I never even saw him drink, though I knew he indulged at least once a month. But just because he showcased to me a picture-perfect image, it didn't mean there wasn't more to the story. Whatever past that haunted him, I feared it was catching up.

I recalled the look of genuine fear glinting in the eyes of my attacker as soon as Luka arrived, running like the devil was hot on his heels.

Even though I was upset with Luka, I felt his absence. I called his phone a dozen times, and all went straight to voicemail. My frustration only grew as I entertained my manic thoughts. *Did I lock all the doors? Did I forget to close the garage?* Tonight would surely be the night I got axe-murdered for failing to check. These thoughts were rampant in my head as I tossed and turned. It was ridiculous.

I got out of bed at four in the morning and walked down the steps to check the locks. Each lock on the front door was bolted shut, but I re-did them for peace of mind. I checked the windows to be safe, too, and drew the curtains open. I stared across at the endless expanse of trees, ginormous and withering in the dark night. Its ambiance chilled me to my core, and I quickly triple-checked the windows were locked.

I shut the curtains, but not before spotting a pair of golden eyes glowing in the distance. I stifled a small scream and yanked the curtains back. *It was nothing, it was nothing,* I said to myself again and again. I was paranoid. Flashes of memory flew to the surface: the animal in the road and at the bar. The animal with eyes the same golden hue.

No, it was nothing. With my run-in with Mr. Crazy, *I* was becoming crazy. While most people fear turning into their parents, I was turning into my brother, paranoid about every threat or danger. Scolding myself, I walked to the kitchen, checking the back door to ensure the locks were done.

An echoing vibration clamored through the room. I gasped and jumped back, throwing my arms around myself. But it was Luka's cell phone buzzing, discarded under the kitchen table. Shakily, I bent down and reached for the phone.

Derek's name illuminated the cracked screen. Eight missed calls and two voicemails. One was from four hours ago, and another only one hour ago.

It wasn't odd for Derek to call Luka, but it was clearly urgent. Whatever was going on, there was no denying the two of them were in on it together.

I pushed down my unease with a gulp and clicked the phone open, ignoring my moral compass, warning me not to snoop. I clicked on the first message from Derek.

"Where the fuck are you? I'm running out of things to say that don't make you seem like a lunatic! If you're going after him, cover your tracks. I'm here tonight to keep an eye on things until you get back."

I dropped the phone, too stunned to do anything else, but I knew two things for sure: Luka was doing something—probably illegal—and Derek lied to me. I took a deep breath, replaying the message over and over in my head.

Face wet with tears, I took a staggering breath and clutched the wall behind me. I slid to the ground and leaned my head against the wall, tipping it back to stare at the ceiling. With each breath, panic rose in me. Something was beginning to unravel, as if the bindings molding my life had been cut. I couldn't grasp it; it was like a hazy fog I could see but not touch.

I forced myself to get up and grab water, craving some normalcy.

Grabbing a glass with trembling hands, I struggled to grip it. I breathed in and out, wiping furiously at my face. I let the water run from the tap and spill from the faucet, fascinated with the steam erupting. Still gripping the glass, I watched it overflow.

A numbing calm settled over me then. One thing was crystal clear: Luka and Derek both lied to me. I didn't know the reason, but I hoped it was a good one. Many things might warrant this type of paranoia and secrecy, but I couldn't entertain it and break the idea I had of my brother and best friend. The conclusion? The two people I trusted most in the world were lying to me.

Pain blistered my senses, and I staggered back as scalding hot water spilled over my hand, but from the looks of the flooding sink, it had been that way for at least a minute. I dropped the glass and it shattered like glitter across the floor. Stepping forward, I held my hand beneath the cold tap to ease the burn, only for new pain to erupt as I stepped on the glass shards. I cried out, falling to my knees before hobbling to a nearby chair.

Not as many shards were embedded as I expected, but I cringed at the thought of removing the pieces. Given I would soon train as a nurse, this was nothing. With a deep breath, I plucked each piece from my foot. I should be more concerned about my scorched skin, but the relief it gave me was worth it. I could think clearly once more. Cleaning myself up, I applied the bandages over my wounds.

I settled back on the couch as the early morning light poured in from the sides of the curtains. A glance at the clock showed it was nearing five in the morning. The earlier distraction did little to silence my thoughts as anger festered from the lies. I felt panicked, not knowing where Luka was. If I was angry with him, I didn't have to worry, but it was hard not to feel both.

Hours passed with me falling in and out of sleep on the couch until it was almost past noon. I didn't want to move. I needed to stay here for when Luka walked in the door. I checked his phone periodically but there was nothing new, and I almost called Derek to demand the truth from him. But I didn't because somehow, Derek was tangled in whatever lies Luka spun, and thus the endless cycle of rage and fear continued.

I wanted to be productive to pass the time, but I could only sit and doze between sleeping and waking. I checked my wounds to ensure they weren't deeper than I thought and peeled the bandage from my foot. Aside from a bloodstain, there was nothing else. I gawked at the smooth, unaltered skin as my mind whirled. The front door opened, and I bolted upright.

Luka walked in, covered in blood.

Blood splattered across his face like flecked paint. His shirt was in tatters, and where it wasn't covered in blood, it was caked with dirt. It was not fresh but dried to a tacky texture, and grass strands wove into his hair, sticking up in every direction. That wasn't the worst of it, because as he stepped inside, he brought in with him an overwhelming stench of rotten eggs. I almost gagged from the intensity of it.

Immediately, his head shot up, and his dark blue eyes widened in surprise. "Maris?" he exclaimed. "Why are you here?"

I was too stunned to speak, watching as he stumbled, tucking his hands behind his head. "Do you see yourself?"

Luka's eyebrows knotted together and he crossed his arms. "I don't see the issue. What did you do to your hand?"

"Seriously, Luka? You disappear and come home *covered* in blood and have the audacity to question *me*? What the hell is going on here, and why are you lying to me?"

Pacing into the kitchen, he tossed his keys on the counter while I followed close behind. He moved toward the sink and turned the tap on, scrubbing furiously at his arms. "I had things to take care of."

"What things?" When he didn't answer, my frustration grew. "Did you kill that man who attacked me?"

I don't know why I asked him that, but I said it. I stood by it.

Luka froze mid-scrub. "Did I—why would you—*dammit!*" He brought his fist down against the sink, and the room shook. I staggered back. "What did Derek tell you?"

"He didn't tell me anything!" I cried, noting his evasion of the question. "What's going on here, Luka? Nothing makes sense. First, it was the wolf in the road, then I was attacked at the bar, and I cut my foot and—" *It miraculously healed within hours without even a ghost of a cut as proof of injury.* "—I know you know something. Just tell me, *please.*"

Luka's palms were face down on the counter, his head hanging low. "I can't," he said softly. "It's too dangerous."

"Fine," I snapped. "Then explain this." I ripped the bandage off my hand. "I let my hand burn under boiling hot water today, and it left me with scalding burns. To top it off, I fell on broken glass, and tore my foot up, but there's no evidence any of it happened. Why?"

A muscle jumped in Luka's jaw, and his voice shook. "This happened today?"

"Yes!"

"This shouldn't be happening," Luka muttered, dragging a hand through his hair. He started to move, shoving past me to head upstairs. "I'm fixing this before it's too late."

"Luka!" I cried out. "Please, just answer me. You're scaring me. You're not making any sense!" I jogged up the steps after him.

"Maris, stop asking questions," Luka warned.

"Why did you give Derek a knife?" I asked.

Luka whirled, eyes wide. "What did Derek tell you?"

"He didn't tell me anything!" I shouted. "Taking a page from your book, I suppose."

Luka roared, smacking his fist into the wall. It went straight through it. He yanked his hand out, and his fingers were disfigured and knuckles bloodied. Panic overrode my anger and I ran forward and grabbed his wrist before he could pull away. Luka stiffened but did not jerk away.

His hand swelled, his fingers jutting out in all directions. Before I could think to get ice or insist he visit the hospital, I watched in horror as his bones cracked together, twisting from their awkward angles back to precision. It looked painful as the skin seamlessly mended, and within seconds, there was no evidence he ever struck the wall, save for the fact of the new hole.

"Maris—" Luka stopped. His eyes focused on the wall behind me, a frown curling at his lips. "This isn't normal. I'm not normal."

I dropped his hand and tore down the steps. I snatched up Luka's car key in the kitchen and quickly entered the garage, knocking aside a worktable while hitting the button on the wall so the door could open as I slipped behind the wheel. Luka appeared by the door in a fury, and I frantically clicked at the locks. Jamming the keys into the ignition, the engine roared to life.

"Maris, stop!" Luka yanked at the handle. "You can't leave like this. Let me explain!"

"No!" I yelled. I put the car in reverse, ignoring the tears streaming from my face. "I can't be here anymore."

I pulled the car out of the garage before slamming against the gas and jolting forward. My whole body shook, unable to fully process what had happened. Luka ran behind me, frantic and yelling, but I closed my eyes against the wave of tears threatening to fall. When I reopened them, I could see Luka in the rearview mirror shrinking from view.

Chapter 5

I drove aimlessly for four hours, regathering control while the threat of an empty gas tank kept me miles from the town borders. But I could run out of gas, and I wouldn't care. If I ended up stuck on the side of the road all night, so be it. My mind replayed Luka's broken hand repairing itself. It made no sense. And the blood that covered him...whose blood had that been? None of it made sense.

I could not fathom what Luka would jeopardize everything for. The not knowing killed me, and while I didn't want to be angry with him, I didn't know how else to feel. More than anything, I hated this tarnished picture I now had of him. If he came clean, maybe I could at least try and understand. Nothing could be so bad as to drive a wedge between us, and that thought trumped all others because all I ever had was Luka. I needed him as much as he needed me.

I stopped at the same red light for the fifth time, having driven in circles to muster a sense of control in all this. I knew how to get back from here. A sudden vibration in my pants pocket jerked me to alertness as I waited for the light to go green. I reached for the cell phone awkwardly with my foot on the brake. I forgot I still had Luka's phone.

Derek. Another piece in this madness.

"Hey," I said stiffly. Silence answered on the other end, followed by heavy breathing. Maybe Derek had pocket dialed by accident.

"Well, you certainly are not who I expected," said a chilling voice.

A car honked behind me, and I realized the light was green. I hit the gas and sped forward, clutching the phone.

"Who is this?" I asked, my heart beating out of my chest.

I felt acutely aware of the growing night sky enveloping the day in black. The familiar back roads were now an aching reminder of the distance to home—the only place I felt safe. Pressing harder on the gas, I guessed I was about five miles away.

"No, who is *this*?" the voice countered, sickly sweet.

Manic laughter filled the silence. A familiar voice sounded in the distance, interrupted by a howl of pain that made me lurch the car to the side of the road and put it in park. My heart pounded. Derek. He roared furiously in the background, his bellows of protest mingled with strangled pain. Then his words came back to me. About meeting the man from the interview.

But Derek wouldn't. Would he? Not without warning...No, Derek would have done exactly this and followed his whims, too blindsided by grief to think rationally.

I opened my mouth to demand who I was speaking to, and then the line went dead. This didn't feel real. Staring out among the forest of trees, I glanced back at the empty road. I needed to get home and go to Luka. Forget everything else for now; Luka would know what to do.

As I twisted the keys in the ignition, a set of headlights approached fast from behind, but before I could think or scream, a fist smashed through the driver's window and pressed against my mouth.

Groggily, my eyelids fluttered open. My whole body felt leaden, unable to carry my weight. A constant ringing buzzed in my ears, and as I lifted my head up, blinking, I failed to make sense of my surroundings. My arms ached, and I soon realized they were chained above my head, stretched like a rubber band while my toes barely scraped the floor. I felt numb yet burning all at once. I had likely been like this for some time to feel so uncomfortable.

The room was dingy, no bigger than a bedroom, and shrouded in shadows, and no windows, making it hard to distinguish anything other than where they'd cuffed me. A light bulb hung from the ceiling by a sketchy-looking wire, swaying slightly. I was underground—possibly in a basement. A blinding pain seared in my head, and I barely stifled a scream.

"Maris?" a deep voice called. "You need to keep it down."

As the pain subsided, I turned to see who spoke. Next to me, I glimpsed the outline of a boy, chained up like me. A dark shadow of stubble traveled down his sharp jawline; bruises decorated his bare chest, and dried blood appeared like scratches across his body. Despite no open wounds, blood dripped over him in spots. Fresh.

His head snapped up, and my body lurched at the golden eyes that beheld me. Flashes of memories seized me—the car accident, the attack, the eyes outside my house—the exact eyes looking back at me now. I fought to keep my breathing even. I didn't believe in coincidences, but this had to be one. Those eyes were from animals, and this was clearly a person. A boy.

Yet the roughish glint in his eyes was like gazing into that of a wild animal, as were his other features—the dark, untamed mane of hair, the tension in his jaw, the jarring scowl. Even in his battered state, tension gripped his body.

"Who are you?" I hissed.

My eyes searched the room for a door—or anything that would offer a clue to where we were. I froze, my mind numbed by denial as breath escaped me. Tossed to the ground like a corpse, battered, bruised, and bloodied, lay Derek. I yanked and writhed against my chains. I needed to get to him.

"Derek!" I cried, jerking against the chains. "Derek—come on! Wake up!"

"He isn't dead!" The boy hissed. "Believe me, if they wanted him dead, he would be."

I closed my eyes, fighting back the tears. There was no relief in finding Derek here—not like that. I loosed a breath before speaking. "Who is *they*? Where are we, and what's going on?"

"If you haven't noticed, I'm chained up like you are," he shot back. "Besides, you're not ready for the answers."

Before I could retaliate, footsteps descended and light poured into the room. I flinched, my head throbbing against the glare. Muffled voices followed as a man emerged into the light.

"And here I thought your sharp tongue was reserved for me," said the man. "I'd be careful with this one, girl." He looked at me, then nodded at the boy. "Dayton's bark is definitely as big as his bite."

The man looked to be the same age as Luka, and he stepped closer with a curious look. He moved like a dancer—unfaltering in his gait. Sweat glimmered at the top of his bare head and dripped down his dark face. His head almost hit the ceiling, and his shoulders nearly tore the fabrics of his shirt. His red eyes were the most disturbing, like ruby orbs searing into my soul.

"Save your taunts, Zayne," Dayton spat, a trickle of blood escaping the corner of his mouth.

Zayne's attention turned from me, but my mind was spinning.

Zayne.

I knew my suspicions were right, but the man Derek found was not standing before me. Figured Derek would get catfished by kidnappers and rope me into his mess. Yet leading Derek here under false pretenses about his family made no sense. Why would he use that as a baseline to lure him in? There were easier ways to kidnap someone without learning their family history. It still begged the question: why would he want to kidnap Derek to begin with? And why bring me into it?

Zayne blinked slowly and dramatically flicked a handkerchief from his pocket to wipe his face clean of Dayton's blood. "Fine then, if that's how you want to be."

Retreating into the darkness, Zayne then returned with a long metal pole sparking with electricity. A cynical look crossed his features, and a hollowness caved in my stomach as I suddenly got the jitters.

"Tell me what you know of the Bestial," demanded Zayne.

"Funny. Being tied up kind of gets in the way of actually meeting him," Dayton growled. "Or her, I suppose. The Bestial could be a woman; I'm not sexist."

Bestial sounded more like a title, not a name. What was it? *Who* was it? I couldn't escape the sickening feeling that whatever was unfolding would begin to change everything I thought I knew.

Zayne smirked. "I know it's the wrong answer, but doing this feels right."

He flung the pole forward and into Dayton's stomach. I gasped as electricity sizzled through him. Dayton did not scream or cry out. His body shook from the shock alone, a vicious snarl his only tell of annoyance. Flinging his head back, Dayton spat at Zayne again.

"Enough!" Zayne shouted, his yell reverberating against the walls. "Where is Lukas Danika?"

Hearing Luka's full name unsettled me to my core. Luka refused to go by Lukas, as that was our father's name, and when he left us, Luka scrubbed away any association with him. By all rights, the name should not be known, but Zayne knew it.

"I'd tell you to go to hell, only I'd rather not see you ever again," Dayton quipped.

Zayne rolled his eyes. "You really are *lovely*, Dayton."

Zayne pressed the pole against Dayton again while I could do nothing except watch helplessly. Back and forth they went, Zayne asking different variations of the same questions and Dayton responding with increasingly sarcastic answers. When Zayne pumped the voltage to its highest capacity, I worried Dayton might crack. He didn't.

Dayton grinned and shook his head. "I could do this all day."

"Believe me, I know. Your tolerance is infuriating, but everyone has a breaking point," Zayne stepped back, then twirled to look at me. "If you won't talk, then we have other methods. You made a friend, right? Well, you may be able to withstand physical torture, but she can't." He advanced toward me, a manic look in his eyes.

I cringed away, casting an anxious look at Dayton, who remained impassive at my predicament. Like, *Oh well, you got yourself into this. You can get yourself out.*

Zayne laughed as the pole neared my chest. I sensed the energy radiating from it.

"What do you want to know about Luka?" I demanded.

"Luka?" Zayne questioned, withdrawing the pole. He assessed me with his beady red eyes as realization washed his features all at once. "Oh, you must be *Maris*. The rumors are true."

"What rumors?"

Zayne crept forward, forgoing his torture device. His red, hungry eyes surveyed me, and as he reached forward, my skin crawled. He brushed a calloused palm against my cheek, and a grin split his features as he inhaled.

"Get off me," I hissed, but I could not escape his touch.

"You are his secret. Yes, it's all making sense. *You* are why he refuses us. He needs to protect you." Zayne crooned, pleased like a child on Christmas morning. "But you walked away from him, he can't protect you. Oh, Kaser is going to be pleased."

Nothing made sense. Who would Luka refuse? Maybe a strange new age cult was trying to recruit Luka.

"Kaser?" Dayton's attention caught. "What does he have to do with this?"

"Hm, so you speak when it's of interest to you," Zayne replied, assessing me with slitted eyes. "How much do you know?"

"I don't know anything!"

"Oh, this is even better than I imagined." Zayne gracefully leaped back, his arrogant grin never wavering. "And now big brother will come to save the day. I admit, your brother is craftier than I thought, Maris. I never imagined myself lucky enough to uncover his most well-guarded secrets."

When Zayne's gaze did not leave mine, I realized what he meant. Luka knew this might happen—that someone might come after him, using me to get to him. That was why he was so paranoid and overbearing. But who was Zayne, and what did he want with Luka?

"It was a gamble to find his Beta and lure him here, but it was a bigger gamble to assume he would come after his Beta. Finding you, well, we assumed you were a member of his inner circle, but now knowing the truth of who you are...he will come for you. I have no doubt."

Beta? He said all these outlandish things without wavering. If Luka came here, he'd be in danger.

"What do you want with him?" I asked.

Zayne laughed outright. "Is it not obvious? We want to kill him."

A gasp fought to escape, but I only shook my head and rattled my chains. "This is sick!"

"You can't kill him," Dayton warned, catching Zayne's attention. "He'll kill you."

Zayne's eyebrows knitted together. "Oh? Him against all the—" His eyes widened. "*Oh,* he is the—which means that they are—" Zayne laughed as he pieced the puzzle together. "They are one and the same. Lukas and the Bestial."

"Took you long enough," Dayton muttered.

My confusion must have been etched across my face, because Zayne turned to me and laughed.

"And she is ignorant to all of this. Utterly oblivious to the history unfolding as we speak." Zayne grinned. "History will remember *me* as the one who took down the Bestial."

"Deflate your ego, hot shot. Your head is already big enough," snarled Dayton.

I couldn't register the lunacy of his words. I just wanted to leave—get Derek and get out. It was a waste of time trying to figure all of this out now. It hurt my head. As I glanced back at Derek, I couldn't tell if his chest rose or fell.

"Leave Luka out of it," I snarled at Zayne.

Amusement flickered in his eyes. "You want to protect him? Cute. Your brother is the orbit that keeps all of this spinning, sweetheart. He is the center of it all."

In a blur, Zayne moved and grabbed the discarded pole, striking out and piercing my skin. I screamed as my body tried to curl in on itself as agonizing pain seized hold of me. The intensity increased, and I writhed for it to stop. A growl rumbled, and as I glanced to see if Derek was awake, I realized it was Dayton raging in his chains.

When the pole was retracted, Zayne prowled closer, his tongue flicking out like a snake and his face inches from mine. I jerked my head forward, teeth bared, and bit down hard into his cheek. He jumped back, dropping the torture device to the ground.

"You bitch," he growled, advancing.

"Stay away from me!"

Zayne halted and jerked his head up, tilting it toward the ceiling. I heard the thud of footsteps in the distance, and a smile of pure glee broke across Zayne's face.

"Showtime."

As Zayne turned back, his gaze fell upon Dayton. I almost forgot he was there, strung up like I was. Zayne reached a table nearby and grabbed a small, pointed dagger, earning an eye-roll from Dayton as if he expected no less.

"You could at least get creative," Dayton drawled. Zayne dragged the blade down Dayton's chest. "Aargh, silver? Fuck you!"

"Oh, do I get creativity points for that?" Zayne smirked. He plunged the dagger deep into Dayton's back, ignoring his hiss of protests. "Try to get that out before the poison kills you."

Zayne spun, dropping a key ring onto a table before disappearing up the stairs he came down.

I counted to ten in my head before I spoke. "Are you okay?" Dayton strained his neck to look at the dagger. "It looks like the whole blade is stuck in," I told him, flinching at the scene of blood and gaping wound. *Maybe I should reconsider the whole nurse thing.*

"Maris," he grumbled.

"How do you know my name?"

"My state-of-the-art observational skills," he snarled. The tone, the anger, all of it stirred a memory awake.

"You!" I shouted. "You were there the night I was attacked!"

It was Dayton that night outside the bar. I had nearly forgotten about him, too distracted by the attack to care. Derek feared him, and it was clear he knew him enough not to trust him. It was no coincidence he was there the night I was attacked, or here now. The only question was if I could trust him—not trust him—or just trust him enough. He, too, was clearly here against his will.

"I tried to warn your dumbass friend about this exact thing happening." Dayton admitted. "And as you can see, we're all in a rather precarious situation because no one wants to listen to me."

I rolled my eyes and inclined my head to peer past him at Derek's unconscious figure slumped against the ground. "Is he okay?"

Dayton hesitated. "He'll survive. He's a fighter."

While it didn't put me at ease, it was a start. "Why is Zayne asking you about my brother? How do you know Derek? Plus, how did you end up here?"

Dayton stayed quiet and glanced around again. He kicked out, just barely, and a clanging below made me look down. Unlike me, his feet were bound, and though he pulled on them, his upper body was paralyzed by the chains.

"Are you a flight risk or something?" I retorted.

Dayton gave a dark chuckle. "I need to get this knife out before the toxins kill me."

"You're joking, right?"

"If I peg you as the joking type then I should re-introduce myself."

Dayton rolled his head with a grim expression, awkwardly twisting his wrists, testing for grip. His fingers barely brushed the loops, but he kept trying. After a few more failed attempts, he slumped.

"What are you trying to do?"

"I'm trying to get the hell out of here."

Like quicksilver, Dayton threw his entire weight forward before crashing to the ground. The crack of bones splintering made the hairs on the nape of my neck rise as he managed to writhe his hands through the tightly bound cuffs with horrifying results. Past the blood, bones protruded from his hands and flesh hung on by threads of muscle. I gagged, my stomach contents threatening to come up.

"Would you keep quiet?"

I fixed him with an icy stare, unable to rid the rising nausea.

With his hands freed, he went to work on the chains at his feet, as if his hands had not been broken a moment ago. My mind spun; how was this possible? I recalled the healing of Luka's hand and figured it was the same sort of trickery. It still didn't make sense, unless I was going crazy and seeing things. That felt like the only plausible explanation. Dayton gritted his teeth as he yanked at the chains, deflating with a curse.

Dayton's eyes widened as one final pull unearthed the chains from the concrete. It clattered, and I tensed, fearing Zayne's return. Dayton stood, looking around as the chains dragged at his ankles. Dayton walked with purpose, toward a table with a glittering key chain atop it. Snatching it up, he freed himself from his confinements before disregarding them again. I opened my mouth to ask how he planned to get the knife out of his back, but he was one step ahead.

Dayton rammed his shoulder into a concrete wall. A loud crack tore the silence, followed by a squelchy pop. Face twisting, he growled and maneuvered the knife out, allowing it to clang to the ground. He rolled his shoulders then reached down to grab it.

"Zayne's too easy to goad." Dayton grinned, the dagger in his palm becoming an extension of himself. "Idiot."

I watched Dayton with wide eyes, wondering what kind of person I was dealing with here. Normal people didn't move or act like he did. He goaded Zayne into stabbing him to obtain a weapon and withstood torture that could have killed him. If he were a normal person, he'd be on the ground from his injuries. I furrowed my brows. What made him different?

Dayton started toward the door then hesitated, glancing back to look at me and shaking his head. His confliction was evident in his eyes, but with the keys in his grip, he strode toward me.

"No, wait," I protested. Dayton pursed his lips, but I cut off his next words. "Help him first, not me."

"You're lucky I'm even helping *you*," he said incredulously.

"Please. He's in worse shape than I am." I cast a worried look in Derek's direction, but it was hard to see him.

Dayton moved to Derek and hunched over him, undoing the cuffs seamlessly, then slapped him back and forth.

"C'mon, pretty boy, wake up," Dayton crooned. I yelled, then froze. Derek stirred, his body jolting.

"Where—" Derek grumbled. Relief flooded through me, quickly overshadowed by the reality of our situation.

"—Yeah, yeah, welcome to Shangri-la," Dayton finished.

Before anymore was said, Dayton moved to me. My body stiffened from our close proximity as Dayton reached my chains. His breath traced my neck, and this close, I glimpsed sweat dripping from the edges of his hairline. His hair tickled my face as he moved his body closer to get a better angle, and his gilded eyes appeared even more prominent up close. He had no shirt on, and I pushed the thought out of my mind when I noticed how well he looked without one.

"How did your hand heal?" I asked, distracting myself.

Dayton clucked his tongue disapprovingly, freeing my from my chains. "Why do you ask so many damn questions?"

I fell, but he caught me at my waist. With Dayton steadying me, I regained my balance as a dizziness washed over me. "I'm not carrying you."

"Like I would even ask," I shot back, pressing a hand to my forehead to regain focus.

"It's the chloroform they used to get you here," croaked Derek. He stood with the same dazed expression, and I crossed over to him, grabbing his wrist to feel his solidity.

"Are you okay?" I asked.

"You shouldn't be here," Derek groaned. "Luka's going to kill me."

"We can talk about it later," I said, squeezing his wrist, though I couldn't even fathom how that conversation would go. I had no idea what to ask or where to begin. "Let's just get out of here, okay?"

"Right, yes." Derek nodded, glancing at me quickly. "Where are we?"

"Stop questioning where we are and worry more about getting the fuck out of here," said Dayton. Commotion sounded from above, and he stiffened, darting up the stairs. "We have to leave now."

"How?" I asked, following him. I gripped Derek's hand, pulling him to trail along behind. "Waltz right in and out the front door?"

"Sorry to fall short on the endeavors of epic escape plans," Dayton snapped, beginning to mess with the doorknob.

I turned to Derek and cast him a worried glance. "What do we do?"

Derek's green eyes gleamed as he assessed Dayton with a level stare. Oddly, it reminded me of a look I'd seen on Luka. "You expect me to believe you aren't working with them?"

"Feel free to rot down here forever," Dayton spat. "See if I give a shit either way."

Dayton turned to me with that same expression of defiance and gave a slow shake of his head. Turning back toward the door, he spared a final glance at Derek. I took a step closer to Dayton, and I squeezed Derek's wrist, pulling him with me.

If Dayton was our only shot of escape, we had to trust him.

"Derek, we need to get out of here," I said.

I walked the rest of the way up, all my fears and anxieties forging their way through my mind. With a tremendous effort, I forced myself not to think of it—not until this was over and I was safe. If I broke down, I did not doubt Dayton would leave me, and I refused to be a dead weight for Derek.

Dayton fiddled with a lock at the door, cursing under his breath. "This is going to hurt like a bitch," he grumbled.

Without warning, he threw his shoulder into the door, striking it hard. The door creaked and groaned as he struck out at it repeatedly. I was afraid the commotion would draw attention, but I didn't think Dayton would appreciate me pointing that out.

"Logically, they want to keep us prisoner down here," Derek remarked. "Why would they make it easy to escape?"

A loud thud from above made me jump. "Can we just get out of here, please?"

"A stellar idea—why didn't I think of that?" Dayton said, throwing himself at the door again.

The door finally gave in, falling backward with a clatter. Dayton stepped back and gestured at the open doorway, which I approached with caution.

"It's now or never, Maris," Dayton said. "I can't protect you if you don't come with me."

He had a warped idea of protection, but I refrained from telling him that, detecting the sincerity in his tone. I nodded and went through slowly, preparing to be thrown into a scene of blood and chaos. My hands shook as I glanced down a dimly lit, narrow hall. A series of doorways scattered either wall, with God knows what behind them. No visible windows, either. Dayton looked both ways, and then back at Derek.

"Go that way, pretty boy." Dayton gestured to the right.

Derek stepped forward and looked down at me. "Stay behind me, okay?"

I nodded and trailed slowly behind, Derek at the front and Dayton in the rear. Dayton clutched the dagger, wielding it at the ready. The floorboards creaked under our weight, and my spine stiffened as a doorknob squeaked.

"*Go*—last door to the right!" hissed Dayton. Derek opened the door, and I heard Dayton suck in a breath of disapproval from behind as he said, "I guess its bad timing to mix up my left from my right."

A large man towered over Derek and tossed him aside like a rag doll. I gasped as Derek jumped up at once, landing a punch to the man's face and sending him stumbling back. The man barreled back without missing a beat. He raised his fist, but Derek caught it, squeezing hard. As bones crunched, Derek kicked him again. Hard. I squealed and scurried back, running into Dayton, who shoved me forward, yelling for me to go. Leaping over the unconscious man's body, I tried not to look at his obviously broken hand.

"Get her out of here!" Derek demanded. "I'll hold them off!"

"No!" I protested as a thundering of footsteps approached. "Are you crazy? They might kill you!"

Dayton hauled me up as I thrashed and kicked, inclining my neck to glimpse at the chaos centering around Derek. He pulled me into what looked like a sunroom with windows covering every inch and showcasing the forest of trees outside. It looked like the dark dead of night outside.

"Let me go!" I demanded, and Dayton did. I fell to my knees, gasping, then leaped up, whirling on him. "What the hell was that? I have to go back! Derek is in trouble!"

"Derek can hold his own," Dayton shot back, blocking the doorway with a glower. "You're not stupid. I know you understand enough of what is going on to not question things yet."

Before I could respond, Dayton's face turned skeptical, and he shot his arm over me. He raised his chin and sniffed the air, his eyes widening. The windows exploded. He moved like a blur, throwing his body over my own and planting a hand behind my head as we struck the ground. His body seized as another explosion went off, making my ears ring.

"What's happening?" I shrieked as he pulled me up. His grip was iron around my wrist—painful—but his quick gait left me to ignore it.

I wanted to turn back and get Derek, the explosion only adding to my unease. Derek couldn't hurt a fly, and the thought of him fighting anyone was unimaginable to me. But I could not fight against Dayton.

Dayton led us outside into the night, the only light escaping through the building's floodlights. I glanced around, grappling for familiarity, but the scenic forest looked like every other. I struggled to keep up and nearly toppled over when he skidded to a stop.

"What?" I asked, and he pushed me against the stone building, shushing me.

Dayton cursed, his straight posture becoming even more rigid. I followed the line of his golden vision and gaped.

Several giant wolves were on the lawn, their jet-black fur melding with the darkness. Their hackles rose, and I glimpsed the proud display of their razor-sharp teeth. Fresh blood dripped from their open mouths, and there was no mistaking these *were* wolves. With instinct kicking in, I turned to bolt the other way.

"No, look," Dayton said. Gripping my shoulders, he forced me to watch.

I nearly screamed. Luka stood in the center of the wolves, a twisted smile curling his lips. Despite being surrounded by a pack of wolves, he looked strange—calm. Throwing his head back, Luka gave a slow laugh. Then he lunged.

Luka's whole body rippled and twisted. Bone melted and grew, and flesh extended like flowing water. His skin turned into deep onyx fur, and his massive paws thundered against the ground. A flash of fangs glinted beneath the moon, and as a snout grew on Luka's face, a low, reverberating growl tore from him, vibrating through the fibers of the earth. Throwing its head back, the wolf let rip a deep howl into the night. I gaped at the beast and took a staggering step back.

I couldn't stop the scream.

Chapter 6

I closed my eyes, envisioning Luka turning into a wolf on replay. Fear snaked up my bones while I battled with denial despite the truth before me. This was far worse than any invention of my imagination. I was out of my mind, propelling headfirst down a path of no return. The idea I had of my brother—of myself—was gone. I had no idea of anything in my life anymore.

Dayton pushed me back against the stone exterior of the house, a hand clasped over my mouth. I tried to speak, but his eyes warned me to be silent. He looked back once and cursed, pulling me around the building and into darkness. Squeals of pain sounded in the distance, intermingled with snapping teeth and vicious growls.

My breath was rampant as I choked, "What the hell was that? What's going on?"

Dayton shook his head. "Are you fight or flight?"

The question caught me off guard, but I answered with shaky confidence. "What do you need me to do?"

A cynical smile briefly passed over him. "I can cause a distraction that will give you a chance to run. It'll only be a moment. Do you understand?"

I nodded, gazing out at the vast forest and narrow road. Neither looked appealing amidst this chaos, but I would run—I would get out of here—despite the panic seizing in my chest. "What about Derek?"

"Don't worry about him."

"No, I won't leave him. He needs to get out safely, too!"

Dayton's lips curled. "I just got you out of there. Don't you even think about going back in."

I crossed my arms. "Don't tell me to abandon my best friend."

Dayton huffed. "Listen, you're smart, that much I can tell. You know enough to realize there are secrets in your life, but it's your brother and best friend keeping them," he said. "I won't defend it, but they want to keep you safe, to protect you. What you just witnessed? That's their reality."

I exhaled slowly and nodded. "Okay, fine. I'll run; I'll leave."

Surprise crossed Dayton's features, and he said, "Okay. Once I leave, count to ten and then *run*."

He began walking away, and I couldn't help but ask, "Why are you helping me?"

Dayton narrowed his gaze, his irises rippling into molten gold until he left me standing there. Stunned I gulped. When I peeked my head around at the chaos of wolves, there was no evidence of him, but a war between wolves unfolding—advancing and snapping at one another. Some stood on their hinds, delivering sickening blows. Luka was among them—a wolf. Somehow. I couldn't wrap my head around it, but I knew it to be true. Could he defend himself? Was he in over his head? His worry for me would make him act irrationally. I forced myself to stay calm, even with my mind exploding. I counted to ten and then took off like a bullet.

My feet hit the ground with shocking force, each step upturning more dirt. I pumped my arms manically, refusing to look back as I sprinted down a dark, inclined road. It felt like hours had passed. I ran into the forest at one point, desperate to keep them off my trail. In the dead of night, I couldn't discern the time, knowing nothing except that I had run for miles without stopping. Still, I never faltered or stopped to look back, even when I stumbled and fell into a pile of mud. I simply got back up. Running was the only thing keeping me from the gravity of my feelings.

When my run became a jog, reality seeped in. My mind was stuck on instant rewind, watching Luka transition into a wolf. How was it possible? Derek and Dayton both displayed an array of inhumane traits, too—strength, healing, preternatural combat skills. Placing my hands on my thighs, I leaned over, gasping.

I forced back tears, blinking at my surroundings. It was hard to see in the dead of night, and I could not make out more than a few feet in front of me. My hands trembled beside me as my mind slowly pushed past my mental shields. I backed up into a tree that I clung to for life support, and as my shoulders sank, I slid down onto the cold, hard ground and cried.

It started as tears, then turned into racking sobs as I gasped and choked to get oxygen to my lungs. It overtook my body, and I held my head in my hands, raking my fingers through my hair. I cried until no sound could escape and the tears subsided. I rocked myself back and forth, the movement a trance. My whole body ached. The thought of moving from this spot weighed me down more, and leaning my head back, I closed my eyes until darkness of a different sort entangled me.

CHAPTER 7

My eyes fluttered open, yet I wondered if I was awake as darkness engulfed me. The surrounding chill was bone-deep, my body curling in on itself for warmth. As I moved, the fabric of a blanket brushed across my skin, and I curled my fingers around it, drawing it closer; I clung to it like my life depended on it, and then I sat up. My head spun, and I closed my eyes, which only intensified the sensation. Everything spun, and as I tried to piece my thoughts together, they spiraled. Nausea rose in me, and I lay back at once.

My hands trembled and my whole body clammed up. Slowly, I rose, and the spinning turned into a dull ache as I inhaled stale air. Despite the cold, anxiety heated my cheeks; my bare feet hit the cold hard floor, and only a sliver of light peeked through the gap in the curtains. I walked to them and clutched the fabric, yanking it back. I pulled the rod from the wall and stumbled backward as it clattered to the ground, upturning dust. I coughed. The morning light blinded me where it broke the darkness.

Staring at the front lawn of my home sent warmth radiating through me. I wrapped my arms around myself, allowing the sunlight to encapsulate me until I glanced down and grimaced. I was wearing dirt-smeared jeans, a tank top, and tennis shoes on my feet. I jerked back, pulling the blankets off my bed to reveal leaves, dirt, and dead bugs. Nausea roiled in me.

Luka. He came home yesterday covered in blood. We had argued, but I couldn't remember why. And Derek...I sent him away, but that felt like yesterday, too. My mind began to spiral.

Rushing across the room, I discarded my clothes as if they were dowsed in acid. I stumbled into the bathroom and locked the door behind me, screwing my eyes shut while turning toward the floor-length mirror. My eyes felt glued together, too afraid of what I would see when they opened.

I opened my eyes at my naked reflection and reeled back. This wasn't me. It had to be a trick; I had to be trapped in some sick and twisted nightmare. Yet a more decisive part of me knew that wasn't true as the reflection looking back at me was indeed my own. Dirt covered me, pale and crusted; I must have been like this for some time now. I dared a step closer, and my hand pressed against my mouth. Flecked blood sprinkled across my skin, like I had been sprayed by it. Over my arms were crimson smudges like handprints, and I touched each one, flinching.

I drew on my memories to fill in the missing pieces, only to come up short. The memory of an ache chased across my belly like a current of electricity as I recalled the wild beating of my heart and the adrenaline coursing through my blood. A flash of a face resurfaced—one I didn't recognize—contorted in a scowl.

I tore my gaze away and turned to the shower. Scalding water gushed from the tap. In moments, blissful heat enveloped me. A stiff washcloth rested on the floor, which I used to vigorously scrub my skin raw with lavender soap. There didn't appear enough to scrub away how unclean I felt. The urge to cry rose inside of me until the water ran clear. My hair was a tangled mess of dirt and leaves, and it took five washes before I was satisfied it was clean. Even then, a sensation of uncleanliness clung to my skin.

I don't know how long the water ran for, but the temperature had dropped to ice long before I got out. The cold floor was harsh beneath my feet. I reached for a towel and, once dried, inspected myself in the mirror to ensure no traces of dirt or blood were left behind. I dressed in dark jeans and my warmest red flannel shirt, even throwing on boots. My tangled hair took longer to comb, but I was meticulous with it and took the time to braid it back.

Slowly, fragments of memory returned. I remembered intense pain rocking my whole body, the sound of bones cracking and tortured cries ripping through the night. There had been...green eyes—Derek had been there. Why? What did he have to do with it? Had he been in danger? None of it made sense, but whatever happened, I knew there was no going back.

Voices drew me out of my head, and I stalked toward the door. My car keys were tossed next to my wallet on the dresser, and with shaking hands, I grabbed both, shoving the wallet into my back pocket. I hesitated, my gaze snagging on my family photo on the dresser. My mom. I pressed the frame face down, and with a final deep breath, I left my bedroom.

The stairs squeaked under my weight. Looking down in the living room, Derek and Luka peered up at me. They both looked normal, I noted. Luka wore regular jeans and a hoodie, and Derek was clad in a simple red flannel and gray sweats. Both were clean-shaven; I could smell their soap and aftershave from here. But something wasn't right. It felt calculated, and one thing they couldn't hide was the haunted looks glinting in their eyes as they watched me.

My heart hammered in my chest, threatening to burst. The same clammy feeling from before washed over me, and I suddenly felt desperate to change and turn back. With great effort, I put one foot in front of the other and continued down the steps. I stayed put at the bottom, keeping a safe distance between us.

"Maris," Luka's voice croaked.

I stared at them, and in a small voice, I said, "How can you stomach it?"

"What?" asked my brother.

"How can you stomach it?" I snapped, staring between the two. A wave of anger rose in me. "Lying! All the time! How could you do this to me?"

"Maris," Derek started, getting up.

Derek was my best friend; when he told me it would be okay, I believed him. But not now. I no longer trusted him or Luka. While my memories were hazy, one thing was crystal clear. They lied to me. Words echoed distantly in my mind, though I couldn't picture the speaker. *There are secrets surrounding your life, but it's your brother and best friend keeping them.*

"Don't!" I yelled, pointing at him. Derek flinched, turning his head like I had slapped him. I summoned a deep breath to contain the sobs brewing. "Stay away from me."

"Maris, if you let me talk, I can explain," said Luka, his voice cracking. I met his gaze, staring into his dark blue large and pleading eyes. He was just as scared as I was.

A memory tugged at me. I whirled, pressing my fingers against my temples to massage them as the memory threatened to pull through. Luka was there that night. Something happened to him. An image formed and then dissolved like vapor. I spun around and stared at the two of them.

Derek started to speak, but Luka held his hand to silence him. "Maris," Luka said calmly, "You need to remember."

My anger almost bested me; I wanted to demand what happened, but when I stared at Luka, the floodgates opened, and the memories pulled through. Overwhelmed, I cried out and fell to my knees. I clutched my head, keys in hand. I was distantly aware of their voices standing over me and my own muffled screams. The pain I endured, the torture—the boy, Dayton, who helped us escape. Derek, tortured, to the point of passing out. All of it rushed back, yet one memory stuck out above all.

I gathered myself together and stood. Elongated teeth—dark, ebony fur—vicious snarls. I shook, then someone grabbed me. Luka. I jerked away, stumbling backward to look at him. The brother I knew and loved suddenly felt like a stranger. I remembered him. I remembered him turning into a wolf.

"What are you?" I shrieked.

"Maris, let me explain—"

"What *are* you?" I repeated, stepping back until I was pressed against the front door.

"Maris—"

"What are you!?" I demanded, the wolf's image vivid in my mind.

Luka turned to Derek standing lamely behind, head down. "Derek, I don't think she can handle the truth."

"You have to tell her," Derek hissed. "She's seen too much; she knows too much. She'll spiral, Luka."

"She can't know."

"She has to!" Derek barked.

They wanted me to forget—to forget what happened to me and to forget whatever Luka was. Luka wanted to act like nothing happened, like when I was first attacked. *No,* I thought furiously. I would know the truth, whatever the cost.

I swung open the door and bolted. I heard the rush of them springing into action behind me as I barreled down the front steps. I stared out at the open terrain of forest, then back at the house where the garage was. I dashed toward it, the keys shaking in my hand. They would not take this from me. Not again. I needed to leave, to make sense of all this and piece it together.

I heard them behind me and spun to face them. I stumbled back wide-eyed, bracing myself against the garage door as a giant wolf landed before me. Its dark fur was a deep ebony, full and thick. There was no kindness in its face as it bore down over me, its figure a staggering six feet taller than myself. Lips curled in a familiar snarl, its blue eyes gazed down at me.

"Luka?" I croaked. The creature lay on the ground beside me, snout even with my face. "What are you?"

With absolute certainty, I knew my eyes were not deceiving me. I took a sharp breath and I watched the fur trade for skin and paws for limbs. Luka materialized out of the wolf crouched before me, as ordinarily as before, clothes and all.

"I'm a werewolf."

CHAPTER 8

"What?" I squawked.

Accepting it as the truth was seemed impossible. How could it be true? How could Luka be both a human and a monstrous creature all at once? I glanced back at Derek who stood behind him, shoulders slumped. Was Derek a wolf, too? I turned, punching in the numbers on the garage door as Luka spoke, half-crazed behind me.

"Please, let me explain," Luka begged.

"Explain what? That you lied?" I said, emotion swelling in my throat. I turned to stare at Luka as the garage door opened, the metal squeaking. "I need space."

"Maris, wait, don't do this!" pleaded Derek.

"What are you doing?" Luka demanded, stepping closer as I opened the driver's side door to my car.

I closed my eyes and took a steady breath. "I'm leaving."

"What do you mean?" Luka asked, slowly drawing closer.

I faced him, knowing tears pricked my eyes. "I'm scared of you, Luka."

Luka's breath caught. His back stiffened and nostrils flared, but he spoke evenly, "Maris, please. You have to let me explain all this."

"No, it's too late," I said. "I don't trust you anymore, Luka."

Luka visibly deflated and stepped forward. "I can't let you just *go*. I've risked too much for you; I've done too much to let you leave me."

"You lied." My voice cracked, my lip quivering. "This is too much—*you're* too much. I'm leaving. I need you to stay away from me."

The words hit their mark, as I knew they would. His stunned silence spoke legions. If I stayed a second longer, he would convince me to stay. But I couldn't, not after everything, so I said the cruelest thing I could think of, though it hurt me probably as much as it hurt him. They were the last words our father said to Luka before leaving us.

Luka grabbed my wrist. I thought he was going to stop me, but he only pressed a pepper spray into my hand. I glanced between Luka and Derek, my heart squeezing in my chest. I took the pepper spray with shaking hands, and as Luka let go, I didn't hesitate to plummet into my car. Numb, I drove off, not allowing the tears to consume me as I left.

I'd been driving aimlessly for hours on end. The back roads of New York were vastly different than the steep roads I stumbled upon before, but I had no idea where I was. I stopped for gas nearly two hours ago and had traveled down this long stretch of road ever since, only crossing paths with a handful of other cars. Considering the dreary, steady trickle of rain, I wasn't surprised.

The uphill drive and winding roads were hard but doable as I tried sifting through my thoughts.

This is irrational. Irresponsible, whispered the devil on my shoulder. Each turn of the wheel further from home made the voice easier to silence.

Watching Luka turn from a wolf and back into himself had me pressing harder against the gas. I couldn't think about that now without terror coiling through my gut. The sheer height of it—*him*—was gigantic, his sharp canines gleaming and his expression one of utter lethality. If it weren't for the eyes, I wouldn't have thought it was Luka, and while I didn't know what I thought he was hiding, never in my wildest dreams could I have foreseen this truth.

I took a deep breath and focused on the road. My body ached, and I realized I hadn't eaten since God knows when. How much time had passed since my abduction? I couldn't figure it out. I had to work hard to stamp the anxiety gnawing away at me, fear rocketing my heart to my throat. I glanced in the review mirror and screamed. A wolf padded along the road, following my tracks—or was it merely a wolf in the woods? Panting, I pulled off into a narrow ditch.

I stumbled out of my car and turned back, clutching the pepper spray, but when a small fox skirted between the bushes, I finally exhaled. Not every animal was a wolf, though I now knew the animal that jumped in the road while Derek drove me home had been a wolf and not a bear. Derek lied. I steadied my breathing and forced myself to move, to stretch my limbs, and clear my head. Maybe a walk would help me.

Darkness enveloped the woods, the only sounds that of the rainfall. The forest stretched for miles; the dewy scent of fresh rain tickled my senses, intermingled with a faint scent of maple. I glanced back toward the road, gauging the distance between where I stood and the woods.

Clammy with anxiety, I stopped by a small stream and knelt beside it. My reflection glinted in the ripples as I splashed water onto my face. When my eyes reopened, a white wolf stared back at me. I screamed and smacked the water, the reflection contorting with the ripples and returning to normal. I bit my lip, forcing myself not to cry. If I started to cry, I wouldn't stop.

Standing, I wiped my hands on the back of my jeans and started heading back toward the car. I froze, the back of my neck prickling. A tree branch snapped and I gasped, taking cover behind a nearby tree and sucking in a breath. I readied myself to run, spinning fast on my heel, and ran into something solid.

"Hello, deary."

I screamed, striking out with my fist, yet he caught my punch, twisting my arm painfully back. He shoved me onto the ground, and I shuffled backward on my elbows as he loomed closer. He had long black hair tied into a bun, with sharp, glass-like features, high cheekbones, and a strong jawline. His red eyes glared down at me, his lips twisting into a smirk.

Flashes of Zayne resurfaced, with the same uncanny red eyes.

I reached for a rock on the ground and lobbed it at him. He caught it inches away from his head, then sent it ricocheting back at me. I ducked, his cooing laughter drawing closer.

"That's no way to treat friends," he crooned.

"Don't flatter yourself," I said through gritted teeth.

A flicker of amusement danced through his features, and he hauled me up faster than I could react, shoving me against a tree and twisting my other arm back. I cried out, trying to shove him away, but to no avail.

He tutted softly in my ear. "A lone wolf—a pup, no less—wandering these parts. Well, it would pique anyone's interest."

I bucked, slamming my head into his. It likely hurt me more than him as I blinked away the stars swimming behind my eyes. His hold lessened enough for me to break free. I ran, my feet slamming against the leaves and branches as he clucked his tongue, leaping over me and landing in a crouch.

"Oh, you're going to make me work for it," his chilling voice teased, a Cheshire cat grin breaking across his features.

I sprinted, and for once I understood why Luka drilled the importance of running into me. I don't know how long I made it before large arms encapsulated me and pressed me against a tree. I tried to scream but his hand covered my mouth. It wasn't the guy from before, but it took a moment for my memory to catch up. A name slowly came to me. Dayton.

I didn't recognize him straightaway, if only because he wasn't covered in blood. He was clean shaven, too, his hair scrubbed clean. He looked kinder, somehow, but then he scowled, and that's when I remembered. Those uncanny golden eyes were connected to all the strange events over the past few weeks.

"Mare?"

"You?" I asked. "How?"

"Again with the asking questions when you're in imminent danger of being killed." A smile barely cracked his lips, and if I were not this close, I might have missed it. Dayton glanced behind me, and his gaze darkened. The man was close. Pulling me by the hand, Dayton shoved me forward. "*Run!*"

"Now, now, don't ruin the fun," drawled the man, his voice near. "I was playing nice."

"Somehow, I struggle to believe that," said Dayton. He turned to me with a feral expression. "Run!"

I knew I *should* run, but my feet didn't, as if my mind had paralyzed me to the spot.

"Whatever," he growled. "Don't say I didn't warn you."

Dayton ran headfirst into danger. He lunged, turning into a wolf in midair. Each paw struck the earth and shattered the ground beneath it. His fur was a chestnut brown, like the hue of his hair; his snout was long, and his lips curled into a snarl, exposing his razor-sharp teeth. His sheer size was bigger than that of a lion, and I quivered at the sight. When Dayton's focus homed in on him, I glimpsed the murderous look in his eyes, and ran.

I took off like a bat out of hell. The ground crunched behind me as I ran, though I dared not to look at who—or what—might be chasing me. Though I was fast, a human's speed was nothing like the creature that trailed me. I glanced back to check if it was Dayton. It wasn't. It was a wolf with ebony fur and red-rimmed eyes.

The downhill path was not easy to navigate, and I tried recalling the direction of my car. Every tree looked the same, and each wrong turn only lured me deeper into the forest. The ground dipped suddenly, and as my feet tangled together, I plummeted down an embankment. Sliding downward, leaves and tree branches stuck in places they shouldn't as I flailed, digging my heels into the ground to decrease my speed until I stopped at the base of a tree. I jumped up and screamed at the black wolf approaching.

"Get the hell away from me," I cried, my words my only defense. Then I remembered the pepper spray Luka gave me and I scrambled for it in my pocket.

The wolf leaped with a snarl, and I threw a hand over my face, pressing down on the nozzle. It sprayed and the wolf jerked back in surprise; I did, too, for landing a good shot.

A dagger flew.

A loud thud ensued as the man who'd chased me fell face down on the ground where the wolf had been, a thick dagger lodged into his head.

Dayton landed beside him and seamlessly pulled the dagger free. He did not stop to wipe the blade clean before barreling toward me and careening me away. I could only blink, my hands trembling as nausea bubbled in my throat. With all the recent curveballs, you'd think I'd be immune to anything—but witnessing a man's murder? That chilled me to my core.

"God. Don't fucking gawk, you're turning ashen," said Dayton, pulling me away. Gripping my wrist, he broke off into a run, and I had no choice except to follow as he practically dragged me with him. I forced my heels into the earth to catch his attention.

He spun. "*What?*"

"Did you have to kill him?" I asked, sensing the hysteria of my words. It was a fair question to ask, though. The man's lifeless body seared into my mind and would be ingrained in my nightmares.

"Killing him was a necessary evil," he replied casually. I studied his blank expression, shocked by his lack of remorse. Dayton watched me, eyebrows furrowed. "Why were you in the Woods of the Damned? Only fools go here."

Woods of the Damned? That was the first time I'd heard of such a thing. *What an odd name.* I looked at Dayton and crossed my arms. "Yet you're here."

Dayton wore clothes as dark as night, his leather jacket splayed over his broad shoulders. Most interesting was the belt looped over his waist, loaded with various weapons; some I could identify—daggers and swords—while others I couldn't, yet they were clearly lethal. That alone should have had me turning and running, yet I stayed.

"I know your brother kept you hidden from this world," Dayton said, striking a hand over his jaw. The tiniest hints of stubble peeked through. "I don't believe he would let you blindly wander into that part of the woods."

"How do you know that?"

"Rumors round the mill." Dayton shrugged.

How could everyone but me know the truth about my life? How could I have been so oblivious, yet strangers knew more about me than I did?

"How come you keep showing up? And seemingly only when I'm in mortal peril?" I added, a tad dramatically. It did not go unnoticed he seemed to know more of me than I did him.

"Ah," he said, dropping his hand and shaking his head. "If I hadn't shown up when I did, there's a good chance you would be dead. Or worse. You're lucky nightfall is still a bit away."

"Let's not beat around the bush. How did you know to be here?" I pressed.

"Right place, right time, I suppose." His tone was light as he walked. "I've saved your life twice now. When are you going to even the score?"

"Who are you really?"

Dayton's posture stiffened and his head shot up, meeting my gaze. His golden eyes pierced into me, and I stepped back. "Dayton," he said roughly. "My name is Dayton, but I already told you that. Though I suppose it's nice to meet you properly, Mare."

"It's Maris."

"If you say so."

Dayton's quips came quickly, delivered with hints of arrogance. He paused his saunter and stood, crossing his arms over his chest and tilting his head. Sun broke through the rain clouds, and the early evening light caught his hair, gilding the dark strands. Again, I couldn't help but notice how ethereal he looked and felt, despite his displaced attitude.

"How do you know who I am?" I asked, snapping back to reality.

"You think rather highly of yourself to assume I do," Dayton said.

I narrowed my eyes, trying to figure out his angle. Dayton had a dangerous edge that he easily flaunted. I wasn't sure of his motives, and frankly, he was a stranger. I had no reason to trust him, except he had saved me twice without question. But he had killed someone, and he strangely showed up everywhere. Was he following me? I had no way of knowing where his true intentions lay.

"Can I trust you?"

Dayton raised his eyebrows, considering. "I'm not the enemy here, though you have a knack for finding them."

"All I know is that in the past few weeks, I've had three people attack me, and somehow you wiggled your way into each of those scenarios. Pardon me if I'm hesitant around strangers." My voice sounded taut, even to my ears.

Dayton's eyes glittered as he contemplated his reply. "Fine, that's fair."

"Why did you save me?" I asked, then added, "How did you know where I would be?"

"Like I already told you," he resumed walking, and up ahead was a road a dozen or so yards away. "Right place, right time."

"I don't believe you."

"I don't blame you." He shrugged. "I wouldn't believe me either if the roles were reversed."

"How do you know my brother?"

"Again, you assume I do," Dayton said. "Why do you keep running into werewolves that want to kill you? Seriously, you officially have a record."

My breath hitched. *Werewolf.* "So, it's all real then? Werewolves?"

Dayton laughed darkly. "I presume you aren't blind and watched me morph into a wolf earlier?" I nodded. "Therein lies your answer."

"Apparently there really is a first time for everything," I muttered.

Dayton halted at the side of the road before crossing it. I looked both ways, though I didn't recognize it. I should go back to my car, I thought, yet I found myself following Dayton, though I wasn't sure why. He jumped into a ditch and pulled out a motorcycle.

"What's that?"

"Another question," said Dayton, wheeling the motorcycle into the road. He leaned against his bike and folded his arms over his chest, smirking. "Fine, this is a motorcycle. It's used to move across distances, similar to a car."

"Would you quit being a smart-ass?" I snapped. Of course that would be the question he decided to answer. "You know what, thanks for saving me but I have to go back to my own car."

Dayton snorted. "Absolutely not."

"I wasn't asking you."

"And I wasn't giving you an option," Dayton returned, rolling his eyes.

"Excuse me?"

Taking note of my tone, Dayton hesitated. "Okay, that was douchey of me. Of course, you get the choice of coming with me or leaving. But you need to understand there are more vicious creatures lurking in these woods than that sorry man I killed. I'm not sticking around to keep saving you, either. If you go back in there, you will die."

"You don't sugarcoat things."

Dayton took my car keys from my hand before I could blink, dropping them to the ground, and repeatedly bashing his boot down hard until they shattered. He reached down and plucked up a small red stone.

"You see this? It's a tracker, put in there by your brother. Do you honestly think he would let you run off on your own after figuring out the truth? He wanted to give you space before bringing you back. He's tracking you, and he's likely not too far behind."

I balked, my heart hammering against my chest as I remembered Luka shifting. The betrayal and the lies all flooded back. "I can't go back to him, not yet."

"Look." Dayton's voice wavered from its previous cockiness. "You have questions; I have answers. Just not here. Come with me, and I can take you someplace safe. I understand you're scared and weary, but if you stay out here alone, you'll get yourself killed."

"Why do you care?" I asked.

"Who said I did?" replied Dayton, holding my gaze for a long moment, wayward strands of hair falling in his eyes. "If you must know, everyone loves a good damsel."

"What are you suggesting?"

He raised his eyebrows, the ghost of a smile on his face. "Come with me and let me help you. I can offer you the answers you want, but not here." He turned, swinging his leg over his motorcycle. Reaching down, he offered me a helmet. "What do you say?"

I held his gaze, contemplating. I couldn't go home, which meant I had nowhere to go, and Dayton here was offering me a solution to both of those problems. But Dayton also just killed someone; with morally good intent or not, murder was murder. The question of trust dangled between us.

"Don't make me regret coming with you," I said. He raised his eyebrows, clearly shocked as I put the helmet over my head and inhaled deeply.

"I'll never make a promise I can't keep." He grinned. I stalked over to him and got onto the back of his bike, sitting awkwardly for a moment until he added, "Hold onto me if you don't want to fly off."

I leaned forward and reached around him. His jacket was worn leather but the flesh beneath was hard muscle. He started the engine, and I tensed, laughter rumbling through him at my unease.

"By the way, I'm not a damsel," I added before we sped off across the road.

CHAPTER 9

I screamed with each acceleration and sharp turn, the speed of his bike like a rocket shooting into oblivion. I suspected Dayton was pushing legal limits, so if the bulk of my helmet smashing into him every few minutes bothered him, then I didn't care. When we slowed enough that my head wasn't spinning, I peered up at the steep mountain ahead of us, surrounded by endless forests. The sunset over the horizon cast a deep-red and orange light across the surfaces as birds flitted about and small creatures scurried between the branches. Even the deer were out, grazing the grounds. It was strange to see these creatures unbothered.

I stared straight ahead as Dayton slowed, turning off the main road. My mouth fell open. A shimmering wall of light glittered between two trees like a gate, warm golden rays radiating from it; it wasn't like anything I had ever seen before. Dayton drove the bike straight through the light, and as we passed through, a cool mist sprinkled over me. I shivered, watching as he took us further along, another glittering veil shooting up between us. My eyes squinted, trying to see beyond it, but there was nothing but endless trees.

"What is that?" I asked over the bike's engine.

"Those are the wards," he replied, coming to a stop in front of a set of iron gates at least fifty feet in height. "They run the length of the property, but you'll soon see what it's protecting."

Wards? Would that be a shield of sorts? Strange, but I was warming up to the idea of strange. Dayton pressed a palm against the stone wall beside the gate, pressing a stone in, and leaving a bloody handprint behind as the gates slowly squealed open.

"You ready?" Dayton asked.

"To get off this bike? Yes."

Dayton revved the engine, and we flew through the gates. I pressed my face against his back and squeezed my eyes shut, bracing for the impact. But I didn't even feel the mist as everything whirled past in a tizzy. Golden lights twirled around us, shimmering in the sunlight, and there was a slight sweetness to the scent, like cotton candy.

Dayton stopped the bike, and I leaped off, dazed, peeling the helmet from my head. A massive building towered overhead, its shocking height dizzying to gaze upon. A staircase that appeared a thousand steps high led to a set of wooden doors. The building was like a castle, dark stone rising high onto the exterior and stretching across small towers, scattering atop the roof at different heights. Windows glinted on every panel of the multiple floors, spreading endlessly each way as the building encapsulated gilded light around and far above. A shield of protection.

"The wards?" I guessed, gazing up in awe.

"Yes," Dayton answered. "Powered by the full moon each month. Only broken with silver stakes."

Full moons and silver stakes. *Alrighty then.*

"Where are we?" I asked, gazing past the building at the miles of trees stretching along the property, set behind the mountain top.

I peeled my eyes away from the beauty to look back at Dayton, who watched me with reluctant bemusement as he covered his motorcycle with a tarp, laying it against the stone pathway. For a quick getaway, it was a convenient spot.

"This is where I live," he said, moving toward the staircase while I hurried to keep pace with him.

"How?"

"How do I live here?" he echoed. "By unlocking the door and going inside?"

I glowered at him. "You know that is not what I meant," I said, taking two steps at a time. "What is this place?"

"This is the Temple of Loup-Garou," said Dayton, "an ancient, sacred fortress to facilitate the healing of the mind, body, and soul."

"That sounds lovely," I said honestly as we reached the top step.

"It's all a bunch of bullshit," Dayton mused, opening the door. "Are you coming?"

He was holding the door for me, I realized. I walked through and into a long hallway. Hanging from the ceiling were ornately decorated chandeliers, with the moon phases twisted into the metal. The black metal was stark against bare-bleached walls, and my feet clicked against the dark wooden floors as I kept up with Dayton. At the end of the hallway, a staircase sat to the right, and to the left was a room with a sitting area, decorated with multiple cushioned chairs and couches which surrounded a large fireplace. One wall was made of only windows, and I gawked at it as I passed.

I scurried ahead to not lose sight of Dayton, who refused to wait for me. He opened another set of doors, this time not bothering to hold it open, and I barely caught it before it slammed shut in my face. Groaning,

I heaved it open, stepping into a large room. Mats lined the floor, and ropes and chains dangled from wooden beams in the ceiling along with various oddly styled punching bags lined up in a row against one wall. Like the other rooms, floor-to-ceiling windows lined the back wall, and tendrils of sunlight leaked through.

What truly caught my attention was the array of weapons lining the wall to my right, promising different types of demise. I stalked toward them, gazing at the selection: blades varying from tiny daggers to full-on swords, bows and arrows, axes and guns. The further I went, the more foreign objects became. Aside from pepper spray, I'd never touched a weapon. Maybe it would be different if I knew how to use them, but even touching something that could kill someone made me think I was in over my head.

Turning around on my heel, I found Dayton watching me with a barely there amused expression. "Is this a weapons room?" I asked.

"Training room, actually. This is just weapons overflow," he answered. "I spend most of my time in this room."

"There are enough weapons here to manage a pretty sizable army," I remarked. "What are you, some sort of commanding chief?"

A figure dropped from the ceiling right in front of me, and I squawked, jumping backward. I stumbled into a smooth table, gripping the sides for support. A tall boy peered down at me, surveying me with piercing green eyes. "Pretty *and* a sense of humor."

If the table wasn't already supporting my weight, I might have stumbled backward again from the uncanny déjà vu I felt while looking at this stranger. I searched his features for any recognizable link, but I'd never seen this person before. If I had, I certainly wouldn't have forgotten him.

He had neon pink hair slicked back atop his head and cut close on the sides his hair was pale blond. Jewelry glinted on his face, a black hoop over his right nostril, and a silver ring slicing through his left eyebrow. Light reflected in a rainbow off his silver-sequined tank top, glittering as he stalked closer. I noticed the smudges of dark eyeliner beneath his eyes.

"Julian Fletcher." He stepped forward, a smile lighting up his features. He outstretched his hand to me, and I warily returned the gesture. "Nice to meet you—?"

He let the question hang, and I realized I needed to speak. "Maris. My name is Maris Bakar."

Julian cast a look at Dayton, who merely shrugged and said, "What was I supposed to do? Leave her in the woods alone?" Dayton moved toward the two of us, shucking off his leather jacket. "She was in the Woods of the Dammed, Jules." I watched them both, confused. "Let's just see how this plays out, okay?"

I frowned and interjected. "What's going on?"

"Nothing," they said in sync.

Though I didn't believe that for a second, I let it go. I had more pressing matters, most of which I had been pushing vehemently down. I glanced behind me at the table I leaned against and moved to sit in a chair. I sat at the front of the table, with Julian to my left, his gaze lingering on Dayton, who leaned against the nearby window edge, head turned.

"It is always exciting seeing how squeamish newcomers are," Julian observed, tilting his head at me. "How much do you know?"

"No," Dayton said, fixing me with a pointed glare. "What do you *think* you know?"

I pondered this for a moment, preparing to unfurl the darkness within me. A part of me wanted to run headfirst into the truth, and another wanted nothing to do with it. I knew what Luka said he was—I saw it with my own eyes. Then there had been Dayton, who turned into a wolf right in front of me. I couldn't deny any of it.

"I had an ordinary life until the night after my shift when I was attacked," I said, looking at Dayton. "You were there that night."

Dayton nodded. "I was tracking the werewolf that attacked you. I tried to warn your friend, but he wasn't listening."

There was more to unpack with that, except my mind was too scattered to prod further. In the back of my mind, I did wonder why this was all coming to light now. Why not sooner? Why did they come after me?

"Well, since that night, I've been attacked, kidnapped, and seen things I can never unsee. Then, I woke up today, and my brother tells me he's a—" I closed my eyes, unable to finish the sentence.

"Werewolf," Dayton said coldly.

"Yes," I loosed a long breath. "In a fictitious sense, I know what it means, but I never considered anything like that to be real. What *does* it mean?"

Dayton and Julian exchanged equal looks of hesitation.

Julian was the first to speak. "Werewolf is a modern way to refer to Lycanthropy, which in its simplest terms means you can transform into a wolf through magical means."

"But how?" I inquired, keeping the shock from my voice.

"The history of our kind is long and complex," Dayton said. "There isn't really a cut and dry explanation for Lycanthropy or its exact origin—there are plenty of rumors, sure, but we only know for certain that there are two ways to become a werewolf."

"You are either born into it or forced into it," Julian explained. "Most of our kind are born, passing it down from generation to generation, and the less pleasant way to become one is by force when an Alpha bites you."

An Alpha bite makes you a werewolf? *I want you to remember this.* The man who attacked me, those were his last words before he bit me. But he had been a human, hadn't he? Or at least, he seemed human. It was nothing—it had to be nothing.

"I'm going to guess on a full moon?" I said, tone dripping with sarcasm. Dayton snorted and shook his head. "What is an Alpha?"

"Alphas are the strongest and most powerful—the leaders of the pack, so to speak. Betas—the second best—are usually the Alpha's right-hand man, and lastly, there are Omegas who make up the entirety of the Cadre, like a pack." Julian explained. "Alphas are powerful beings; you're either an Alpha by killing an existing Alpha and inheriting their power, or the natural pecking order deems you worthy. But most Alpha's kill for the power. The status."

It seemed oddly like a natural wolf pack, then, and I wondered whether wolves had mimicked werewolves, or vice versa. Linking werewolves with ordinary creatures made it easier to understand. Plus, it lessened the shock of the truth.

"Then there are dormant wolves and Fenrir." Dayton scowled. "Foul creatures, Fenrir are. They are humans that want the bite when they don't have the curse."

"Fenrir?" I tried to mimic how Dayton pronounced it: *fen-rear.* "What is that?"

"They're a breed of werewolves," Dayton explained. "Foul, loathsome, and disgusting creatures."

"You could be empathetic," Julian added. "Not all Fenrir willingly choose that path."

"It makes no difference when it comes to killing them," said Dayton callously.

"Can we backpedal?" I interjected.

Julian turned to me with easy patience. "Werewolves are born by either having two parents who are werewolves, or one parent who is and one who isn't. The werewolf gene is always dominant, and the result of a human and a werewolf defaults to a werewolf, but a dormant werewolf. Essentially, a dormant werewolf is one whose curse has not been activated until bitten by an Alpha werewolf."

"Wait," I said, "you lost me."

Julian chuckled and stood to cross the room, open a cabinet, then return with a paper and pen. He scratched the pen at the paper, and then turned it to me.

"A werewolf plus another werewolf equals another werewolf." He gestured to the scribbled diagram, designed like a family tree. I nodded. "Alright then. You take one werewolf parent out and make that a human. A human with a werewolf creates a dormant werewolf, which simply put is a werewolf without the curse."

Dormant had to be what Luka was—what I was. If we were dormant, that meant one of our parents had been a werewolf, but which one? It could have been either, I supposed. I never knew my mom, but that didn't mean she couldn't have been. As for my dad, he was an asshole, but there was no reason why it couldn't have been him, either.

"Curse?" I asked.

"The bite is considered a curse when you're not born into it. There is no difference really between being born into it or not, except most dormant werewolves don't know of this world, so it can come as a shock," Dayton explained.

A feeling I know all too well.

"Which brings us back to Fenrir—humans bitten by a werewolf yet possess no werewolf lineage. The bite drives them to madness. They are half-human, half-wolf creatures who are strong, mindless, and lethal as all hell. The only way to control them is to kill them." Julian spoke without judgment in his tone, but I glimpsed the haunted look in his eyes as he spoke.

Fenrir sounded terrifying. Who would willingly choose that life? But what did I know? *Very little,* considering I was learning all of this now. My head began to ache.

"Where does my brother fall into this?" I asked, bracing for the answer. A collective silence filled the room.

"It's hard to say, really," Dayton said after a moment. "Luka is the legends you tell over campfires—a myth of nightmares. Parents use the story of him to scare little kids into obedience. If you know him, you know he's not someone you want to be your enemy."

Luka had a temper, but that didn't sound like him. But maybe his perception just didn't align into the version of Luka I knew—the version only I knew. Another reminder I didn't know my brother, not really.

"Why? Why does he terrify people?" I asked.

"Luka is the Bestial."

That name. Zayne said it, too, and that was what Zayne pieced together that night. Luka's real identity. I was the one who unintentionally aided him in figuring it out. It unsettled me to know I might have inadvertently put Luka in danger. Despite my anger with him now, I would never want to hurt him.

"I'm confused about this whole Luka and the Bestial thing. I don't quite understand the difference."

"The Bestial is a title given to him based off the rumors of his crimes," said Julian.

"Think of the Bestial as the stage name—the persona Luka hides behind," Dayton added. "No one knows who the Bestial is; they know Luka to be a strong Alpha, but he hides behind the alias, therefore, there's no one to hold accountable for the crimes committed."

"What's the point?" I asked, as the truth sunk in. He'd lived two lives, keeping me separate from his world.

"I assume to keep you safe, to—"

"—keep me separate from the world he hid from me," I cut Dayton off. "Yeah, I got it."

My head spun. There was no way the man Dayton just described was my brother. When I thought of Luka, I recalled my older brother who raised me alone without parental guidance; my brother who made me coffee every morning and cooked me breakfast, who helped me with my math homework despite knowing nothing about it. That was exactly what he wanted for me, I realized. A normal life away from this one because this life was messy. Emotion welled in me, and I pushed it back.

"This world can be messy," Dayton said. "I don't know why he chose to keep you in the dark. Maybe because he emerged within the human world, and not the Moon Court, so it allowed him to live by his own law."

"What do you mean?"

"It's rare for a dormant werewolf to emerge without the Werewolf Council's knowledge. Luka slipped through the cracks, and by the time the Council realized who he was, he knew enough about them to defy against them," Dayton explained.

Moon Courts and Werewolf Councils—uncanny things I knew nothing about. I couldn't help but notice the way he spoke about Luka as if he knew him.

"If Luka is as secretive as you say, how do you know him?" I asked.

Dayton stilled, and as he observed me, I saw the wheels turning in his head. He continued to scrutinize me with his stare. "I don't know him; I just make it my business to know things."

Any more questions down that road would be unwelcome, so I let it go. "You mention a Council and a Court?" I asked.

Julian perked up and supplied, "The Moon Court is a place within our homeland of Lycan, and residing there is the Werewolf Council which governs us."

"Lycan as in Lycanthropy?" I asked.

"Exactly," Julian agreed. "Lycan is like its own country. It's small and remote, across the globe past Romania. Not on any maps, though. It's hidden from humans. Lycan is the homeland, the Moon Court is the capital, and the Council governs us."

I swallowed. It was wild to think there was a whole other country hidden from the world, and the otherworldliness of it all was hard to wrap my mind around. I only nodded, then asked, "This house... how does that work?"

"Like I explained before, this is the Temple of Loup-Garou. It's a sanctuary for other werewolves," Dayton explained. "Jules and I were assigned to be guardians of the Temple by the Council, and here we are."

"Are there other..." I paused. "Werewolves?"

"Sometimes. At the moment, no," Julian continued. "The werewolf population in these areas has been fleeting over the past years. Plus, werewolves tend to stick with their Cadre, but if they need aid, that's what the Temple is for. But there have been more Fenrir sightings in these parts than anything."

"Zayne was a werewolf?" I asked, remembering his creepy red eyes. Dayton nodded. "And the man that attacked me at the bar was also a werewolf?"

"Now you're getting it," Dayton said.

"What did they want with me?"

Dayton and Julian shared another look, but Dayton must have noticed my brows furrow and interjected.

"There is a man. His name is Kaser. There are rumors he is rising to power quickly," Dayton said, but I sensed his hesitation as he did.

My shock was stunted as I quickly said, "Zayne mentioned that name. Kaser. Did they know who I was? Is that why they took me? Am I in danger?"

Julian interrupted just as quick. "Kaser was a man whose father did diabolical things. He was a stain in our history, but that's nothing to get into now. Kaser is not someone I would be overly worried about."

"What did his father do?"

"Nothing worth speaking of," said Dayton sharply. "Kaser is nothing to be concerned about. He isn't interested in you, that's if he even knows of your existence. Kaser is a problem for the Wolf Council to deal with."

"But Zayne—"

"—was a thickheaded moron whose ego got him killed," Dayton snapped. "He died before he was able to even relay the message. You're safe."

Dayton held my gaze; I trusted him enough not to lie to me, but safe felt like a loose word to use right now. I hadn't been safe since the night I was first attacked—the night that started all of this.

"What happens if someone else finds me and tries to take me?" I asked. "I mean, I was attacked outside of work. Who's to say that won't happen again? That man bit me."

"That was just an Alpha looking to pick a fight with your brother, hoping to overpower him," said Dayton absently.

An Alpha. I jerked back, retreating from the table.

"Mare, wait—" Dayton began, but I silenced him with a look.

A panic I couldn't control erupted in me. I clutched a hand to my chest; this was not happening. I was *not* a werewolf; I could accept that Luka and Derek were, but not me. This was not my world. I was supposed to go to school in the fall, start my classes, and try to build a normal life with a normal career. My breath caught, and my hands trembled.

"Mare," Dayton spoke cautiously, peeling from his spot by the window. "What's wrong?"

"I-I think I'm having a panic attack," I stammered. "I need something that will center my fear, clear my head."

"What are you panicking about?" Dayton asked, slowly approaching me. "The truth? Because that's not going to change. Panicking about it doesn't change it."

"My whole life has just been upended!" I argued.

"I don't give a shit," he snarled, holding my gaze.

"I need to smoke," Julian announced, rising from his chair. "Things are getting dramatic, and I don't deal well with stress."

Dayton shook his head, turning away from me. He reached into a case and produced a series of daggers, unwavering from that slightly pissed-off stance as he glanced back. "If you're going to be mad, at least channel it into something useful," he said, holding out a series of daggers. Each blade was at least six inches, and the hilt glittered with red stones.

"No," I said. "I don't want to use that."

"Why?"

"Because it could kill someone," I hissed. "They're dangerous."

"Yeah, that's kind of the point," said Dayton. He grabbed my elbow and gently guided me forward in front of a set of targets. "Look, these are easy. I promise they won't hurt you or anyone else."

Dayton flung each dagger in rapid succession, each artfully landing on six different bullseyes. My eyes widened as he summoned them back with a flick of his wrist and, turning to me, he held them out again.

"How do you summon them back?" I asked.

"Magic," he replied. Dayton peeled a black band from around his wrist and grabbed my own. It felt warm and snug around my wrist. "Each of these daggers has a tracker embedded in it, and these bands summon them. It's a simple backtrack spell."

"Simple, huh?"

Dayton narrowed his gaze. "I want you to practice throwing these. It does not matter how well you aim. This is just for the distraction. When you are done, you can summon them back."

"I don't know about this," I said, but he raised his eyebrows in challenge.

"I promise its safe."

"Fine," I said. "But remember that you pissed me off and then decided to put weapons in my hand."

My mind felt like it was teetering on the edge of a dangerous cliff. I was tempted to grab the blade and squeeze it until it broke skin, to invite in the pain and allow it to center me. But Dayton's relentless words echoed in my head, and I stepped beside him, poised to aim.

Despite Dayton's words of "not needing to be good," he set the bar pretty high. He produced multiple small knives from a belt around his waist and the same black band I had on my wrist. He pointed at several targets—sacks with various sized circles around them—arranged at different heights along the wall and let them sail one after another. Each hit the target's center without fail. He explained where I should aim and the easiest ones to hit.

When I finally dared to throw one, I felt Dayton watching me. My palms were sweaty as I focused on the target, the knife heavy in my hand. I hesitated, then reeled my arm back and threw. It missed. I threw another one. The same. Again, no dice. Frustration boiled in me; I was on my last two, and I chucked the last one with no luck.

I flicked my wrist as Dayton had instructed to summon them back, but I must have done it wrong. All six knives came barreling back like a boomerang. On instinct, I leaped to the ground and heard the knives clattering behind me.

I got up, pointing a finger at Dayton. "This was stupid, and you know it." Out of the corner of my eye, something ricocheted toward me. I spun and caught the knife poised to hit me. Once the hilt was in my hand, I ripped off the black band and shoved it at Dayton along with the dagger. "How did I catch that?"

He lazily flicked his wrist to summon the remaining wayward daggers as he drawled, "Mare, you ask all the wrong questions. You know how you did that."

Dayton was right. He seemed to *always* be right. The truth was, I caught the knife because of the thing I was too afraid to face.

"I'm a werewolf." The words came out slow; there was no taking them back once they were said.

Dayton nodded slowly. "That's why I brought you here. To be fair, I thought you knew. You have this energy radiating off you that just screams newborn."

"Newborn?"

"New wolf," he explained. "When you first start to transition, you go through a series of events. You're exhibiting all the signs. Out of control emotions, rash decisions, an imminent danger to yourself." He spoke each word with precision. "Most new wolves end up dead because they don't realize what's happening to them."

"Ah," a voice said. I glanced past Dayton to find Julian had reappeared. "You've told her, I see."

Julian's scent was intoxicating: smokiness intertwined with a subtle sweetness of menthol that hit you immediately, mixed with a pungent reek of alcohol. Bitter like cheap vodka. The smell made my head spin.

"Dude, you picked the two worst vices and banded them together," Dayton grumbled, wrinkling his nose. The pair shared a look of such familiarity I felt like I was missing something. "At least my coping mechanisms won't kill me."

"Are you guys brothers?" I asked, averting the attention from my newborn status.

"Not by blood," Julian said, frowning. "We're each other's found family. We grew up in Court together and now we live here together, but as I hear myself say that, there are probably quite a few people that suspect we're gay."

"Would that be a bad thing?"

Julian laughed. "Depends on who you ask I suppose. I exemplify the characteristics of a freewheeling bisexual because I proudly am."

"The pricks dwelling in that Court can gossip all they want about us," Dayton said with a sneer. "It's the only thing they're good at."

"Where does this leave me? What do I do about being a—" I glanced away from them, unable to say the word.

"You stay here and let us help you. Train you," said Julian. "This is our area of expertise."

"What if I choose not to?" I asked. I wanted to weigh all my options. A part of me wished Luka and Derek hadn't lied to me, that they could train me. It was too late for that; I wasn't ready to go back and face them.

"Then, you go back out there and die," said Dayton unwaveringly.

My temper rose at his crassness. "This is crazy! I was supposed to go to school. It was going to be mundane, ordinary." My voice caught, and I shook my head. "I wasn't supposed to be a werewolf."

Dayton's gaze wavered, assessing me. With that razor edge in his tone, he said, "That life is over. This is your life now; you can't change it. Your brother has many enemies. Rumors spread like wildfire, and it won't be long before someone else figures out who you are. It will be more people like Zayne, only he was child's play compared to most of what is out there."

Dejected against what I knew deep down to be true, I said, "You certainly don't beat around the bush."

"Lies are cheap. The truth is free." He shrugged then prowled closer, his golden gaze flicking over me in judgment. "It's your call, Mare. What will it be?"

The challenge in his tone was what had me saying, "Fine. Where can I stay?"

Chapter 10

I jolted awake at the sound of an explosion. The barren room absorbed the noise, reverberating across the windowpanes. Of course, after trying desperately to sleep, I would be awakened by some insane explosion. That was my life now, I supposed.

I glanced at the clock on the wall; it was the middle of the night. Only hours had passed since Dayton showed me to this guest bedroom, and I hadn't seen him or Julian since.

As another explosion sounded, I scrambled from the bed, put on a pair of slippers, and crossed the hardwood floor. Maybe this was a normal thing I'd get used to, things exploding in the night. I opened the door and turned down the long hall, greeted by Julian, who walked out of his room.

He smelt faintly of smoke and nearly fell over as we collided. "Wrong way." He grabbed my shoulders to steer me around and pushed past me sloppily as I followed suit.

The more I followed, the more lost I became. This house was a maze, and it was hard to keep up with the various twists and turns of each echoing hallway. Paintings decorated the walls, with brief inscriptions beneath each one. They were mostly the same: wolves, wolves in battle, or wolves staring up at a full moon. We reached a staircase, and Julian leaped from the top step, landing gracefully down at the bottom. I was not attempting acrobatics of any sort, however, and jogged down the steps behind him.

"What is going on?" I asked, running to keep up. Distantly, I heard a shrieking wail replaying on a loop.

Julian halted at the door to outside and opened it cautiously. Slowly, he walked in, holding the door open for me to pass while a loud blaring alarm rung into the night. The air outside was crisp, and my breath steamed when I exhaled. We stood on a porch that wrapped around the entire Temple, lit by bronze torches along the banister. I crossed my arms and followed Julian's gaze where, in the distance, I saw a figure and detected the slightest muffle of voices. Before I could ask anything, another boom sounded, and a chilling realization washed over me as a pained cry tore through the night. Someone was being shot.

"Shit," Julian said.

Julian stood in front of me, blocking my view, as he dug into his pocket and took out a dark flask. He unscrewed the top and brought it to his lips, taking a long swig.

"It's three o'clock in the morning," I chastised him.

"You want a swig?" He grinned.

Ignoring his question, I shot two of my own. "What's going on? Where is Dayton?"

Julian shook his head and took another long gulp. "He is, um, well, he's shooting someone, it seems. One moment." He held a finger up and closed his eyes. "Perfect. I'll be right back."

Julian disappeared into the shadows of the night while I paced around to try to displace the discomfort nestling inside of me. Waking up in the middle of the night to someone being shot was not something I wanted to get used to, but who—or what—was being shot? Could it be those Fenrir creatures? Or perhaps another werewolf after me to get to Luka? I shuddered. This felt so unreal, so otherworldly. Dayton appeared before I could dwell any further.

He appeared stoic, a slight dusting of blood scattered across his face. He approached me and cupped my shoulders, shoving me back inside. "I should have warned you about going out at night."

Once inside the kitchen, I whirled on him, locking gazes. "Who were you shooting?"

His eyes darkened, and I felt myself shrink. "Your friend's here."

"What? Who?" I asked. When he turned from me, I grabbed his shoulder. "Hey, you told me you would tell me the truth. I can handle the truth."

"Fine." He turned on me, his eyes feral, and as he stalked closer, I backed up. "Your friend, *Derek*, trespassed here tonight. If he weren't your friend, I would have already put a bullet between his eyes."

Stunned, I faltered before I spoke, "Let me talk to him. He will listen to me. Anything you need to know, I'll find it out. You don't need to hurt him."

"This is how we do things."

"You're barbaric then."

"We've forgone the practice of slicing off fingers and toes each time wolves step out of line," Dayton snarled. "I like to think of us as modern werewolves."

I inhaled deeply, struggling to keep my cool. "I'm going to talk to him."

"I think you should," Dayton agreed.

"God forbid he breathes wrong and incurs your wrath," I muttered, following him outside.

"It warms me that you already understand me so."

Dayton jumped over the banister on the large porch and glanced back at me as if he were waiting for me to copy. Apparently, werewolves had an aversion to stairs. Not me. I took the stairs like a civil person, then followed Dayton down a short pathway leading to a tall stone building with a door fixed with silver bars like a jail cell.

Leaning against the stone was Julian, a lit cigarette between his lips. When he saw me, his green eyes flickered with amusement as he blew smoke in my direction. It was both sweet and intoxicating, like menthol. I coughed and moved away.

"Really, Jules?" Dayton scolded, thwacking the air.

"It's your fault for having high expectations I have no interest in living up to," Julian drawled, inhaling more smoke.

The two boys beside one another were a jarring contrast. Stiff and taut, Dayton looked ready to pounce at a moment's notice while Julian, loose-limbed and carefree, grinned like the devil. Intertwined personalities like a black cat against a golden retriever. There was a balance between them, though, like they evened one another out.

"Did you get anything?" Dayton asked.

Julian shrugged and stubbed his cigarette on the ground. "No, he is protected. Makes sense considering he's in Luka's ranks."

"What are you talking about?" I asked.

"Your friend is, uh," Julian hesitated. "Not easy to get through to."

"What do you mean?"

They shared a look. Julian shrugged and Dayton frowned.

"What, are you reading each other's minds?" I snorted.

"How about you just go talk to your friend?" Dayton said, stepping aside and gesturing at the cell. "Hm?"

"Whatever," I muttered, storming ahead.

"Be careful," Dayton warned, hand hovering over his gun.

"He's not going to hurt me." I insisted. "He's my best friend."

Dayton's eyes narrowed as he said, "Don't forget he lied to you just as much as your brother did."

I hated that he was right. It was true. Hated that my best friend was a part of this tangled web of lies. Luka's omission of the truth felt hard enough, but Derek was supposed to be there for me through anything. None of this was right.

Dayton opened the door behind him, the hinges squealing like nails on a chalkboard. I gulped and stepped through, immediately aware of the chill. The room was small, the floor was covered in hay, and it smelled like old, stagnant water. The door behind me slammed, and I jumped further into the room. A small window was placed atop the wall where it met the ceiling, and from the bars, Derek dangled.

"Derek?" I said, surprised by the thick emotion in my voice.

Derek dropped from the window and stared at me. Blood soaked the front of his shirt, wet and fresh, and a furious look contorted his features. But when he saw me, his features softened and he looked like my best friend again. He barreled toward me, clinging to me like his life depended on it, despite his cries of pain from our embrace. I stiffened.

"Maris." His voice was strangled as he held me tighter, burying his face in my hair. "I'm surprised you're here—surprised but relieved."

He let go, and I took a step back. His bloodied shirt was in tatters. "What happened to you?"

His eyes darkened, and he glanced behind me. "Your new buddy shot me. He used silver bullets like a bastard, which means it takes longer to heal."

"You say that like I should understand it," I said bitterly.

Derek twisted his hands together before him. "Right, sorry. Silver is toxic to us—in some cases, lethal—but not in this one," he added, watching my expression shift.

He ripped the shirt over his head, pointing at two similar bullet wounds on both shoulders. I expected to feel more pity.

"I told him he was wrong to do that," I said feebly, as if that would help.

"Do you realize who he is?" Derek asked. "The gravity of danger you're in by being with him?"

"No, Derek. I don't. How on earth would I know that?" I snapped. "Besides, where was I supposed to go?"

"Home! Come back home, Maris," he pleaded, eyes watering as he jutted his lip out.

"Why?" I roared. Anger seized me, hitting harder than I expected, and my following words were bitter. "I don't have a home anymore, Derek. You lied to me; Luka lied to me. That is not something I can just forgive and forget!"

"It's not that simple."

"No, it is." My words were ice cold. "And God, you were *tracking* me?"

Derek's eyebrows scrunched together. "How did you figure that out?"

"*That's* what you want to know?" I yelled, rolling my eyes.

"Luka wanted to protect you from all this."

"Look how well that ended up. You know what the worst part is?" I glared at him. "You were the person I trusted most in this world, and looking at you now, I just see a stranger."

Derek cowered, averting my gaze. "Maris," he said, his voice low, almost a whisper. "I don't know what I can say to make this okay."

My hands trembled, tears stinging the backs of my eyes. How could Derek think he could make this okay again? The damage was done, and I was done being lied to.

"Leave." My voice was low. "Leave and stay out of my life. If I come back, it will be of my own accord."

Derek's head snapped up, his eyes brimming with unshed tears. I forced myself to look away before I changed my mind. "Maris, don't draw this line. Please," he choked.

"Please, Derek."

I heard his shaky intake of breath before he pushed past me and out the door. I slid down the wall, sitting on the cold, hard ground. I rested my head between my legs and tangled my hands in my hair. The emotion physically hurt, as if my chest might burst open from the pain. My own heart backfired; any fragments of normalcy I had left were now gone. The horrible truth was, there was no more normal for me. Any life I thought I could have—the dreams I thought I would pursue—they were all gone.

I sobbed, clenching my body until the pain went away.

— ◦ —

I stayed there until the sun rose, my mind numb. Sending Derek away was a rash decision, but it was the right one. This phantom feeling stirred inside me like I had lost a limb, and in a way, I had. I had cast away everything I trusted and knew; my old life of ignorance was gone, and I would never get it back. I had no idea if I'd ever even be able to go to school to try to live a normal life as a nurse. For so long, that was all I had wanted.

Yet that dream felt like sand, slipping through the hourglass. I had to get a grapple on this new reality first before considering school again. Starting fresh would mean a clean slate. Maybe I could go back one day, but there was no point dwelling on it. I needed to figure out what to do next.

I rose from the cell and stretched my sore, stiff limbs. The door was shut, and with a great effort, I heaved it open. Dayton and Julian never said anything to me after I sent Derek away, nor did they try to get me out. I respected that they let me be. I needed my moment to grieve my old life. Alone.

Once outside, I was surprised to see a thin fog above the grass. I trampled through it, my feet cold and wet. I probably looked insane in my attire, and I could only imagine what my hair looked like. I was not trying to impress anyone, and after the past few weeks, things like my appearance seemed trivial.

The stairs creaked under my weight as I ascended them. In the daylight, the black wood was stark—everything around here was dark, actually—ominous. The space around the back patio seemed large enough to host sizable events or parties, and it was odd to think only two boys lived here.

"You know why, Jules!" Dayton yelled. When Julian remained silent, Dayton spoke again. "Yeah, that's what I thought."

I opened the back door and walked into the kitchen. I immediately felt like I was intruding. Seated atop two barstools were Dayton and Julian. I hoped to turn away unnoticed, which I soon realized was impossible. Julian stood from the table visibly upset, his green eyes clouded in fury. He made no remarks as he pushed past me outside, and I gulped as I entered the room, Dayton stirring his coffee with a grunt.

"Mare," he said curtly, not looking up. "Help yourself to coffee and anything else you would like."

I walked toward a coffee pot on the counter, tracing my fingers across the dark marble and grabbing an unused mug next to the pot. I poured a cup, spotted a sugar bowl, and heaped a spoonful in the liquid. There was no cream lying around, and instead of searching awkwardly for it, I added another scoop of sugar and hoped for the best.

I took a bitter sip and scrunched my nose. Breaking the silence, I asked, "If werewolves are real, does that make everything else real?"

Dayton paused, looking up at me. "What do you mean?"

"Vampires, witches, fairies, that sort of thing?" I said, taking another sip of the coffee. The sugar began to mask the bitterness.

He cocked his head sideways in thought, a ray of sunshine catching his hair and highlighting his golden hues. "Well," he began, "vampires exist, but they are a dying race. They haven't been spotted for over a decade. Witches exist, too, but they keep to themselves. Fairies died out years ago. Their offspring still exists, however—pixies and nixies, nasty little creatures, though. Only useful if you know how to persuade them."

"What about beyond life?" I asked. "God and angels and heaven."

Dayton shrugged. "Your guess is as good as mine."

I never attended church, and I rarely dwelled upon creation itself or the thought of something "bigger." Luka never taught it to me, having outwardly expressed he was an atheist. I never knew if my parents were religious, either, and if I thought too deeply about creation or prayer, my head would hurt. Probably more so now, considering all I knew. I do like to think there was some afterlife, though. Somewhere we went that wasn't completely horrid.

"What happened to your friend?" he asked.

I took another distracting sip and sat at the barstool next to Dayton. "I sent him away."

"You don't sound like that was a choice made with conviction," he remarked, looking down at me with an eyebrow raised.

"It wasn't. It was rash, but the lines between this life and my old life are too muddled." I set the mug aside, twisting my fingers together. "I don't know that I'm making the right choices in anything."

Dayton chuckled darkly. "Agonizing over it won't help. Overthinking is a disease that eats away at your mind if you let it."

The way he spoke made him sound both incredibly old and young. When he seemed amused, it was never truly real. His golden gaze held a haunted glint, and his smiles were barely there—crooked and imperceptible. The lightness in him bounced off his rough exterior, and I tried to imagine Dayton living more carefree, alighting all his features to capacity, but I couldn't. He reminded me of a soldier returned from war, never quite the same as he once was.

"How old are you?" I asked.

Dayton surveyed me with that judgmental stare. "Five hundred and twenty-two."

I nearly choked on my coffee. "What?"

Dayton's mouth twisted in a smirk. "You'll believe anything I say, huh?"

"It's not nice to tease people who don't know any better."

Dayton shrugged. "I'm only twenty-three."

"What about your parents?"

His already straight posture went rigid. "You ask a lot of questions," he mused. "My parents were both murdered when I was eighteen."

His straightforward answer of such a heavy statement had me saying, "I didn't know; I wouldn't have asked, I—I'm sorry."

"Don't pity me, Mare. It's not something to get hung up over. It means nothing to me; don't let it mean anything to you," he said vexatiously, watching me. Sharp malice glittered in his golden eyes, and I staggered back. He stood, placing his mug in the sink before turning toward the door.

Confused, I watched him leave. I felt as though I somehow offended him but couldn't understand how. I followed him. Outside was still chilly and Dayton walked fast. I could barely keep up with him without practically running, which was hard in only slippers. The grounds outside were vast, littered with plush grass, large boulders, trees, and even jagged pathways. The early morning sunlight breaking through the trees cast an array of shadows over everything. Dayton stopped in front of a series of trees lined with bulls-eyes.

"What are you doing?" I asked.

"I thought it was implied I wanted to be alone," he quipped, reaching into the belt at his waist where he withdrew a series of daggers. "I'm practicing. You can never be too skilled. I throw knives every day for four hours to ensure my aim never falters."

"That seems excessive."

Dayton threw each blade faster than the speed of light. His muscles rippled beneath his shirt with each movement, tight and unruly. I followed the direction of the target and saw each blade nestled in the bullseye. His easy maneuver when summoning back the daggers seemed as natural as breathing. His lips curled into a snarl as he shook his head, but if there was an error in his aim, it was slight. Dayton summoned the daggers with that same band around his wrist. I don't know why I watched him, but it was entrancing to watch the knives soar flawlessly through the air.

I leaned against a tree and said, "You're confusing, you know? Yesterday, you practically begged me to come with you, and now you seem to want me to leave."

"Believe me, if it were not for those out to get you, I'd tell you to do just that," he snarled.

I spun to leave, no longer interested in being graced by his foul mood, but as I walked away, I halted. A strange tingling traced my skin and unexpected pain shot down my fingertips, as if my fingernails were ripped off. I glanced down; claws ripped beneath my nail beds, jutting out through the flesh. My knees buckled under me from the sight, and I cried out, unable to form words around the white-hot agony searing through me.

"Mare, look at me!" Dayton demanded, suddenly at my side.

My spinal column reverberated, twisting painfully.

"What is happening?" I shrieked.

My jaw ached intensely, pain beating against my gums. My heart thundered in my chest as I realized what was happening to me. Against my will, my body began to shift. I wasn't ready—I wasn't prepared. The idea felt jarring enough as it was.

"Look at me!" Dayton repeated. I did, his golden eyes aglow. "Stop panicking. Let the panic go, and the change will stop." His words were so powerful I felt compelled to listen. Slowly, my breath became less labored, and the pain dialed down to a dull ache. "Stop panicking."

Then, just like that, the pain was gone. I knelt on the ground, panting, fear no longer rattling my bones. "Was I..." I whispered, unable to finish the sentence.

"Yes, you were turning into your wolf," he said, offering his hand.

"How?" I asked, taking it. I let him pull me up.

"Intense, rash emotions tend to pull at the wolf; they're heightened for newborns," Dayton explained, stepping away from me.

"What did you do?"

"I made you submit to my will," he said, and before I could ask, he continued, "Normally it's your Alpha that keeps a newborn in line. I'm no Alpha, but I have a basic understanding of how it works."

"Why did you do it?"

A rogue grin split his face, no doubt suppressing the temptation to reply with snark. "You're a newborn wolf teetering on the edge of losing control. Someone must keep you in line. It just so happens to be me."

"What happens if I lose control?" I made myself ask, despite not wanting to hear the answer.

"A multitude of unpleasant things could rain down on you. The path you're heading down is an expedited road to getting yourself killed. You wouldn't last three days on your own."

In my mind's eye, I pictured Dayton's ease when aiming his knives and recalled his warrior-like instincts against threats. That type of skill was not obtained overnight. It was taught. "Teach me."

If Dayton was surprised, he didn't show it. He stalked closer, making a low tutting noise in his throat. "Teach you, huh? Why should I do that?"

"You're the one readily pointing out how much I lack in the skills department," I said, crossing my arms and meeting his gaze. "Teach me to fight."

Dayton looked down at me with a predatory glint in his eyes, with only inches separating us. I wondered if I pushed too far, but I didn't care.

Either way, he would do what he wanted. After a long moment, Dayton's nostrils flared as he slowly shook his head.

"I won't be easy on you. Everything you know will be challenged," snarled Dayton.

"I never asked for easy."

"You're eager, but are you willing to be taught?" he asked. "Training means staying here and committing yourself to this new life. Are you sure you want that?"

My thoughts turned to Luka, who infuriated me by knowing I was vulnerable and rendering me so because of his lies. I thought of how helpless I was to defend myself against these threats. With going to school being on the back burner, it seemed like an easy choice. Plus, I had left Luka, and I sent Derek away last night—all pieces of the life I knew dwindled away. If I did this, it would be my choice.

"Yes, I want this," I said with certainty.

"Fine," Dayton agreed. "We start tomorrow. Six o'clock sharp."

I looked Dayton up and down before turning to walk away. "You better impress me."

Chapter 11

After my encounter with Dayton, I didn't see him or Julian for the rest of the day. I didn't look for them either, preferring to stay in the confinements of my room. The long night had me tossing and turning, nightmares forcing me awake. I had to hurl myself to the bathroom twice to vomit my guts up. In my dreams, wolves chased me; I'd been defenseless, then met my untimely demise. Fear rattled my bones, and even reminding myself it was a nightmare didn't help. As much as I wanted to accept this new life, I struggled not to fear it. It would take time to adjust, which I suspected was true, but I wished it was easier.

I peeled myself out of the sweat-soaked sheets and glanced at the clock on the wall. It was five in the morning. Inwardly groaning, I reminded myself I was responsible for this; after all, I'd convinced Dayton to train me. Plus, I would sooner be damned than be even a minute late to my first training session with him. I didn't know what to expect out of these sessions. I liked keeping my body moving, used to the repetition and endurance of running.

The guest room was a decent size; a queen-sized bed was pushed against a wall in the middle of the room with sheer curtains surrounding the perimeter. Two worn leather armchairs sat adjacent from each other next to the floor length windows, and a plush rug of deep maroon laid across the dark hardwood in front of the bed. The bathroom attached had a standard sized shower, toilet, and porcelain sink. Various shower supplies were tucked beneath it, set beside a stack of towels, and even a set of toothbrushes, toothpaste, and mouthwash. As crazy as the notion of werewolves is, as least they kept track of their personal hygiene.

I showered quickly, and soon stared into the wardrobe, deciding what to wear. The closet was filled with styles ranging from simple workout clothes to fighting leathers to ordinary T-shirts and leggings—an assortment of sizes to accommodate all individuals, varying from extra large to extra small. I sorted through them, finding sizes for both male and female. As the Temple was a sanctuary, it made sense.

I settled on loose pants, a black T-shirt, and tennis shoes. I didn't know what Dayton's training entailed, so this felt like a safe option. Braiding my hair back was a tedious task this early in the day, and my eyes drooped as I attempted to focus. I leaned over the chestnut oak vanity, staring at my reflection. A white wolf flashed.

I gasped and stumbled back, and when I dared look again, my reflection had returned. My eyes lingered over my body, which felt alien to me now, the pain that ripped through me yesterday fresh in my mind. I imagined my body shifting into another being, struggling to understand how another creature lingered beneath my skin. I shuddered and, tearing away from the mirror, I left the room.

I scoured the endless halls until I found the staircase and went down, trying to remember where the training room was located. I finally found it; it was the same room Dayton first brought me to, and it made sense to train in the training room. The room held an eerie silence, and I flinched against the sound of my shoes on the polished floor.

The morning sun began to shine light into the room, glinting off the polished weapons and casting shadows from the trees. I paced the room, wiping my palms against my thighs. A glance at the clock showed it had just turned six. Something coiled in my stomach, and I fought the urge to leave and forget this madness. I almost did until something dropped from the ceiling. The scream barely registered as Dayton shoved me, grabbed my arm, and flipped me around.

I landed hard on the ground, knocking the breath clean out of me. He pinned my arm, and I forced my eyes open, greeted by Dayton's snarling rage. His body was expertly positioned over my own, and his weight positioned in places to keep me down. I was acutely aware of where his body touched mine, hot like lava against my skin. I wiggled my arm free enough to grasp his bicep, but it was like trying to grip a boulder.

"Get off me!" I tried to wiggle myself free, but my efforts were futile. Dayton slinked off me and shook his head while I scrambled up, gasping.

"Situational awareness, staying on guard, and reacting defensively and immediately. You failed on all three counts," he grumbled. "Three keys to even fathom surviving being a werewolf."

His clothes were similar to my own, I realized. The all-black attire was like a uniform for him, but the training clothes hugged his body tight around the swells of his muscles and across his stomach and arms. I pointedly looked away.

"Can you stop defaulting to death as the only outcome for me?"

"Do you think you would survive in this world on your own?" he asked, and at my silence, he nodded. "That's what I thought. Since its clear you aren't equipped to do anything too vigorous yet, we can start with the basics. Running. It will help to build your stamina, especially since that one maneuver had you wheezing for breath." With raised eyebrows, he looked me up and down. "You ready to run like a werewolf?"

Relief trickled through me; at least I could do one thing right. "I already excel at running."

"Not the way I run," Dayton countered.

Dayton stalked toward a door at the back end of the training room, and it flew back from behind him. I caught it and forced it open, scurrying to keep up with his strides. He led us into the woods and into the cold, crisp air, the chill biting against my exposed skin. Dayton flew down the path, bending low-hanging branches and letting them ricochet into my face. I bit my tongue to keep from any rude remarks.

"Isn't running a pretty universal concept?" I asked.

"You know how to run like a human, but you're not a human anymore," he explained. "You won't last five minutes running these courses."

Dayton came to a sudden halt, and I nearly toppled into him. With a glare, I looked to where he pointed. In a break between the trees, there were three paths marked. Each had different intensities: a flat plane, a downhill feat, and an uphill battle.

I should have stayed in bed.

"It's your pick which one you want to do," Dayton said, starting a backward jog. I couldn't help but notice the coil of muscles along his arms and the hard ripples of his stomach exposed beneath his thin shirt. "Think about building up that stamina to outrun your enemies."

"And if I outrun you?" I countered.

Dayton shook his head, then disappeared up the path. I picked the straightforward path, hoping to avoid him. I started with a fair pace, and I thought I had a good groove going until the path progressively narrowed and heightened. I watched my footing; the pathway was clearly meant to challenge me, dotted with jagged rocks jutting up in all directions, threatening to take me down. Multiple low-hanging branches snagged and scraped my skin.

Given this was the easier path, it was quite a hike. I didn't put it past Dayton to lie about which path was which and to trick me into taking a harder route. Sweat began beading down my back and dripping down my face in no time. The higher I went, the harder it was to gather breath into my lungs. I pushed myself as I hadn't even made it to the end, and I had a feeling the end was nowhere near.

Another set of footsteps sounded from behind, and I turned. Through bleary eyes, I could make out Julian running up beside me dressed in shorts, sneakers, and a pair of black sunglasses. Thin lines of black ink traced his chest, and the closer Julian got, I noticed a sway in his steps.

"Pardon my appearance," Julian said, facing me with red-rimmed eyes. He pulled his sunglasses down. "Long night."

"Are you high?" I asked, shaking my head.

"Certainly not." Julian feigned insult, clutching a hand to his chest. "Anymore, at least, if that makes you feel better. No, now I'm just nursing one hell of a hangover."

I didn't question the green glitter in his hair or the rumple on the back of his shorts.

"You have Dayton in a mood," Julian commented. "The effect you have on him is amusing."

"What does that mean?" I asked, jumping over a large rock in the path.

"You ruffle his uptight feathers." Julian smirked. We veered toward a downhill path, and I had to slow down to not tumble forward. "Dayton keeps to himself. He trains, he works, and he guards the territory lines. You show up, and now his world is all askew."

"First of all, I didn't just 'show up,'" I said, increasing my speed. "He found me. He followed me into the woods. He dragged me to this place, yet now that I'm here, he acts like I'm some huge inconvenience."

My words only ignited my anger, and Julian laughed under his breath beside me. Maybe it was just proximity, but a slight wheeze rattled in Julian's breath as he kept up the pace. His gait was slightly wobbled, and I half expected him to topple over.

"That's Dayton for you," he said. "Being with people for more than five minutes gives him headaches, and people who question everything he says? You made his hit list before he created it."

"Gee, how did I get so lucky?" I rolled my eyes.

"It's refreshing not to be on the receiving end of Dayton's moods for once," Julian said. "No offense."

"Is he always so... *prickly*?" I asked, searching for the right word.

"You've come to notice that, yeah? Dayton has a funny way of showing he cares by acting like he doesn't."

"That's an oxymoron," I pointed out.

"No, that's Dayton. You get used to it after a while."

The trees thickened around us like a shield. The path darkened, and I kept my senses open. I noted the varying objects—rocks and fallen trees littering the pathway.

"How do you live with him?"

"Ten-mile mark," Julian said as we veered around a rock to the right. I was shocked to hear I had made it ten miles already. "I manage because Dayton's all I've got."

"Let me guess, your parents are dead, too?" I asked without thinking.

Julian barked a laugh without humor. "They could be, for all I know. They gave me up when I was a kid. My history is complicated and all kinds of fucked up, but it's not worth getting into."

Julian stopped and grappled for balance against a tree, a coughing fit arising as his body seized. He clutched tightly to his chest, and I turned to run back toward him. He held a hand out.

"I'm fine." Julian stood up straight once more. "Smoker's cough is all." Frown lines creased his eyes, and I noticed how ashen he looked. He wiped the back of his mouth. A trickle of blood stained his hand.

"Julian, are you—"

"I promise I'm alright," he insisted. "I haven't smoked yet today; my lungs are in protest from too much fresh air. Go on ahead, and I'll catch up." Before I could say anything else, he produced a pack of cigarettes from his pocket and brought one to his lips.

I continued the rest of the run alone, counting the mile markers as I passed. When I finished the first lap, it had been fifteen miles. I was surprised. My normal run rounded between three to six miles. When I crossed the ending, Dayton leaned against a tree, his arms crossed.

"I did it," I gasped, resting my hands on my knees. Dayton tossed a water bottle to the ground at my feet. I picked it up and guzzled the contents. "Well?"

"You're still not in control fully," Dayton observed, studying me. "However, I'm mildly surprised. None of these courses are for beginners, and while your time could improve, you made it out in decent enough time."

His play on words felt calculated, like he wanted to be sincere but not sincere enough to appear like a decent guy. I shook my head and said, "Considering that was almost nice of you, I'll take it."

"Don't get used to it," Dayton said coyly.

"I'm pretty used to running, honestly," I told him. A slight breeze trickled through, rustling the branches and upturning leaves. "Luka always went on about the importance of endurance built through running."

"Sounds about right." Dayton nodded. "Plus, running is a good outlet to center your emotions against the shift."

"Now what?" I asked.

"Now, the real training begins."

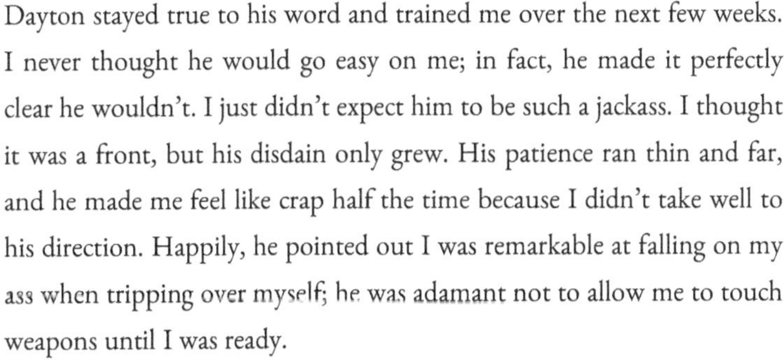

Dayton stayed true to his word and trained me over the next few weeks. I never thought he would go easy on me; in fact, he made it perfectly clear he wouldn't. I just didn't expect him to be such a jackass. I thought it was a front, but his disdain only grew. His patience ran thin and far, and he made me feel like crap half the time because I didn't take well to his direction. Happily, he pointed out I was remarkable at falling on my ass when tripping over myself; he was adamant not to allow me to touch weapons until I was ready.

Despite it all, I welcomed the distraction. I had been here nearly two weeks already, and time had flown. However, it was strange to be apart from Luka, and I often wondered about him. He had to be worried sick, and it seemed off that he hadn't already found me. Derek no doubt relayed the message to Luka, but a part of me still thought he would come. Maybe I was too quick to jump the gun, too hasty to draw a line between us that Luka wouldn't cross. Despite knowing Luka was wrong to lie to me, I missed him. I was not ready to face him again, but there was an ache without him. It felt wrong.

Landing hard on my back swiftly chased away all thought. Dayton was teaching me basic moves—emphasis on *trying*. Today's lesson involved willingly flinging yourself from insane heights and landing safely. Much to Dayton's annoyance, I was afraid to drop fifty feet from the air.

I stood up dizzily and said, "How is this at all useful again?"

Dayton answered by kicking my legs from beneath me. I gasped as the air rushed from my lungs and my back smacked against the mat. Hovering over me, Dayton said, "Rule number one: stop questioning everything I say. Rule number two: always be on guard or die."

"Can you just kill me and get it over with?" I asked, watching the ceiling spin.

Dayton glared. "Do you really want me to answer that?"

I stood up again and huffed, turning from him. Dayton's footsteps sounded behind me, and I spun, but he was already there, twisting my arm back and flinging me upward. I hated being thrown around like a rag doll. Once again, Dayton had me with my back against the mat and a wooden sword pointed at my chest above my heart.

"If I wanted to kill you, I could think of fifty different ways simply by having this advantage," he snarled. "You don't want to give your enemy the upper hand by turning your back."

"Alright, alright," I said, defeated. "I get it."

He let me up, his gaze unrelenting. "You always need to be prepared for anything."

Dayton advanced, and I threw my arms in front of myself and ducked. After he taught me a series of self-defense basics, I'd mistakenly voiced I was getting the hang of it. He soon humbled me. I hadn't been quick enough, and Dayton left me with a black eye; his warped philosophy was that an actual attacker wouldn't hesitate, and it would improve my reaction time.

I unsheathed my wooden sword and aimed it at Dayton, who grabbed the hilt and flung it from my grasp in seconds.

"Really?" I groaned.

Dayton caught it in the air and backed me up against a wall, the fake sword pressed at my throat. This close, I could see the sweat dripping from his temples and smell the toothpaste on his breath.

"Dead," he said lowly, his breath tickling my cheek.

"C'mon, Dayton. Cut her some slack," said Julian, acting as our mediator—mostly to keep Dayton in check. "She has been making some progress."

"Thank you," I said.

My gaze didn't stray from Dayton. I hated looking away first, and even more, I hated standing so close together I could feel his heat. Slowly, I reached up and pushed the wooden sword away, leaving only air between us. Dayton scowled and walked away.

"She's only making progress on how to get killed quicker," Dayton snapped.

I growled, jolting forward and kicking my leg out under Dayton—a move he taught me. For once, he fell, landing on his back. I caught the wooden sword that soared from his hand, and landed on top of him, sword aimed at his throat.

"Dead," I said, feeling triumphant.

Dayton held my gaze, lips upturned into a barely-there sneer. I slinked off him and backed away while he shot up in a huffy rage, cursing under his breath.

"Dude, she got you," Julian wheezed, and Dayton's sharp glance had his amusement slip away. "Don't be a sourpuss. Besides, when should we teach her the fun stuff?"

"She isn't ready," Dayton said, an edge to his voice.

"Ready for what?" I asked.

Julian crossed the room gracefully, assessing me. "I'm afraid if I say it, Dayton might rip my tongue out."

"Jules," Dayton warned, stepping between Julian and me.

Julian's emerald eyes glowed, and his smile widened into a grin, allowing long, sharp canines to grow. Something about the mischievous glint in his gaze scratched at my brain, digging for a memory that wasn't there. I stumbled, nearly falling at Julian's implication for what he intended to teach me. The reason for the training was to control it, not willingly turn into *it*.

"No," I said, my voice a whisper. "Not now."

In a flash, those teeth disappeared, his eyes muting to their normal green hue. "You'll have to learn eventually."

"When she's ready, I will teach her," said Dayton, his tone low with warning.

"I'm shocked you aren't pushing this," Julian said.

Dayton prowled closer to Julian, standing taller by a matter of inches. "It's her choice. When she's ready, I'll teach her. Until then, the answer is no."

It unnerved me how swiftly Dayton's moods shifted, yet it somehow endeared me to him, too, to hear him respect my choice. I'd never tell him that, but the little things reminded me that no matter how foul he could be, he had some redeeming qualities.

Julian's retort was ready on his lips, but he froze. Dayton's ears perked, tilting his head toward the open window. Something flew in like a rocket, landing on the ground with a clatter. It was a circular ball, no bigger than a baseball, and it was on fire. Dayton was on it like a moth to a flame, and before I could speak, he reached down. It escaped him and flew directly at me.

I screeched and stumbled back as the flaming ball landed in my hands. I expected to feel pain and immediately dropped it, yet at my touch, the flames dwindled and the ball disintegrated into ash. I balked at the envelope left in my palms, addressed to me in a neat inscription. Dayton was already there when I looked up, snatching the envelope from me. He cursed.

Julian tutted and stepped forward, grabbing the envelope with a tissue. "Enchanted to only open at her touch, clever."

"What is that?" I asked, still balking at the fact it had been a flaming ball moments before.

"Fire letters," Julian said, holding it out for me again. "Old forms of communication from a time before technology, like a carrier pigeon but with magic. The magic delivers it to the recipient wherever they are in the world. In this case, an extra enchantment was added to the letter to ensure the contents were confidential for the recipient."

"Yeah, well, I've ignored the last dozen letters they've sent. It was only a matter of time before they found a workaround," snarled Dayton.

Daggers suddenly flew into Dayton's hands, and he began to throw them. Each soared with extreme accuracy and never failed to miss the intended target.

"Okay, but who sent it?" I asked. "Why to me, and why the confidentiality?"

"How about you open it and find out?" Dayton jabbed.

Exasperated, I complied. It was a thick envelope, sealed with a waxed crescent of overlapping moons. The letter inside was scrawled on with yellowed paper and messy black ink.

Maris Bakar,

The Wolf Council would like to formally invite you to the Moon Court. As a newly turned werewolf, a formal introduction to this new world helps to ease the transitional period. There is much we would like to discuss with you alone.

With hopes of being acquainted soon, on willing terms,

The Wolf Council

I read it twice over before reading it aloud.

"That sounds ominous," I said at last.

Julian grunted in agreement and stepped toward Dayton, who reeled on him, propelling a dagger toward him. My eyes widened as Julian ducked and swore.

"No, no. We cannot let her go," said Dayton, shaking his head.

"They will just keep coming if she doesn't," Julian countered.

"Let them for all I care! I've been itching for a good fight." Silence and then, "I can certainly try, Jules."

"Why do you care?" Julian asked.

Dayton drew his shoulders back and summoned his daggers from the targets. Stiffly, he put them away, his hands steady. Pointedly, he refused to look at anyone, but I saw his angry glare. Slowly, he stepped back and turned to me.

"The Wolf Council are an utterly insane group of werewolves ignorant to everything that does not fit their idyllic image," he explained. Julian nodded along, carefully watching Dayton.

"What does willing terms mean?" I asked. "Are they going to take me if I'm unwilling? What do they even want with me?"

"Yes to the first part. If they decide they want to meet you, it's decided," said Julian. "They want to know what you know of the Bestial."

"Why don't they find Luka then?"

Dayton shook his head. "They know you have an inkling of a connection to the Bestial, but what they don't know is that Luka is the Bestial."

"How do they not know it is him?" I asked.

"Luka stays hidden beneath the skin of his wolf. He's an Alpha, which means he has a deeper connection to his wolf. To be honest, I barely understand it, but I suspect it's something you can only experience, but Luka and his wolf have a deep bond. They are both the same and not the same," Dayton explained.

"That bond reflects how powerful your brother really is," Julian said. "The world knows extraordinarily little of Luka; he stays away from the court, and he lives outside the law just enough to keep the peace. There is more speculation about him than anything else, really. No doubt the Council has tried to wrangle him to their ranks with obvious futile results."

"So, finding out he has harbored a secret sister that no one knew about means they want me to exploit him, even inadvertently," I said, beginning to understand.

"Yes and no," said Julian. "Everyone wants Luka on their side, but he's notorious for not picking sides. With you, it's like a slab of clay; everyone thinks by getting to you, they can mold him to their will. They want to force his hand, confirm what they suspect."

"But what do they want him for?"

"Power is what it all boils down to. Who has the most of it, and who has control over it." Dayton shook his head. "Luka is the wrong person to mess with."

Again, I couldn't help wondering about the familiarity in Dayton's tone when he spoke of Luka as if speaking of an old friend with a long-faded fondness. When I'd asked him how he'd known Luka, he denied that he did. I couldn't figure it out.

"The Council is looking for a grab of power. They want Luka as he's an example of what having too much power means." Julian rolled his eyes and drank from his flask. "They are too moronic to even see what's already in front of them."

"Enough, Jules," Dayton warned. "It doesn't matter; no one is going to the Council. I'll go there and talk to them myself if that's what it takes for them to leave you the hell alone."

"Missing the comfort of your old cell?" Julian quipped. "You know they won't back off on this."

Dayton's hatred of this Council didn't seem baseless, but a part of me wondered if I should go. If anything, it would allow me to immerse into this world further and learn more about the culture I was now a part of. Yet there was a reason Luka stayed away, but could they truly be that bad? Ignoring their request would only work for so long.

"They want me," I said. "Let me go, and maybe we can get them to back off."

"They'll use this meeting to feel you out for weaknesses and determine how to manipulate you. You don't know, but I know firsthand you can't be exposed to them." Dayton scowled, tracing a hand down his jaw. "There's a reason Luka never revealed himself to them. He knows how batshit they are, and he's watching them from a distance."

"They will find a way to get to her either way, Dayton," Julian argued. "Let it be on your terms and not theirs."

"*Jules*," Dayton ground out.

"You think I want this any more than you? You know I have as much animosity for them as you. But you must think with a clear head and think *logically*," Julian pushed forward before Dayton interjected. "You know we can't ignore this. You of all people are smarter than this."

Dayton met his gaze, exhaling deeply, and after a long moment, he conceded. "You're not going alone. When we get there, you don't speak. You ask no questions. You look at no one. If someone even looks at you funny, you tell me."

"Fine," I said, crossing my arms over my chest. "When do we leave?"

Chapter 12

I spent the rest of the day alone, gathering my thoughts. What was I getting myself into? Lately, I felt like I was playing a losing game, yet this world was enthralling, captivating me at every turn. Going to the Wolf Council would further entrap me into this world, and I thought about Dayton's resistance and wondered if he was right; his usual feral rage felt heightened. Was it possible for him to become more unhinged? We would be leaving just past one in the morning, arriving as the day began.

Julian said Lycan was its own country somewhere past Romania, and considering that wasn't exactly within driving distance, I had no clue of how he planned to get there. I imagined taking a plane but I couldn't picture Dayton making it past TSA without being arrested, and I doubted Julian could make it more than an hour without a cigarette.

While I twisted my hair into a tight knot, a loud knock came at my door. I crossed the room and opened it to find Dayton, clad in all black fighting leathers. It fitted him well, giving heed to the muscles beneath. Strapped across his back were two swords, the only visible weapons, and I suspected coiled in his pockets and grooves were at least two dozen more weapons, likely more lethal.

"You ready?" he asked flippantly, his eyes lazily roaming over me.

I reached to grab a green sweater and loosed a shaky breath. I walked out, following Dayton down the hall. The halls were lit by silvery flames encased in wolf-head torches; a strange choice in décor, I thought. Dayton prowled the long corridors with a feline grace and equal quiet, but it was uncanny to walk that lightly on your feet. My boots squeaked on the polished hardwood.

"What's your deal with the Council?" I asked curiously as we descended the stairs.

Dayton's lips thinned as he pondered his response. "I grew up in the Court. It's a vile place full of manipulative bastards. The Council cares more about individuals of status as opposed to qualified werewolves."

"Status?"

"The Council is like royalty. It's a pristine position, and most would kill for an opportunity to be a part of it. Politically, having a seat on the Council gives you influence over other werewolves, Alpha's, even Cadres," Dayton explained. "Status wise, a Council seat guarantees invites to the most lavish parties and hanging in the circles of society's elite. They're all a bunch of socialites."

"You sound like you speak from experience," I observed, baiting him. He plowed ahead of me, taking the lead.

"Wouldn't you like to know?" Dayton halted by the front door. Refusing to look at me, he said, "Mare, when you talk to them, you have to be careful with how you word things."

"Why?"

"They'll know if you lie," Dayton explained. "But dancing around the truth never hurt anyone. They don't know who the Bestial is. They have reason to believe it's Luka, but not the evidence. Remember, you have the advantage pressed to you. If they ask if you know who the Bestial is, you say no. It's not a lie. You have never met the Bestial."

"How do they detect lies?" I asked.

"Supernatural sense of hearing," said Dayton. "They can listen to your heartbeat, which tends to increase with the stress of telling a lie."

As bizarre as it seemed, I believed it. I'd been shocked the other day after waking up to a faucet running. I thought I'd left the bathroom taps on. When I investigated it, they were off. In fact, what I heard was Julian in the kitchen making coffee on the other side of the Temple. Dayton told me I'd eventually be able to lean into my senses rather than be overwhelmed by them, but like everything else, I'd have to learn.

"What did Luka do that makes him a fugitive?" I asked.

Dayton glowered and shook his head, turning to walk out the door. "Luka and the Bestial are two separate entities. By law, Luka is an upstanding citizen; the Bestial is the troublemaker. The Council doesn't know who the Bestial is for sure, and that keeps Luka safe."

"This is all confusing to keep up with."

"Once you see him as the Bestial, it will be easier to understand," Dayton said.

We descended the front steps where Julian waited with a lit cigarette between his fingertips. Like Dayton, he was head to toe in fighting leathers with a bow and arrow slung across his back. I could not help but notice the loose fitting of his clothes, and I wondered if it was purposeful. Julian had no middle ground; he was a total wild card. He wore a winning smile upon seeing us and took a last drag on his cigarette.

"I take it you must be talking about your charming brother?" Julian chipped in.

Bounding into the forest, I followed. The darkness was eerie tonight, the sky a pitiless black. It was mindboggling that Dayton could navigate this, but I knew he was tapping into his wolf eyesight. I tried channeling it, hoping to see more than the outlines of trees. Yet as I did, my mind throbbed, so I stopped.

"How do you know Luka again?"

"I've told you, I don't know Luka." Dayton called back.

"What does the Bestial do that makes him... bad?"

Julian laughed. "Luka is very well connected. I wouldn't consider him good or bad, but he's the person people go to to make other people disappear."

"Disappear?"

"Disappear, like dead, Mare. No longer breathing, their families forever shifted, their life extinguished by Luka," Dayton said, not holding back.

Envisioning Luka through Dayton's perspective made me sick to my stomach. Luka couldn't—*wouldn't*—kill anyone, not the Luka I knew, not the older brother who raised and protected me. He wouldn't. He wasn't like that. Why would he kill anyone? When did he have the time? I considered Derek's role in all this; he must have been a part of it all, too. Did he ever question the morality of it all? Or did he take it as it was? I'd like to think Derek was above that, but clearly my thoughts as of late had little reflection on reality.

"He's a killer? A cold-blooded killer?" I blinked.

"As opposed to what?" Dayton spat, dragging a hand down his jaw. "While it might not be right morally, it's justified. He's not killing innocent people. The people he kills are scum; they deserve what they get, and the world is better off without them poisoning it." The certainty in his voice made it hard to argue. "He's one of the good guys. Maybe not in the eyes of the law, or cases of wrong versus right, but for everything that matters, he's a good guy."

"How do you know?" I asked.

"Like I told you before, I make it my business to know things," Dayton said, sauntering ahead. He called back and said, "We'll be there soon. Better not to get caught up."

I stayed silent after that, the information sinking in. Who really was Luka? I felt naïve, now discovering Luka had somehow hidden this from me. It was a lot to take in—to navigate. My older brother, who protected and cared for me, was also made of nightmares, notorious for killing in the werewolf community. I felt it deep in my bones then, the shifting of my reality.

"He can be harsh sometimes," Julian said, falling in stride beside me, cigarette dangling between his lips.

Leaves crunched beneath us as we walked, a slight breeze swaying the low-hanging branches. The branches looked like clawed hands reaching to grab you in its clutches. I crossed my arms over my chest and peered up at Julian.

"He certainly doesn't beat around the bush, but it doesn't change the truth that my brother is who I'm really upset with." I exhaled. "How are we getting there?"

"Lycan?" Julian asked. "A portal will take us."

"Portal?"

"A portal is like a magical threshold for traveling between places. It's tricky, though. One wrong move and you could end up in limbo. No one has ever made it back from that unscathed," Julian explained and then added, "But I wouldn't worry about that. It'll just take us to The Moon Court in Lycan."

"The hidden country exclusive for werewolves," I said. "I'm still struggling to wrap my mind around that."

Julian chuckled. "Once you see it, it'll be easier to understand."

Ahead, an outline of a building appeared, small like a shed. Dayton marched forward, moonlight breaking between the trees above him. I noticed the grip of a gun at his side.

"Why does he carry endless amounts of weapons?" I asked. Dayton glanced back before storming on.

"We always have to be prepared. As Dayton says, 'We can't always think with our claws.'" Julian raised his eyebrows, tilting his head back and forth. "Go down fighting or not at all. Angel with a shotgun running on pride."

"That's neurotic."

"A werewolf, in other words. It's our lifestyle; we've been trained since kids to be defenders." Julian shrugged. "Keep in mind your crazy is our normal. Though it's fascinating how naïve you are to this world. I've never met another wolf who didn't know they were one. As crazy as this is for you, it's also crazy for us. The Wolf Council will pick you up for that peculiarity, too."

I clicked my tongue and made no further comment. Most people knew they were werewolves as their families didn't lie to them about it. Why had Luka lied? Did it have anything to do with our parents? Our mom dies, and a few years after that, our father leaves, and all the while, there was this world stuck in the middle of it. There was a missing piece to all this, and whatever it was held the answers to understanding. Only one person knew the truth, but I wasn't ready to face Luka again.

Dayton stood away from us, leaning against a wall. Gray stone crumbled away at a small building with a low-set entrance, one that looked like we had to crawl through it. Various vines and thorns crawled up the sides, intertwined with moss, and a large metal lock adorned the rickety wooden door.

Dayton stepped forward with a dagger in his hand as Julian ambled toward him, hand outstretched. I smelled it before I realized what was going on. Dayton sliced his palm and then Julian's, collecting the mingled blood in a small vial. My eyebrows drew together, but I continued to watch. Dayton grabbed the lock against the door and poured the vial of blood over it. When he pulled back, the door flew open.

"It's charmed by blood," Dayton explained before I asked. "The Council regulates portal travel so not anyone can use it. Wouldn't want fugitives running into a portal and storming through Lycan in a rage. Portals are only placed in Temples and whoever guards the Temple controls it."

"Temples?"

"Yeah," said Dayton. "There isn't just one Temple, they're scattered across the globe, and each have their own guardians. The Temple isn't just like a halfway house for wayward wolves. It's also a safe haven for ancient relics—textbooks—history of our kind. All sorts of stuff are harbored in the Temples."

I had noticed odd things within the Temple: the library shelving a variety of books, everything from different poisons and treatments, to weapons and killing in one blow. I never looked beyond that, discouraged by the titles.

"I'm going to smoke," Julian announced, cigarette on his lips. "Portal travel makes me uneasy; I need to calm the nerves."

Dayton didn't hide his scowl as he walked inside without comment. I followed, swallowed in the cold, lingering darkness as the only light filtering through emerged from a tall doorway entrapped in a silvery mist.

It looked like a floating veil, enticing and dangerous. The farther I went, the grander it became, situated upon a black marble podium between two white columns. Along the edges of the podium were inscriptions in a language I didn't understand.

"What does this say?" I mused, trailing my fingers alongside the words.

Dayton came up close behind me, his breath on my neck. "Naïve little wolves who don't listen die," he whispered. "Back up, you don't want to get too close to it."

"It doesn't really say that," I hissed.

"*'Bless the passage of the Moons Children with safety and fortitude,'* he said, still close in my ear. A chill went down my spine. "A bunch of bullshit, really."

"I think that's a nice sentiment."

Dayton rolled his eyes. "Remember what I told you. Follow my lead and let me do most of the talking. Moons save us if you can't keep your opinions to yourself." He strained the last part, peering knowingly down at me.

"I'll be fine," I said. "Besides, I'm not alone. You'll be there, and I trust you."

Dayton's gaze darkened but he made no comment. He only stepped onto the podium and reached his hand to help me up. I took it, his grip warm and reassuring. I looked at him, unsure of what to do next.

"Hold on tight, Mare."

Gripping my shoulders, Dayton shoved me face-first into the portal. The instant rush surprised me as I launched off my feet. A scream rose but refused to surface. Everything spun wildly out of control, and the scenery was forever changing with each passing second, none of which I could focus on enough to remember. Fear struck me, chilling my bones, and when my feet hit solid ground, I kept my eyes squeezed shut. When I dared to open them, I stood on light, fluffy snow, and I invited the air into my lungs.

"State your name and business!" The abruptness of the declaration forced me to focus.

A man stood inches from me, pointing a long sword at my chest. His lips turned scathingly upwards. Before I could react, Dayton jerked me backward.

"Point that sword at her again and see how well that ends for you, Istvan," Dayton growled.

"Lord Cadman," the guard—Istvan—greeted, maintaining the same hard stance. "It's been too long since the Court has been graced by your presence."

There was a whooshing noise behind him, and Julian tumbled through the portal, his hair sticking up every which way while another cigarette dangled unlit on his lips. He stood up straight, grinning.

"Istvan." Julian nodded toward the guard. "Good to see you again. Always a pleasure. Pardon Dayton. You know how prickly he can be."

"State your business, Lord Cadman," Istvan requested. Istvan wore a uniform of gray and red, stretching tight around his middle. He had shoulder-length hair drawn into a ponytail.

"Drop the Lord from my title," Dayton said stiffly. "It's been long since stripped from me."

Lord? That sounded far too civil to suit him. Lords were polite, even-tempered— civilized. Dayton was rude, hot tempered, and feral at times.

Julian slinked around Istvan, grinning as he knocked back a flask. "Ah, that was needed. Anyway, we're here to have an audience with the Wolf Council."

"Neither of you look like Maris Bakar to me," Istvan growled, peering past Dayton to where I stood behind him.

"Maybe stop swinging that sword at every shadow that spooks you," Dayton said curtly. "And I don't remember telling you her name."

"You know how rumors fly around here," Istvan said with a scrutinizing glare. "Whispers say you're awfully protective of this newborn."

"Then I'd lower that sword if I were you," Dayton said with lethal calm.

I wasn't surprised by Dayton's uncanny protectiveness, though I didn't quite understand it. Why would he extend his protection to me? Nonetheless, I would take it.

Istvan narrowed his eyes and beckoned for Dayton to step aside, who did with snarling reluctance. Dayton left a foot of distance between us while Istvan lowered his sword and stepped toward me with an assessing gaze. When he raised his arm, I fumbled back.

"Don't touch her," Dayton growled from beside me.

Istvan threw his hands up and slunk away down the long, snowy pathway. Dayton stomped ahead with me hurrying to catch up. Wolves prowled between the trees, watching us with predatory ease. Each one looked different, from the jarring size differences to their unique colorings, a tangle of ebony and onyx furs, yellow and blue eyes. Each one had the same snarl as we passed. I gulped and inched closer to Dayton. A few of the giant wolves dared a closer look, and I had to train my gaze ahead.

"Hey, Dayton?" I whispered. He inclined his head toward me. "Remember you told me to tell you if anyone looked at me funny? Well, these wolves are looking at me like I'm a meal."

The corners of his mouth turned up, but he only said, "Mare, relax. They can smell your fear."

"Where are we going?"

"No talking. Make this trip painless for yourself," he muttered.

That was going to be exceedingly difficult for me.

The trees surrounding us felt more intimidating than the wolves. Thick trunks stretched at least thirty feet and towered over us menacingly. Dark bark wrinkled up the base, the size of logs. The forest expanded endlessly over hills and mountain terrain. Ahead, outlines of buildings stood beneath a layer of mist. We approached an ancient stone wall wrapped around the forest. It had seen better days.

Istvan halted to unlock a gate, drawing out a blade and cutting his palm before pressing it against the lock. It popped open and he gestured us all through, and once inside, the whole dynamic changed. The inside felt empty, hollow, with our footsteps echoing with each shuffle forward. Black stone crept up each wall, and the deeper we went in, the more unsettled I became.

Tapestries billowed as we passed, weaved with maroon threads and interlaced with gold to form circlets of the moon phases. Similar to those at the Temple, wolf head torches glowed with silver flames, but the eyes on the wolves' heads were scarlet. Sharply, Istvan stopped, and I nearly ran into him.

"There will be no weapons in the council room," Istvan said, reaching down to produce a sizable bucket. "Please, place your weapons in here."

"No weapons? Since when?" Dayton protested.

"Just play nice, Dayton," Julian said, smelling freshly of alcohol as he pocketed his flask. He stepped up and began undoing his bow strap and setting aside his quiver. He withdrew a small dagger, alongside a coil of wire from his pockets, then handed them over. He looked at me and said, "The wire heats as you tighten it; it makes for easy kills when you have the element of surprise."

Wondering why he would think he needed such a weapon here, my head spun. Dayton stepped forward looking less than pleased and unsheathed the swords from his back to toss them into the bucket. He removed his gun from his side and another hidden in the back of his pants, glaring as they clattered alongside the rest. Istvan gave him his boots a pointed look. Scowling, Dayton reached down and removed multiple daggers, darts, and arrowheads from the buckles of his shoes. Lastly, he unbuckled his weapons belt and dropped it in.

"Happy?" he shot.

"Ecstatic." Istvan grinned. "What about the girl?"

"Couldn't even hurt a fly; she's wildly uncoordinated," chimed Dayton. "She isn't carrying anything."

"I might have to do a more extensive check on her before allowing you in," Istvan drawled, his gaze sauntering over my body. I recoiled and stepped back.

Dayton's answering snarl rumbled through the hall. "You even breathe in her direction and I'll snap your spine so creatively, any more thoughts like that will forever be in vain."

Dayton stepped closer to me, and my body relaxed as his towering form practically hid me from view.

"Still, such anger you hold," Istvan huffed.

"It begs to stick around from time to time," Dayton retorted.

Istvan led us down another hall, winding down endless corridors rivaling the Temple's. Adorned on the walls were portraits of people, all varying through the ages. Women dressed in tight bodices and large, flowing dresses next to men in suits with their hair slicked back. At the bottom were inscriptions stating their names and time periods. One picture stood out—an old man dressed similarly to Dayton with battle leathers, while the rest of the portrait had been marred by three slashes cutting the portrait into ribbons. Claw marks. The inscription looked burned; I could only make out a first name: Dante.

Dayton caught me looking at it and shook his head curtly. I didn't ask, despite the poking curiosity. We stopped at a monstrous oak door, which Istvan opened, stepping aside to bow his head.

"I present to you the Wolf Council," Istvan announced.

Chapter 13

As soon as I walked through the doors, the atmosphere dropped. It was like a crypt; the fine stone walls were bare. Dull, greenish candles hung overhead and had me squinting, and no sound echoed in the room. A large, round table was placed in the center of the room with ornate dark green chairs, lavishly designed. I stepped in cautiously and looked back at Dayton, whose jaw was set and eyes hard as he stared ahead. Following his gaze, a soft "oh" formed on my lips.

A woman sat in one of the notably grander chairs. Despite her small frame, she wore an elegant onyx gown with a plunging neckline, her night-black hair pulled into a complex-looking bun atop her head. Her wine-red lips twirled into a generous smile as we approached the table, her dark gaze surveying us.

"My, my, look what the cat dragged in," she drawled, her voice edged with mischief.

We all sat while she stood, slowly walking toward us. If I had to guess, I'd peg her to be no older than twenty-five. Her gown rippled as she moved, dancing behind her in the shadows. She was beautiful in the way roses were, pretty to look at yet dangerous to touch. Halting by Dayton, she placed a hand under his chin. He was stiff as a board.

"Dayton, darling, it has simply been too long. You used to visit me all the time when you lived in Court." She pouted, but I sensed the predator beneath her, itching to pounce. "You seem different since our last acquaintance."

Then, the strangest thing happened. Dayton transformed. His usual feral disposition was no longer as he mimicked that of a near upstanding citizen, his mouth stretching into a wide smile that practically had my jaw to the floor from its fakeness. Dayton stood, and the woman offered a hand, which Dayton accepted, kissing the top gently. I gripped my hands and glanced away. I prayed I was putting on the best stoic expression because I felt like my eyeballs fell from their sockets.

"Always the pleasure, Claire," said Dayton sweetly, addressing her casually like he would a friend. Dayton sat back down and caught my eye with cunning. He was playing a strange game.

"Now, Julian," Claire drawled, sauntering toward Julian. He made no effort to play nice, eyes stonily fixed on her. She studied him coolly, placing a finger under Julian's chin to tilt his face upward. "You are still quite a looker, darling. Those eyes..." She narrowed her dark eyes at him, her tongue between her teeth.

"Thank you," said Julian curtly. "It is always a pleasure, Lady Evermore of the Wolves."

She threw her head back and laughed. "Pish posh with the formalities. I know I'm part of the Council; I don't need the refresher. Call me Claire."

"Well," Julian said, allowing the word to hang in the abyss for a moment. "It is a pleasure to meet you. Perhaps when the fake niceties are forgone, we can do away with the formalities."

Dayton sucked in a breath. If I hadn't been acutely aware of him, I wouldn't have noticed. Having expected such behavior from Dayton, I was stunned by Julian's bluntness. Julian was the mild-mannered one. The tension simmered as Julian glared daggers at Claire, whose dark gaze sharpened on him.

"My, my, I rather like you, Julian." Claire's eyes never strayed off him as she trailed a long red fingernail across his jaw.

Her attention shifted then upon noticing me. My blood went cold, and goosebumps erupted across my arms. Her look was sharp like glass, and her gaze remained unmoving; she was soaking in every detail, and as she strode toward me, her heels clicked. My hands began to shake, and I wanted to look away, but I felt that casting my eyes from her would not be well-received. She clearly enjoyed being the center of attention.

"Oh, those eyes," she said at last, coming to a standstill beside me. This close, I could smell her perfume—intoxicatingly sweet. My heart hammered out of my chest, and my hands clammed up with sweat. "A precise shade of sapphire."

Talking about my eye color was the last thing I expected. "Thank you," I whispered, unable to find my voice.

She whirled past me and back to her chair, where she draped herself across it. It was strange seeing her sit this casually. Yet again, her whole demeanor was bizarre—eerie, even.

"You'll have to pardon the absence of the rest of the Council." Claire shook her head. "An abysmal situation is being dealt with, politics and all that riffraff. Plus, with an empty council seat in our future, you understand how people get around elections."

I recalled Dayton's description of the Council and how people desperately sought seats. I counted the seats around the table. Thirteen. An odd number for if the votes were to ever come to a tie. I couldn't imagine more than just Claire here; I might have fainted from fear if they were anything like her.

"Their absence is certainly disappointing," said Dayton, and his words sounded sincere. "Next time."

"Dayton, dear, I found it very unfortunate to learn you harbored a newborn and did not make a record of it." Claire faced him, pouting. "Especially someone as special as Maris."

She said "special" like I was a golden ticket. I expected this—yes—but I didn't like the grimy feeling of being used for information.

Once again, Dayton offered her a smile, the gesture wildly out of place. "That was my mistake, a lapse in judgment," he smoothly explained. "I was under the belief the Wolf Council was only interested once the newborn shifts."

"Normally, yes. But like I said, Maris is special." Claire shook her head at Dayton and tsked, her eyes narrowing. "You are lucky I was able to plead a case for you this time. The strings I had to pull were strenuous, and then you went ahead and ignored our ample requests for a meeting. Darling, you have gotten out of touch."

"I realize how it must seem," Dayton agreed.

"Especially looking at your tangled history," she added, gaze shifting to me. I took a slow breath to compose myself. I didn't understand what she was implying, but if Dayton wanted to tell me himself, he would have.

Dayton nodded, his winning smile morphing into a snarl. "That was a long time ago, I assure you. I had no intentions beyond getting Mare—" He cleared his throat. "*Maris* situated."

She watched him thoughtfully before her gaze fell on me once more. "I have heard lots about you, Maris. However, nothing beyond whispers and rumors. You are acquainted with an interesting group of wolves, so seeing you in the flesh is astounding." She beamed, crossing her arms.

"I never knew of this world until a few weeks ago," I said. "I don't have much to tell you if you want information."

Claire snorted. "Well, I think you may know more than you realize. I mean Lukas Danika is your brother. That in itself is a glittering fascination."

"It's just Luka," I corrected, yet it was strange she referred to him as Danika, not Bakar, given she knew I was Maris Bakar.

"I must ask, why did he shield you from this world?" she crooned. I hated Claire's act, the bravado and beating around the bush.

"You'd have to ask him," I said stiffly. "I never knew of this world."

"Claire, you're scaring poor Maris," Dayton chimed, shifting in his seat. "She is still frightened to be around werewolves."

She strummed her fingers against the chair, lazily holding her head back. "My apologies, Maris. How rude I must sound! Lukas Danika, however, is of interest," she hummed.

"I'm not talking about my brother," I whispered, looking away from her.

Claire laughed. "It wasn't your brother I was asking you about."

She unfurled a folder from beside her and slid it toward me. Pasted on the front was the name *Lukas Danika*. I opened it, but only enough to glimpse a photo before shoving it back toward Claire. She giggled, then; she knew exactly who this person was to me.

"That man is—" I stopped and considered my words. "He gave me life, that is all."

My father was a man I rarely thought about. I tried not to mess with the memories I had of him. I didn't know or ever have an interest in him, and Luka rarely spoke of him.

"Lukas Danika is your father?" Claire asked.

"He is not my father. He lost all right to that the day he walked out of my life. My brother raised me and took care of me. He gains the right to that title far more than that excuse of a man." My words came out sharp and clipped, and by Dayton's sharp intake of breath, I might have pushed too far. But where my father was concerned, my temper always went astray.

"Well, I just find it utterly shocking that your father leads the Hunt of the Wolves," Claire said.

I froze.

"What do you mean?"

"Werewolf hunters," Dayton interjected before Claire could. "He is the leader of the sadistic group of humans who know of our kind and actively seek to kill us."

I considered this. Nothing shocked me with my father, yet hearing he engaged in a group centered around killing werewolves did, especially as Luka was the exact thing he set on murdering. But if my father was a werewolf hunter, I doubted he was a werewolf, which would make my mother the one who passed down the genes to Luka and me. The real question was if my mother was a werewolf, why had she married a werewolf hunter?

"Makes one wonder," Claire chirped, "if he perhaps knew of your wolf lineage.

"I don't care to talk about him anymore," I said lowly as this new information churned in my stomach.

"Fine, then let me get a timeline settled in my head. You were raised by your brother. At what age?" Claire asked. I told her nine, prompting her to ask about my age now. I told her. Twenty-one. "For nearly twelve years, you have had no clue about this world? Not even an inkling of suspicion?" I let my silence be the answer. "Still, it seems unbelievable, the oddity of your situation."

"I never asked you to believe me," I hissed.

Claire looked taken aback, placing a hand on her chest as if my words hurt her. I looked over at Dayton, who glanced at Julian, whose head downturned to hide his grin.

"You certainly have the natural temperament of the wolves," she quipped.

A retort was ready on my lips, but Dayton interjected. "Claire, Maris does not mean to act rudely. As we know, she is new to this world; she's still unaware of certain customs." I glared daggers at Dayton, finding it ironic he was acting like a poster boy for "well-mannered" while I was scrutinized.

"Don't fret, little warrior," Claire said. "She's still learning. She is quite a curious case. How about this, Maris? I show you everything we know about your brother, and you confirm what is true?"

She did not allow me to answer before a Cheshire cat grin broke across her face. She leaned forward and pulled out another black folder, pushing it toward me. It was a thin folder with question marks where the names should be, and I cautiously pulled it toward me to open it. I recalled Dayton's earlier warning that they could detect lies.

Inside was a single piece of paper, and various things were on it. A blurry picture of Luka, hat low on his face and sunglasses concealing his features; he must have been sixteen here. I realized this was an entire report on Luka, yet the Council knew startlingly little about him. There were some crass comments about his sour personality and unwillingness to work with others, and his home address, middle name, phone number, and birthday were all wrong. A blank section read "Cadre" while a column for his status guessed he was an Alpha, with an array of question marks scrawled beside it. The family member section was also blank.

"As you can see, there is little knowledge about your brother. The fact that you have existed this whole time, hidden from us, is astounding. Luka has a knack for secrets," Claire said. "I believe he has multiple aliases, but there's one, in particular, that is of interest to me. Tell me, did your brother ever refer to the name Bestial?"

I pushed the folder back and glared. "I have no idea. Anything about his life as a werewolf is more of a mystery to me than you."

She watched me thoughtfully for a long while before answering. "Blood runs thicker than water," she said, her voice losing its charm.

Julian, who had been quiet for a while, made a disgruntled noise in the back of his throat and straightened once he realized the attention had shifted.

"Something to add, Mr. Fletcher?" Claire asked.

He met her glare. "I find it interesting your fascination with a myth of a werewolf. It's time that you and the whole goddamn council opened their eyes." Julian sneered. Dayton's eyes widened, his knuckles turning white.

"What are you insinuating, Mr. Fletcher?" Claire asked, no longer disguising her irritation.

Julian snorted and shook his head. "My, my, Lady Evermore. You really do have your head in the sand. You can't really tell me you haven't received the weekly reports and chosen to ignore them?" His words were hard, and he stood on his feet, hands against the table.

"Ah," Claire said, her posture stiff. "You have not let that go, it seems."

"Maybe if the Council weren't all such narcissistic morons, I wouldn't have had to worry about it," Julian hissed. Dayton put his head in his hands. "Kaser Odessa is rising to power again, and you know it."

That name again. Zayne had mentioned it, too, but Dayton had shrugged it off. He'd said he'd been a terrible man but never explained more about it. My stomach hollowed realizing Dayton might not have told me the entire truth.

"Such claims are haughty without evidence, Mr. Fletcher," Claire fumed.

"Evidence? What of the Fenrir sightings? Even one being sighted should be of interest to the Council! Yet you've ignored the dozens sent to you over the past months," Julian continued.

"Fenrir are not a threat to us anymore," Claire said calmly, resting her palms flat against the table.

"You ignorant bitch." Julian sneered. "When Kaser comes back, I hope you all suffer."

"*Jules*," Dayton chided, standing and reaching to smack his friend.

"Enough!" Claire screeched, unleashing her hidden anger. "I will not be insulted in my own court! Guards, take him away!"

Piles of guards flooded the room, waiting for her commands; they dressed like Istvan in red and gray uniforms. Unlike Istvan, these guards looked younger and more able-bodied. They swarmed Julian, who raised his arms in submission, the disdain never leaving his features. He never once disguised his evident loathing for Claire. One guard pointed a crossbow at Julian's spine as they pushed him out of the room.

I was not foolish enough to push the mention of that name again, but I knew there was more to it than Dayton had revealed. It was the third time the name was spoken like a curse and brushed away without a second thought. Whoever Kaser was, I wanted to know. I glanced at Dayton, taut as a bowstring in his chair.

"Now, where were we?" She tucked a wayward piece of her dark hair back. "Maris, I must say, you know a shocking number of interesting wolves for someone so out of touch with her own heritage. Derek Knight, a wolf your age. You know him?"

Flashes of Derek from the last night I saw him returned. I wrung my hands. "What about Derek?"

"A wolf who is also resistant to attempts of—*alliances* with the Council." Claire clicked her tongue.

"Considering he knows my brother, I don't know why you seem shocked."

"So, Derek is Luka's Beta then." Claire hummed appreciatively, scrawling on her sheet. I cursed myself for the slight slip of the tongue. "A report came through regarding Derek from an anonymous source. Apparently he has gone missing." Her words were teasing—playful, almost—as she slowly flicked through a small stack of pages.

I froze in my seat. "What?"

"Werewolves go missing all the time. They come back, or they don't. We never really enforce resources to finding them. It's a losing game." Claire smiled.

"When did the report come in?" I asked, heart hammering.

"Two weeks ago or so?" She shrugged. "Maybe more, maybe less."

Two weeks ago was when I last saw Derek at the Temple before sending him away. Was I the reason he went missing? Did something terrible happen to him? Had he gotten himself kidnapped like he had with Zayne? The possibilities were endless, but if me sending him away had caused this, I would never forgive myself.

"Thank you for informing us of this. We appreciate the extra insight," Dayton interjected, the fakeness wavering in his tone. I watched him, but he refused to meet my eye. "I believe you have done quite a thorough job with your evaluation of Maris."

"It is refreshing to have my kindest intentions recognized." Claire watched Dayton thoughtfully, seemingly captivated by him. "Darling, I have missed you dearly."

Dayton's smile was stiff. "Traveling between realms can become exhausting, not to mention time-consuming," he explained. "Besides, I already have my hands full with this one." He directed his gaze at me, the harshness beneath his persona faltering.

"Why, you could both come back to the Courts and play," she declared, clapping her hands together. "I do miss the way you warmed my bed." She pouted her lips again.

Their interactions made sense then, their history clear. My skin heated, and I clenched my fists, wishing very much to be somewhere else. Dayton's sexual history was his own business.

Dayton's answer came slowly and carefully. "If I perhaps will come back one day, it will not be to entertain you." I noticed he was carefully evading the use of promises. "The past is the past."

"Oh, how much you resemble Daniel," she crooned. "Yet I am sorry to say he would be disappointed in how you turned out."

That seemed to be the tether breaking Dayton's leash. The scowl I was used to darkened as he snapped, "Don't you dare speak of him like you knew him. You are no more than a child yourself. Anything you think to know is from whispers and rumors."

Claire made a low *hmpf* in her throat, then swiveled her attention to me. "Maris. Being a newborn wolf, the Council made a preempt decision to have you moved from the Temple of Loup-Garou into the safety of the Moon Court."

"What?" I said, outraged. "I'm *not* living here."

"You can't force her to live here," Dayton protested. "She hasn't even shifted yet. We don't know that she ever will."

"Without any Cadre affiliation, nothing is keeping Maris at the Temple." Claire's eyes slipped to Dayton and narrowed before swiveling to me. "Dayton knows as well as I that it's only a matter of time before you shift because you *will.* Failure to comply will mark you as a renegade wolf, meaning we would have authority to kill on sight."

"No," Dayton snarled. He stood, eyes glowing. "You will not do that."

I jerked away from the table, sending the chair skittering back. Dayton kept his gaze between me and Claire, unmoving. My breath erupted in short pants as I began to pace.

"Dayton, stand down," Claire ordered. "You are no Alpha. You saw to the fact you have no Cadre. You may as well be a renegade yourself."

"Wait a minute," I said. "You can't just decide these things for me."

Claire rolled her eyes. "Actually, I can. But with your cooperation, Maris, I will promise you one other thing. I will send search parties across the globe to search for your beloved best friend, Derek. Any questions about your brother would be dropped, and you would have a spotless slate here at Court."

I considered this, noticing the temptation of her words. Find Derek—wherever he was—and bring him back safely. Protect Luka from the Moon Court and give him a clean slate. Agreeing felt like the right thing to do, but it also felt way too easy. I looked to Dayton, who inched closer to me, and my breathing slowed. Desperation laced his golden gaze. I had to fight this.

"You don't seem to be giving me much choice," I argued. "It hardly seems like a fair bargain."

"Politics, darling." Claire shrugged.

"No," Dayton said again. "Maris will not be going to the Moon Court because I'm entitling myself as her Consort."

I glanced at Dayton, confused, but he wouldn't look at me.

Claire curled her lip. "Consort is quite a title for a girl you barely know."

"It is a title that I take with the utmost respect of the bond it shall forge," Dayton continued. "You know as well as I that the Consort bond is a bond you cannot be separated from."

Consort? I'd never heard of the term, yet Dayton spoke courageously and with conviction like it was the only thing he could say to make Claire waver. The prospect of his words unsettled me. A shared bond with Dayton? Why would he even propose such a thing?

"Is it a bond or a curse? Both are abhorrent. Why muddle your reputation further, Dayton?"

"It's my reputation to muddle."

"The Consort bond is nearly as close as a mating bond. For that reason, it has been centuries since a Consort bond was made. Are you willing to risk all it entails?"

"I'm willing to lay my life before hers: protect her, guard her, whatever it takes." Dayton's scowl never wavered, his sincerity clear. "Relay the message to the rest of the Council to leave us be until I see it fit to return to the Court. Proof of the bond will be sent to you in a day's time."

His words again were spoken with such intensity. Protect me, guard me—lay his *life* before me? That felt way too much to ask of anyone, especially Dayton. Yet, I supposed he had been doing most of those things, in some form or another.

"Well, I hope to be the fly on the wall once Luka realizes whose claws are sunk into his sister's back," Claire purred. "Though, I'm sure Maris knows nothing of how you knew Luka."

I whirled to face Dayton then, his teeth bared at Claire. It was all the confirmation I needed. She was telling the truth. My heart sank. It was all too much again, too real.

"The truth is the truth, Dayton," Claire said. "Don't be mad because she knows only a fraction of your broken past."

"Enough," Dayton snapped, eyes beginning to glow.

"You are a slippery beast. I hope you realize what you have done." Claire stood, glaring as she slithered toward the door at the back wall. "This meeting is dismissed."

Once I heard the click of the lock, I spun and ran for the door we'd come through, ignoring Dayton's protests. I pushed past guards, mumbled apologies, and ignored the irritated comments of passersby; I shoved through crowds of people, wondering where the hell they all came from. I couldn't freak out here, not in Court surrounded by strangers. The hallways were long, and the more twists and turns I made, the more trapped I felt in this maze. This whole trip had been a mistake; I wanted to forget all of it.

"Mare!" Someone distantly called my name. "Mare!" Dayton. "*Maris!*"

Someone pulled my arm roughly behind me, and I shrieked in protest. I stared up at Dayton, who pulled me back. Any lingering politeness in him had gone. He ran toward a wall and shoved into it where a door I had not noticed before opened. Inside was a closet, the space so small I was pressed up against Dayton.

"You knew this would happen." I refused to look at him, already hating the strain in my voice.

"I did." Dayton's eyebrows were raised as he looked down at me.

"Is that all you have to say?" I snapped. "You played a pretty convincing part back there. You're a wonderful actor."

Dayton rolled his eyes. "I had to play the part. It's all games to them, Claire especially. You're lucky the rest of the Council were not there. They are each uniquely vicious. You should be thanking me that I finagled you out of their clutches."

"What is a Consort?" I asked, the idea of it jangling in my head. The way Claire spoke of it felt confusing—wrong. *Is it a bond or a curse?*

Dayton ran a hand down his jaw and shook his head. "It is complex and—just complex." He hesitated. "I can tell you more about it, but not here with listening ears."

"Fine."

"Are you—are you okay?" Dayton asked slowly, as if afraid to know the answer.

"Yes, I'm fine," I snapped, and then backtracked. "Claire just brought up a lot of stuff, stuff I don't normally think about. My parents—my father, really. I don't know him, so it's easy to forget him, but I can't forget the stuff he did, especially to Luka. And to know he's a werewolf hunter..."

Dayton bit his lip, glancing sideways. "Yeah, complicated relationships with parents I get."

I recalled Dayton telling me his parents had died. Having a bad, irreparable relationship with your family was tragic, but in my case, I had no interest in ever seeing my father again. I couldn't care less if he died, but I remembered how Dayton initially reacted about his parents. Dayton was clearly haunted by a past he could not fix, but Dayton wouldn't welcome questions, so I didn't ask.

"Then there's Derek missing." I sighed. "I don't know what I'll do."

Dayton's face contorted in confusion. "What do you mean?"

"He's my best friend, and he's missing." I huffed. "I can't ignore that; I have to find him."

"You mean you want to embark on a mission to find him?" Dayton laughed, but it was hollow. Upon noticing my expression, he added, "Oh, you aren't kidding."

He said it like the notion was crazy, but to me, it was a no brainer. Ignoring it felt more displaced than anything. "I know I'm new to this world, and maybe naïve at times, but Derek is my best friend. I'd do anything for him."

Dayton watched me with a level gaze, contemplating, and after a moment, he conceded. "Fine, I see how important he is to you. I can't make promises, but I'll see what I can do."

I sighed in relief. "Thank you, Dayton."

Dayton glanced up at the ceiling and into the light. "Speaking of friends, I'd like to strangle my moronic one. Jules likely got himself kicked out of the Court with a temporary ban. He is most likely already back at the Temple," he said.

"What was his problem?" I asked. "He flipped his lid—and that name... Kaser? What was that about?"

"Oh, you never ask simple questions." Dayton's face strained before he continued. "I may have downplayed the threat of Kaser to you initially. I didn't want—I didn't want you to be worried about your safety because of Kaser's interest in you, despite only being interested in you because of Luka."

At the mention of Luka, I lifted my head to look at Dayton. His gaze was stony, no inkling of how or what he felt exposed. "You lied to me about Luka."

"No, I never lied," he said. "You asked me how I know Luka. I don't know Luka, but I knew Luka. Past tense."

"That's a sneaky way of evading the truth," I remarked. I wasn't really surprised; Dayton was the one who told me to watch for careful wordplay. I just never expected him to hold back on me with stuff like that.

"Ask me no questions, and I tell you no lies." He shrugged. "You'll pick up on wordplay eventually."

"It's all games and careful manipulation," I said, casting my eyes down. "How do I know who to trust?"

"Mare, look at me." Dayton rested a finger under my chin, and I jutted my head up to meet his steely gaze. "I will never lie to you. I promise you that."

Somehow, I believed him. I nodded, swallowing hard.

My mind was too addled to fully comprehend the gravity of all that went down. I wanted nothing more than to leave here with the truths I had to deal with. I wished Claire was bluffing about Derek, but deep down, I knew otherwise. I recalled the harsh words I said to him last, and dread festered in my stomach. A man I knew little about was dangerous and interested in me, and all these loose ends led back to one thing—one person. Luka.

I didn't know what to make of that.

Chapter 14

Leaving through the portal ignited the same wave of dizziness, like the feeling of my flesh and bones torn apart. Bouts of nausea rose inside me, and I did my best to push it down. We landed in the same cramped space the portal had been, crouching awkwardly on the marble podium. Slowly, I rose, leaning against the wall for support. My head spun, and I squeezed my eyes shut, gathering my breath to regain my composure.

"Do you ever get used to that?" I asked, cautiously stepping forward.

Dayton watched me closely with sharp eyes, as if waiting for me to collapse. "Being thrust through a magic veil taking you halfway across the world and back in seconds?" He shook his head. "No, not really."

We walked outside, the lingering nausea chased away by the crisp air. Early morning light broke through the branches of the trees, and Julian stood further ahead as Dayton predicted. He leaned lazily against a tree, one of many outside the Temple, and grinned at our approach. He held a lit cigarette between his fingers, the end glowing scarlet as we joined him. Dayton scowled.

"Yeah, I know it's a bad habit." Julian shrugged. "But deeply repressing your emotions to the point of numbness is no healthier, my friend."

Dayton ignored this and veered ahead, taking the lead. "That was an abysmal waste of time."

"Not a complete waste. I'm sure gossip is now alight, even with your brief appearance." Julian sneered. "The title-stripped Lord back at Courts."

"What does that mean?" I asked.

"Lord is just a title—like Alpha, Beta—only politically driven, not pack," Dayton explained. "Lord essentially means you have a more elevated presence at the Court. More connections."

"And you were a Lord?"

"Past tense," Julian said. "Don't ask him anything else; his temper gets the better of him."

I let it go, knowing Dayton enough by now to understand his reluctance to open up.

"Besides, the pricks at Court will most likely talk about the dumbass kicked out by Claire, the most politically influential member on the Council. What the hell is wrong with you?" Dayton sneered.

"They will get the whole race killed with their inability to see the truth," Julian said, any preface of humor gone. "I could hear her. Her blindness is appalling. They all think we're living in this rose-colored world and they refuse to see what's right in front of them!"

"There's a way to talk to them without coming off as a dick." Dayton scoffed.

"That's rich coming from you, possibly the biggest dick I know," Julian said, and I laughed. "Your upbringing shines in Court, your Lordship. We are all just lucky Claire's favorite boy toy was there to distract her," Julian snapped.

"Guys, stop it," I intervened. "It was a horrible trip. Just leave it at that. Arguing amongst ourselves is pointless."

Julian answered by digging into his pocket and pulling out his flask, not hesitating to take a deep gulp. His swaggering steps made me wonder how many times the metal had met his lips today. I recalled his drinking earlier and smelled the bitter scent of alcohol on his breath.

"You know, moderation is healthy," I told him.

"Julian has a vastly different definition of moderation," said Dayton.

"I see no reason to stop," Julian said. "I'm not a danger to myself or others in my drunken state. If anything, I'm more of a danger without my vices pumping through my system." Julian scoffed lightly. "Until my diet of energy drinks, alcohol, tobacco, and only eating on Tuesday catches up with me, I think I'll be okay."

"Why Tuesday?" I asked idly.

"Taco Tuesday." He grinned.

I shook my head but halted at the exact moment Dayton froze. I inhaled deeply, grimacing at the stench of rotten eggs. I nearly gagged from the smell, an uneasy feeling crawling up my spine. Dayton's sword was out in a flash, his eyes brighter than I had ever seen.

"Dayton," Julian said, glancing to his friend for direction.

"Get Maris to the Temple. I'll handle it," Dayton commanded. He took off in a blur, running into the woods.

"Julian, what is out there?" I asked, unable to hide my rising panic.

"Fenrir." He spat the word. "I have to get you out of here or I'll never hear the end of it."

Tearing from where he stood, Julian moved at warped speeds. I stilled momentarily before kicking myself into gear, trailing fast behind him. I glanced back in the direction where Dayton had taken off, searching for him but coming up short. Julian glanced back at me once, then slowed his pace to grab my arm to pull me along. Apparently, in the face of real danger, my mind and body didn't understand the severity. Julian flew around a tree, coming to a skittering stop. He swore as he dropped to the ground with me beside him; we were just in front of the Temple's front steps.

Julian shook his head and whispered, "The wards are down. I have to get them back up. Stay here; I'll be back in just a hop, skip and jump."

Baffled, I could do nothing but comply and stare at what was happening just a few yards before me.

Dayton stood in a small clearing outside the Temple, perhaps ten or so yards from me. Surrounding him were three wolf-like creatures. They were strange. They stood on their hind legs and had long snouts for faces. Their bodies appeared creepily human, with patches of fur dotting across them. Their backs were arched in defense as they moved slowly toward Dayton. They were like baby deer attempting to walk for the first time, only the more they moved, the steadier they were. They had long, sharp claws where fingers should be.

Fenrir, Julian said. Humans bitten by werewolves who were unable to withstand it, becoming these creatures instead. I shuddered and nearly ran, except common sense forced me to stay put.

Dayton assessed the situation with dark eyes. He held his sword out steady before him. There was nothing of the person I was coming to know. His stance was taut as he was poised to strike out like a snake. Shadows and moonlight cascaded over him, exposing his manic expression. In his eyes, rage broiled, finally coming to a head when he stepped toward the creatures.

"Did no one ever tell you? It's not wise to bring claws to a sword fight." A cynical smile crept over his lips, the adrenaline of the upcoming battle washing over him. He struck out with his sword, piercing a nearby Fenrir.

Then all hell broke loose.

Blood showered down like an open floodgate, and Dayton, the perpetrator, was streaked in it. The creature lunged, its maw exposed, ready to bite with its vicious teeth. In response, Dayton whipped his sword around, and to my utter astonishment, drove the blade right through the Fenrir's head. I bit back a scream of sheer horror as the Fenrir transformed into a human against the blade, tossed aside by Dayton as though it were nothing more than a bothersome gnat.

The thunk of the corpse's body hitting the ground reverberated. Cold, dead eyes of a young boy stared up at me, forever unseeing. The body lurched, bones cracking and healing, as a clawing rasp tore from his throat. They stilled, and then the body imploded. Black gore rained down, plummeting toward me thick and hot. The putrid stench made me gag and reel backward as it drenched my face.

Black gore covered every viable inch of Dayton, who dropped his sword and threw back his head, the gore sprinkling from his hair as he laughed. His laugh of death paused the battle unfolding as the creatures seemed to practice caution.

Dayton reprised his role as another creature advanced. Panting heavily, he took on the next threat, lunging high as two Fenrir came at him at once. They bounded into one another, with Dayton landing atop one. Dayton yanked on the scruff of fur, hacking at the protesting creature with his bare hands, yet the yelps of protest did not stop Dayton. He held firmly onto the Fenrir, as if he could tear it apart in two with only his hands. Behind him, another one came running, propelling toward him at supernatural speed.

I looked around frantically for Julian, searching for help. He was nowhere to be seen. Dayton was about to be skewered by the Fenrir's claws. My blood chilled as I cast an anxious glance back at Dayton still fighting the other Fenrir like a bull rider, unaware of the other about to leap on him. I shot up, unable to watch any longer.

I ran toward him.

"Dayton, behind you!" I screeched.

Dayton released the Fenrir, and it whirled on him. Both Fenrir were on Dayton, and claws teared down his chest, slashing him open as easily as ripping paper. My stomach sank at what I caused. Dayton snarled, cursing at the Fenrir. My heart pounded, and I dove for a tree branch, throwing it at one of the Fenrir with all my strength. It thunked against its hind, the creature swiveling back toward me.

Dark, depthless eyes rested on me, and I stumbled back, tripping over myself. I gawked as the creature rose on its haunches and lunged. It landed atop me, its weight forcing me hard to the ground. Its force made my arm snap back, and white-hot pain erupted. Their snout was against my neck, sniffing deeply as if to remember my scent, yet its snarl was short-lived as it was wrenched off me.

My eyes flew open as Dayton dragged the creature away by the scruff of its neck. Dayton had his sword once more, malice glinting in his gaze. My hand automatically went to my mouth, suppressing a scream as Dayton raged, slicing the creature's throat clean open. Again, it thudded, its body human once again. The body bucked and imploded into black gore, but I could only watch, sick to my stomach, as my body writhed. I wiped the gore from my face, trembling.

When Dayton looked down at me, I wished he hadn't. His feral rage was unmuted—relentless. The gore was a thick second skin. His eyes, despite glowing that golden hue, were empty. Unwavering, unfeeling, with no traces of remorse or humanity, as if the death unleashed here was not by his doing.

I staggered back, my spiked heartrate beating against my sternum like a drum. I spun around, closing my eyes and breathing harshly through my mouth to calm down. I started to walk away, but my steps swayed, and hot tears streamed down my cheeks.

A glittering light exploded around us like a gilded halo as the wards shot like a shield, entrapping us in the safety of the Temple. Before I could witness more horrors, two frail hands grasped me up, pulling me away.

"Don't look. Moons above, don't look," Julian's voice said behind me.

Distantly, I heard Dayton's battle cry as Julian pulled me away. Everything was a blur, and suddenly, I was stumbling up the stairs while Julian fumbled to open the door. I walked through the Temple, still clutching to him. He led us into the kitchen, releasing me as he moved to tear the curtains shut, cursing under his breath. I slinked onto the floor, my back against the wall.

"I didn't know—I thought it was going to kill him, but I made it worse." That was all I managed to say, my head in my hands. "But he killed them so violently."

"You didn't know, how could you? You acted with good intentions, but it was dangerous." Julian sighed, discarding what looked like silver stakes on the counter. "Dayton did what had to be done. It's not all rainbows and sunshine, but if he hadn't done that, we would all be dead."

"The blood, the amount of blood..." I said slowly, my voice catching as the bloody images flashed in my memory. I glanced at the gore still fresh on my body.

Julian rummaged around, producing a rag, and running cold water over it, handing it to me.

I pressed the cloth over my face, repulsed by the black gore covering my body. When I finished with it, Julian sat beside me and offered his flask. I considered taking a swig but shook my head. Julian shrugged and took a long gulp. We sat silent for a long while as a few tears escaped me. I gulped and pressed my head back, staring up at the ceiling.

"I know it wasn't pretty," Julian said slowly. "You shouldn't have had to see that."

I thought for a moment about my next words. "He was ruthless."

"Dayton is complicated," he said uncertainly. "Dayton carries this barely leashed violence inside of him. I'm truly sorry you had to see that."

I had watched Dayton fight before, even witnessed him killing that man in the woods. That had been different; he hadn't acted so violently then. The glint in his eyes had been borderline possessive, like the rage had taken complete control of him, blocking out all sensible thought. He looked like he enjoyed killing the Fenrir. I shuddered.

"Why did they come here?" I asked.

Julian chuckled huskily. "Fenrir are only able to obey orders. Think of them as people enslaved to the wolf. The wolf side of them needs an Alpha to lead them. My guess is they were sent here to find someone." He took another swig. "Whoever sent them here knew how to break the wards: silver stakes in each cardinal point, struck in order."

"Who would send those creatures?"

"Kaser Odessa," Julian said bitterly.

"What's the deal with him?" I asked. "I'm guessing no one likes him much?"

"Like is a very loose term. It's complicated—he's complicated." Julian exhaled. "It all started years ago with Dante Odessa who held a notably elevated position on the Council."

"Let me guess—a crazier relative?" I chimed sarcastically.

Julian snorted.

"Yes, no families are normal when it comes to werewolves," said Julian. "But Dante Odessa was Kaser's father. Dante was young, charismatic, charming—a poster boy for young wolves to look up to. Dante had a way of speaking that made you want to listen to him, to believe him. If Dante said the sky was green and grass was blue, people would take it as fact. His ideas started small. Frivolous things, really. He believed an Alpha's power should be regulated—a registration system enforced for werewolves, forbidding them from marrying and interbreeding with humans. None of what he said was feasible to obtain, but people supported him nonetheless.

"Despite his faults, he still has supporters after all these years. One group held more sway than the rest; he had an inner circle of friends, a pack of elite werewolves, they called themselves the werewolves of comradery. Ironic being that they all had specific talents of varying torture," Julian explained. "Shetani, the white wolf, bold and brazen with lethal cunning. Her twin brother, Kato, was a sadistic torturer, particularly to those defying the group. Lastly, Brontes and Ashni, the thunder and lightning duo, who were famous for their ability of destruction. They thought themselves to be the werewolf's salvation from werewolves themselves."

"The Council never did anything about it?" I asked, baffled.

"Initially, no, because his antics were less noticeable in the beginning. His Cadre was not the lethal pack of wolves we now have presented to the world. Dante wanted more; he wanted better for werewolves, and he thought he knew better. Within the last few decades, werewolf numbers are less and less. It's not to say we are a dying race by any means, but more werewolves are born dormant, waiting for the curse to be triggered. There are werewolves scattered across the globe. It's natural for us to eventually intermingle with humans and conceive, and as a result, we get dormant wolves." Julian peered down at me, an eyebrow raised. "As you know, dormant wolves are ignorant to the curse until it's triggered by an Alpha's bite. I suspect there are plenty of werewolves in the world without an inkling of what they are."

Julian paused, glancing up. I had been that ignorant dormant wolf, and a part of me yearned for the simplicity of that life again but I knew, deep down, that knowing the truth was better.

"I'm getting sidetracked—back to Dante. He wanted more werewolves and thought he could replenish the race. He was poised to attack humans, the problem being most humans are too frail to accept the bite, so it rejects them. Thus, the bite turns on them and creates what you saw today. Fenrir. It's a sad state of being, really. No one knows how much of the human is left in there. It's why a quick death is best for them."

"Dante made those creatures?" I asked.

"Under the preface of moral goodness, yes. Dante loved werewolves. That never changed, but his ideas for us as a race were too big, too much. Dante wanted to overthrow the Council and rein with his Cadre, creating werewolves as he saw fit, changing dormant wolves against their will. Scary enough, he almost did. He had created enough of a following outside his Cadre to make it possible. The plan fell through when an Alpha came in and killed Dante." Julian gave me a knowing look.

"The Bestial," I said. "Luka killed him."

"Dante's fatal mistake was thinking he could overtake the Bestial. He tried to recruit Luka. He wanted him as a part of his Cadre, but Luka is too powerful to exist within a Cadre like them; he's too domineering. Dante took his refusal and tried to kill Luka and failed. Luka, too smart for his own good, knew the destruction someone like Dante would cause long before anyone else saw it. He planned to kill him at the right moment to show the world who the Bestial was and stop Dante before he created more terror. It was smart; he let the world know of the powerful Bestial without revealing the man under the skin."

"You said the Fenrir were sent here tonight, looking for someone," I said. "Luka killing Dante probably didn't sit right with his Cadre. I'm venturing a guess here that they were after me?"

"You are a smart girl, Maris." Julian grinned. "But I don't believe the Cadre is after you. After that night, the Council captured who remained of his Cadre. They have since been locked up in Sköll, a special prison for werewolves that's eons away. But Dante had a son. Kaser Odessa: someone vastly different from Dante—forgettable. After his father died, no one heard of what happened to Kaser. He fell off the radar completely, and with the ruckus Dante caused, the Council was inclined to let Kaser slip between the cracks. They didn't want to go looking for trouble. Now, we're here today, and past patterns are returning. Missing people, missing werewolves, all with dead ends. I believe Kaser is back, keeping a low profile and attempting to finish what his father started."

"If Kaser is alive, he wouldn't take too kindly to Luka. If he's alive and doing this to people and werewolves then—" I stopped as a harrowing realization dawned on me. "Derek is missing," I said, standing up. "If he's back and seeking revenge on Luka, it all makes sense."

"When did he go missing?" Julian asked, standing with me.

"That's enough, Jules."

I spun on my heel, facing Dayton who stood in the kitchen dripping in sweat, blood, and gore. The high from his battle was gone, replaced by his usual scowl. Hair fell into his face, the ends dripping with his blood. Stepping forward, he unsheathed his sword, forcing it down on the counter, where black goop splattered.

"Dayton, maybe you shouldn't—" Julian started.

"Did you enjoy the show?" Dayton growled, shoving more dirtied weapons onto the countertop.

The horrible images of Dayton flooded back. "You killed them." My voice wavered, stuck between fear and disgust. "*Ruthlessly.*"

"It was them or me," he hissed, whipping his head to look at me. "Those creatures have no business in this world. They're lawless killers. They have no remorse."

"What about you?" I challenged. "Do you feel remorse? Because you certainly act like you don't."

His lip curled; I'd clearly struck a chord.

"Did it scare you to see me like that?" he spat, raising his eyebrows. He stepped closer to me, and I stepped back, closer to the wall. "Guess what, Mare? You're right. I don't care that I killed them, and I would do it again in a heartbeat."

I glared. No light flickered in his eyes, just unwavering, cold darkness. Slowly, he crept forward, a predator, assessing where—and how best—to strike. As his chest rose and fell, I whiffed a scent of copper. Iron. I glanced at the open wounds of claw marks across his chest slowly fading. Dayton took notice and tore his shirt back.

"This is your fault," Dayton hissed, prodding at the gashes on his chest that bled profoundly, yet he didn't seem fazed. "You nearly got me killed."

"I'm sorry," I said. "I thought they were going to kill you. I didn't know."

Dayton stepped closer. One more step, and there'd be no space left between us. "I had it under control. You were in the way! Stupidly throwing yourself where you don't belong."

"Dayton, don't be so hard on her," said Julian.

Dayton's next words, directed at me, were a kindled flame of fury. "If I had died, it would have been your fault."

The words hit me like a slap in the face. I didn't have a response; I was too taken aback. Instead, I gulped and pushed past Dayton hard, ignoring the hot tears springing to my vision.

CHAPTER 15

*N*o! I screeched, the protest tearing from my throat. *No!* Luka stood over me, blood pouring down on him in sheets. The monstrous creatures—the Fenrir—were coming. I was useless, unable to help. All I could do was scream. *No!* A useless word. Pathetic. Luka stayed there, still as a statue, grinning and shaking his head. *No.* They struck, Fenrir toppling over him; I could only watch as they tore his flesh, ripping his skin into pieces like shredded paper. Limbs were wrenched off one after another, and his guttural protests were all I heard.

I shot up, gasping for air, my surroundings the only relief from the terror coiling inside me. The bedsheets crumpled, sticking to my body, layered in sweat. My stomach lurched, and I ran out of bed toward the bathroom. I barely made it before I hurled my guts up. My body bucked, turning in on itself and pouring out the contents of my stomach until nothing more than bile came up.

Slowly, I rose, clutching the sink for support. I turned the tap to cold, splashing my face and rinsing my mouth. My hands shook, unable to be calmed. I glanced at my reflection and then cast my eyes away. It was only a dream—a nightmare, really, yet telling myself that didn't chase away the intensity that shook me to my core. I was used to being dammed by dreams that felt like reality, but they never had me hurtling out of bed to find the nearest toilet.

I walked back into the room and glared at the bed. A glance at the clock and showed it was past one in the morning, and all was quiet. After yesterday's events, I had stayed holed up in this room for the entire day, unable to see or be with anyone. Dayton's words still stung, and I was glad not to see him. A part of me felt shameful for throwing myself into the battle, but I feared he might die. So many came to him at once, but I was useless in battle, no more than deadweight.

A sudden rap at the door had me jumping out of my skin again. I crossed the room and padded my bare feet over the floor. I yanked the door open to see Dayton standing on the other end, gripping his knife white-knuckled. He must have been roused from sleep since he was clad in only shorts, his hard stomach exposed, rippling with the results of many strict workout routines, I assumed. I rolled my eyes and turned away.

"There's no one here to kill," I said, "unless you have finally tired of me. I didn't mean to wake you up, either. Go back to doing whatever it is you do."

"Fine, next time you're screaming bloody murder, I'll ignore you," he snapped, pocketing the knife.

I crossed my arms and turned to face him, but he was walking away. "Dayton, wait," I called out suddenly.

Dayton paused in the doorway, his back to me. "Yes?"

"I—" My words came up short; I didn't know why I asked him to stay. He turned to face me, his gaze dark. "I'm sorry about before. I wasn't thinking, and it was reckless."

Dayton rolled his shoulders back as he answered. "A couple of Fenrir wouldn't have killed me, regardless of your interference, but seeing you throw yourself into the midst of it just threw me off."

"What does it mean, if they're back?"

Slowly, Dayton stepped into the room, his golden eyes watching me with a careful guard in his expression, keeping his walls up. "Julian explained it pretty well, I think. In short, Kaser's most likely trying to rise to power again, with a chip on his shoulder about your brother. To go after you means he would force Luka's hand in the game."

"Do you think Luka knows any of this?"

Dayton rested a hand on the back of his neck. "To some degree, I'm sure he does. He's notorious for gathering information, and if he realizes the gravity of the situation, especially with Fenrir coming back, then he's lying low about it." Dayton's voice wavered.

"You don't believe that," I said.

Dayton huffed a laugh. "No, I don't. If Luka knew, he would've stopped you from leaving. It's only been emerging the past few weeks; I was investigating leads based on rumors. The Alpha who bit you was hired by Zayne. In turn, Zayne was in Kaser's ear, and that's why I was there both times. But now with the Alpha and Zayne dead and Fenrir suddenly popping up, this all circles around you."

Dayton watched me as he paced. Hearing that didn't shock me, but it unsettled me. I didn't like being the missing piece. I took a deep breath as Dayton went on.

"It's maddening because I can't figure out why Luka isn't acting. It isn't like him to not do something. I must assume he doesn't know, which is just as scary."

"Then we have to tell him," I said at once, my mind racing. "If this is about Luka, and he doesn't know, then he needs to."

I spoke with certainty, despite the uncertainty I felt. After all, he lied to me—he hid this whole *life* from me. But he was Luka, my older brother, my first defender. Despite everything that happened, he continued to be there for me and protect me. I left him, but I'd go back if he were ever in danger. No doubt about that.

"I agree," Dayton said. He paused his pacing, leaning against a wall. "It's fair to say I'm not your brother's favorite person, and it's entirely possible he might kill me on sight."

I looked at Dayton, baffled. "Why?"

His jaw clenched before he spoke. "There's bad blood between us. No one is entirely blameless, especially not me, but I won't get into it. Luka needs to know."

My curiosity piqued, but I didn't prod further on Dayton's tangled history with Luka. Whatever happened clearly wasn't bad enough to cause a permanent rift, otherwise Dayton wouldn't have agreed to warn him. I was getting to know Dayton in spades, but the massive chip on his shoulder told me he wasn't the type to open up. I wasn't even sure I wanted to know more; the more you knew about a person, the closer you became, and Dayton was no doubt a dangerous person to be close to.

Despite that, something still bothered me—something I felt needed to be addressed. "Do you truly not care?" I asked. "About killing Fenrir?"

"No, I don't. Nothing has changed since yesterday when I told you the first time. They deserved what they got," he said, his words clipped. Yet I knew his heart wasn't in it when I looked up to find his golden eyes downcast, his shoulders slumped. For a minute—just a minute—it was easy to forget he was a major jerk.

"Does anyone really deserve that?" I asked.

Dayton shook his head. "You must be able to see the difference between the life of an innocent and the life of those who *take* innocence. They would kill all in their path if no one stopped them. It wasn't a choice for me." Dayton hesitated, watching me. "Believe me when I say I never wanted you to see that side of me."

Again, Dayton's words tossed into a pool of confusion. Dayton was a wild card, his words unpredictable. One moment he was pure venom, and the next he was nearly human. A part of me wanted to challenge him, to desperately try to figure out his end game. Yet pressing him would only result in another of his outbursts; I was having doubts—lingering worries. Dayton knew how to hurt people, and it came easy for him. But Dayton never wanted me in harm's way, which only added to my confusion.

I gripped the rail of the bed frame behind me. "But how can you do that and feel nothing? Are you so wounded that showing a sliver of guilt is a toll on your pride?"

"Pride?" he barked, huffing a laugh. "It's hardly about that."

"Then what is it?" I challenged.

Wildness flickered in his gaze. "Why do you think there's more to it?"

"Because not even you are that cruel without just cause," I said. "Yes, you can be cruel, and yes, you can be rude, but that doesn't mean you're a bad person."

Dayton snorted and shook his head, running a hand through his dark hair. "Good and bad, right and wrong. I teeter a dangerous line between both." He exhaled. "You hit the nail on the head about...well, you could see through me when I killed those Fenrir. With them there, it's never a question of what I will do."

"Why?" I asked. I stepped from the bed frame and got closer to him.

"My life, my past... it's all fucked up," said Dayton. "I often think I did something shitty in a past life to deserve this. I told you my parents are dead, right?"

"Yes," I said.

"I don't really want to get into it, but I'll tell you enough to understand," Dayton said. "I had a family; I even had a brother; now, I only have myself. They all died, and I witnessed each of their ends. In part because of Fenrir, yes, but what happened to them was my fault."

I thought my next words over carefully; I wanted to respect his wishes to not speak on this, but I wanted clarity. "So... seeing the Fenrir brings back bad memories for you, igniting your—" *slightly terrifying, murderous rage,* "—anger?"

"Yes," Dayton confirmed. "I changed when all that happened to me; it was as if a part of me died with them. Most days, I feel like I'm just functioning, doing what is expected: eat, train, sleep, and repeat. If breathing wasn't automatic, I would forget to do it. It's like I live in this numbing trance of existing, like a never-ending nightmare."

"Is that really living at all?"

Dayton prowled closer, and I almost stepped back, but something stopped me. He hovered closer, hands opening and closing at his sides. "If you asked me that three weeks ago, I would have said yes."

"What changed?"

"I met you, and it was like I woke up," Dayton admitted. My breath caught in my throat, my heart hammering. "My life is reckless; I don't hesitate or second guess myself, and then you came along, and suddenly I'm considering how what I do and say affects others."

"What do you mean?" I asked, voice thin. I hadn't explicitly done anything to try to change him.

"The damn Fenrir. I went to bed tonight thinking about how I acted while killing them. I know killing them was right, but did I have to act so ruthless?" Dayton scowled. "It's maddening, and I see that it scares you—that *I* scare you. You looked at me like I'm a monster."

Now it was my turn to shake my head. "No, Dayton. I looked at you like you're an asshole. I'm only beginning to understand this world and you, and truthfully, I'm thankful for you. I would be dead—or worse off—without you."

"There you go again, making me question myself. I should be sure of myself." He stalked closer, and I smelled his mint toothpaste and lingering traces of soap. He looked down at me, eyelids heavy. "Mare, you get under my skin in a way that shakes me to my core. Enough that I entitled myself your Consort."

A chill skittered down my spine. Consort. I felt a pull around my middle, like an invisible string drawing me closer to him. Our eyes locked, and I didn't shy from the rawness in his gaze. My heart thundered in my chest, my palms clammy.

"Why did you do that?" I asked.

"Because the thought of you unprotected in this world drives me mad. It shouldn't—I should not care, but seeing you in danger scares me," Dayton said, a wildness to his voice.

My face flushed, and I wanted to turn my gaze away. "What is a Consort?"

He smiled; it seemed genuine but out of practice. "Consort means protector of the wolf, and protector of the innocent. It's a bond forged between souls by magic older than the legends of werewolves. It twines souls together, and it's a sacred bond, enacted rarely. The Consort bond is higher than the law. The protector and protected cannot be separated."

I gulped. Yesterday, I would have questioned if Dayton even had a soul, and now we were talking about our souls intertwining. This bond Dayton wanted with me—well, there was no denying it was intense. I didn't know what to make of it.

"And you want to be my Consort?"

"Yes," he said at once, his voice raspy. "You should refuse me, turn me away."

"Why?"

Dayton's golden eyes blazed. "What if I told you I was no good for you and this was only going to hurt? That the fire in me would only burn you? Would you still walk in?"

There was poison in his mind; I could see it. It was as if the poison told him to say these things, hoping I would validate them. An icy chill went through me. I hated that he thought so low of himself. That type of mental war could break the strongest of people. I shook my head, refusing.

"I would walk in," I said firmly. "I would with you. I trust you."

Dayton brought himself closer, his gaze searching mine for any untruths. He brought his head down, his breath hot on my neck. He was nearly touching me, and I wanted to reach for him. I wanted to reach out—touch him, hold him. I did none of those things.

"I would stay by your side as your Consort: a guide to this world. A protector, friend, flame in the dark, whatever I needed to be, I would be that."

"You would be my protector," I echoed.

"Mare, I don't want to pressure you into anything. The bond it will forge between us is a sacred bond that I will uphold with the utmost respect," he said with sincerity. "It's a bond that will entwine the life force between us. I would sense any danger and harm coming your way, even if it's only a moment away from harming you."

"Does it work both ways?" I asked.

"No," Dayton said. "The protector and protected, remember?"

"It sounds like a lot." I hesitated, mulling over his explanation in my head. "But if I said no, the Council takes me to the Moon Court?"

"I don't have the jurisdiction to fight them," Dayton said.

I weighed the options. Trust Dayton enough that I'd twine my life with his, or be forced into living at the Moon Court. Everything with Claire flooded back, all her comments and quips. It was not me she wanted, but Luka. He would have a clean slate, and they'd even search for Derek. It sounded like a no brainer—the easier choice. But Dayton didn't want that for me; in fact, he was adamantly against it. I knew Dayton.

I trusted Dayton.

"Yes, I want this," I said, quickly before I changed my mind.

Dayton grinned, and it suited him better than his usual scowl. Dayton reached into his pocket and pulled out his knife, cutting the blade down his palm. Blood trickled down his wrist. "It's enacted with a blood oath. If you want this, we both have to say the words."

I nodded my head, offering my palm to him. My heart beat frantically in my chest as Dayton grabbed my palm and sliced it. The pain was gentle and shallow. Holding my palm in his, our fingers interlaced, his touch hot and electric. His gaze traced my expression, equally wild. Where our skin touched, it felt alive, and nearly wiped the breath from me.

"First, I vow to protect you, and then you entitle me as your Consort," he said, pressing his forehead against my own.

"That seems awfully simple for something this serious," I quipped, trying to distract myself from how close we were to one other.

"Mare," Dayton rumbled, tightening his grip on my fingers.

"Yes, Dayton?"

A muscle jumped in his jaw. "I vow to protect you, Maris, from any danger bestowed upon you. To jump into the fire first and to lay my life before yours. In the name of the sacred Consort bond, I declare myself worthy to be your protector."

The temperature dropped, and I looked up at Dayton, his gilded gaze softening. Our bodies practically touched everywhere else as well as our hands, and I felt Dayton's heat melting over me. My heart hammered, and I tried to steady it, knowing he could hear. This closeness—the intimacy between us—made me want to break all barriers.

I took a steadying breath and said, "I entitle you, Dayton, to be my Consort."

Dayton's eyes glowed, and I saw my blue gaze reflected in them. I inhaled sharply as a jolt went up my arm, white lines spindling upward and encasing my body. The white lights over me mirrored those streaming across Dayton, except his markings were black. Where our hands were bound, something tugged in my chest, pulling me toward him. I gasped at the dark ink splayed in intricate patterns over my arm. Dayton's right arm was now adorned with the markings of the bond, etched in dark twirls.

"How?" I asked.

"Magic," he said ominously. Dayton stepped back, as if realizing the space—or lack thereof—between us. "I forgot about the tattoo part."

I gazed at my arm, loosing a breath. The tattoo started at my fingertips and stopped by my elbow, twin to the one Dayton now possessed. Dark swirling patterns formed; clean stark lines intertwining with one other.

"Easy thing to forget, I suppose," I muttered.

"The tattoo is the markings of the bond forged. Anyone that sees it will know," Dayton said. "It will grow in time as the bond grows."

"Grows?"

"The tattoo is a reflection of how strong the bond is. The closer the bonded pair grow, the bigger the tattoo gets," he explained. "It doesn't always grow, though. It can stay the same."

I exhaled, unsure how to feel about that. "That's it now?"

"Seems simple, I know, but the bond will become more apparent in time," Dayton said. "Thank you for allowing me this."

"Thank you for deeming me someone worth protecting," I said, smiling. "This means the Council will back off now."

"Yes," he said. "I will send the Council word of the bond tomorrow. They might not back off entirely, but they can't interfere now. They must go through me."

"Thank you," I said sincerely. "Truly. For everything."

Dayton nodded and moved to leave. He hesitated at the doorway, his hand stilled on the knob. "Goodnight, Mare."

Swiftly, Dayton walked out, shutting the door silently behind him. I stared at the place where he had been moments before, pondering everything that happened. It felt both overwhelming and refreshing all at once. Dayton had shared parts of himself with me tonight, something that didn't happen often, if at all.

What had I gotten myself into?

Chapter 16

I couldn't sleep after the events from the previous night, both from fear and the fact I couldn't stop staring at the tattoo now running up my arm. I marveled at it. It felt strangely alive, the coiled tendrils flowing in intricate patterns from my palm. Had I made the right decision accepting Dayton as my Consort? It didn't feel wrong, and maybe it was the only thing that made sense since coming into this new world. It felt dangerous, though, to link myself to Dayton in a way I didn't fully understand. Why would Dayton even want an inseparable bond with me? To willingly protect me for eternity? He gained nothing from it. I wondered if it had anything to do with Luka and their past. From Dayton's brief synopsis, he'd told me bad blood existed in their past, but how bad was *bad*?

I ran from dawn until noon to clear my head despite my bone-deep, aching protests. I thought of Dayton's judgment if I didn't maintain the stamina I had slowly built, mocking me: "Enemies don't care if you're tired. If they want you dead, you'll be dead."

The prospect of what I would soon face gave me the jitters. Going back to Luka—to what I left behind—wouldn't be easy. I needed to warn him, yet I still felt guilty about the way we left things. Even though he lied, it didn't make me feel better. I never let him explain. I left him, afraid of the truth. It was wrong of me. Childish.

I wondered if Luka would have more answers about Derek and how he disappeared. I thought about him long into the night, yet I couldn't shake this sinking feeling that he went searching for answers about his family. It worried me to think he'd chase more leads, especially after what happened with Zayne. Derek was stubborn and determined, a lethal combination. The night Derek came here, I assumed he'd come looking for me, but Derek had been surprised to find me. What else had he hoped to find? The portal, to get to Lycan? I had no idea.

I huffed a breath and chided myself for losing focus. I dangled from a rope I was attempting to climb with little success. Not even halfway up, my muscles protested against my weight, and the thought of falling only added to my anxiety. Gritting my teeth, I made it up one more notch, sweat dripping down my face.

"You're halfway to not falling, Maris," called Julian's cheery voice from below. Julian had taken over Dayton's training for today, which was unnerving given last night's events. Maybe he'd changed his mind about the Consort business, realizing he hated me after all.

"You know, Julian," I grunted, reaching for the next notch. Palms sweaty, I slipped, screaming as I plummeted. The impact of the ground against my spine had me groaning as I got up. "You are *not* helpful."

"There's a reason Dayton is the better teacher," said Julian, offering his hand. I noticed his fingernails were painted, each a different shade of pastel. "Alright, try again."

I grunted as I stood, peering at Julian. He changed his hair color overnight, the longer strands on top now a neon green and the rest still white blond. It was an interesting change, but it boded well with his multiple facial piercings. Today, he wore a sparkling silver tank top with armholes cut low on the sides.

"Why don't you try it?" I challenged, stepping aside.

Julian grabbed the rope and skillfully climbed it without a word, further proving his point. I flushed; he made it seem easy. His lean muscles quickly worked the rope, and as he swiftly reached the top, he grinned down at me. Julian launched himself down, flipping midair and landing gracefully like a cat.

"I don't think I will ever be able to do that," I groaned.

"Don't knock it until you try it," Julian said, before falling into a fitful cough. It seemed heavy and thick, and he stepped away, his face growing red. "Smoker's cough," he choked.

It didn't sound like that to me, but I didn't comment. His spluttering cough faded into a dry choke, and I crossed the room to grab an ice-cold bottle from the small fridge. Julian knew my intention and met me in three strokes. He downed the whole thing in about ten seconds before collapsing onto the chair and bracing his knees with his hands.

"Are you alright?" I asked, sitting beside him.

His green eyes watched me thoughtfully as he spoke. "I have a bad habit of doing things that aren't inherently good for me." He folded his hands out in front of him. "Nice tattoo, by the way."

"Dayton told you?"

"Not in so many words," Julian said, stretching as he added, "I have a sixth sense for that type of stuff."

"I notice you seem to pick up on everything," I said open-endedly, hoping he might fill in the blanks.

"I'm amused Dayton committed to the bond. I thought it was just his desperate way of keeping you from the Council while he figured something else out. Ah, it would be like Dayton to unleash old curses, though." Julian said. He stood. "Speak of the devil."

I followed Julian's gaze, confused, until light footsteps in the outside hall drew closer. The door opened and Dayton stepped in. He appeared strangely mundane compared to his usual soldier-like wear. He wore simple clothes, dark jeans, a black T-shirt, and a worn leather jacket. I couldn't help but notice how his shirt hugged his muscles, reminding me of how he looked last night shirtless. I tore my gaze away, scolding myself. Julian coughed to hide his laughter.

"I see the training is going well. Sitting on your ass will really come in handy against enemies intent on killing you," said Dayton, coming toward us. "Though I suppose I did ask the most distracted person I know to fill in for me."

"I'm not sure if I should be insulted or flattered," Julian pondered. "We were actually practicing, believe it or not."

"Yeah, Julian had me climbing the rope of death." I glanced at the rope with disdain. "Seriously, when can I start learning how to use weapons?"

"Pathetically eager," Dayton said, glancing down at me. "You are nowhere near ready to even hold a weapon. If you were smart, you would consider my lessons as weapons."

"Your lessons teach me how to get my ass kicked."

Out of the corner of my eye, Dayton's hand flew, and I shot my hand up, grabbing his wrist at once. I grinned but was foolish to think I could best him. Catching me off guard, his foot kicked out, taking the chair from under me. I cursed, smacking against the hard floor.

"You're still learning," he said, flipping up the fallen chair and sitting on it backwards. "Though I suppose once your wolf comes out, the rest will start to be easier."

Another prospect I was dreading. The notion of turning into a wolf made me sick to my stomach; I thought of bones growing and bodies breaking, imagining the pain rippling through me. The one time it happened—or started to before Dayton intervened—had freaked me out enough, and that was a small transition, nothing compared to turning into a full-fledged wolf. I couldn't bring myself to ask any questions about it, too afraid of the answers.

I could feel it. In my bones, and down to my very essence, it stirred. Not a darkness stirring, but a new life waiting to ignite. I had been leaning into that life—this life. Until I was ready, the life would stay stirring, waiting, lingering. By accepting that part of me, I would forge my existence anew.

"Why learn hand-to-hand combat when you can turn into a wolf?" I asked.

"Relying solely on the best-oiled weapon in your arsenal is the easiest way—"

"To get yourself killed?"

"Burnt out, actually." Dayton gave me a pointed look. "Wielding too much magic will cause your body to wear down, and then you'll get yourself killed. Also, more likely than not, your enemy will try to eradicate you from the wolf. Some elements affect us—hurt us—and cause us to transform back to our human form."

"Wolfsbane, silver powder, mountain ash. Am I missing anything? Oh, silver bullets," Julian listed idly. "Though those are usually aimed at our head."

"Silver or not, I think a bullet aimed at your head would kill you," I pointed out.

Dayton chuckled. "The point is that everything Julian listed could temporarily stunt your wolf."

"Okay, so hand-to-hand combat is important then," I said. "Duly noted."

Dayton flicked his hand outward at me, extending his long and pointy claws to their full length before retracting them. "It can look like this once you learn control."

"How do I learn control?" I asked, peering at my own hands and flexing my fingers.

"Practice, time, and patience," he said. "Most of which we'll be out of by the day's end if visiting your brother proves to be as unpleasant as I imagine."

"We're going back today?" I asked, not entirely shocked.

Dayton nodded. "He hasn't been spotted in over a week, which doesn't mean much coming from him. If he wants to be seen, he will be, and vice versa. I'm taking a guess to say he's simply staying off the radar, keeping his head low."

There was a certain comfort in Dayton's words, a familiarity. He obviously knew my brother well. It was comforting, like someone who might know your breakfast habits or coffee preferences, except Dayton knew Luka's battle strategies and operational moves. Knowing someone that well didn't happen overnight, but Dayton made it clear things were no longer pleasant between him and Luka.

"You make it sound like driving right up to his wards will be pleasant," Julian muttered.

"Oh, I'm perfectly aware Luka will try to kill me on sight," said Dayton.

I posed my next question carefully. "Why does Luka hate you, Dayton?"

Dayton looked at me with his golden gaze, the beginnings of a scowl on his lips. "I betrayed Luka's trust. He let me into his Cadre against his initial judgment, and I proved him right."

I studied his guarded expression that invited no further questions on the topic. I let it go, resting my head in my hands. "God, give me the strength to get through today."

Julian placed a hand on my shoulder and gave it a squeeze. "You've got this, Maris. Remember, he is the same Luka, you know. He just transforms into a wolf as a side hustle."

I laughed and stood up. "Side hustle. Got it."

Dayton watched me with harsh intensity, then inhaled slowly. "If going back proves fruitless, we can leave. It will be your call, Mare. Just say the word and we're gone, no questions asked."

I offered him a small smile in response, my nerves too bundled for words. Deep down, I feared I had drawn a line in the sand between me and Luka, a line he wouldn't cross. Luka was stubborn. Proud. As much as he loved me and wanted to protect me, I might have pushed too far by running away. For me to just come clamoring back, with Dayton who he didn't like...who knew how'd he react?

Dayton strode toward the weapons and started assembling his belt. Julian came up behind him, assuming a similar stance. They each took a variety of different weapons; Julian seemed to prefer the showier weapons, like bow and arrows, and long swords. Dayton equipped himself with smaller yet equally lethal tools.

"Go with the short sword. I feel like it would be the least painful to be tortured with," Julian added, watching his friend.

"Yeah, you would know," Dayton said automatically.

Julian's breath caught, his grip on his sword white knuckled. His green, usually kind eyes turned cold. "That was cruel. Even for you." He shoved away from the weapons rack and was out the doors in two strides.

"Jules, wait!" Dayton called. "I didn't mean it like that."

"What did you say to him?" I asked, perplexed.

"Nothing." Dayton snapped, running toward the door where Julian left.

There was still much I didn't know about these two boys, and the stark tattoo on my arm now bound me to one. It was a bizarre notion, given how my life had been only a few weeks ago. My life had changed more drastically than I ever imagined it could. The thought of attending college felt stale compared to this new life. Monsters, magic, werewolves, and Derek being missing. Maybe I could hit my head hard enough to forget it all.

That was unlikely, though. Besides, I couldn't deny the calling in my bones that this was the path intended for me. It may not have been the easier or advisable path, but it was one I was meant to be on. I peered at the swirling ink of my tattoo, and knew I had to persevere.

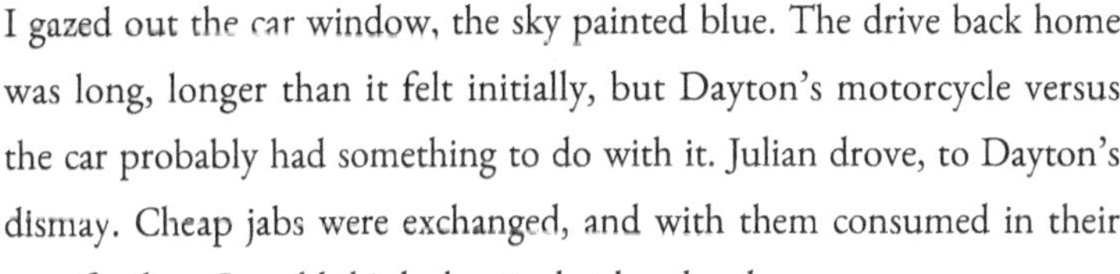

I gazed out the car window, the sky painted blue. The drive back home was long, longer than it felt initially, but Dayton's motorcycle versus the car probably had something to do with it. Julian drove, to Dayton's dismay. Cheap jabs were exchanged, and with them consumed in their own feuding, I could think about what lay ahead.

I mulled over the thought of returning to Luka, given all I knew about him now, which only added to the anxiety slowly brewing inside me. With my head against the seat, I took a long breath, the wheels turning in my head as to what to say to Luka. I was still angry with him. I wanted to yell and scream and be furious with him for keeping this world from me. Yet at the same time, I understood his reasonings after experiencing the dangers firsthand: the Wolf Council, the Fenrir, all the elements of this life he wanted to shield me from.

Julian turned off the highway and onto bumpy back roads. My palms were sweaty, and I clutched my hand into a fist, my fingernails digging into my palm. My mind started to race. What if he didn't want me back? What if he was too angry with me for running away? How bad was the blood between him and my new companions?

"Mare, you should pay attention to your surroundings," Dayton chirped, catching my attention. I glanced up to where he glared at me through the rearview mirror. "Keep your senses on high alert. You always want to have the upper hand if an enemy is near."

Julian turned the wheel. "Give her a break, Dayton."

Dayton looked ready to retort, then thought better of it. "If Kaser is rising to power, he will be seeking revenge for his father's death," Dayton countered. "Usually revenge in our world is life for a life. There's no reason to be easy about it."

"It hardly seems fair an evil werewolf is hunting me down because my brother killed his father," I said.

"If the Council listened to us, things wouldn't have to be as bad," Julian mused, rolling to a stop and looking both ways. "But they want proof."

"The Fenrir coming after us *is* proof," I said as we hit a bump in the road.

"Proof that someone is creating Fenrir once more," Dayton said. "Not proof that Kaser is the one sending them."

"It's all political," Julian said. "Their image was tarnished by Dante, and they don't want to risk it again for a fool's tale."

"Jules, the road!" Dayton barked. He leaned over and jerked the wheel.

Julian hit the brakes hard enough that my seatbelt caught and burned my neck. Dayton swore under his breath, unbuckling his seatbelt as the car veered off the road. My heart sank like an anchor in my chest when I saw who stopped us.

Luka stood in front of the car, eyes glowing deep blue.

He let out a howl of rage.

CHAPTER 17

I had never seen Luka look quite so picturesque. Anger radiated from him, and his cold blue eyes promised no mercy. Despite his terrifying demeanor, it suited him. He was completely in his element, content with being utterly lethal. It was scary, but what made it more unnerving was who had his full attention.

Dayton.

"Luka," I croaked, unbuckling the seat belt with shaking hands.

"This ought to be interesting," Julian exhaled and flew from the car, adopting a firm stance behind Dayton.

"What's up, Chief?" Dayton drawled. He smirked like a roguish wolf set free.

My hands were clammy as I opened the car door. Luka started towards Dayton. His teeth elongated as he snarled, his claws flexed and ready to strike. I scrambled out of the car at a speed I didn't know was possible and lurched forward to stand between them. Instantly, Luka halted.

"Maris." His tone was clipped, yet his guard never wavered as his gaze remained beyond me. "Do you know who you are protecting?"

"Luka, you have to listen to me," I said. Though my heart thudded, I kept my voice steady. Despite my fear, I would not back down. I would not let Luka harm Dayton.

"Move before I move you myself," he ordered in a voice different from his own. Luka's gaze bore down onto me, and I flinched.

Suddenly, I stepped aside, pushed by a force outside of my will. Alpha. Luka was an Alpha, and from what I'd been told, he was a strong one. I gritted my teeth, trying to shake my head—trying to resist—but even attempts to move my legs were futile. He could not stop me from glaring at him as he forced me aside to allow a clearer view of Dayton.

Between one moment and the next, Luka moved and shoved Dayton against the car, denting the passenger's side door. "I don't make empty threats! The last time I saw you, I told you that if I saw you again, you'd wish you were dead." His voice boomed through the trees.

Dayton's strangled laugh was pitiless. "Kill me then. I dare you."

Julian leaped in the air and landed squarely on the car roof, his green eyes aglow. "Be careful, Luka."

Luka's attention didn't stray from Dayton as he seethed. "This is not your fight, Julian."

Luka was a blur of movement, yanking Dayton by the shirtfront and throwing him against a tree. His back hit the bark and a crack tore the silence as the trunk bore the brunt of the impact. Luka drew his arm back, readying to strike Dayton, who grinned as if welcoming his rage.

"Luka, stop it!" I lurched toward them.

Luka hesitated. "Maris, stay out of this."

"Don't worry, Mare. He won't kill me in front of you," Dayton said, unfazed.

"This doesn't have to be bloody," Julian called.

Luka growled and punched Dayton square in the face, and the fracturing of bones made my stomach churn. He again grabbed Dayton by the shirtfront, launching him against the tree. The whole tree swayed, with Dayton collapsed beneath it, releasing a strangled gurgle of pain. Luka stormed away, pacing like a caged lion while Dayton rose, wiping the blood from his face with the back of his hand.

"Just a light maiming then?" Dayton quipped, a ghostly smile twisting his lips. "You've lost your touch, Chief."

I groaned in unison with Julian, who leaped down, assuming a defensive stance in front of Dayton. Instinctively, I stood in front of both of them; Luka wouldn't dare hurt me. He flashed me a brutal look, void of feeling.

Luka let out another howl of rage.

"All these years later and you still can't control your anger," Dayton mocked. "Is the Bestial's downfall the ghosts of the past?"

Aghast, I glared back at Dayton, who only shrugged.

"Still mouthy as ever," snarled Luka.

Luka pushed past Julian and me, propelling toward Dayton. He had Dayton at his mercy once again, arms pinned behind his back. He must have hidden a blade as it was now unsheathed, poised at Dayton's throat. Julian's gaze narrowed on the hilt of the dagger, and I looked, recognizing the emeralds encrusted on the hilt. The same dagger Derek had all those weeks ago.

"Lukas, may I dare point out what you have overlooked?" purred a familiar voice from above.

I followed the sound to where a woman perched in the trees, clad in all white, her opal eyes aglow. She sauntered from the tree and landed silently on her feet. Thin scars ran the length of her neck downward, her small, delicate frame and ageless eyes boring into each of us. I recognized her, of course, usually a silent assailant. Renetta. The last person I expected to see. She stopped beside Luka, who still held Dayton firmly, assessing him quietly.

"You owe him her life," Renetta crooned. "Look to Maris."

Reluctantly, Luka released a smirking Dayton. Luka gazed at my arm, his eyes narrowed. I stepped back, but it was too late. Luka quickly shot his hand out and grabbed my wrist, a growl rising in his throat. He beheld the tattoo and then whirled back to face Dayton.

"You saved her?" Luka demanded. "Why?"

"Repentance." Dayton sneered. Blood dripped from his mouth.

I tilted my head, confused. What had Dayton done that required Luka's forgiveness? As Luka snarled, forgiveness seemed off the cards.

Luka lunged, and I yelled out in protest. I thought Dayton had exaggerated my brother's disdain. I scrambled back as Luka transformed into a wolf before my eyes. Someone yelled as I lunged in front of Dayton, whose arms grasped my own, whipping me aside with force so intense I saw black in seconds.

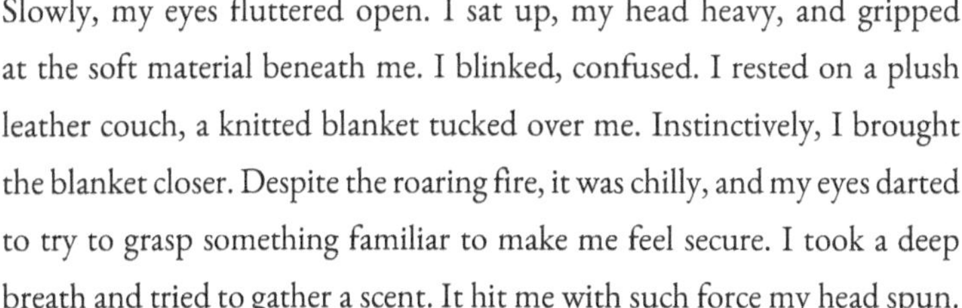

Slowly, my eyes fluttered open. I sat up, my head heavy, and gripped at the soft material beneath me. I blinked, confused. I rested on a plush leather couch, a knitted blanket tucked over me. Instinctively, I brought the blanket closer. Despite the roaring fire, it was chilly, and my eyes darted to try to grasp something familiar to make me feel secure. I took a deep breath and tried to gather a scent. It hit me with such force my head spun. I was home.

I leaped up and the blanket fell to the floor with a whoosh. This was Luka's private domain; I had never been inside it before. It was always off-limits, a space only he had access to. I drank in the room at once. Knowing my brother, this might be the last time I saw it. A large oak desk occupied most of the space, and a few personalized items were scattered across the smooth surface. Above, a sword was on display. I peered closely at it and saw the initials *L.G.D.* inscribed on the hilt. It glinted against the light of the fire, freshly polished.

"That was our father's weapon of choice," a voice called.

I nearly jumped out of my skin, spinning to find Luka standing in the doorway. I wondered how long he had stood there watching me. No anger rippled through his features; his eyes were soft, shadows cast beneath his eyes. His posture was relaxed, shoulders slumped, and he appeared kinder, more like the brother I knew, opposed to the Alpha. Moving soundlessly, Luka picked up the sword to examine it with scornful, blue eyes. He set it back in place.

"This whole office was his, actually," he said. He trailed his fingers along the opposite wall before stopping to look up at a picture of a dark, large wolf. "When he left us, I managed to discard most of his things. I wanted to tear this room apart, but I couldn't. It was this big aching reminder of who he was and how he left." Luka let out a strangled laugh. "He was still our dad, though, through it all."

I turned from Luka to take in the rest of the room. Our father's office. I hated thinking about him, knowing what he did to Luka. I hated him more knowing he was the leader of the werewolf hunt. Briefly, I wondered if Luka knew that. He probably did, though I doubt it was something Luka planned on sharing with me.

I walked past the oversized chair with an impossibly long back. It was a deep emerald, adorned with green cushions. The walls were a crimson red with various maps and animals, primarily wolves, all in golden frames. I trailed my fingers over the desk and stopped at a picture of Luka and me. I was nothing more than an infant, but Luka was shockingly young, too, with a genuine smile lighting his face as he held me. So much about him changed after our mom died, and his young innocence in this picture made me sad. Completely oblivious to the weight of the world to be placed on his shoulders. I looked at him, a grown man with stubble across his jaw and a haggard look in his blue eyes.

"Luka," I choked, unable to disguise the whine in my voice.

I crossed the room and lunged at him, grasping him tightly. He stilled, clearly not expecting this reaction out of me. I had surprised myself, even, but when he squeezed me back, holding me in this tight embrace, all the tension trickled out of me. Luka may have been the root cause of all this uproar, but he was still my brother.

"I'm sorry I hurt you," Luka said, patting my hair as if ensuring I was in one piece. He let me go and stepped back. "The wound will take longer to heal. Alphas have a way of leaving a mark."

I turned to find a small mirror and looked into it. Over my right eye was a black bruise, slowly fading yet yellowing around the outer parts. "You punched me?"

"To be fair, I didn't expect you to jump in front of him," he said. He crossed the room and sat on the windowsill, looking out. Outside it was dark, nearly pitch-black. "You scared me."

"It was impulsive," I said, stepping back and sitting on the couch. I had felt an instinctual pull to protect Dayton, one I didn't understand.

Luka seemed contemplative as he said, "You look different, Maris."

I laughed without humor. "I am different, Luka. I'm a werewolf now."

"Yes, that I can see. You reek of a newborn." He turned to look at me, twisting a bracelet between his fingers. "It's surreal to be talking to you about this. This world was always supposed to be separate from you. You were never supposed to be tangled with it."

Anger gutted me all at once. "You didn't have the right to make that choice for me," I said, shuddering. "I'm scared, Luka. Being in this world scares me."

He observed me, gauging my reaction before he responded. "This world is scary, Maris. Nothing about it is sunshine and rainbows. Why do you think I hid you away?"

"Hiding me did nothing for me!" I shouted, yet it was more of a frantic plea. "What I have seen, and what I now know, it's terrifying. But it was ten times more terrifying being unprepared."

"Maris—"

"—Unless you have a good explanation, save it."

Luka took a trembling breath. "I understand why you're upset, but listen to my side of this," he said. Again, he was fidgeting with his bracelet and not meeting my eyes. "Please."

I took a deep breath and let my defenses down. "Okay. Talk."

"This started with our parents—our mother. She was born and raised as a werewolf in the Moon Court before she met our father." I figured as much, but I was glad for the confirmation. It made sense, given our father was intent on killing werewolves. "She came from a line of pure-bred werewolves who considered themselves better than others. Purebred werewolves are rare; nearly every werewolf nowadays has some human lineage mixed in with them." Luka peeled away from the window, begin-ning to pace. "The circle of purebred werewolves is small. Realistically, the only way to keep the blood untainted, as they say, would be to procreate within families."

I shuddered. "I never want to hear you say the word 'procreate' again."

Luka grinned but otherwise ignored me. "When our mother met and fell in love with our father, it was not well received, nor was her decision to marry him. It was abhorrent to our grandfather, and he threatened to kill our father. Missed opportunity, really, but beside the point. She told our father what she was and who her family was. The only way she could safely marry was to polarize herself entirely from all she knew and start a new life in the human world under a new name. They became Moira and Lukas Danika, two humans young and in love, starting a family in a rural town of New York."

I had some inkling of where this was going, but I let Luka continue.

"It took a long time before her life caught up to her—nearly ten years. I told you she died of an illness, but that was an easier truth to bear. Instead, when I was nine, our grandfather found out where she was, and he sent a search party of werewolves to hunt and kill her. She knew he was coming and forced our father to take me and you and run. He didn't want to, and I remember their fight was brutal. He wanted to protect her from her family, fearing they would kill her while she didn't want her family to know of us, fearing the same. She won in the end, and he took us and ran." Luka gulped. "When he went back, he took me. He told me I needed to see what kind of monsters killed her, but they didn't just kill her. They brutalized her and they—they—I'll spare you the details. Our father became consumed with revenge on all werewolves for what they did. He told me in every fever pitch of rage he had that it was monsters that killed her, and he would have his revenge."

I didn't know what to make of that. In some ways, I didn't blame my father for seeking revenge on all werewolves, especially if what my grandfather did was true. Yet it felt strange to feel any sort of pity for him after taking Luka, his young son, to see her dead body. That was sick. Twisted.

"When I turned fifteen, he realized I was a dormant werewolf. Even without the curse triggered, there are signs of the wolf lineage in your blood—mood swings close to a full moon, your body changing, even your senses are heightened, albeit marginally compared to the real thing. Most humans chalk up the signs to puberty, none the wiser of the truth. But our father knew the truth, and once he realized that, it sealed his hatred of me into finality. I always had issues with him, even when Mom was alive. We butted heads like ranging bulls."

I watched as Luka told this story, his face ashen. In the light of the fire, a haunted look gleamed in his sapphire eyes.

"Just the threat that I might someday be bitten and turned into a werewolf repulsed him. He hated werewolves with ferocity, and he decided it would be better to have me killed than risk triggering the curse. One day, he drove me deep into the Woods of the Damned and dropped me off into the middle of it before leaving me entirely. He arranged for someone to have me killed."

My blood ran cold. Of course I knew our father disliked Luka, hurting him both emotionally and physically as we grew up. But to want his son dead and coerce a plan to execute it? There was no excuse. For any of it.

"He did what?"

"Our father wanted me dead. He hired someone to do it. One thing I never quite understood, though, was why he arranged for an Alpha werewolf to kill me. Maybe he planned to kill the Alpha after me—who knows? But the Alpha told me why he was there; the Alpha hadn't thought I would fight back. The Alpha managed to bite me, and initially, I didn't understand what that meant, but it came as a shock to our father when I turned up back at the house. I killed the Alpha." Luka's hands trembled by his sides, and it was strange to see my brother vulnerable, visibly not okay. "I don't even know how I managed it, but I wanted to survive, and I did."

Luka gave a hollow laugh.

"Stunned would be putting it lightly when I came back alive. For the first time, he was afraid of me. I don't know what his plan was for you. Maybe he wanted to wait to see if the signs were there for you, and have you killed like he tried to for me...I don't know. I do know that when I got back, I gave him a choice. He could leave and forget us entirely, or I would kill him, too."

"Luka, oh my god," I said, unable to find the words. I stared at him, stunned.

Fifteen. He had been fifteen and forced to kill someone to defend himself. That burden would be heavy for anyone, but *God*, Luka was fifteen.

"I became a killer, an Alpha werewolf, and a father all in one night." Luka raked a shaking hand through his hair. "Sometimes I regret not killing him. Does that make me sick?"

I couldn't muster a reply right away. When I did, my voice was low. "I didn't realize what you went through."

"That was the point, Maris." His tone held an edge. "After I turned, there were many obstacles I had to navigate. My only lead in edgewise was that I wasn't entirely ignorant to the world of werewolves. I knew that killing an Alpha gave you their power, and that I had that power. At the time, many people wanted it; they saw an easy opportunity to get power from a kid who no one believed should have it.

"The Alpha I killed owned the bar, and his Cadre made up the staff. They wanted me dead. They *hated* me. I feared them so much that I was barely around. I had you to worry about raising, and I wasn't keen on dying," He laughed humorlessly, gazing out the window. "Very quickly, I realized I was good at one thing: killing. After a year with the Cadre, they made their move against me. They threatened you first, and that was the final straw. I knew what needed to be done. I killed them all, and from the bloodshed, the Bestial was born."

From what I had been told about Luka, I wasn't entirely surprised to hear it, yet learning it from him directly chilled me to my bones. It was a long time before he spoke again.

"Maris, I kept you from all this because it's horrifying. I have killed more people than I care to admit, and yes, while the people I have killed will not be missed, it still takes a toll. I was terrified half the time. And you... I couldn't let his life taint you like it tainted me." He dragged a hand down his face. "I wanted a normal life for you, as normal as it could be, anyway."

Hearing Luka's story left me at an impasse. It was easy to peg someone as a bad guy before you heard their side. I was angry with him, and Derek, too. I recalled one of the last things I said to Derek before I sent him away. *Leave and stay out of my life.* That might have been the last thing I said to him because now he was gone. Missing. I could not make the same mistake twice.

Luka's gaze met mine. He seemed sad, yet in a way that made him strong. "I'm not sorry that I never told you. This life was not meant for you. Now, we're at a point of no return, and we must deal with it."

I swallowed back the thick emotion in my throat. "I'm sorry you ever had to make those kinds of choices. I know there was nothing I could have done to make it better, but knowing you dealt with all that while raising me...it couldn't have been easy."

Luka moved to kneel beside me, lifting my chin so we were at eye-level. "It was never a choice for me to raise you. Understand?"

I nodded, and stood, reaching for Luka, who held me in a tight embrace, lightly kissing the top of my head. Eventually, he pulled back from me. I leaned against the arm of the couch and sighed.

I had originally come here to inform Luka that Derek was missing, and it ate away at me. I felt like a sitting duck, and I hoped Luka could provide some insight, or maybe he knew where Derek was. I opened my mouth to bring it up, but Luka spoke first.

"Not to ruin a nice moment, but I must bring up the topic of your questionable company," said Luka.

"What do you mean?" I asked, though I knew perfectly well what he meant.

"Dayton Cadman is an unworthy weasel," Luka said, as if trying to keep his anger in check. "I don't trust him, not one bit."

"Why?" Dayton could be described in many ways and as many things, but not that. Dayton was rude and obnoxious, but he was loyal and kind—sometimes.

Luka hesitated. "He betrayed my trust; he betrayed me. That's all there is to it."

"When you say betray—"

"—I'm not getting into it. I don't trust him, and I will never make that mistake again."

"Well, Dayton is the one who has helped me through all this," I said. "Without question, without reason. He was there, and I'm not willing to forget that."

"God, Dayton is sneaky," Luka muttered. "He's using you to get to me, Maris."

"No," I said automatically. "Dayton wouldn't do that."

"That tattoo on your arm already keeps you from going against him," Luka stated. "That is ancient magic inked on your skin."

"A blood oath," I said. Oddly, saying the words aloud made the notion sound even wilder. Dayton had said the bond would become apparent in time, and I wondered if this was what he meant. The need to defend and protect him. "The Council wanted to take me and force me into the Court. Dayton took a blood oath for me; he entitled himself as my Consort to keep me from them."

Luka's nostrils flared at the mention of the Council. "Maris, did you stop to think that pledging blindly to have someone protect you might not be a smart idea? In a world where you don't understand half the shit going on?" Luka said, his hands in fists by his side. "He wanted to be your Consort because he knows I cannot turn him away now."

"Why?"

"Because being a Consort is not as simple as a title," Luka explained. "It is binding magic. Dayton will endure whatever harm is bestowed to you. That black eye you're sporting, he has it, too. You two are bonded, and that type of bond only grows deeper."

Chills shivered down my spine. Cut me, and he bleeds. "I know what I agreed to."

"I don't trust him, Maris," Luka said again.

I felt torn watching Luka. With Dayton, I was in between liking and tolerating him, but something had forged between us in the brief time I'd known him—something I couldn't abandon on the principles of split loyalties, especially when neither party was keen on divulging details of their animosity.

"I trust him, Luka."

Luka shook his head and said, "I trusted him once, too."

Silence followed, so quiet you could hear a pin drop. I remembered then the reason I came back to warn Luka.

"Did you know Derek is missing?" I asked.

"I had a hunch something had happened to him," Luka said. He turned away from me, resigned. "He and I had somewhat of a disagreement regarding his absurd quest to find his family. Since the fight, he hasn't returned. But it isn't particularly odd behavior for him to leave to blow off steam, though he's never usually gone for this long."

"He found me," I said. "It was a few weeks ago, but he still did."

Luka scowled and pulled out his cellphone from his jean pocket, his fingers swiping across the screen. He lifted the phone to his ear and began pacing, answering the phone with a hushed voice. He spoke a language I didn't understand or recognize, his vowels and enunciation thick and firm. I never knew he was bilingual. His expression grew grim as his mouth shut into a thin line, his eyebrows furrowed in frustration.

"What's going on?" I asked.

Luka raised a hand to silence me before ripping the phone from his ear and smacking it on the desk with a clang. He crossed the room and rested his hand against the wall beside the fireplace, and as he did, all the wall pictures flipped. A high-pitched chime sounded through the room as monitors appeared. I realized then that I was looking at surveillance footage outside the house. I stood up to get a closer look. On one of the screens, Julian sat on the front porch, smoking a cigarette.

"Just because this was Dad's old office didn't mean I couldn't upgrade it." Luka shrugged, a slight smile tugging at his lips. "I talked to one of my contacts, Randall. He's forwarding me information about a young werewolf asking around about his family."

Luka sat at the desk chair and clicked through a computer monitor that hadn't been there before. "You think Derek was looking for his family?"

"I think Derek was desperate for answers. Derek, being born a werewolf, was always convinced there was a supernatural reason for his family's disappearance, and even though everyone claimed his family was dead, it wasn't a good enough reason to drop it," he said. "I think Derek took advantage of the time away from me."

"Derek chased the lead to Zayne; he thought it was connected to his family."

Luka grunted. "Zayne tricked Derek; he knew how desperate he was for answers. I don't think Zayne knew anything about his family. Derek was just naïve."

"There was an interview with Zayne that Derek found."

"A fabricated interview from a fabricated newspaper on a fabricated website," Luka said adamantly. "I know it sounds like a stretch, but they knew Derek was desperate, and they were just as desperate to find me."

"Oh, Derek," I moaned, sadness stirring in my stomach.

"This is why I never let him follow leads. Plus, we always had more pressing matters, like keeping you hidden from this world and explaining away my long departures." Luka said, intently staring at the screen. He loosed a frustrated breath. "C'mon, Derek."

I whirled around to look at the screen, but it was so bright I had to squint to see the image Randall sent. The picture was pixelated, clearly blown up to zoom in closer. I would recognize Derek from anywhere. The disconcerting part was watching his bloodied body being dragged away.

Chapter 18

Seeing my best friend in such a disgruntled state spurred me to save him. As much as I wanted to spring into immediate action, I couldn't tear my eyes from the picture of Derek drenched in blood. Something twisted in my chest, and a low noise reverberated in my throat. The people who dragged him away had towering, beefy frames and masks covering their faces. It could have been anyone.

"Who would do this?" I asked, eyes shifting to Luka.

He hesitated, appearing to contemplate his next words. "Derek is a young wolf, and he's kind of an airhead at times. This picture is from a bar in New York City. It could easily be that he pissed off some older, more seasoned werewolves."

"Seasoned?"

Luka gestured wildly with his hands. "Experienced, spicy, volatile. You get the idea."

"Could it have anything to do with you?" I asked.

Luka gave me a sidelong look before saying, "I doubt it. Derek wouldn't compromise his position of knowing who I am."

I saw an opportunity then. "I have a theory about Derek actually, and who might've taken him."

Luka seemed surprised and arched one eyebrow. "Oh?"

I told Luka of the Fenrir, the missing werewolves, and Julian's theory on past behaviors returning once again. I mentioned Kaser and the suspicion that he may come to power, but when I brought up how Luka might be tied into all this, he didn't seem fazed. Luka listened intently the whole time, nodding.

"I had a strange feeling about all this, even more so when Zayne took you. I didn't want to pry further after you ran off; I feared that somehow you would get caught in the middle of it. Well, I guess I was wrong on that account." Luka sighed. "I'm going to have to cool the jets on my Cadre. They sense the displaced ranks with Derek gone and they're itching to replace him as Beta."

"*Replace him*? He isn't dead," I said incredulously.

Luka chuckled and shook his head. "Being the Beta to an Alpha in any pack is considered an elite position. The Alpha hand picks their second-in-command, and the relationship between an Alpha and their Beta is a strong one. It's stronger than any brotherhood, deeper than any friendship; they're your partners in battle, someone you can always count on."

"What does that have to do with replacing Derek?"

"Well, without your Beta, the Alpha is considered weaker. I don't see that in myself, personally, but no pack wants a weak Alpha—especially my Cadre. I've only let a few into my inner circle, and they're protective. Rico, especially, but he's always been a brute."

"Rico from the bar?" I asked. Given his moody and aggressive disposition, it didn't surprise me to learn he was also a werewolf. He fit right in. While I never disliked Rico, he always scared me, so hearing he was a part of Luka's Cadre made sense.

"Yeah, him. As you may have guessed, the bar is more of a preface to keep my Cadre together," explained Luka. "I can't always be around to keep them in line. That's why I have Derek, but with him gone, it's complicated. Renetta is good at keeping them in line when I'm not around, but it's a matter I need to address."

"Well, it won't be an issue when we get Derek back," I said surely.

Luka whipped his head up, his eyes steely. I felt the atmosphere shift, a cold stillness leaking in. He turned his head upward, nostrils flared as he moved to look out the window. He jerked away and cursed, shooting across the room. He slammed a hand down on the desk, extinguishing all the screens.

I straightened and breathed in, yet I couldn't detect anything. Even as I looked outside into the darkening day, there was nothing out of the ordinary. Either my senses weren't as good as Luka's, or his were just exceptional. Regardless, something was up.

Luka barreled toward the door with me quick on his heels. Two long, strangled howls called from outside as Luka made it swiftly to the back door, yanking it open. With the day ending, seeing in the fading light was difficult, but I could smell something. The stench of rotting eggs wafted thick in the air, and unease washed over me. A large wolf with brown fur streaked into the woods, and I had a few notions of who it was. Luka lunged and shifted into his wolf skin mid-jump, becoming a shadow as he entered the night.

Another howl pierced through the forest, a high-pitched, pained cry I didn't recognize. I sprinted to where Luka had charged, challenging his supernatural speed. However, I came up short, stumbling over something slick. In the heartbeat that it took for me to look, I looked away just as quick. Blood, thick and fresh, coated the ground in pools. I trailed my line of vision toward Luka, who prowled in his wolf alias, circling a pile of wolf bodies. I hoped they were dead because even from here I could see they were dismembered and bloodied beyond recognition.

I couldn't tell from the bodies if they were Fenrir or not—humans, perhaps? No. If anything, they'd be werewolves. Panic seeped through me as I thought about Dayton and Julian. While I trusted they could defend themselves, it didn't make them untouchable. I inspected the pile of bodies that looked and smelled fresh, the blood freely pouring from their open wounds. The vacant loss of life in their eyes chilled me. They were not my friends, but emotion still knotted in my throat. I tried turning away but I stayed grounded, staring ahead. Luka jerked his giant head toward me, a snarl on his lips, and I turned away from him. I wanted to go back; it was a mistake to come here.

However, my attention snagged on the pile of dead wolves. Cautiously, I stepped closer and the stench of freshly flowing blood filled my nose. I bounded forward, leaping over the dead wolves while Luka barreled toward me. He missed me by inches. A faint gurgle sounded in the distance, and a thick trail of blood led into the woods. I followed it and came up short, finding a young girl leaning against a tree with tears streaking her face.

She looked like she bathed in blood. It streaked across her face more prominent as she beheld me with fearful, hazel eyes. Fallen tears streaked lines through the blood on her cheeks. She was a small girl with a dark complexion and unruly black hair pushed in every direction; she looked young—maybe nineteen or so. I fell to my knees beside her and instinctively offered a helping hand. She swatted me, claws raking against my face. I jerked away, pain lighting my senses on fire, but when I opened my eyes, she was on her knees, doubled over.

"Maris, back away!" Luka barked from behind. He came up beside me and practically tossed me aside. "You shouldn't have followed me!"

Before I could retort, I was yanked away. I looked up to find Dayton. "Get off me!" I screeched.

"Are you insane?" Dayton bellowed. He pushed me further away from Luka and the girl. "There are Fenrir out there, you shouldn't be prancing off into the woods!"

"I didn't know that," I grumbled. "But she needs help. She's hurt."

"Mare, it's not like you could've helped her," Dayton said harshly.

Three gashes sliced his face below the dark bruise residing under his eye, yellow and fading. Like mine. The lines of his face were pulled—strained and taut. He scowled, his eyes flashing gold. I held that unyielding stare.

"What happened to you?" I asked.

"It'll heal," Dayton replied.

"That's not what I asked you."

"I didn't ask you to worry about me," he snapped, peering over my shoulder. "Chief, you okay?"

I spun to see Luka in his human skin, lifting the girl into his arms and running past us. Her body was limp, and Luka's eyes glowed as he ran at unnatural speeds toward the house.

Dayton and I exchanged a look and followed, the two of us racing through the woods and after Luka. I didn't realize how far out I had gone, but once the back porch was in sight, I nearly jumped to it. Luka stood over the girl and placed her on the table where she splayed out, unmoving. The wounds across her arms and chest remained unhealed yet slowly stitched together. It was odd. This strange girl appeared out of nowhere. I didn't recognize her, but Julian did. He ran toward the girl and dropped his cigarette, his eyes wild.

"*Dayton, no!*" Julian roared.

Two words I don't think were ever spoken with agreement.

I hadn't even noticed Dayton approach the girl until he extended his claws with a savage expression. Everyone moved to grab him, but Dayton was quick. Scraping his claws against the back of her neck, she jolted awake, gasping for breath. Dayton stepped back, his hand dripping with blood.

"What the fuck?" Julian gaped, lunging at Dayton. Luka stepped between them, catching Julian by the shoulder, but it didn't stop Julian from ambling on. "Claws in the spine is barbaric! God, one misplaced claw could have been detrimental."

Luka released Julian with a huff, then turned on Dayton. "You could've killed her!"

"We don't have time to wait! If Fenrir are back in full force, she might have some insight," Dayton shot back. "Besides, I know who she is."

"Seriously, Dayton?" squeaked a high-pitched voice. I glanced down at the girl. "That really hurt, you asshole, not to mention you could've *killed me.*"

"So I've been told," Dayton drawled. "If it were anyone but you, Kyler, I might have re-considered."

"Are you okay?" Julian asked. He peered down at her but didn't step any closer.

Luka and I exchanged confused looks. Clearly he had no idea who she was either, though Julian and Dayton seemed to. Who was she? I intervened.

"Guys, what is going on?" I asked.

Surprisingly, it was Kyler who spoke. "I know these two idiots. I'd even caution to say they're my friends, but Julian more so than Dayton. My Alpha was seeking the Temple—we were only passing through. We weren't expecting to run into Fenrir. They killed my whole Cadre back there. Oh, I'm Kyler by the way, Kyler Collins."

There was a lot to unpack with that statement, so I said, "What were you looking for?"

"I don't know. Even if I did, I don't trust any of you to elaborate further," Kyler quipped, assessing me levelly.

"Who was your Alpha?" asked Luka.

"Are *you* an Alpha?" Kyler countered.

Luka huffed a laugh, grinning like the devil. He shook his head. "What do you think, honey?"

"Demarco is her Alpha," intervened Julian. "But if you're all that's left, Ky, does that mean Demarco is dead?"

"No real loss. He was more of an asshole than Dayton, and *that's* impressive," Kyler crooned, eyes narrowing in on me. I stepped back, uncomfortable with her sharp assessment.

"I've always considered it an honor to be judged by you, Kyler," Dayton jabbed.

Kyler's eyes narrowed into slits as she stepped closer to me. "There's something different about you... it's not just that you're a newborn, either." She inhaled. "What the hell are you?"

Something about the straightforward way in which she spoke had me stepping back. Soundlessly, Dayton came up from behind me and gripped my elbow, my body relaxing into his touch. I glanced down. Dayton's knuckles were white.

"Enough," Luka said. "This is my property, and my home, and *I'm* the Alpha. We discuss things on my terms here. First, I'm cleaning up the bodies, and then we can all talk."

CHAPTER 19

Luka dismissed everyone to seek shelter in the outside basement. Apparently he was hell-bent on no one being inside the house except for himself and me. Though I didn't entirely understand his logic, I didn't question him. The inside of the basement was roomy enough, with a separate shower, bed, and two couches.

Kyler paid no mind to any of this, though. She sat, blinking, as if the initial shock had worn off and she was now realizing the truth. She had lost everyone. I offered her some of my clothes. She seemed slightly smaller than me, but it was better than her shredded, bloodied garments. Kyler undressed and stepped into the shower, shutting the door firmly behind her.

I sank into the battered orange couch and massaged my temples. Julian sauntered forward, nestling on the sofa across from me, his long legs splayed out. Tilting his head back, he stretched as the door creaked open. Dayton walked in, aromas of smoke and ash trailing alongside him. He assessed the room with a scowl.

"Where did you run off to?" I asked, watching as he prowled in.

Dayton stood in the shadows, pressing his head against the wall. His clothes were sweat-stained and streaked with dirt and blood. His face had since healed yet flecks of dried blood remained as reminders of his injury.

His mouth twisted cruelly into a scowl. "I had to help take care of the bodies."

Images of the dead wolves flashed behind my eyes, and I flinched. "You burned them?" I guessed.

"I didn't have the time to dig eight graves for wolves I don't know, so yeah," he quipped, his voice hoarse with fatigue. "Though I suppose I could've left them to rot for the vultures to pick and pluck at them. Circle of life and all."

"Dayton," Julian groaned, pinching the bridge of his nose. "Is it fruit-less to say your attitude helps no one?"

"Who is Kyler?" I asked, poking for a subject change.

Julian was about to speak, but Dayton beat him to it. "An old friend from our time at the Moon Court. Like she said, she's less my friend than Julian's. They have a sporadic love affair that always ends in her leaving Julian like a broken-hearted puppy. It's been at least two years since she last disappeared, and my opinion only sinks deeper with time."

An interesting pairing, I supposed. Kyler had been sharp and unafraid to speak her mind. Julian was softer spoken and quick with his jests to lighten the mood—a happy-go-lucky type. Opposites attract, I supposed. I hadn't forgotten what Kyler said about me being more than just a newborn, yet I allowed it to simmer on the back burner. I refused to dwell on what she meant.

"You make it sound like she's some horrible person who I let walk all over me," Julian said. "I have some self-respect, fleeting as it may be."

"Your words, not mine." Dayton shrugged.

"Kyler isn't that bad," Julian said, turning to me. "She's nice and down to earth when you get to know her. Just don't get on her bad side like Mr. Sunshine over there."

Dayton rolled his eyes, and I laughed.

"She seems frightened," I said. "And given her whole Cadre just died, I don't blame her."

Julian nodded and leaned back, reaching into his pocket for his flask. He brought it to his lips while Dayton glared at him. Julian shrugged, and Dayton shook his head. I glanced between the two of them.

"No, Jules," he said, agitated. A brief silence followed before Dayton continued. "I don't care that he suspects it. I still don't trust him."

I narrowed my eyes, confused. Their ability to communicate with just a look baffled me. They did it often at the Temple but were never this blatant. After another pause, Julian sat up.

"What does that have to do with anything?" Dayton asked.

Julian smirked, wayward strands of his colored hair falling into his eyes as he shook his head. He cast another look at Dayton, eyebrows raised. For the first time, I sensed something different between them.

"What kind of Morse code do you two have?" I asked. "It's like you have this unspoken communication."

Julian grinned wickedly, planting his feet on the floor and leaning forward to brace his knees. Dayton inclined his head. "Are you sure about this, Jules?"

Julian nodded before facing me. "I should preface this by saying that this knowledge I have extended to only a few. I have a certain talent that allows me to finagle moral boundaries to my own advantage."

A sinking feeling crept over me at his ominous words. I cocked my head and gave him an inquiring look. "This is either going to be detrimentally scary or detrimentally bad."

"The prospect is scary, but the reality is only bad for me," Julian explained, inhaling deeply. "I can read minds."

I pursed my lips. "Read minds?"

Julian nodded slowly. "As in I always know what you're thinking. I can hear it in my own mind, all the thoughts you think and the hidden intrusive thoughts that never make the surface," he explained. "I could communicate with you telepathically if I wanted to."

The questions buzzing in my head were imminent. I wasn't sure how to feel about that, now I knew Julian could read my inner thoughts. Your mind was the one thing that was entirely yours, so to unwittingly share that part of yourself felt wrong.

"Jules doesn't pry," Dayton said, looking at me. "It's a bit uncanny what he can do, but he's honest, and he doesn't share anything he may know."

I believed that, of course. It was Julian; he wasn't a gossip. "I don't understand what you mean about communicating telepathically."

Julian grinned. "Let me show you instead."

It happened quickly, a whispered echo in my mind that sounded like Julian through a microphone, yet interference made the words difficult to uncover.

"*Maris.*"

I leaped up and squealed, clapping a hand over my mouth. "*How?*" I gasped. Only then I realized I hadn't spoken.

It was surreal to hear him in my head and to respond with a simple thought. His voice echoed, like reverberating off surfaces in a large room. Distant, yet still audible. I realized this was how Dayton and Julian spoke with each other, and I wondered if they realized they interchanged between normal speech and mind-speaking sometimes.

"*You have your boy in a tizzy today.*" Again, Julian's voice wrapped around my head.

I'd hardly call Dayton my boy. Dayton gave himself to others in jagged pieces like a feral cat. He trusted only enough, and never entirely. One false move forced him to recoil and attack, anchored by that untamed wildness.

"*He is not my boy. He only has himself to blame for being an ass,*" I echoed back. The sensation of hearing my own voice clear in my head made my skin tingle.

"*He is plenty good at blaming himself.*"

I looked at Julian and voiced aloud a piece of the puzzle that had finally clicked into place. "This is why you smoke, isn't it? And why you drink?"

"Clever girl." He nodded in approval. "Most people write me off as an addict. With any gift, it comes with difficulties. I cannot control who I hear in a room full of people. Right now, I have your wild thoughts and Dayton's foul mood screaming at me at once."

Dayton rolled his eyes but made no comment.

"The alcohol stops it, and the cigarettes temper it?" I guessed.

"Correct. I cannot always be drunk, and sometimes—most times—I just need to think. All these voices in my head can make a guy go crazy." He untwisted the top of his flask. "There are a lot of people here right now, therefore..." Raising the flask, he tipped it backward into his mouth.

"I still think you can control it," Dayton said. "Letting yourself waste away into nothing is a pathetic path of acceptance."

"We've been down that road, Dayton," Julian said, a distinct edge of annoyance in his tone. "Of all people, you know hope is a miserable road to travel."

Dayton bared his teeth and started forward, then halted. He scowled and turned away, returning to his preferred shadows. Julian shifted his feet and laid back, gazing upward.

"How is it possible?" I asked, attempting to diffuse the tension.

Julian let out a low whistle, chuckling joylessly. "That is something I don't tread on too much. I quickly realized that even amongst beasts like us, being odd is dangerous. Few know of my ability, and I would prefer to keep it that way."

"Do other werewolves have abilities like that?"

Julian laughed. "No, it's an exclusive sort of purgatory, my mind and me. A Midas touch that I never asked for if you will."

Before I replied, the bathroom door cracked open and light leaked in. Kyler stood with her hands on her hips, assessing each of us. Unsurprisingly, she looked remarkably different than before without the blood and gore. She appeared softer, her dark hair twisted into a bun atop her head. Raising her chin, she broadcast her distinctively pretty features: high cheekbones and a dark complexion that highlighted her hazel eyes. She approached Dayton first, sizing him up as the leader.

"I want to speak to your Alpha," she requested.

Dayton laughed with no humor. "You know I don't have a damn Alpha."

"Enough, Dayton," Luka's strong voice bellowed. My brother stood by the open doors; he loomed over all of us before jumping down into the crowded space, his eyes glowing brightly. He approached Kyler, who held his stare. "I'm the Alpha," Luka said, voice dripping with dominance. "Dayton isn't a part of my pack. Any ill behavior he presents isn't a reflection of me."

Kyler shrank at his stare, chin dipping and eyes lowered. Luka towered further over her until her neck dropped down, and she bared her exposed nape to him. Slowly, like a predator already having caught its prey, Luka circled Kyler, a display of pure animalistic dominance. I wanted to interject, but it wouldn't be well received. Luka was showing he was the Alpha that everyone feared.

Dayton and Julian both watched the exchange, with Julian seeming ready to jump off the couch to step between them. Luka stopped before her, growling low. Kyler remained shrunken in on herself—wary.

"Who are you?" demanded Luka.

"My name is Kyler," she said, but not fearfully. "Lukas Bakar."

If Luka was shocked she knew his name, he didn't show it. He merely replied, "It's just Luka."

As Luka backed away, Kyler let her shoulders relax and her posture slacken. She backed up and leaned against a wall, wiping her palms against her jeans. Luka kept an eye on her, however, refusing to let down his guard.

"There are rumors about you. That you were a human before and became a powerful Alpha seemingly overnight," Kyler said. "My Alpha told stories about you. You're like the Alpha of Alphas."

I could see her curiosity of unsaid words. The rumors that Luka was more than just a powerful Alpha, that he was the Bestial. But that was Luka's secret to tell and keep.

Luka shrugged. "It's not as big of a deal as you make it sound."

"Luka, you're far too humble. You could give someone a mere look and have them trembling." Julian snorted. "You're literally the most lethal and dangerous werewolf to ever walk this earth."

"I never believed you were real," Kyler said, still awestruck. "It's an honor to meet you."

I recognized the shift in Luka's expression as his eyebrows scrunched together and his jaw clenched; his temper would soon erupt. I interjected, "I know my brother is a big deal in this world, but here he is. He's just Luka. An average guy."

"Your brother... oh, the rumor is true then. You're Maris," Kyler said to me.

"What rumors?" Dayton asked. I was surprised he spoke, even more so when he peeled away from his spot in the shadows. I wondered why my name would be known; I wasn't anybody special.

"I'm most certainly not talking to you," Kyler said in disgust. "Your impatient werewolf ass nearly got me killed, but maybe that was what you hoped for."

"Maybe you should get your priorities straight, sweetheart," Dayton shot back. "Considering your whole pack's ashes are being blown through the wind as we speak."

My eyes widened. Snarling, Kyler lunged, claws outs. Julian leaped up, grabbing her shoulders and pushing her against the wall despite her thrashing. Her eyes were yellow and frantic as Dayton laughed at the ruckus he had caused. Kyler broke free of Julian's restraints and lunged at Dayton again, who caught her wrists.

A growl erupted suddenly, and the whole room trembled. Everyone froze as Luka's eyes projected his deep-rooted power as he allowed it to radiate from him. Luka stepped forward, another low rumble threatening the roof as chunks of dust and plaster broke free.

"That is *enough*." His voice oozed authority. "Release her."

Dayton and Kyler held one another's stare, neither moving.

"*Dayton*," Luka's voice rang out with that unquestionable authority.

"You're not my Alpha anymore, Luka." Dayton contorted. He released Kyler and spun on Luka. "You don't get to use your power on me anymore."

"Enough, all of you," I said.

I stepped forward, but Dayton angled himself between Kyler and me. I shot him a look, but he ignored it and gave a slight shake of his head. He would not meet my gaze yet continued to side eye both Luka and Kyler.

"Men." Kyler rolled her eyes. "Untrusting of anything and everything that moves."

Julian snorted. "Funny from the girl whose claws came out that easily."

Kyler turned her nose at Julian and glanced away from him. I had never been comfortable around girls growing up, which was probably why I was so weary. Growing up with only boys made it easier to relate to them, but I felt wary around this girl. She seemed nice enough, and if she had ill intentions, we had more than enough means to find them out.

"You said there was something different about Maris," Luka said, narrowing his eyes. "What did you mean?"

"I did," said Kyler, "and I meant it, too. Something about her is different; I can feel it in her aura."

"My what?" I asked.

"My mother was a seer, and my father was a werewolf," Kyler explained.

"A seer is essentially someone who can see the supernatural on a deeper level," Dayton added before I asked. "Supernatural beings have energies that surround them called auras. A seer can see your aura."

"Simply put," Kyler muttered. "I'm a werewolf with the ability to see auras, and while most are the same for each supernatural being, yours is different."

"Different how?" I asked.

Kyler pursed her lips, and after a pause, she reluctantly answered, "There's a reckless energy I sense in you. It's common amongst newborns, but there's something slightly wilder about it. I can't pinpoint exactly what it is, but it's like there's some base level of protection engraved in you."

"That sounds like the Consort bond," I said, glancing down at my tattoo. When I looked up, Dayton watched me, puzzled. "I share it with Dayton."

Kyler snorted. "You should get your head examined for signs of lunacy," she said. "But no, strange and old as that bond is, it's not the bond that makes your aura different."

"That's enough. What you are describing sounds like a newborn to me," Luka said, sounding unconvinced. "If you can't pinpoint anything to back your claim, why should we believe it?"

"Not everything is as it seems," Kyler argued. "You may be a powerful Alpha—an enemy no one wants—but there are still things even beyond your understanding."

Luka's blue eyes sliced into Kyler but he made no further comment.

"What does it mean though? Why me?" I asked.

"You certainly are covering all your Ws," Dayton muttered under his breath.

"I can't tell you what I don't know," Kyler said.

I stepped away from Dayton, leaning against the wall as the gravity of her words hit close to home. I forced myself to breathe, clutching my hand to my chest. The idea that there was something different about me—something special—weighed heavy on my mind. Another responsibility I didn't ask for, nor want.

"Mare?"

I peeled my eyes open to find Dayton staring back at me. "I'm fine. This is all a little overwhelming," I admitted.

"Enough of this for now." Luka fixed Kyler with a look. "My turn for questions. Who was your Alpha?"

Kyler's posture stiffened, and she was silent a moment before answering. "I already told you. Demarco. Vincent Demarco."

Dayton glanced back at me briefly before saying, "Why were Fenrir after your pack?"

"No," Kyler said. "I've never trusted you. I will only speak to the Alpha."

Luka grinned. "That's good as I don't trust him either. Bit of a hothead." He shrugged. "However, he brings up a good point. Why were they after you?"

"I don't know. Like I said, we were just passing through. Demarco was looking for the Temple; he wanted to get to the Moon Court as quickly as possible. I don't know why," she explained. "They just attacked us—well, they tried to take us initially."

"How many wolves were in your Cadre?" Luka asked.

Kyler looked immediately uncomfortable. "There were nine of us. Now there's one."

Luka gave a low whistle. "That's a lot of werewolves."

Kyler shrugged. "Needless to say, males who attempt to assert their dominance no longer faze me."

"You haven't lost your spunk." Julian laughed.

Kyler grinned at Julian, who returned the gesture before casting his gaze away.

"Alright then, riddle me this," Dayton said. "How come they killed them and spared you?"

I interjected. "Dayton, c'mon. Stop throwing that in her face."

"No, Mare. It's a good point. You just trust too easily," he said, his words certain. "Fenrir don't have a history of leaving behind leftovers."

Kyler's eyes went yellow once more, and Luka jumped in. "No more, you two, enough. Though however rude he is, his point is true."

Jaw clenched, Kyler looked to Luka. "They wanted me to relay a message." She licked her lips and turned away from us all. "They said that Kaser is coming, and this time, he is after the blood of the Bestial."

CHAPTER 20

The silence was palpable. People knew who Luka was; he was a powerful Alpha who lived outside the law, while the Bestial was a powerful werewolf who hid behind the alias, running rogue into the night and killing evil werewolves. Not many people knew they were the same, even though they might have suspected. From Kyler's confused expression, I doubted she realized she stood in his presence.

Dayton chuckled dryly, dragging a hand down his face. "Presumptuous of them to assume you worthy of relaying the message."

"Enough, Dayton," Luka hissed.

Dayton narrowed his gaze before saluting Luka. "Sure. Whatever you say, Chief."

Luka rolled his eyes and said, "Kyler, you're welcome to stay here if you wish. It will be nightfall. We can rest and reconvene in the morning."

Luka departed, not looking back while Kyler stared blankly at the rest of us. "Did I miss something?"

Julian shrugged. "He's a bit moody about that topic, best to let it go than entertain it."

Dayton stalked out, too. I moved to follow him, glancing back once at Julian, who chatted away with Kyler, grinning. Once outside, I shivered, my teeth chattering. The sky was dark, aside from the splatter of stars illuminating the night. Dayton's gait was fast as he crossed the lawn.

"Dayton, wait!"

He halted in his tracks and spun to face me, glowering as I approached. You would have thought I kicked a puppy into oncoming traffic. "What?"

"Are you alright?"

His face contorted. "What kind of question is that?"

I huffed. Of course he would be this difficult. "A genuine question," I said. "I feel bad about the way Luka acted before we got here. I don't know your history, but I don't think anyone deserves to be treated like that."

"Don't apologize for him on my behalf, Mare," said Dayton.

"I'm not," I protested, though maybe I had been. "I just want to make sure you're okay."

"I'm fine," he snapped. "I'm more annoyed that you threw yourself between me and Luka and got punched in the face. Did I explain the Consort thing? Protector and protected?"

"Yeah, I know. It was stupid." I exhaled. "But I lived, so no worries."

Dayton chuckled. "I don't think I'll ever not worry about you."

"Then I'm sorry to be the cause of your eternal suffering." I grinned.

Dayton glanced away, pursing his lips to hide a smile. "It's getting late; you should rest. It's been a long day."

"I can show you to the spare room," I said, inclining my head toward the house.

"Oh, no," Dayton said. "I can't go inside."

"What?"

"You heard me," Dayton said. "Luka's property, Luka's rules. He doesn't like me, but he has no choice now but to tolerate me. He doesn't want unwanted guests in his house, and that's his right. It's his domain."

"That ludicrous," I balked. "I'm going to talk to him."

I stormed toward the front porch, but Dayton caught me by the shoulder, pulling me back. "Don't, Mare. It's not worth your breath. I promise I'm okay with it."

"But—"

"—there are some perks to being a werewolf," Dayton interjected, "like turning into a literal wolf. I'll be okay."

Before I could speak again, Dayton turned, shedding his human skin. Fur sprouted, forming into a thick, dark coat as he sprung ahead, like a void in the night. He stalked around the edge of the house before nestling outside my bedroom window. I hated that he was exiled to sleep outside, though he didn't seem to mind. I doubted he'd ever admit it if he did.

Dejected, I headed inside and trod up the rickety stairs, peering at the creepy garden gnome Luka had bought years ago. The once vibrant paint was now worn after years beneath the elements; it looked faded and peeled, like a zombie gnome. I reached into my pocket for the house keys before I realized they weren't there. Of course they weren't, because I hadn't been home in weeks.

I knocked on the door for the first time in my life. Luka answered.

"No keys." I shrugged at his puzzled expression. He stepped back to let me in. I started for the stairs but paused and glanced back at Luka. "Is it really necessary to make Dayton stay outside?"

Luka finished locking the door and grinned. "Dogs stay in the doghouse."

Another night of nightmares plagued me, yet this time about Derek. He looked to be in a town square of sorts, chained on a podium with his arms and legs weighed down with thick iron. He wore only shorts, his exposed skin covered in lacerations ranging from claw marks to knife wounds. Humans swarmed, protesting and screaming allegations at him. They chanted, demanding Derek to remember the forgotten brother. They spat at him; they told him he had disgraced the gift, and when they finally slit his throat, I awoke, covered in sweat. I ran to the toilet. I stayed awake after that, my throat raw and swollen, my mind abuzz. I stared up at the ceiling, watching the fan spin in circles and counting the pacing of my breaths.

When tendrils of light poured through the curtains, I flung the blankets off, unable to stay another moment in bed. I stalked downstairs to find Luka in his office. The fireplace behind him dwindled with embers, and Luka slumped, asleep, over his desk. Even asleep, he looked exhausted, his posture rigid as if ready to jump up and attack at a moment's notice. He had always been this way. I just assumed it was the struggles of normal life he dealt with. I felt torn between the ignorance I had and knowledge of what I now knew. I wish I had known, to try and ease some of the burden. Quietly, I left the room. It would be a matter of time before he rose.

Outside, the morning air was damp, and dew covered the lawn like teardrops. I looked to where Dayton had been, and only an imprint remained of where he had laid. I peered around and into the forest, but he was nowhere to be seen. That was not to say he wasn't here; he was always somewhere—watching. Waiting. I was still disgruntled Luka made him sleep outside, but Dayton had neither protested nor seemed bothered by it.

I considered checking the basement for him, yet one step past the basement door made me reconsider. Julian seemed to occupy the room with Kyler, and their suggestive sounds and scents told me enough. I ran far in the other direction.

Alone, I ran through the forest. I stayed on the path Luka marked for me all those years ago. It was strange running it now. The straight path, unobscured by obstacles or difficulties, felt too easy now. Dayton's idea of running had me begging for breath after a few minutes, and though it was definitely having an impact, I would never admit that aloud. By my fifth lap, I had run three miles, the sun out in full force. I squinted as I rounded the corner and tripped.

I caught myself, squealing, yet my elbows bore the fall. I huffed, rolling to see what I tumbled over. There was nothing except upturned leaves, but sunlight glinted across something covered with dirt and leaves. I strode closer and reached down to grab it. A silver stake. It was as long as my forearm, and the tip looked melted away as if seared against a hot surface. I remember the stake in Julian's arms when he explained how they could be used to break down wards.

But why would it be here?

I took off like a bat out of hell, running back toward the house. I hadn't gone far, but I must have teetered on the property lines as the forest blurred around me. I wanted to scream for help, knowing the others would hear me, but I feared it might draw attention to whoever had broken the wards. The house was in my sights, and I sprinted toward it until someone knocked me aside.

Clutching my heart, all breath escaped me, and I whipped my head in the direction of the figure who plowed me down. In the blur of movement, I could identify the terrifying silhouette of a Fenrir. I scrambled back, gaping as six more flew past. I leaped up to follow after them as they headed toward the house. The rotting smell sent chills down my spine as Fenrir scattered like confetti over the front lawn.

Before I could get too close, a familiar brown wolf soared overhead. Dayton landed in front of me. I beheld his massive form, still daunting to behold. His coat, golden in the morning sun, matched his molten eyes. He stalked toward me, his hackles raised. His ferocity reminded me of his mean streak when pushed or challenged. This was the first true test of our bond. Protector and protected.

"The wards are down." I held up the stake, as if it weren't already obvious.

I stepped back and, without warning, Dayton tore off after them.

Luka came out of the house at a sprint, lunging into wolf form. Even from this distance, the size of him was superior—terrifying. Considering how disastrous last time went when I intervened, I stayed back and let them take care of it. Watching the bloodshed was also not something I was keen on doing. The basement door burst open, and Kyler streaked across the battlefield. For a moment, I thought she might join in the fight, but as she ran towards the woods, I knew she was fleeing.

Instinctually, I followed. I didn't fully register I was running until I was halfway there. My legs seeming to move on their own accord, compelling me to intervene, to stop her. Kyler was within twenty feet of me when a Fenrir stopped her pursuit. She fell backwards as the Fenrir hurtled toward me, and I dodged its outstretched claws by inches. With no choice but to run, I sprinted back, stealing a final glance at the Fenrir. It stared at me, as if a glaze of understanding clicked into place behind its pitiless eyes. I kept moving. Dayton bellowed my name in the distance, a bark of warning to stay put. My tattoo appeared to hiss its approval.

To stay put and what? Be attacked by Fenrir? Nope. I ran toward Kyler again, who was distantly ahead. I was astonished by her speed. I yelled at her to stop running, but to no avail, and the further I chased her, the harder the tattoo pulsed against my arm. Kyler shrunk, a distant figure. The woods darkened, but the sun was still out beyond the trees that veiled us. My frustration grew until I heard Kyler scream. I skidded to an abrupt stop.

A strange female emerged behind a tree, holding a dagger to Kyler's throat. I froze. A manic look of enjoyment glinted in her red eyes, artfully painted with black eyeliner. Her eyeliner wings looked sharp enough to cut glass. Each ringlet of her white-blonde hair bounced with her movements, and she moved like a jack in the box, ready to lunge at a moment's notice.

"Looky here, little sissy, all by her lonesome," taunted the female. Her voice was high-pitched like a baby. "What to do, indeed. It's been so long since I could play."

I cursed a list of profanities Luka would disapprove of despite me learning them from him.

The female released Kyler, as if disinterested, then rushed to me in a blur. She shoved me against a tree, gripping my ponytail and jutting my throat toward her. Rising panic threatened me, but I forced it down. Not now, not yet. I struggled against her iron grip.

"Who are you?" I choked.

She threw her head back and let out a bark of laughter. "They call me Shetani."

The name tickled my brain, and Julian's words flooded back. *Shetani, the white wolf, bold and brazen with lethal cunning.* A member of Dante's original Cadre who, according to Julian, was supposed to be in prison.

Shetani released me, and I fell, gasping. She yanked me up by my hair again, and I heard someone shuffling behind me. I glimpsed Kyler on the ground, gaping, not daring to move. Great. I chased after the girl that runs from battle and freezes in a confrontation. I bucked out against Shetani, feebly kicking her shins. She clearly hadn't expected any resistance and laughed through her shock.

"You fight back," she growled, releasing me. My hair slackened, and my mind reeled. "Let's see what you're made of then."

"I wasn't made for backing down." I sneered.

I rose to my feet. Pain shot through my arms, travelling directly to my fingers. I clenched my jaw, my fingers twisting and writhing. I whimpered as my fingernails shifted, and when I glanced down, I was shocked to find claws where my fingers should be.

Shetani advanced, and I dodged her. I surprised myself as I leaped into the air and landed behind where she stood. I ran at her and tore my claws down her back, violence erupting in me like a volcano. She screeched and whirled, her lips curled back. She moved rapidly and slapped me hard across the cheek, shoving me backward. I kicked out again. We rolled around on the ground, landing painful blows on each other.

I only froze when she pinned my legs beneath me. Shetani caressed the tip of a silver dagger at the hollow of my throat, peering down on me with an uncaged wildness alight in her eyes. "You are a scrapper, sissy. I'm surprised. Sloppy but determined."

"I told you I wasn't made for backing down," I growled.

"Killing you would be pathetically easy. Just enough pressure against the hilt and you'd be bleeding out." Her lips curved into a knowing sneer, pressing against the hilt just enough to nick my skin. I hissed and bared my teeth. She squealed. "Oh, to see the look on Lukas' face!"

"Leave him out of this," I spat.

Shetani grinned like a woman having just escaped the psych ward, though, I supposed that wasn't far off. "No big brother to save you now, sissy."

"Guess again."

Luka emerged, his blue eyes aglow. Anger rippled off him in waves. He stood alone, and we were too thick into the forest to detect the others. The blood coating Luka was like an extension of himself, even more terrifying than usual. I swallowed back my fear; I only hoped Dayton and Julian were alright.

Luka had Shetani off me, dragging her by the scruff. She yowled, thrashing and dropping her dagger. Unbothered, Luka ventured forward. I stood up at once, a trickle of blood running from my neck. I scrambled to Kyler who watched the scene unfold like a deer in headlights. I grabbed her by the arm and urged her to move. She sprang into action, following my lead.

"We need to go back to the house!" I yelled as we ran. "What did you think running was going to do anyways?"

"Not the time!" she countered. "Besides, you just fought with Shetani."

"Yeah, I noticed," I said. "Nice of you to jump in, by the way."

"Yeah, fat chance. Shetani is one of the most dangerous werewolves there is," Kyler said. "I wouldn't have intervened if she had my entire family held hostage, but she's found her match with your brother."

"Well, she didn't seem all that scary to me," I said. "If you ask me, I think she talks too much."

Speak of the devil. Shetani soared and landed before us. I stopped short, stumbling backward. Kyler didn't think twice and kept running, but I was glad. One less person to worry about. Shetani quickly advanced, and I barely had time to clamber back.

Baring her pointy teeth, Shetani crawled closer. Luka lunged, knocking her down with one swift blow, but she was down for only a moment before she threw Luka off her and resumed her attack on me. Luka growled and punched the ground. The earth trembled beneath us, the nearby trees leaning as their roots jutted from the soil. Shetani lost her balance and fell forward, but not before hurling a dagger at me. I caught it as it approached my chest, and she shrieked, furious, but Luka shoved her back with bone-crushing force.

Luka had her against a tree, gripping her by the neck with one hand. Her face reddened, and she thrashed against him. I stood, maintaining a distance away from the pair for precaution. Luka's face was unrecognizable, his teeth bared and his eyes glowing a dark, angry blue. His free hand exposed long, pointed claws, dripping in blood.

"I've waited a long time to kill you," he snarled, his voice low. "*Shetani.*"

Shetani thrashed weakly as her face turned a bluish-purple, her limbs beginning to slacken. "Kaser," Shetani gurgled. "He knows."

Luka let her go at once. She gasped for breath, and he kicked her in the stomach, sending her flying. She smacked into a large boulder, the crack of her bones ripping through the forest. Luka soared, grabbing hold of her leg, and twisting it back until it snapped. Shetani howled, and nausea roiled inside me.

Luka's claws shot out and he extended his arm, readying for the final blow.

"Don't!" I screeched, surprising myself. Luka, about to strike, stopped. "You can't just kill her; there must be another option."

"Maris, she has committed terrible crimes and hasn't thought twice about it," growled Luka.

"So be better than her," I pleaded. "You can't just kill people; you don't get to play judge and jury."

Before Luka could reply, Shetani yanked at a red stone amulet from around her neck.

Luka's eyes widened, and he sprung forward. "No!"

Shetani winked at Luka, beaming, and touched the stone. One blink and she was gone. Luka roared, his frustration rattling the trees to their roots. Someone pulled me backward, and I spun upon recognizing Dayton's familiar scent. A sense of relief washed over me. He gripped my shoulders, assessing me for injury. His thumb traced my throat where Shetani's blade nicked it, his own neck a mirror as blood trickled down it. Dayton scowled and started dragging me away.

"What the hell were you thinking, Mare?"

"Kyler was fleeing; I thought she was in danger!" I said, jerking from him. "I can walk by myself."

"That's Shetani," he grumbled. "She could've killed you!"

"I held my own against her."

"What does that mean?" Genuine shock halted Dayton's movements. "You fought Shetani?"

"Should I have let her kill me?" I said, exasperated. Dayton raised his eyebrows, disbelieving. "What? She attacked me first."

"She isn't someone you want as your enemy." Dayton shook his head. "She is lethal—hell, you saw her! Even Luka was struggling against her."

"He didn't look like he was struggling," I said. "Shetani is insane, but there was something off about her. She was sloppy."

"Shetani is supposed to be locked up far from here," Dayton said, shaking his head again. "It was still stupid to run off like that."

"Well, I didn't die. I really don't see the big deal."

Dayton pursed his lips, hiding a grin. "You're a piece of work."

"How did she find us, anyway?"

"That's a fantastic question, but one I have no answer for," he admitted. "What I do know is that it isn't safe here anymore."

We continued in silence, approaching the scene of the house. The lawn was a mess of upturned dirt and dead Fenrir bodies. Julian was busy pouring what looked like gasoline over their corpses, a cigarette lit between his lips. At our approach, he grinned. If anyone were to light a cigarette while pouring gasoline, it would be Julian.

"Well, that was fun," he said, chucking the empty canister aside. "We should do it again sometime. Preferably with pre-gaming to keep things interesting."

Kyler sat on the porch, resting her head in between her legs. I wondered why she had fled and wondered about her blatant disinterest to fight. It wasn't the time for questions.

"Jesus, Maris. You should have let me kill her!" Luka roared, emerging from the woods. He marched towards me, his eyes glowing. Dayton angled himself between us, hand hovering near his dagger.

"You can't just kill people Luka!" I shot back.

"It's what I do; it's who I am. I don't kill housewives with children; I kill criminals!" he thundered.

"Enough," Dayton interjected. "She is still new to this world. Bloodshed is never an easy thing to stomach, innocent or not."

I was shocked Dayton had sided with me, though I understood where Luka was coming from. It was too much of a gray area for me to be okay with it. Life or death were too big of an enormity, one that no one should mess with.

Kyler's head popped up from where she sat on the porch, "Why would Shetani be after you anyway?"

Dayton smirked. "Put the pieces together, Ky. The Fenrir, the message, now Shetani?"

Kyler shot up wide eyed. "Shit. You're him—the Bestial. Well, that explains your vibrant aura."

Luka growled and started pacing. "It seems my past is coming back to haunt me," he said, looking to me. "You see how dangerous someone like her is? You see why I never wanted you in this world?"

The past several weeks were a sped-up film reel in my mind. Yeah, I could see; I understood the dangers plenty. I wouldn't want anyone that I loved involved in this, but what I hated more was being in the dark, defenseless against all the danger. I didn't voice any of this, though. What was the point in wasting my breath?

"We aren't safe here, Chief," Dayton said, narrowing his eyes at Luka.

Luka's nostrils flared at the nickname, and Dayton grinned. He enjoyed being an asshole.

Scowling, Luka dragged a hand down his face. "Fuck," he said. "I hate when you're right."

"It has to happen every so often." Dayton shrugged. "Where do you want to go?"

Luka glared at Dayton, reading between the lines of his words. The Temple. By not asking Luka outright, Luka could draw the conclusion as if it were his idea. It would be the easiest, most obvious choice, and there was plenty of space to accommodate everyone—not to mention the wards and the weapons to use in defense if we were attacked again. But it was Dayton's domain, and Luka was in control here. My brother was never keen on delegating.

Not to mention, Luka would be forced to stay with Dayton, possibly even work with him. Yet I knew Luka well enough to understand that he wouldn't even entertain the idea if he truly despised Dayton.

Slowly, Luka shook his head at Dayton, and the corners of Dayton's mouth upturned in a smirk.

Chapter 21

Luka was stubborn. Despite Dayton arguing it was the safest option, Luka had listed all the reasons why he didn't want to go to the Temple. In fact, Luka wanted to oppose everything Dayton said, and the constant back and forth of sarcastic remarks had my head spinning. I didn't add my two cents in, but I thought the Temple was the better option, if only for the ample space to accommodate everyone. I told Luka I would be going with Dayton regardless, and finally, he conceded. He was hesitant of the Temple because of the Council, but Dayton claimed he knew how to evade them.

I walked down the wooden porch steps with a duffle bag slung over my shoulder. The cool midday air enveloped my body as I strode through the grass toward Luka's black Jeep. Not for the first time, I wondered if this would be the last time I would see my home. The thought didn't sit well with me, nor did the lingering anxiety it brought. Chills trickled down my spine at the reality of my life and everything that had changed in it.

Now, my reality revolved around full moons, worrying about turning into a wolf, and finding who took Derek, all the while navigating my strange bond with a boy my brother despised.

I fell to the flats of my feet and huffed. Hair fell loose from my ponytail, and I blew it back, struggling to fit my small duffle bag along with Luka's crap in the trunk. I reached up on my tiptoes, determined to make it fit, even if I reached a little higher. I jumped and pushed the bag, and as I did, a body pressed up close behind me and maneuvered it into place.

"Really, Dayton?" I spun to face Dayton, who merely shrugged. Inches separated us, yet it felt like were opposing sides of two magnets. No matter how close we were, we'd never be able to touch, yet the pull was hard to resist.

"Even when I'm nice, I'm wrong," he said, smirking.

"I would've eventually gotten it," I said, offering a small smile. I stepped back. "But thank you."

Dayton shook his head as he watched me. He looked worse for wear today; his shirt was torn and dirty, and exhaustion lined his eyes. Stubble creeped across his sharp jawline, and his hair was a mess.

"You look drained," I said. When he didn't answer, I added, "I feel like this is more than you signed up for. Fenrir, Shetani, Kaser. I understand if you want to back out."

"I'm in this with you now," he said swiftly, holding up his tattooed arm.

"I just feel like I'm asking too much of you," I said, unable to meet his gaze.

Dayton stepped forward and reached out, his hand catching a loose strand of hair and tucking it behind my ear. His touch sent warmth through me. Our gazes locked, and I was pulled into the burning magnetic field that was Dayton. Every piece of him was dizzying and utterly consuming; around him, it was a struggle to remember to breathe. Realizing what he had done, he stepped back and cleared his throat.

"You haven't asked anything of me. Everything I've done is because I wanted to."

I exhaled. "Then at least let me get you a new shirt."

He glanced down as if only just realizing the state of his attire. He stripped, taking off his dark leather jacket and tearing off his shirt—literally. I gaped at him, wide-eyed, as he stood in the middle of the lawn in just his jeans and boots. I spun away as heat rose in my face, remembering the lines of his muscled, hard stomach.

"Dayton!"

"It's not something you haven't already seen."

"Just because I've seen you without your shirt on does not warrant a strip show," I protested, yet damned myself as I turned back toward him, keeping my gaze eye-level with his.

"I always thought I'd be a spectacular stripper," Dayton said, leaning beside me as he zipped up his jacket. "In another life that didn't involve—well, all of this."

"You don't have the temperament or manners for that." I paused and laughed at the thought, yet another thought sobered my mood. "I was going to go to college before all this. I got accepted into a school only a few weeks ago."

Dayton stared ahead, his arms crossed. "You could still go," he said. "This life is not always like this. At least, it doesn't have to be."

Now that I knew the truth, the thought of going to school felt impossible. Juggling classes would be stressful enough without worrying about what I'd do once a month when the moon rose, and that's without the added pressure of werewolves hunting me down. It would be too much for anyone.

"It's too different now. I know the truth, and that will never change." I sighed, tilting my head. "Would you have wanted a different life?"

He straightened at the question. "I've never had any thoughts about having another life. This is my life, and dreaming of a different one is senseless. Fantasies lead to misery," he said. "In this life, or any made-up one, I am who I am."

"And just who is that, exactly?"

I expected my question to be met with fury, and I waited for its delivery. But at that moment, Luka clamored out the front door, carrying more bags brimming with weapons.

"What's the plan when we get to the Temple?" I asked him.

"Not sure, exactly," Luka answered. "I've got to make a few calls, pull in some favors. I've been theorizing what happened to Derek."

"Yeah?" I asked. I had gone to bed with a raging headache last night, my mind running wild with worry about Derek and what he might be going through.

"Don't jump to any conclusions, but I think Derek's disappearance and Kaser might be intertangled," Luka said.

"That would make sense," agreed Dayton. "Kaser is clearly after you. If he caught your Beta, he might want to use him as collateral to lure you out."

While they were only speaking theories, the notion made me sick. More than anything, I wanted to get Derek back safely, but if this Kaser person had him, that would complicate an already over-complicated situation. I pressed my fingers against my temples as it started to pulse.

Julian strolled toward us while chatting with Kyler beside him. He laughed at something she said, the pair grinning at one another. I felt the ease between them. People who mutually respected one another. Considering how Dayton described their relationship, this surprised me, though

I wouldn't meddle. Grinning broadly, Julian approached, his green eyes brightening. Beside me, I heard Luka's low grunt of disapproval.

"Hey, be nice." I nudged him.

"Are we ready to go?" Julian asked, twirling a set of keys.

Kyler snatched the keys from Julian. "I'm driving. Your driving makes me carsick."

"Ouch," Julian feigned offense.

Julian and Kyler would drive the car we originally came here in. The outside was scratched, the hood dented, and one of the windows shattered. Though as long as it drove, I supposed it was fine. Dayton wanted to travel in wolf form to expend some energy while ensuring we weren't followed. It was odd, I thought, but that was Dayton.

Luka shut the trunk, rocking the Jeep. "Don't take backroads where you can avoid it. If Fenrir are stalking the area, they're likely to strike where it would draw less attention."

"I can't tell if you think I'm stupid for thinking I don't know that or if you're being genuinely helpful," said Julian.

"It's because he's an Alpha," Kyler remarked. "A good Alpha, anyway. He can't help but take charge and give direction; it's as natural as breathing for him."

"Pretty much nailed it on the head," said Luka. He turned to look at Julian without judgment yet appeared to study him. "What's your deal?"

Julian's green eyes narrowed. "You already know. Why ask?"

Luka smiled. "It's still rude to act like I know better, even when I do."

"You ask questions to provoke more tidbits of information and build upon your existing knowledge," said Julian. "I don't know how your mind is guarded against me, but I can still finagle the surface."

"Interesting to see just how powerful you are," drawled Luka. "You have immeasurable power far beyond your mind tricks."

"Luka," Dayton warned, glancing between the pair.

I sensed the tension rising. Julian, normally even-tempered, wasn't so much now, and Luka's smirking didn't help. I turned to Luka, but he quickly circled Julian, his eyes glowing. Kyler and I backed up in unison, keen to stay clear of the possible crossfire.

Luka paused his prowl and laughed. "Julian, you need to learn to control your powers before it either controls you or someone else does."

"Manipulation is what gave me these powers. I never asked for this," Julian said through gritted teeth. He tore his gaze from Luka. "You don't understand the repercussions of these powers, but I do." Julian's protest glinted in his eyes as he stepped forward.

"Enough, Luka. Leave him alone," I said, facing Julian. "You don't have to do anything you don't want to."

Julian shook his head and clapped his hands. *It's a nice sentiment,* Julian's words whispered in my mind. He glanced at Kyler, then jerked his head back, and together they walked to the car and took off. If he was upset beyond his cryptic words, he didn't say.

"You shouldn't have pushed him," Dayton snapped.

"He needs to stop being coddled," Luka answered coldly. "Julian is more powerful than he lets on."

"He hates his magic!"

"Julian was manipulated at an early age by Dante. Whatever Dante did to him gave him the powers he has, but his mind reading and telepathy are only at the surface of what he can do. But Julian refuses to mess with it—he always has. With Kaser returning, I can't help but fear Julian might be pulled into a battle he doesn't want to fight and he won't be prepared," Luka explained.

"Look, you can say and do whatever you want to me, but if you try to drag Julian into this, it won't end well for you. I'll make sure of that," hissed Dayton, voice full of menace. He scowled, glaring at Luka.

Luka snarled, and I stepped between them. "Enough. No more throwing wolf rage at each other," I glanced back at Luka. "You have to stop being all Alpha all the time. I know you can be decent and kind when you want to be. You must learn to play nice; they're my friends."

"For now," said Luka, gaze locked on Dayton. Their confusing rocky past was hard to navigate, and though I hated playing mediator, it worked.

Without another word, Dayton morphed into his wolf form and disappeared into the woods. Luka opened the passenger door to his Jeep, beckoning me inside. He slid into the leather seat on the driver's side, grumbling incoherently under his breath. I sensed Luka's storm brewing, having grown up with it. He revved the engine to life and banged his fist against the steering wheel. I jumped but didn't dare comment.

"Be straight with me. Did Dayton force you to take that oath to him?" Luka asked, gesturing to my tattoo.

"Really?" I balked. "I'm not an idiot, and Dayton wouldn't force me to do anything."

"Dayton might surprise you on what he would and wouldn't do," said Luka, his hands tightening on the steering wheel. "I trusted Dayton with my life once, and we were close. He was my—"

Luka hesitated before finishing his sentence.

"He was your what?" I pressed.

"Dayton was my Beta," Luka admitted, exhaling.

Beta. Dayton had been Luka's Beta. In hindsight, it made sense, really. All their taunts and jabs conveyed their familiarity—two people who knew each other well enough to understand how the other person ticked. They understood how to get under each other's skin.

"My first Beta," Luka continued. "When he betrayed me, it was a big blow. I never saw it coming; I never suspected it. Now, I can't help but think that he is using you to get to me again. But I will *not* allow him to put you at risk because of me."

How had things turned so sour between them?

"Dayton may have his faults, but he is honest in his intentions with me," I said. "I trust him, which is enough for me, and if you trust me, it has to be enough for you."

Luka appeared indecisive as we sped down the long stretch of road back to the Temple. "No, it's not enough, and it has nothing to with me trusting you but everything to do with me loathing him."

"What did he do to warrant your unwavering anger?" I finally asked, fed up with all the secrets.

"Dayton tried to kill me!" Luka snapped, as if it was the first time he had said the words aloud.

Shock struck me, rendering me too stunned into speechlessness. I could only manage one word, which came out softly: "Why?"

"I don't know why," admitted Luka. "I never found out, and Dayton covered his tracks, a trick he learned from me. When I met him, he was running from a past that haunted him long before his parents died. All I know for certain is that Dayton has a dark past. Don't fall victim to it."

Long before his parents died. Had his brother died before or after them? To lose your whole family was an unimaginable notion, and I knew

Dayton blamed himself for their deaths. I also knew that's why he acted like he did: always pissed off and ruthless in battle.

I looked down at the swirling lines against my arm and traced a finger over them. I closed my eyes, picturing Dayton—his scowl, his arrogance, his way with words. All of it. Something pulled me toward him; it was unexplainable, but there. I believed Luka, but I trusted Dayton.

Maybe I was the one who was a fool.

CHAPTER 22

The car ride was quiet for the rest of the journey. My thoughts ran so deep that I didn't even notice when the car slowed.

In the rearview mirror, Dayton followed in his wolf skin. While I knew Dayton was a merciless killer, I couldn't wrap my head around what Luka said. Dayton killing Luka didn't seem right. Displaced, almost. There had to be more to it.

Driving towards the Temple, as opposed to hurtling through on a motorcycle, allowed me to take in the scenery. For one, I didn't realize how deep in the woods it was, and the closer we approached the gates, the more I noticed the endless trees shrouding the light. The Jeep slowed. Red button-topped mushrooms sprouted from the ground, dotted with white. Low-hanging branches billowed with the breeze, as did the dusty pink flower buds, not yet in bloom.

The wards shot skywards and descended like a glittering veil around the perimeter of the Temple that stretched far back beyond the woods. It opened like a yawn when Dayton pressed his bloodied palm against the gate to allow us through. Once Luka parked, I leaped out, letting the cool air hit my face. Dayton jogged toward us, his eyebrows drawn together.

"What the fuck?" he said, running through the grass and up the grand staircase.

Luka was hot on Dayton's tail, with me trailing behind. Kyler pulled up to the Temple, and Julian was halfway out of the car before even putting it into park. I could make out an outline of a person at the top of the stairs and smelled blood. As I raced up them, blood smeared the steps, like the person had dragged themselves up it. A cold feeling crept up my spine.

Dayton already had one arm around the stranger's shoulder, hauling them up. It was a man, his face stark-white and eyes bloodshot. Deep gashes trailed down his front, and strips of his shirt clung to his sweat-soaked skin. A tousle of dark curls fell in ringlets around his face as he panted like a dying animal. Luka shouldered the door and held it open.

"Neville," Julian huffed, joining us. He grabbed the stranger's other shoulder, and together the three of them helped him inside.

"Which way is the infirmary?" Luka asked. "Those gashes look bad, inflicted either by silver or an Alpha."

"Down the stairs to the left," instructed Dayton.

Kyler marched behind, like she was on a mission, blowing past everyone and making a beeline down the stairs. The sterile, white lights in the infirmary were blinding; the walls were stark, and the floors were free of scuffs. Shelving adorned a back wall, lined with vials and contents with various substances inside. From the ceiling hung plants that swung as I brushed past, tickling my arm. I held the door open as Dayton and Julian walked in and dropped Neville onto a hospital bed. It looked like it had a cast-iron frame, the simple design reminding me of hospital beds you'd see in old war movies. At least twelve beds ran on each side of the room, lined against the walls.

Luka and Kyler rummaged through the cabinets, speaking amongst themselves as they gathered supplies. I gulped and stepped back, frozen in terror. I had no idea how to react.

Neville trembled on the bed, his teeth chattering. In the blinding lights, his wound was more apparent. Deep gashes oozed black goop instead of blood, and it smelt acidic, like fresh tar on a highway.

Dayton ripped the tatters of Neville's shirt off and tossed it into a waste bin. He backed away as Kyler scooched in with a long needle filled with a golden-like substance. Luka stood at the ready behind, with a rolling cart beside him, set up with gauze, bandages, and other needles filled with the same liquid.

Dayton crossed to where I stood and steered me gently out of the room. "Hey, are you okay?" he whispered.

The infirmary door shut and extinguished all light, aside from the silver-flamed torches along the halls. "Me? What about him? He looks like he's dying."

Dayton's face soured. "I don't know what happened to him. Like Luka said, maybe it was his Alpha, or maybe a wound inflicted by silver." A blood-curdling scream tore from the room, and I flinched. "Mare, look at me."

My body trembled, but I forced myself to meet his gaze.

"Why don't you go upstairs? This is upsetting you. If anything changes with him, good or bad, I'll let you know."

I started to nod, just as Neville screeched, "*Shetani—Kaser—moon-stones!*"

Holding me by my shoulders, Dayton pressed me gently against the wall.

"Let me go, Dayton. He knows something," I said.

"He's injured and possibly dying," Dayton chided. "If he makes it through the next hour, he should be fine and we can question him then."

I huffed reluctantly but conceded. He was right. The infirmary door opened, and Julian popped his head out before letting the door seal behind him. Flask in hand, he brought it halfway to his lips then paused, eyebrows raised as he looked at me then Dayton, who stepped back, scowling.

"I got kicked out," Julian said. "Kyler knows her way around medicine and wants Luka as backup in case she might need his Alpha-ness. Plus, he seems to know his way around an infirmary, which is a bonus."

"Luka taught himself the ins and outs of basic medical knowledge," said Dayton. Considering I wanted to pursue a career as a nurse, it was interesting Luka never shared that with me—but I digress. "Neville, well, I just hope he comes out okay."

"He looks different," Julian added. "Haggard."

Dayton snorted. "He's a renegade werewolf who lives alone in the middle of nowhere with no one to bother him. I'm jealous of that in a way."

I was about to ask who he was before Julian spoke again. "Neville is an acquaintance from our days at the Court. I haven't seen him in years, but you know, nothing but well wishes for the guy. He was turned into a werewolf as a teenager, which is interesting, given he was a witch."

My eyebrows drew together. "How's that possible?"

Julian shrugged. "It's not. Werewolf magic concealed his witch powers, rendering them useless."

I thought about Derek and how Luka and Dayton theorized that Kaser might have taken him. If they were right, would Neville know something? He'd belched the names of Kaser and Shetani, so he knew something about them.

Time moved slowly as we all sat in wait outside the infirmary. I wondered how Neville got here in his injured state and why he came here at all. Strictly speaking, the Temple was a sanctuary for all werewolves, but the timing seemed off.

Julian left for a smoke break more than once, always coming back with the putrid yet tolerable stench of tobacco. Dayton paced back and forth, sometimes leaving, then coming back. I could make out Luka and Kyler's muffled voices echoing from the other side.

I was rocking back and forth on my heels when Luka opened the door and announced it was safe to enter. I practically fell through the doorway. Luka glared at me in warning, as if telling me to behave, though I was desperate for answers about Derek. Kyler sat on a chair overlooking a tiny window that showed a view of the early evening sun outside. Julian sauntered in behind me, and Dayton leaned in the doorway, glowering.

At the bed, Neville sat up, propped by pillows. His whole chest was covered in white bandages where a tinge of red sliced through his middle. He looked less haunted; color had returned to his face, revealing his tanned complexion. His eyes studied me carefully, dark and assessing as Dayton strode up behind me, standing close by. Neville cocked his head, his dark eyes surveying us.

"Oh my, is that you, Dayton? You certainly have grown. What's it been, five years?" Neville chirped, despite the hoarseness of his voice.

I whirled to look at Dayton, who stared straight ahead. "Neville," he said. "I would say it's nice to see you again, but I don't lie."

Neville waggled his brows and snapped his teeth playfully. "Still as vexatious as ever." His gaze fell onto me while his nostrils flared. "You're new. Hello, Maris."

"How do you know me?" I asked.

"Your entrance into this world has been nothing short of subtle, my dear." Neville chuckled. Luka cleared his voice, flashing Neville a pointed look. "Right, Lukas never wanted you in this world. He won't take kindly to strangers questioning you."

"It's Luka," he corrected, moving to sit on a small swivel chair at the edge of the bed. Luka looked too large for it, like he sat on furniture for dolls. Luka straightened, his elbows resting on the bed frame as he glared at Neville.

"Lukas was your given name at birth," Neville said provokingly. "There is power in a name."

Luka smiled sourly, adopting a persona of calm that only came with significant restraint. "Call me Luka."

Neville raised a single eyebrow. "Fine, then. *Luka.*"

"What happened to you?" Kyler asked from her corner in the room. Color had drained from her face, and she looked ready to pass out from exhaustion.

Neville adverted his gaze and thrummed his fingers soundlessly on the bedsheets. "I was attacked at my home by Shetani. She was demanding information on certain relics to give to her master Kaser."

I gulped. Shetani seemed to be on a violent spree; I remembered what Julian said about having her locked away in prison. I supposed she was making up for lost time now that she was free.

"Why did you come here? How did you manage to get here?" asked Dayton.

"Why? Well, the Temple is an open sanctuary for werewolves in distress. It was disheartening to get here to find it abandoned by you two. I laid dying on the steps for hours," grumbled Neville. "I have half a mind not to report you to the Council for insubordination."

"I checked the cameras. You were only out there for thirty minutes before we got back," snapped Dayton.

"Enough," Luka said. His voice was quiet, yet everyone's chatter halted at once. With his gaze never averting from Neville, he said, "Tell me everything you know about Kaser Odessa."

The amusement faded from Neville's eyes. "Oh dear. What makes you think I know anything about him?"

"Shetani. If she attacked you, that means you're on Kaser's radar, and you're only on his radar if you know something you shouldn't," said Luka. "Your wounds weren't fresh either; I'd guess you were injured anywhere from six to eight hours ago before hauling your sorry ass here."

I was halfway between surprised and amazed Luka had gathered that much information in the short time Neville had been here. Luka was considered a big deal in the werewolf world, and I could see why.

Neville grinned like a Cheshire cat. Unease washed over me at this man's mischievous nature. "My, my. You are very perceptive."

"With thinning patience," growled Luka. "Answer my questions."

Neville sighed. "I don't know much about Kaser, but I know what he is after; he thought he could recruit me to help him on his mission." He paused before continuing. "Kaser was under the impression I could help him find the Infinite Artifacts."

There was a collective intake of breath from everyone but me. I sensed—and not for the first time—I was the only one in the dark as to what the Infinite Artifacts were.

"What? Why?" asked Dayton, stepping forward. Luka shot him a warning look.

"I don't know. We have about as much proof they exist as we do about the man upstairs," Neville explained. "He is after power that he can obtain in a limited time. He is under the impression that finding these Artifacts will grant it to him."

"What are these Artifacts?" I asked.

Julian chimed in to answer. "Assuming the Artifacts are real...they are powerful objects rumored to be tied to the existence of werewolves, but there's no proof they really exist, though I'm not one to doubt whispers and rumors. Everything starts from something."

Kyler, who looked slightly shell-shocked, said, "If we just entertain the idea that they're real, what would Kaser want with them?"

"Powerful objects, evil villain?" Neville raised his eyebrows. "It's fairly obvious, I think."

"No one has answered what they actually are," I interjected. "I'm still a little behind here."

Luka glanced away from me and stood up, pacing the length of the room and grumbling to himself.

"Records of our existence date back centuries. Mostly fragmented history is all we have to link to the official creation of werewolves—legends and myths. Some are thought to be truthful, though it's really a mesh of blurred lines. Ancient archives of the old language have been discovered but deciphering them has proven difficult. It's taken years with a skilled team of experts to shed light on the little we know," explained Luka. "There is a relic with unique magical properties that only connects to the beginning of our creation, and the end."

"The Moonstone," muttered Dayton.

Neville had screamed that word before. I didn't say anything and let Luka continue.

"Yes, the Moonstone." He agreed. "The Moonstone is believed to be the start of our creation. Anyone with half a brain would want to know why an ancient stone changed the actual fibers of our beings, yet no one has ever found it. There are only whispers, all which lead to dead ends." Luka stilled his pacing and shook his head. "The problem with the Moonstone was that the power was too great for one person to bear. The magic in it drove the bearer of the stone to madness. The stone was split into pieces and placed in mundane objects cast into society."

"And that is what the Infinite Artifacts are. Vessels for the Moonstone to hide in plain sight," added Dayton. "It could be a sword that gives the user sure strike or a mirror that blurs all flaws. A pen that never runs out of ink. You get the idea."

"So, in theory, if Kaser gets hold of these Artifacts, it'll give him power because of the Moonstone?" I said, making sure I followed.

"Exactly," agreed Neville. "But the magic can be unpredictable."

"Unless you learn to control it," Dayton said, glancing at Julian.

"What made him think you could help him?" Luka asked.

"He thought I'd know more than I do because of my witch magic. I don't have that magic anymore as it died when I changed," Neville shrugged. "I only know he wanted information regarding the Artifacts, but I had little to tell him. He is working fast, and he has many pieces on the game board in play."

"You said there was not much to tell him," I interjected. "But there was something?"

Neville's posture straightened. "Yes. The Moonstone he seeks was broken into four parts. I will not get into how I know that, just trust that I do. Four parts; four Artifacts."

"And Shetani tried to kill you, so you'd take that information to your grave," added Dayton. "This is so sick and twisted."

"Silver tipped claws coated with wolfsbane to leave a mark on me," Neville agreed, wincing and clutching his chest. "I give her points for creativity."

Kyler stood and walked toward him, glowering back at all of us. "He isn't well. He needs rest. No more questioning him."

"Fine with me, I need a smoke anyway," Julian chirped, already halfway to the door.

Luka seemed ready to protest, but then thought better of it as Kyler shooed us all out of the room, and we clamored out one by one. Dayton stayed close behind me, his warmth radiating toward me.

"That was a nice observation on his wordplay," said Dayton as we walked up the stairs.

"Yes, good catch," Luka confirmed. He glanced back at me approvingly.

Being praised for something trivial by both Dayton and Luka felt strangely satisfying, as if I might be able to find a place for myself in this strange new world after all. At the top of the stairs, we all stood in the entryway and shared a look.

"What's the next play, Chief?" asked Dayton.

Luka frowned but said, "I don't know. I don't like this business about the Moonstones. If Kaser is after them, it makes a grim situation grimmer. He has Fenrir at his disposal, plus Shetani to do his dirty work. There's something missing—a vital piece in all this."

"What about Derek?" I asked.

"I just hope Derek isn't unwittingly at the center." Luka dragged a hand down his face. "I need to make some calls, check in on my Cadre and update them. I need to do some research as well. I assume there's a library here?" Dayton nodded. "Alright. We can call reconvene in a few hours, wash up and rest."

Chapter 23

Hot water gushed over me, and I relished being clean after washing my hair five times to get rid of dried blood and dirt. It disturbed me to think how long I'd walked around like that with no one saying anything about it. Even after, I still felt like it was there. It was only a matter of time before someone attacked me again. I wondered if cutting my hair would be better. My long locks felt like a part of me but were easy to use against me in a fight.

Stepping out of the shower, the chill of the air settled across my skin. I shivered and reached for the pile of clothes to change. It was strange, but I felt better wearing my own clothes from home. Training clothes felt like armor compared to my leggings and oversized shirts.

I gazed at my reflection in the mirror and sighed. The bags under my eyes were prominent, fueled by lack of sleep. Over the last two nights, nightmares plagued me, yet my dreams had never felt so real or vivid before.

I forced my gaze away from the mirror to stop myself from further scrutiny. I ambled out of the bathroom, my wet hair cascading from the towel and onto my shirt. Tossing the towel aside, I walked to the plush armchair and sunk into it. This room had grown on me the more time I spent in it. It was less alien and felt cozier despite being bigger than my room at home. Closing my eyes for a moment, I enjoyed the silence.

A knock came at the door.

Dayton walked in and peered around curiously. Before I could speak, he did. "Hey."

"What's up?" I asked, surprised to see him.

"Nothing." He glanced at the ground and shrugged. "Neville's still knocked out from the drugs Kyler gave him. Julian is passed out in his room. I'd talk to Kyler, but we don't get along too well."

I thought about all we had learned from Neville. Kaser was chasing after the Infinite Artifacts to gather the Moonstones, and I thought of Derek then, too, and wondered how he was tied into all this.

Dayton entered the room to sit on the footrest across from me. "It wouldn't kill you to be nice," I said.

"I'm plenty nice." he said, a tiny smile playing on his lips. He was clean-shaven and smelled of soap and pine. His dark hair was swept back today and exposed the intensity of his gaze.

"Does it bother you to know your words hurt people?" I asked.

Dayton's golden eyes flicked to me. "Not usually, no."

Thoughts of Dayton surfaced, though I didn't want to dwell on it. It felt wrong to know his past with Luka; he had only ever been open with me about his family's death, which came with vulnerability. It felt like an invasion to know more, yet I so desperately did. It felt like admitting betrayal. There was a shape to Dayton: cracks in his foundation, Band-Aids over bullet holes.

"How are you?" Dayton asked before I said anything else.

"I'm as well as I can be, I suppose." I said.

"Are you sure?" he questioned, knitting his eyebrows close together. "You seem tired."

I laughed. "A bit closer to exhaustion, actually. The nightmares are keeping me awake."

Dayton stared straight ahead at the wall, resting his elbows on his knees. "It happened again?" There was an edge in his tone.

I crossed the room to look out the window; the bright sun glittered outside. "Yes," I whispered.

Wordlessly, Dayton approached and leaned against the windows with his arms crossed over his chest. He peered down at me. "Are you sure you're alright?"

I looked up at him then, acutely aware of the inches of space between us. The concern over his features nearly made me break, cracking the sturdy walls of my questionable well-being. But if I broke down and felt everything I suppressed, I wouldn't stop. "I'm okay."

Dayton reached a hand out and placed a finger under my chin. His touch made me shiver as his fingers trailed slowly down my jawline. "C'mon, Mare."

"Dayton, we need to talk."

He took a sharp intake of breath and turned from me. His hand automatically unsheathed his daggers, and he withdrew his arm back to aim. As Julian appeared in the doorway, he ducked and swore at the blade propelling toward him.

"Jesus, Jules." Dayton scowled, summoning back his dagger in one swift flick.

"Why does your first thought always go to attack the intruder?" Julian asked sarcastically. "Can it never be, 'how are you?' or 'how can I help?'"

"I think I'm more surprised he didn't sense you." I laughed, expelling the tension from my body.

Dayton's scowl deepened. "I was distracted."

My heart rate increased traitorously in my chest.

"I can see that plenty," said Julian, waggling his brows. Heat rose to my face. I noted Julian's clothes: a black glittering tank top adorned with little skulls. His hair was different again, too, a stark white streaked with purple.

"What's up with your ever-changing hair?" I asked.

Julian tipped his head back and laughed. "It's a cloaking salve I use." He reached into his pocket and pulled out a small tin. "It's meant to dissuade your actual appearance. Meant for like undercover missions, but handy for my daily mental spirals."

"You go through that stuff too much." Dayton frowned. "Just pick a color and stick with it."

Julian gave him a knowing look. "Deep down in your shredded soul, you know you want it, just to try." He winked then turned to leave. "Oh, Luka wants to talk to you, Maris."

"What does Luka want?" Dayton asked, following Julian.

I padded behind them both, my bare feet plodding against the cold hardwood. Our voices echoed through the dimly lit hall as we walked. "Luka could want a triage of things. I never know what to expect," I said.

Dayton made a disgruntled noise. "Maybe he'll try and warn you away from me again."

"Oh, I don't think I'll be that lucky," I joked.

"Luck, huh?" Dayton smirked.

Julian stopped walking and grabbed a lit candlestick from a table against the wall. He whirled, pointing the flames at the two of us. "Whatever this is that's happening now, stop. I think Luka might actually *kill* Dayton if he suspected there was more than just an old bond between you."

My face flushed at Julian's implications. I didn't feel that way about Dayton; he was my friend. No, that wasn't the right word. He was my Consort. It felt natural to get along with him—to some degree, at least.

Dayton scowled. "Enough, Jules."

Rolling his green eyes, Julian continued walking. Luka wasn't far. We found him hanging upside down from a beam on the ceiling in the training room, reading a book. He made it look effortless. It was laughable. I imagined myself trying that, though I'd have to choose a gravestone for after. I tilted my head up to read the title of the book. Luka's blue eyes met mine and he grinned, dropping down and gracefully flipping to land soundlessly on his feet.

"I just know I'll never be able to do that," I said.

Luka laughed and pocketed the book he was reading. "Sure, you will. One day."

"Right now, worry more about entering a room without sounding like a stampeding herd of elephants," Dayton commented, leaning beside the fireplace.

"Elephants. Really?"

He shrugged. "Clumsy lion?"

"Fish out of water?" added Luka.

"Okay, okay. I get it. I'm loud," I said. "Stealth isn't my strong point."

"It'll all come into place eventually. You just have to be patient and willing to learn," said Luka. He wandered toward the rack of weapons, trailing a finger over them as he passed. "This is quite the collection."

"The Council knows how to provide," Dayton said nonchalantly, eyeing Luka with suspicion. "Feel free to use what you'd like."

At Dayton's mention of the Council, I felt uneasy. To my knowledge, we hadn't heard from them since Dayton stayed true to his word and became my Consort. I assumed he told them like he'd said. Perhaps that was the end of them for now, but I doubted it would be the last time they bothered us.

Luka plucked a long sword from the wall, looking more lethal than usual. Weapon in hand, it appeared like an extension of himself. While some people had a natural disposition for mundane hobbies like cooking or cleaning, Luka was naturally predisposed for inflicting death.

"These are dangerous weapons. Do you ever actually use these?" Luka asked.

"Not as often as we might like," Julian chimed, one eye on Dayton. "Personally, I think they are better displayed than executed."

Dayton moved to adopt his usual stance before the targets, daggers in hand. The nifty band he wore remained around his wrist, and he tossed the knives effortlessly into each target. The simplicity of his movements was like clockwork: rhythmic and always bringing the same result.

"What's up, Chief?" Dayton asked, letting the final knife go.

I shook my head as Luka's hand froze over a pair of two sharp blades. He turned to glare at Dayton. "What did I say about calling me that?"

"How about General?" Dayton let another soar. "Major? Lord of the Wolves? I think Captain has a nice ring to it."

Luka was a blur of motion and threw a dagger without hesitation. It whirled wickedly fast past Dayton's head and nestled into the target with perfect precision. Dayton reached his hand up to his ear, blood trickling down the tip.

"So, just Chief then?" taunted Dayton.

A growl of pure annoyance escaped Luka and he turned from Dayton, shaking his head.

"Dayton," Julian moaned. "Stop pushing his buttons, or so help me, I'll let him attack you. God knows he's well within his rights."

The doors to the training room creaked open, and Kyler walked in. She wore jeans and a cream-colored sweater, her hair tied in a bun atop her head. She appeared rested, her eyes no longer crazed and terrified. She peered around, silently assessing everyone until her gaze softened on Julian.

"Neville is still resting," she said. "His wounds are healing nicely, though."

Luka began to say something, but a round object soared in through one of the open windows. It blew past Luka, and he caught it with a curse, and dropped it just as quickly. It flew toward me, and I caught it with a screech, the orange flames dwindling in my palms. A fire letter addressed to me. I groaned, remembering the last time I received one of these from the Council.

"It's for me," I announced, meeting Luka's eyes. He looked pensive and walked toward me while I flipped the letter. It was enclosed with a plain red wax seal. No sender information was provided.

"Go on. Open it," said Dayton.

I unfolded the thick piece of paper and read over the words on the page. It was written in neat cursive letters, and I reread it twice before I was able to make any sense of it. After the third time, I read the words aloud.

"Come and seek it where the found is lost

To find it, look to where gone is time

Moonstones by Moonstones

In the interim, Derek suffers in wait

K. O"

Kaser Odessa.

Kaser had Derek. The letter proved it, and the letter was addressed to me. Yet the confirmation that Kaser had a hand in Derek's disappearance felt like a sick joke. Kaser knew by addressing the letter to me and mentioning Derek he would lure me into his scheme. I hated to say it, but it worked.

Luka asked me to repeat it, then said, "He's speaking in riddles."

If Luka didn't understand the letter, we were all screwed. It made no sense to me; it seemed designed to mislead for how little it made sense. The only straightforward line had been the last, and even then, it felt convoluted.

"Are you surprised?" Dayton asked.

Luka paced the room and circled the training mats. "I figured Kaser would attempt to go after the Moonstone, which is why I summoned you here to begin with. That letter sounds like he wants us to go after the Moonstone for him, but why would he address it to Maris?"

"Let me make sure I understand still," I interjected. "The Moonstone that supposedly created werewolves was split into four pieces and put into various objects because its power was too great to handle, creating Infinite Artifacts?" Luka nodded. "Could Kaser want to find the Infinite Artifacts to assemble the Moonstone again?"

"When you put it that plainly, it's both genius and utterly grim," Julian said, then shuddered.

"The idea of Kaser with any piece of the Moonstone doesn't sit well with me," said Luka. "The extent of its powers is unknown; therefore, it should be treated as limitless."

It didn't sit well with me, either. Why could he want them? Did he want to fulfill Dante's legacy? Take control of werewolves? Dante had planned to force dormant werewolves into transitioning. Would the Moonstone make that easier? Could it make him invincible?

"Okay, but what does all of this have to do with the note?" asked Kyler.

"*Moonstones by Moonstones. In the interim, Derek suffers in wait.* It's obvious. Kaser can wait, but it will be Derek who suffers." Dayton squared his shoulders. "Kaser wants Maris to go on his Moonstone wild-goose chase under the guise it will somehow aid her to finding Derek."

Moonstones by Moonstones. In the interim, Derek suffers in wait.

Luka paused and took one look at my face before starting to speak. "No. I see it on your face. You want to entertain this note and go after this fallacy."

"But Derek—"

"—is a fool for getting caught," Luka cut me off. "I'll be dammed if I let you go down with him."

"I'm not suggesting that," I said. "But what if—"

"No," snapped Luka, cutting me off again. "No what ifs. Be in this world if you must, Maris, but you will not have anything to do with Kaser. I'll die ten times over before involving you in his schemes."

"Maybe she's right. We can't just abandon the guy," Julian added. "Foolish or not, no one should be left to Kaser's mercy."

"*Jules,*" Dayton hissed.

"What? I'm just saying."

Luka crossed the room in two strides and snatched the note from me, and my protests died on my lips when I watched him toss it into the fireplace, the letter becoming nothing more than a burning pile of ash. A blaze of anger rose in me, but Dayton gripped my wrist hard before I could speak.

"Mare, listen to him," Dayton said. "Luka's right."

I yanked my arm from him and stormed out of the room.

"Come and seek him where the found is lost?" I muttered. "Or was it lost is found?" Frustration pooled through me as I scribbled out the riddle. "Time is sound?" Only one line I remembered clearly: '*Moonstones by Moonstones. In the interim, Derek suffers and waits.*' I circled it boldly in red marker.

Leaning back against the pillows of the bed, I sighed, trying to ignore the crawling ache in my neck from sitting hunched over paper for hours. Early evening light crept through the windows, shadowing the room in blue. Luka was against this entire proposition; his instincts were too hardwired to protect me, but it wasn't about me anymore. It was about Derek. He was a prisoner, so not jumping on the chance to get him back was ridiculous. I couldn't abandon him.

I refocused and glanced at the progress I had made with the riddle. The words were jumbled, and while I understood the premise, it lacked sophistication.

A soft voice spoke my name from the doorway. It took me a second to realize it was all in my head. I looked up to where Julian leaned against the frame, balancing a mountain of books in his arms. I was about to speak before he placed a finger to his lips and shook his head. He walked out, shutting the door firmly behind him.

"*Follow me. Be discreet,*" his voice echoed.

I gathered up the paper and silently followed him. Noiselessly, he padded down the hall, and with one hand, he opened a small hidden door that blended into the wall. He quickly ushered me inside and shut it behind him. We stood before a long narrow staircase, and I glanced at him questioningly, but still followed along. It seemed to shrink the higher we went, and I hunched over to fit through.

At the top, Julian glanced back at me, grinning. "This part is really cool."

He pushed slightly against the wall, and the wall sank inward. I gaped as a door that had never been there before appeared. Julian opened it and stepped back to let me enter.

The inside reminded me of an attic with dusty and musty cloths covering most surfaces. Each corner collected cobwebs, but I didn't look too closely at what else tangled within it. Next to a window on one wall were three shelves lined with paintbrushes, oil paints, and glasses besides empty or half-filled liquor bottles.

"Secret attic room. The furthest point in the house from everyone," remarked Julian, setting the books down at a table. "We can talk freely here without fear of being overheard."

"Are you sure?" I asked him wearily.

"Positive. The only voice I can hear is yours." Julian tapped his head. "If I can't hear them, they can't hear us."

I looked at the liquor bottles and paint. "I guess you come up here often?"

"Only when I want true peace and quiet," said Julian. He pulled a sheet free, revealing a small oak table beneath. I coughed at the upturned dust, but Julian paid it no mind. "Being drunk all the time can be considered dangerous to some."

"What's with the paint?" I asked.

"That?" Julian pulled up two chairs. "The singular time I saw a therapist, she recommended it. She claimed I had a talent for it and said it might be 'healthy' for me," he said with air quotes before slumping into the chair. "Waste of time and money, but I gave it the old college try."

Julian talked freely without consideration, and though he wasn't outright drunk, I knew he was feeling it.

"Why did you bring me here?" I asked.

"I want to help you." He splayed books across the table. "Something about this riddle feels off to me, and helping you feels right."

"Thank you. I appreciate it." I smiled. "I don't mean to be headstrong or naïve, but I just want to do what's right, and abandoning Derek just—I just can't do it."

"I get it," Julian agreed. "Dayton and Luka, they have their differences, but they're not so different. God forbid either of them realize it."

He hit the nail on the head with that one. The more I saw them together, the more easily I pictured how they had worked together before. Seamlessly, I imagined. Some people just clicked, and Dayton and Luka were a pair that worked better together than apart. So what really drove a wedge between them, and why had Dayton tried to kill him?

"How did you ever get through to Dayton?" I asked. "He's gentler with you. Less cruel."

Julian grinned sympathetically and lifted his head. "I never really did. I listened to him. I paid attention."

"Every time I feel like I gain an inch, he jumps three feet." I sighed.

"I knew Dayton before his families' deaths. He used to be this animated, funny kid, full of life. The life of the party." Julian smiled. "While he still looks like himself, he's someone else. A person that even I'm still getting to know. Every day is a surprise with him. I just know he's going through something that I will never understand."

I thought over his words for a moment. Dayton was a juxtaposition of ever-changing moods. One moment, he showed a sliver of compassion, and the next, he was lost in a fiery rage. There was no telling what his temperament might be.

"He was a beast before you showed up," Julian added. "He still is, but it's almost tempered. You're able to see through the front he puts up. It amuses me to watch the two of you."

"Why?" I asked. Julian gave me a pointed look; he could see right through me.

"He wants you to be safe, and you keep running into wild situations at will." Julian shrugged. "You rile him up, and he doesn't know how to handle it."

"I don't mean to," I said. "Why do you put up with his rudeness?"

"He was there for me in my darkest days. I still have the scars to prove it." Julian gripped his right wrist. "Dayton might be goddamn rude, but he would move heaven and hell for those he cares about."

Pain glinted behind Julian's eyes. He had a calming nature, like the golden hour at sunset. He was there to make you laugh and find light in the darkness, like the easy friendship I shared with Derek, the easiness that breaks through the toughest of people. It made sense that Dayton had Julian.

"Alright," I said, turning from him. "This riddle. Where do we start?"

Julian plucked a book from his stack, his finger tracing the page. He began flicking through pages fast like lightning. Something about his expression felt familiar, but I couldn't place it. Julian scrawled across a page and pushed it toward me.

"'*Come and seek him, only where the found is lost,*'" I said.

"*Found is lost,*" Julian muttered under his breath.

"Maybe that goes with the '*Find us where gone is time*'?"

"Speak it aloud."

"*Come and seek him, only where the found is lost. Find us where gone is time.*" I spoke slowly, enunciating each word.

"Where is time gone?" Julian grumbled. "That doesn't even make sense. Time is a constant thread. It can't be flipped on or off."

"Maybe it's metaphorical?" I suggested. "It could be referring to the essence of time. Gone is time could also mean a certain time frame?"

Julian furrowed his eyebrows in thought. "Maybe, but that seems too simple. Kaser is clever. He will make you think until you wish you couldn't." He trailed his fingers over another book. "*Found is lost. Gone is time,*" he muttered. "It says to seek him there..."

"Maybe it's backwards," I said. "It's a riddle, right? Maybe the lost is found, and time is gone."

Julian shot his head up fast, his green eyes wild. "The Temple is more than a sanctuary for werewolves. We keep ancient archives of extensive history. I remember learning the history of a particular group in school, but I'm not sure if my theory is right."

He scowled and tossed the book aside and grabbed another, flipping through the pages. Making a low noise in his throat, he shook his head and clicked his tongue. He rapidly flipped through pages, Julian's eyes moving fast over the words. I glanced over his shoulder at the blurred lines while Julian muttered a slew of vulgar words before finally pointing at a page.

"Nixies!" he exclaimed. "'*Come and seek him, only where the found is lost. Find us where the time is gone!*' It's Nixies!"

I stared at him blankly. "Nixies?"

"Lemme tell you, I feel incredibly thick for not figuring it out sooner." Julian skimmed excitedly through the pages. "'*The realm of Nixies can be accessed through any body of water as long as the voyager keeps hold of the stone artifact of the Fae.*'"

"What are you talking about?" I wasn't following.

"Ah, sorry. sorry," Julian glanced up from the book. "I get absent minded sometimes—forgetful. Anyway, Nixies are tricksters; they're shapeshifting mermaids and cousins of the Fae, though Fae no longer exist. The realm of Nixies isn't in one place. It just exists and can only be accessed with the right tools."

After grappling with the world of werewolves, I didn't feel shocked by his revelation of other supernatural beings. I felt compelled to know more. I tried to wrap my head around an image of what they might look like but couldn't imagine anything that didn't resemble the Loch Ness monster.

"Why would Kaser be leading us to them?" I asked.

"The Infinite Artifacts—the Moonstone—it would be a genius spot to hide it. Werewolves don't tread in the land of Nixies; we are too domineering and rough. The Nixies are peaceful folk; they prefer solitude. There's an agreed understanding that they are to be left alone." Julian paused and gave me a look of warning. "But just because they're gentle doesn't mean they're not lethal."

"So, theoretically, we go there—although we're unwelcome—we find and steal an Infinite Artifact, and somehow, we get out alive, all because

Kaser wants the Artifact, and I want Derek back?" I sighed and rubbed my temples. "It can't be easy, can it?"

"It could be with the right tools. It might not be simple, but it's not impossible," Julian mused. "The Temple is like a supernatural powerhouse. There are access points for each realm within the grounds. You take the Fae stone, go to the lake, and an entrance appears."

"Fae stone?"

"A stone enchanted by Fae magic, given freely to other supernaturals at their discretion," Julian said as if it were the most obvious thing. "There's not many left since there isn't Fae magic to enchant them anymore. But we have one, and it could offer you entry to their realm."

"And then there's a guided pathway leading straight to the Artifact?" I asked hopefully.

"Funny." Julian grinned. "You ask for an audience with the leader, whom I believe is Nøkkeroser now. You request his help. If he sends you away, threaten to poison his lands with silver toxins; oddly, that's a universal poison amongst the supernatural."

Ordinarily, I'd like to think I wouldn't consider any of this: frolicking to foreign lands, poisoning innocents. Yet Derek's life was at stake, and that made this an extraordinary circumstance. I couldn't feel bad about bending my morals. Not for him.

"Um, would threatening them really be the wisest move?" I asked. "It might make them angry."

"It's only a threat." Julian shrugged. "You won't really poison the waters; it would kill them and then we'd have a war."

"I don't know," I admitted. "I can't do this by myself, but if I go to Luka with this, he'll just dismiss me. I wish Dayton would be more willing to help."

"I would offer my service, but I'd get us both killed," said Julian. "I know my way around weapons, but I'm no solider like Dayton."

The door suddenly flew open. "What is going on up here?"

I stared at Julian, appalled; he said he'd know if anyone was coming. I gambled on turning around, and when I did, Dayton stomped into the room like an aggressive bear, his hands in fists and his muscles tensed; dark fabric stretched over the swells of his arms.

"Ah, Dayton." Julian didn't turn to face him. "Normally, your presence wouldn't be as... unsettling."

"Oh? And why is that?" Dayton snarled.

"What gave us away? Was it sneaking around? The exchanged looks of sympathy?" Julian ambled. "Just let me know, so I can be better about it next time."

"*Jules*," Dayton growled. "What's going on?"

"I want to find the Artifact and exchange it for Derek," I answered. "The riddle leads us to the Nixies realm, and it's worth following. I don't know why Kaser wanted it to be me, but I'm willing to try."

"*Mare*," Dayton said, sounding perplexed, frustrated, and confused all at once. "Have you lost your goddamn mind?"

I stood up to face him, crossing my arms over my chest. "Maybe," I said. "But I can't sit around waiting for something bad to happen, not when I know Derek's in danger. Maybe it's foolish to pursue, but if Derek's well-being is on the line, it's not a question for me."

"Mare," Dayton said, more patiently this time, despite his hands white-knuckled at his sides. "I'm asking you as your Consort to think rationally here. Please."

Desperation glinted in his golden eyes, begging me to yield.

"You're asking me to stay back and do nothing when I know Derek is danger," I argued. "I'm not craving a dangerous quest out of boredom."

"If something happens and you get hurt—" Dayton's temper fumed. "I won't even say what I might do."

"I have to do this," I said. "But I would like it if you went with me, Dayton."

Dayton's eyes softened marginally, and he dragged a hand down his face. "Well, I won't sit back and let you walk into a suicide mission." He loosed a breath. "Tell me what you've found."

Chapter 24

Although Dayton agreed to help, he thought the whole idea was a disastrous one. But he didn't go back on his word. In his room, he assembled the various weapons he thought we might need. Julian helped, too, scampering off to collect the Fae stone; he even procured a silver bullet that he melted down in case we needed to resort to threats.

I finished getting myself together. I plaited my hair and zipped up my jacket, my hands trembling as I reached for the mug of coffee that had long since cooled. I choked down the stale remnants in a futile attempt to chase exhaustion as the clock on the wall struck midnight. I streaked across the room and yanked the curtains shut, extinguishing all light, then quietly, I left.

I ventured down the narrow halls and stole nervous glances over my shoulder. Julian planned to distract Luka—how, I didn't know—but Julian seemed confident enough in his ability. While I didn't doubt Julian per se, Luka was scarily stealthy, especially if he suspected something was amiss. I descended the stairs, peering into the entryway for Dayton. My foot missed the last step, and I clapped a hand over my mouth to keep from squealing, catching myself on the corner of a side table. The sharp end sliced my palm from the impact, and I squeezed my hand shut.

No more than two seconds later, Dayton appeared at the top of the stairs, practically floating down like a ghost for all the noise he made. I tried to hide my hand behind my back, but he grabbed my elbow and pulled my hand to him. His touch was warm, sending tingles up my arms, and if it weren't for the fierce look in his eyes, I might have protested.

"If you can't manage to walk down the steps without hurting yourself, then maybe we shouldn't go," he hissed.

I rolled my eyes and snapped my hand back. "It's annoying that I can't be hurt without you knowing. I just tripped."

Dayton was clad in black fighting leathers, with two twin blades strapped to his back. At his waist, he carried his weapons belt, and I noticed the glittering opal stones on the hilt. Even his tightly laced boots had extra throwing knives concealed in hidden compartments. He ran a hand through his tousled hair and scowled.

"Go over the plan again," I said.

He reached into his weapons belt and pulled out a shimmering, milky white stone. "This is an ancient Fae stone that will guide us into the Nixie realm. It's like a fragment of the portal we went through to get to Lycan. Think of it as a key."

"And the Temple just had that?" I asked.

I sensed his thinning patience, but he answered me anyway. "The Temple is one of the most well-guarded werewolf sanctuaries there is, and aside from being a sanctuary, it protects ancient relics and artifacts from getting into the wrong hands."

I nodded. "If you didn't have the key, what's in the lake?"

"I don't know? An open terrain of water?" he jabbed. "No more questions. We don't have a lot of time before Luka interferes."

As if on cue, a long howl sounded in the distance—once, and then twice.

Dayton took off toward the garage, and I followed. Tearing open the door, he twirled a pair of keys around his fingers in seconds. He jumped over the glossy exterior of his motorcycle with the ease of someone used to the rush and whirlwind of a quick getaway. Throwing a helmet at me, I caught it and jumped on.

"The death bike, really?" I exclaimed. He hadn't divulged this part of the plan.

Dayton laughed, and the sound of it shocked me. He was so careful in everything he did—from every word to every glance—the sound of his laugh was like his mask had slipped, parts of his true self leaking through.

"Luka will be scenting for my wolf, not my death bike. It will give us a little extra leeway," he said. "C'mon, we don't have a lot of time."

I hesitantly grabbed onto Dayton's waist. The last time I had been in this position was when Dayton found me in the woods and took me to the Temple. From his attitude alone, I'd half wondered then if I was holding onto a ticking time bomb. I didn't doubt that Dayton still was, but I had more confidence that if—or when—he exploded, it wouldn't be at me.

Dayton revved the engine of the bike as the garage door squealed open. We took off like a rocket. My stomach lurched, and I closed my eyes, pressing the bulk of the helmet into Dayton's back. The engine purred as he willed it to go faster, and despite the whirl of air blocking other noise, the thudding of paws against the earth was loud enough to break through. Snarls and howls sounded from close behind. Luka was gaining on us.

"We have about a two-minute jump on Luka," Dayton shouted over the engine's roar. "But the second the lake is in view, you have to run like a bat out of hell."

I tightened my grip around Dayton and nodded. Before us, the lake materialized, but it seemed too far. Luka would surely catch up to us.

As if reading my mind, Dayton jerked the bike to the left, and as he did, his whole body tensed. The brakes squealed as he threw his weight to the right, yet I lost my grip at the sudden stop and flew backward. I tumbled over the earth, leaves crunching beneath me as grass stained my clothes and twigs scratched my skin. My spine smacked against the base of a tree and breath sliced through me as I gasped.

"Mare!"

Dayton was at my side in moments to help me up, gently gripping my elbow to steady me.

"I'm okay," I wheezed upon seeing his troubled expression. "Really. I'll be okay."

My body felt better despite the dull ache echoing through my bones from shock. I looked to what stopped us and gasped. We overlooked the edge of a clifftop, which Dayton almost sent us off. There was no way the bike could have made the jump without proper momentum.

"We have to jump," said Dayton. He took several steps back.

"What?" I screeched. "Are you insane?"

"Mare, *your* idea is insane, but I'm entertaining it. We're werewolves, and we're going to jump this," said Dayton. After a quick inhale, he took off.

I screamed as he ran forward and leapt off the cliff's edge. My heart thudded in my chest as I expected gravity to do its worst. Dayton's claws flashed in the moonlight as he reached the other side, grappling the earth with his claws to keep from plummeting. I watched him swing up to the other side and shout for me to go.

Much nearer than ever before, I heard Luka gaining on us. I thought desperately of Derek. He was the reason why I was doing this. I had to jump.

I took a breath of courage, then ran forward and leaped. I screamed like a banshee, and my limbs flailed in the air. My heart dropped when I realized I was going down faster than a sinking ship. I missed the other side by at least two feet... all of that to sacrifice myself to the earth.

I locked eyes with Dayton and sensed his rising panic. He threw himself toward the edge, his arm outstretched. He wouldn't make it in time. I gasped when his sweaty palms tightened over my wrist as he held me dangling over the cliff's edge. In seconds, he yanked me up, my body wobbling like Jello as we stumbled back. I fell atop Dayton, catching myself on his chest with my elbows. We both panted, hearts beating too fast. Our gazes locked, sucking the air from both of us, as if something pulled us closer together. It felt entirely all-consuming being this close to Dayton with our foreheads nearly touching. Dayton leaned his head back and closed his eyes, inhaling deeply.

I pushed away from Dayton, allowing normal airflow to return to my lungs. He stood as alert as ever, his nostrils flaring as he inhaled. He didn't have to say it. We both took off toward the lake. My heart pounded as I heard Luka's approach. He was so close. His thunderous steps drew near, and I was starting to doubt the logistics of this plan.

Dayton pointed toward a small wooden dock, shouting something about a boat. The dock itself appeared rickety; smothered in moss, vines crawled up the wooden rails, and a thick layer of algae coated the ground of the dock. Ordinarily, I would have slipped, but the boots I had on protected me. We clamored to the dock as the unsteady wood squeaked beneath our weight. At the end of the dock, a cream-colored rowboat floated in the water.

Dayton fumbled in his pocket; he glanced back and cursed. I followed his gaze to the shore. Luka. He barreled over to us in wolf form, his blue eyes glowing.

With the Fae stone in his hand, Dayton looked down at me. "The portal will only stay open for a few moments. We have to move quickly. Do you understand?"

I nodded. Dayton flicked his wrist, and the stone skipped across the water's surface. With each ripple, the water rumbled and gurgled as if being awakened. Light emerged from the boiling water and then at once, it burst, spraying water over us as the lake separated to reveal a glittering veil in the distance.

Dayton hurtled forward, jumping off the dock and into the small rowboat. I followed, grabbing his hand to lower myself down. The boat rocked atop the water, but Dayton didn't hesitate to slice the rope anchoring us to the dock. He yanked the oars and took us through the veil, a sweet-smelling mist settling over us. It closed like a curtain as we crossed, but not before I glimpsed the outline of Luka on the dock and heard his echoing howl of rage.

The water we glided atop was crystal clear. Willowing branches of pastel pinks and blues overhung the river's pass, the weeping arches like a canopy, enclosing us. An air of peace welcomed us, a land undisturbed by violence or gore. It was a nice change of pace.

I glanced at Dayton, who threw his head back, laughing. I stared in utter astonishment as he continued to laugh, hearty and deep, then slowly, he composed himself, the laughter dwindling like the fading of a whistle. I wanted him to laugh again.

"That was insane," Dayton balked, awestruck. He leaned forward, and for a second, I thought he was going to grab me, but he gripped the oars instead and we slowly started to move. "I can't believe you convinced me to do that; I can't believe we escaped *Luka*!"

I expelled a long breath. "It was getting dicey there at the end," I said, glancing down. The Fae stone sat at the bottom of the boat, and I reached for it, handing it to Dayton. "Here, we'll need this to get out."

Dayton glanced at the stone and then at me. "You hold onto it, I trust you."

I nearly fell off the side of the boat. For someone so guarded and reserved, it felt like a privilege to be trusted by Dayton, and whatever friendship we were forming, it now seemed solidified. I grinned at him and peered at the scenic view.

"This place is gorgeous," I said. Neon-colored lily pads floated past us; the vibrant colors reminded me of Julian's ever-changing hair. "Look at all of this."

In the water's reflection, I could see Dayton, but he was looking at me. I turned toward him, and he sucked in a breath, turning away.

"What are those?" I asked, pointing toward the water at small creatures zigzagging around the boat. They gathered like a school of fish, keeping pace with us while sloshing through the water. They were no more than three or four inches, cobalt blue, with sharp gills at their sides.

"Naiads," Dayton said, frowning at them. "Don't pay attention to them; they crave attention. They're hatchlings of Nixies; they're like toddlers. Mischievous buggers."

"Where are the Nixies?"

Dayton gazed ahead, narrowing his golden eyes while peering into the distance.

I screamed as a long, pointed object propelled toward me at eye-level. My hands shot up, and I managed to catch it. It was a trident, at least three feet in length, with three sharp and jagged prongs. It vibrated in my hands from the impact, a low hum emitting from it. I gulped. It would have pierced my throat if I hadn't seen it; it came out of nowhere.

Still balking, I dropped it and glanced at Dayton, surprised by his own lack of reaction. He appeared frozen, as if fear seized his insides and held his body hostage. In my peripheral, another trident soared, but this time, aimed at Dayton.

"Dayton, move!" I screeched, barreling into him.

He winced as the trident narrowly missed me, but not before slicing my cheek. Dayton's shoulder took the brunt of the fall, and his body tensed as if realizing the severity of what happened. His eyes were wild as he touched his cheek, his wound matching mine. In a blur, he pushed me off him and grabbed the oars. He glided over the water with precision and had us shoreside in moments. Leaping out of the boat, Dayton stormed onto land, with me following quick on his heels.

He whirled on me and I staggered back. "What the fuck was that?"

I blinked before realizing he was referring to me. Was he angry I saved him? "We were under attack, and you froze," I said. "You didn't see the trident and you weren't moving!"

"So, you thought the most logical thing to do was to throw yourself into the line of fire?" he thundered. "You could've gotten your head severed from your body!"

"You could have died." I crossed my arms over her chest.

He made a disgruntled noise and began walking into the woods for cover. "You don't get to hurt yourself on account of my well-being. That's not an option. It's out of the picture."

I shook my head and fell into step beside him. "Too bad."

"Too bad? No, no, not 'too bad.' Are you out of your mind?"

I rolled my eyes. Overhead, thick vines blocked our path. Dayton drew his sword and started cutting them away.

"You're not thinking clearly," I said. "You're just mad because you didn't see it."

"I'm mad because I'm the one who's supposed to get hurt, not you!"

I understood his point from a Consort point of view—protector and protected, and all that—but still, I said, "Too bad, Dayton. I wasn't going to watch you die. You could at least say thank you."

He snorted, cutting back more vines. "Yes, thank you for taking me on your suicide mission."

"Why are you cutting the vines away?" I ignored his sarcasm, trying to keep the edge from my voice.

"They're in the way," he grumbled, cutting another bunch.

"If this were my homeland, I wouldn't take kindly to strangers tearing it apart."

"I'm not looking to make friends," he snarled.

"If I asked you to stop, would you?"

He ripped more vines apart. "You haven't asked."

"Please stop it," I said. "You're just angry."

He shook his head. "Yeah, well, I can only imagine why."

I bit my tongue to keep from my sharp reply. We continued in silence. It always seemed one step forward and three steps back with Dayton; maybe I didn't know him as well as I thought. If only he'd be willing to let me piece together the puzzles in his head, to pull on the threads in his mind. I focused on the exotic greenery and surrounding flowers, yet Dayton's sword slicing every two seconds made it difficult.

"Did you try to kill Luka?" I asked, surprising us both.

Dayton sucked in a breath. "Luka told you?"

"I'm more surprised that you didn't," I said, unable to keep the waver from my voice. "You didn't answer the question either."

Dayton appeared to carefully think through his answer. "It's not that simple."

"I doubt anything is ever simple when it comes to you, Dayton." I ducked under a low branch.

"Is this really the best time to be having this conversation?" he asked. "We're in imminent danger here."

I laughed. "We're *always* in imminent danger. Really, what is the difference?"

I noticed his smile trying to break through. "You seem to be a common factor when it comes to the danger."

A figure moved ahead in the opposite direction. I glimpsed the sharp points of ears and a button nose. Another zipped past, moving swiftly through the trees and vines like objects passing through water. The creatures were a brilliant shade of cobalt, their movements stealthy amid the shadows. If Dayton noticed, he didn't comment.

"No thanks to you," I said. I bit my bottom lip as I considered my words. "I don't know what happened between you and Luka, but I know that if you wanted Luka dead, he would be."

Dayton spun so quickly I didn't realize what happened until I was on the ground with him pressed atop me. I almost yelled at him to get off, yet his sharp glare kept me quiet as he peered around with steel in his eyes, seeing something I obviously hadn't.

"They're watching us," he whispered.

"Being on the ground does what then?" I snapped.

I shoved him off, and he let go of me without preamble. As Dayton moved to stand, he noticed—at the same time I did—a pool of mud encasing his legs. I swore it hadn't been there moments before. Each movement he made dragged him further into the wet, sticky mud.

"Get me something to grab onto!" he said.

My eyes widened as he sunk deeper. I searched for something to grab, deciding on a large stick wedged within the soil. I held it out to him, just as a trident whizzed in front of me, piercing the stick and sending it soaring. Dayton growled, searching for the culprit. He was nearly waist deep.

"Here, take my hand." I crouched and reached for him.

"No!" he yelled. "Jesus, stay back. I don't need you stuck in here, too."

I rolled my eyes and grabbed a low hanging vine instead. This was thicker, like rope, and I tested its sturdiness with both hands before throwing it at Dayton, who caught it. The second he did, it crumbled to nothing.

"Hm, maybe if you hadn't been cutting them away earlier, they would have helped," I said, raising my chin.

"Mare, I'm literally *sinking* to my death," he snarled. "You could be a little more helpful."

"Okay, fine," I said. "For your headstone, do you want it to say, 'Death by drowning in a pile of mud' or 'Death by stubbornly refusing to take Maris' hand?'"

Dayton glared, and I loosed an exasperated breath.

"Dayton, c'mon. Just take my hand." I reached out to him, practically pleading as the mud rose to his chest. "Let me help you. Please."

Reluctantly, he took my hand. His grip in mine was strong, and for a second, I thought he'd accidentally pull me into it. Digging my heels into the earth, I pulled, feeling the strain of the mud as it suctioned him deeper into its clutches. I clenched my jaw and growled until the mud started to bubble. I steeled my mind to the task at hand, and with one hefty pull, I yanked Dayton free. He rose out of it, grunting in pain as his shoulder popped. He stumbled and landed on his knees. Staring down at himself, a thick layer of mud drenched his clothes.

Panting, Dayton stood and reached for a weapon on instinct. He paused, glancing down at himself and then the mud. "You've got to be kidding me!"

"What?"

Dayton shook his head and prowled past me to where the trident had landed. Mud squished in his shoes as he walked and picked up the trident. It seemed small in his hands as he tested its weight, whirling it and holding it up like he planned to throw it.

"I smell like shit. The shithole ate my weapons, and now I only have this shitty pointed stick that needs sharpening." Dayton shook his head and stormed past me.

I suppressed the urge to laugh. "You're still a werewolf. That counts for something."

Dayton didn't bother replying and stormed ahead in silence. He attempted to slice down the overhanging vines and branches with the trident, but it seemed an impossible feat. It was better this way. I feared we annoyed the Nixies already with his behavior.

I tried to tap into my senses and strained to hear or scent them but came up short. I could only hear the running of water in the distance and smell the overwhelming scent of flowers. I thought I detected a giggle behind me, but it was too faint to be sure. Instead, I focused on keeping up with Dayton, who quickened his gait.

He stopped at a large waterfall, and I gasped, straining my neck to peer at the massive structure crafted from jagged silver stones. Crystal blue water spilled from the top and gushed through the middle, pooling into a larger river at the bottom, where rocks protruded in all sizes and directions. The shore was small, layered in various dark pebbles. In the water, figures moved. I looked to Dayton.

"Dayton," I said uneasily. I reached to grab his wrist and pulled him back. "What is that?"

Dayton searched the water, then stood before me and raised the trident. "Nixies. We walked into their nest."

That sounded right, considering our luck so far. A scaly creature with jagged teeth leaped from the water toward us, wielding a sharp trident identical to the one Dayton held. Dayton snarled and struck the nixie, who released a loud, high-pitched wail, falling to the ground in a slump. I winced as blood pooled from the creature who lay unmoving on the ground.

Dayton reached into a pocket in his jacket and held the vial of the melted silver bullet Julian had made. It still didn't feel right to use it—even if it was just a threat—but I said nothing as six more Nixies emerged from the water. Each wore identical looks of rage, their dark, pitiless eyes glaring and mouths foaming at the sight of us. Dayton's own fangs extended and his sharp claws unfurled. Unanimously, they all hissed. The Nixies were strange, gangly creatures with green and blue scales and large bug eyes. They closed in on us.

"One more step, and I drop this," Dayton warned, uncorking the vial of silver. The Nixies hissed, and Dayton made a show of tipping the vial, almost spilling it. The Nixies' only defense was their tridents they raised toward us. "Hear us out before you run us out."

Another figure protruded from the water, and my spine straightened. Dayton followed my gaze to where another Nixie broke the surface. This one was notably bigger than the others and glowered darkly at us. A golden crown perched atop his head, waist-length black hair spilling over his scaly body like ink. He assessed us with eyes narrowed to slits, possessing a trident easily twice his size. He stepped away from the rest, who lowered their weapons as he strode slowly toward us. Dayton rumbled in warning.

"The Moons Children are not welcome here," said the Nixie, his voice deep and raspy. "Who are you?"

"That isn't your business. It's your problem if you step closer to us with that thing. I will not hesitate to fight you," Dayton said with venom. "I like my odds."

I suppressed the urge to chide Dayton for his rudeness.

The large Nixie man laughed, and the rest joined in. "Brave words to use against me."

"I know who you are, Nøkkeroser," said Dayton with a twisted smile, inching toward him. "I'm looking for someone who is most likely up to no good and asking questions he should not ask."

Nøkkeroser narrowed his eyes. "You talk about another up to no good, yet you come here demanding things and threatening my people? Ruining our sacred lands." The water shifted behind them, and I turned to where a herd of Nixies swam towards us. Dayton pressed closer to me.

"We're looking for Kaser Odessa," I blurted, stepping in front of Dayton. He grabbed my wrist, forcing me still, yet I continued to face Nøkkeroser and imbued calmness into my voice. "Do you know him?"

Nøkkeroser stepped forward, watching me with curious eyes. He extended his large trident toward me, and I did my best to keep my cool as my heart rattled in my chest. Touching the trident to my chin, Nøkkeroser lifted my gaze to meet his.

Dayton pulled me back behind him. "Don't touch her."

"Does the little wolf have a weakness?" Nøkkeroser cooed, refusing to take his eyes off me. "No longer brave now, are you, with your damsel being threatened?"

"I'm no damsel," I snarled.

He continued to study me like pages in a book. "Hmm, well, you're familiar, but I know we've never met." He scrunched his caterpillar eyebrows together. "Oh, I see it. It's all in the eyes. You're Lukas Bakar's sister."

"What's your point?"

"He is a friend of mine," Nøkkeroser said, almost hesitantly. "The young Alpha has made a name for himself over the years."

That didn't surprise me in the least. If Luka was half as powerful as everyone said, it made sense he'd have connections with the strangest of folk. Yet if someone like Nøkkeroser could easily identify me as Luka's sister, who knew what would happen if the wrong person did?

"Luka has no friends," Dayton interjected, swinging his trident. "He has made that clear."

"Friend, ally, all the same," dismissed Nøkkeroser, tilting his head. "We see, and we trust." He stared at Dayton. "You're unkind and arrogant. You expect trust yet refuse it in return. I cannot help you. Daresay, if you leave now, we will leave you untouched and allow you both safe departure."

Nøkkeroser started to slither back into the water, yet a shot of desperation flashed through me. He was my only chance to save Derek, and he slowly slipped away with the other Nixies who sank beneath the water's surface.

"Wait!" I bellowed. "You spoke of my friend and his arrogance, but not of mine. You can still help me."

Nøkkeroser shook his head. "Clever girl." He grinned savagely. "I know what you seek; many before have trudged these lands for it."

"Please." I stepped forward. "I need to save someone important to me, or else he might die."

"Others have sought it," Nøkkeroser warned. "Others seek it now."

Kaser, no doubt. That didn't make sense, though. Why send us here if he planned to send someone else from his Cadre? I pushed the thought aside and refocused on Nøkkeroser.

"If you can help us in any way, it wouldn't be forgotten," I said.

"When you die on your quest, then I get nothing out of this," he said with a sneer.

"What do you want?" Dayton added curtly, holding out the vial. "You want this?"

Nøkkeroser's gaze narrowed. "Civilizations are not destroyed by one thing; it starts as a wound, then it grows infected," he said, glancing between Dayton and me. "You must destroy that wound before it gets worse; before there's nothing left to be done."

Yeah, like that's not freaking ominous.

Nøkkeroser took the vial from Dayton, dropping it into an invisible pocket at his side. He slithered back like a snake over water, slowing sinking into its depths. As he did, the waterfall yawned open behind him, and the waters stilled. Not even a ripple passed through. The water crashed before us suddenly, and the impact sent us both flying. Dayton grabbed me and pulled me closer to his chest as the water consumed us.

302

CHAPTER 25

It felt like broken guitar strings cutting my throat as I screamed. Water cocooned us like a blanket as fear pumped through my veins. Dayton's arms remained around my body, holding me to him. He took the brunt of the impact as we collided against hard stone. He grunted as we skidded to a halt. We both stayed put, panting. Dayton was the first to move, gliding his hands up my back and around my arms, stroking the top of my head.

Assessing me through his long curling eyelashes, a wild look glinted in his golden eyes. "Are you alright?" he asked.

I only managed a slight nod, my voice caught in my throat. He stared at me for another moment, tracing a finger along the side of my face. His touch sent tingles through me, and I shivered. I needed to move off him. Wobbling, I stood up, and so did Dayton, running a hand through his messy hair that curled at the ends. I bit my lower lip and looked away from him.

The cave was dark, illuminated only by the light from the water that launched us here. It glowed, appearing ethereal, like a pool of electric blue ink. Droplets of water from the ceiling echoed as they fell. Dark, dank stone surrounded us, and a rusty smell like old pennies filled my senses. The chill combined with the wetness of my clothes made me shiver.

"Mare, here." Dayton came forward, shucking his jacket off. I started to protest, but his gaze stopped me. He tucked the jacket around my shoulders, and I relished the comfort of it.

"Thank you," I croaked.

Dayton looked around the cave, tracing his fingers over the stone. I looked at the small pool of water, peering inside. It was clear blue, like the water Nøkkeroser and the other Nixies had emerged from. I crouched, reaching for it. The cool liquid pooled over my palm, and I squinted at its depths. How was it possible to be thrown from water so shallow?

"I think we're underground." My voice echoed.

"What clued you into that?" said Dayton sarcastically.

Long cylindrical stones protruded from the ceiling into points; water dripped from them, and a droplet fell on my cheek. I brushed it away and began to pace the cave. It was small, and it didn't take long to reach the back. I clicked my tongue, trying to suppress my irritation at insisting on an adventure that heeded little results.

"Well, Mare. Now what?" asked Dayton. "We're here. We made it through the Nixie realm. You got us sent to where we needed to be. What's the next move?"

While Dayton didn't seem frustrated, I knew him well enough to read between the lines. "I don't know," I said truthfully. "I didn't think we'd be thrown into a cave. I thought that maybe you might have some insight once we got here."

Dayton rested both his hands behind his head. "I don't have all the answers; I'm not like Luka," he said. "We have to find one of the Infinite Artifacts to begin piecing together the Moonstone. That's all we have to go on."

"Okay, okay," I said, studying the walls. "There has to be a reason we were brought here. It has to mean something."

I traced my fingers over the rough, jagged stones. Small lines etched into the rocks—undecipherable scratches. I glanced around at the other walls to find similar markings, and before I beckoned Dayton, he stood directly behind me.

"Could this mean anything?" I asked.

A shrill, high-pitched laugh ricocheted across the cave. Dayton whipped around, immediately on the defense. He backed up, using his body to shield mine against the cave wall. Without any weapons, he seemed oddly vulnerable. The girlish giggle erupted again, and the water began to ripple. Dayton lunged toward it, his claws extended.

Yet the air changed once he moved from my side. I stiffened as hands wrapped around my neck, claws kissing my throat. I didn't dare move. The perpetrator cackled again, and this time, the familiarity of it shook me to my core.

Dayton was a swarm of unwavering anger; he turned toward us, his rage ignited. As he moved, his teeth lengthened to fangs and his nails to claws. His irises rippled into molten gold, and his low growl shook the cave, the stone rumbling beneath him with each step.

"Shetani," he growled.

Of course. The person I begged Luka not to kill now had her claws at my throat. Just my luck.

Shetani giggled before breaking her silence. "I see I've struck a chord in you," her shrill voice boomed. "Before anyone wastes their breath asking, Kaser sent me. He has his own means to export his followers in and out of where he wants them."

"Why did he send you?" I asked, despite my precarious position. "He sent us to do his dirty work."

"I'm here to ensure it's done and act as motivation if it isn't," she answered. "Case in point, it has taken you far too long to get to this point, therefore..."

Shetani moved her claws to grab my braid, yanking hard. I writhed to escape her, which only amused her more. Clutching my hair tightly, she exposed my throat further, open and vulnerable. She hummed, her claws teasing my throat again. Dayton lunged at her but halted with great restraint. One well-placed puncture would have me bleeding out. Shetani pressed a single claw into my neck.

"You never had the guts for merciless death. That was always Kato's specialty. He was the live wire," said Dayton, his voice stone cold. "Besides, if Kaser wanted her dead, he wouldn't have sent us on a goose chase."

Shetani stiffened behind me, Dayton's words throwing her off-kilter. "I can still hurt her," she seethed, raking her claws over my cheek. She threw me to the ground.

I cried out, hot blood spilling down my face while Shetani cackled at my anguish. I fell to my knees, yet with each passing second, the pain dulled. Dayton advanced on Shetani, crimson dripping down his face, too.

"The rumors are true, then. She's a two-for-one deal," Shetani purred and darted out of Dayton's reach. "Cut her, and you bleed, Mr. Consort. Well, hurting her just became that much more fun."

I distantly wondered if the Nixies watched this escapade, wondering whether to intervene. Somehow, I doubted it.

A battle cry echoed behind me as Shetani formed a wolf, with fur as bright as freshly fallen snow. Dayton advanced, a challenge rippling from his angered features. They paced the cave like dancers, each move practiced and precise. Dayton dodged a blow, yet Shetani gained an opening, pushing down with massive paws against his chest. They moved too fast for me to even consider finding an opening. Dayton flew hard across the cave, landing against the wall with a grunt while Shetani towered above him, sharp teeth bared into a snarl.

Dayton laughed jadedly. "Do it, Shetani. *Kill me.*"

"*No!*" I shrieked desperately.

Ice coated my veins, and the rage had claws curling from my fingertips. The sensation felt like razor blades slicing off the tips of my fingers. I had only a moment to balk before launching myself at Shetani, my claws extended. My canines protruded, too, the pain like biting into a jawbreaker. It felt like something guided me, willing me by force to land on Shetani's back. I raked my claws against her spine and she yelped, bucking in protest. She threw me off, and I splashed into the water. My side throbbed where I landed. I stepped back as Shetani advanced through the rippling waves and she transitioned back into the wild girl with bouncy white curls and wild eyes.

"Brave, even without your big brother to save the day," she snarled.

Shetani didn't manage more than two strides before Dayton intervened once again and their fight resumed—this time in the water. A light on the wall caught my attention from where water splashed against it. I scrambled onto the shore, grazing my fingers over the wall's surface, a glowing trail left behind from where the water touched it. A language I couldn't understand was etched into the wall, a scrawled passage written in stone.

A sharp howl drew my attention, and I spun. Dayton and Shetani circled one another like cat and mouse; Shetani was a wolf once again while Dayton was himself, bloodied and panting, yet he didn't seem willing to back down anytime soon. With Shetani's back was to me, Dayton's eyes flickered to my own for the briefest of moments, the feral wolf livid behind his eyes and begging to unleash. I jabbed my thumb back toward the wall, and his gaze quickly traced it.

Shetani reared on me then, her massive paws crushing me to the ground. I gasped desperately for air as she assessed the wall, her eyes rapidly reading over the text. Weak and tired, I couldn't fight her off.

"Stand down," said Dayton, his voice low—dangerous.

Shetani's lips curled, and she flicked out her tongue. His words challenged her, so she stood taller, her red eyes boastful as she sauntered off me. I wheezed, my hands immediately rubbing my throat as I sat up. Shetani changed back to her human skin with such ease shocked me. She kept an equal distance between Dayton and me, as if readying to pounce on either of us. Unsheathing a dagger from her belt, it gleamed silver in the light.

"You can read the old language, right?" Shetani crooned at Dayton. "You had the fancy education and all."

Dayton's eyes flicked between Shetani, the dagger, and me. "Step away from Maris before I make you."

She threw her head back and cackled. "It requires a sacrifice to get the Artifact. If it can't be Maris, then it must be you."

Shetani's dagger flew. I didn't even register moving until I shoved Shetani down to the ground, screaming. Everything moved in slow-motion as the dagger spun toward Dayton's heart. I hit the hilt with the back of my hand, and white light ricocheted off it.

A shrill ringing echoed around us, and blinding light blanketed the cave. It lasted only moments before the noise and light winked out at once, with only Dayton and me left. Wide-eyed, I looked around, expecting to see Shetani reappear. She never did. I smelled iron, and I ran to reach Dayton.

He looked as dazed as I felt, but at his side, the hilt of the dagger protruded. If I hadn't intervened, it would have embedded his heart, likely killing him within minutes. I rushed forward and caught Dayton as he fell to his knees. He fumbled, trying to grab hold of the blade, but I reached it for him. Our hands met the hilt simultaneously, and I stared at him, his eyes wide. Panic rose in me knowing he had been so close to death, and he was still hurt, though I never fathomed an outcome like this. I never would have come here if I thought I'd be putting Dayton in danger.

"No," I whispered. "Let me see it first."

Dayton's gaze snapped to my own, unfocused and diluted. "Wolfsbane is toxic to werewolves, sometimes lethal," he said lowly. "It's laced in wolfsbane; that's why it's—" he hissed, leaning back against the wall. "This is a silver blade. I'm double dipped in poison."

I stared at the blade covered in a mixture of blood and purple powder. "What does that mean?"

Dayton clutched his side, wincing. Dark laughter escaped him. "Death is really giving me a run for its money tonight."

I smelled the blood pouring from his wound and met his surly gaze. "You're not dying."

"What did you do?" he asked. "You were nowhere near that blade, and you aren't trained enough to move that fast. Don't get me started on where Shetani went."

"Shetani left on her own accord, just like she came," I said. "The rest, well, maybe I just picked things up faster than you realized."

Dayton raised his eyebrows, clearly disbelieving, yet said, "Regardless, she got me. I'm dying."

"No," I protested. "I'm going to fix this."

He ran a bloodied hand through his tousled hair, staining it. "Mare, there's nothing to be done."

"Doing nothing does just that," I said through gritted teeth, a hot spring of tears rushing behind my eyes. I blinked rapidly to keep them at bay. "Show me the wound."

The intensity of his gaze was distracting, but not as distracting as Dayton undoing his gear and tossing it aside. While his bare chest was not something I hadn't already seen, it felt oddly intimate as I sat close beside him. The blood of healed wounds dripped across his skin as his chest rose and fell in uneven breaths. The tattoo, proof of our bond, swirled from his right arm and across his chest, now climbing up his neck. My gaze wandered to where his hand clutched his side. I pulled his hand away.

Black goop spurted from the sides of the blade. Dayton grimaced as I swiped a thumb across it, the wet, thick substance like honey between my fingers. I examined the wound more closely; the hilt was practically buried in him along with the blade. Swallowing my worry, I reached my hand out, tingles running through me like sparks of electricity.

"Mare," said Dayton, warning in his tone. "You know what you're doing?"

"I never went to nursing school, but I know some stuff. Wolfsbane is poison, and it's contaminating your bloodstream," I explained. Talking helped to soothe my trembling nerves. "That dagger is coated in poison, and the longer it contaminates you without removal, the more likely infection will set in."

"The poison is the bigger concern," said Dayton. "I can't get infections as werewolf healing prevents it."

I nodded and glanced at his discarded shirt, torn and bloodied. I turned from him to slip off my borrowed jacket and peel my wet shirt off, my skin protesting as goosebumps roamed my arms. I ignored them and knelt beside the water, wringing out my shirt with trembling hands. Once satisfied it was as clean as it could be, I turned back toward Dayton. He didn't even balk at my appearance in just jeans, boots, and a black sports bra.

"You look a little pale," he said.

I shook my head. "This is going to hurt."

I reached for the hilt and yanked it out. Bones and muscles writhed with the movement as Dayton let out a low noise of pain, the only sign of his discomfort. Once the dagger was out, I gaped at its size. The blade had to be six inches long, coated in blood and gore. I let it clatter to the ground and took the shirt, pressing it against his wound.

"Can you feel the pressure I'm applying?" I asked, unable to keep the fear from my voice.

"Yes," Dayton gurgled. I noticed his complexion paled and gulped. "You might be better off just leaving me here and saving yourself."

My eyes snapped to his. "I won't leave you here to die. This Consort business is a two-way street."

He held my gaze. "That wasn't the deal."

"Too bad," I said, hands shaking. "Besides, it isn't like I can just up and leave you here."

Dayton shrugged. "The writing on the wall says you need a sacrifice to find the Artifact. It seems simple to me. Let me die, get your Artifact, and get your friend back."

"Dayton," I growled, refusing his death wish that now dangled over the both of us. I couldn't even entertain his crazy proposal. I couldn't leave

Dayton here anymore than I could leave Derek in Kaser's hands. "Please, there has to be something else I can do."

Dayton looked at me like he really me saw for the first time. "Burning out the wolfsbane would do it," he croaked. "Heat, fire, anything of the sort, really."

"Of course," I said. "Fire or heat in a cave surrounded by ice and water."

"Julian would have been the wiser choice to bring," Dayton croaked. "His survival interests far surpass my own. Plus, he never leaves home without a lighter."

It annoyed me how Dayton could be so brazen while his life hung in the balance. Death was no joke. I couldn't stand by and watch him die; I couldn't walk away from him.

Dayton's stare wavered, and he leaned his head back, eyes closing as the rise and fall of his chest slowed. "I'm sorry," he said. "I'm scaring you, I realize that. I just can't bring myself to care about—" He paused, searching for words.

"Your own well-being?" I finished for him.

Dayton's mouth quirked up slightly. "You could bond with Julian over the shared frustrations I cause you both." I pulled the shirt back an inch and reapplied it with more pressure as the blood still dripped. "I wasn't always so cynical about death."

"What changed?"

"Everything" said Dayton gruffly. "You asked me before if I tried to kill Luka and I danced around the answer because it's one of many grievances I've never atoned for. The truth is, I did try to kill Luka, and it's exactly how it sounds, but just not how it seems."

I blinked down at him, confused by his sudden admission.

"Before Luka, I had everything until it was nothing. Everything that I did have is gone, and it's my fault." Dayton swallowed hard. "My past is fucked up, Mare."

Hearing him admit that was difficult to bear, yet if he wanted to talk about his past, it had to be on his own terms. Not Luka's, not Julian's.

"You don't have to tell me anything, Dayton. I won't judge you either way."

"I want to tell you," he said. "Please, let me."

I nodded.

"I had an older brother. His name was Daniel, and I looked up to him as a kid. My father was the Captain of the Guard, a prestigious position amongst the Court. We grew up in the Moon Court amid the most elite werewolves. Daniel was politically driven like my father wanted him to be, and when he turned eighteen, he would inherit the title of lord. So, he was a good boy; he followed the rules and did what was expected of him. I didn't give a rat's ass about politics, and instead, I lavished on the benefits of court life: attention, admiration, parties, booze. I was young, dumb, attractive, and adored, and I felt untouchable."

Strangely, I could picture a younger version of Dayton, yet nothing about who he was reflected that. But I could see it. I recalled our time at the Moon Court when Istvan called Dayton a Lord. The title seemed too prestigious for someone as wild as Dayton. If Dayton had been all those things, what changed him so drastically into the person sitting before me now?

"Daniel often told me he envied me and how much easier things were for me. He had expectations to uphold and people to impress; most importantly, our father. The weight of everyone's expectations was a heavy burden to carry, but he only revealed that to me. Our father was a good man, driven and wanting the best for his kids. He told me he wanted me to be as good as Daniel, in case Daniel turned out to not be good enough. While Daniel submitted to our father's wishes without complaint, to no one's surprise, I talked back. If Daniel didn't get in with the best Cadre, I had to. If Daniel didn't graduate top of his class, I had to. You get the idea. I told my dad he was a fool to think Daniel wouldn't be good enough for any of that, and an idiot to think I'd ever want it. It was the only thing we ever fought about.

"When Daniel turned eighteen, he could inherit the title of lord so long as he proved a brave and worthy werewolf when put before the Council. This was seven years ago, when Dante was a proud member of society. Fenrir were at an all-time peak and hard to kill. My father had a plan for Daniel to find and kill a group of Fenrir living in the caves of Mount Lycan. If he did it and succeeded, he'd be a lord, and there was no doubt he would be victorious. On the night Daniel was supposed to leave for his hunt, he admitted to me that the thought of being shackled to that Court forever sickened him. He saw no way out, and despite my protests telling him to speak up, he wouldn't. I threatened to be his voice and to tell our father his true feelings, and it was the only time he shouted at me. He told me he had to do this; he had to be perfect to earn our father's love."

Dayton never opened his eyes as he spoke, yet his breathing appeared to be evening out. I peeled back the shirt again and noticed less blood loss. I only hoped that was a good sign.

"I told him he was a spineless, moronic dumbass and that I hoped he realized it before he was too far gone. He left on his hunt in a tizzy and didn't say another word to me. I followed him—discreetly. At first, I wanted to talk him out of doing it, but I knew my temper wouldn't help with that. Then, I thought I could just stop him, knock him out and drag him back home. He would have hated me for that, too, so in the end, none of that happened. When Daniel found the Fenrir nest, well, it was more than the couple my father said it would be. There was at least a dozen. He didn't attack them outright; he was smarter than that. I watched him from afar, not wanting to interfere. He drew them out, one by one, and took them out individually. It was a good tactic—it worked, even—until one came up from behind him. He didn't see it, but I did."

Dayton paused for a long moment before continuing. Opening his eyes, he stared straight ahead, his eyes void of emotion as he steeled himself. His breath dropped to short pants, and he faltered while trying to find the words.

"I killed the Fenrir in one neat blow to the head with a knife. Daniel had been shocked to see me, and I was proud. Proud I just saved my big brother from death. I was so goddamn proud that I didn't hear the Fenrir coming from behind me, but Daniel saw them, and pushed me out of the way. He was wounded, badly, and the Fenrir didn't stop coming at him. I couldn't stop it either because more were coming, and Daniel told me to run to save myself. I didn't want to, but there were so many Fenrir.

"I ran and all the while Daniel's screams echoed in my head. When I got back home, my dad was preparing celebrations for when Daniel returned. Only, he was never coming back, and it was my fault. I couldn't face my parents and admit what I did. I wrote a letter explaining everything, and then I ran far from Lycan. I threw myself into a portal and prayed I would get far, far away. I don't know where I ended up, but I found myself in the woods alone. I turned into my wolf skin to travel, and I stayed that way for weeks. Until I met Luka."

Dayton dragged a hand down his face and slowly shook his head. I didn't know what to think of his story. Losing your brother was one thing, but like that? The violence of it alone terrified me, but the thought of hearing Luka's screams as he slowly died sickened me. I understood then why Dayton was so cold and merciless. Dayton versus the world.

"I was caught amid a ravaging pack of Fenrir; I held my own pretty well, fueled by pure rage. I hated those creatures. But one misstep had me in death's grip and nearly killed me. I must have ventured into Luka's territory unknowingly because he came in guns blazing and swiftly killed each Fenrir. I was amazed by his power, and when Luka asked me who I was, I told him. He asked if I had anywhere to go, and I said no. Just the fact he had no idea who I was enticed me to him. He held no preconceived notions of me: that I was a kin slayer and a fuckup. I was simply Dayton. Luka was not as untrusting as the man he is today, and he allowed me a place in his Cadre.

"Luka's Cadre, though made up of only a few wolves, welcomed me. Renetta and Rico were there; they were the two that stuck with Luka through the years. At the time, he had no Beta, which I thought was odd, but I never commented on it. They were an outlawed Cadre who lived outside of the Council's jurisdiction under Luka's order. Being invited into Luka's world of secrets and careful lies was a tangled web, yet I craved change. Everything in my life transformed. Luka helped to temper me, teaching me a better way of redirecting my anger and controlling my attitude. After my first year with him, I felt comfortable enough to let my guard down and admit what I had run from. He didn't judge me or tell me it was my fault; he did the opposite.

"He said what happened to Daniel wasn't my fault. It was a tragic accident. He told me that my reaction was because I had suffered a traumatic ordeal, and I never considered it to be traumatic because all I focused on was it being my fault. He wanted me to go back home, but I refused. I couldn't go back and face my father, and I needed Luka—more than anyone—to understand that. Luka understood and dropped it, and the next day, he asked me to be his Beta. I was shocked; I would be Luka's first Beta. The connection we shared felt deeper than any brotherhood. We just clicked, and we worked so well together; we understood each other from just a look. Warrior partners. I owe a lot to Luka; he met me at my lowest point and helped me to rise again."

Dayton gave a bitter laugh. Knowing Dayton and Luka had, at one point, shared such closeness was baffling to imagine, seeing how they felt about each other now.

"Another year went by, and the situation with Dante was turning dire. I knew it was bad when Luka wanted to involve himself. He stayed out of Court politics, but it was becoming more than that. He wanted to show the world who the Bestial was; he wanted to kill Dante. After that admission, I don't know how, but somehow Dante learned of Luka's true identity and his plans to kill him," Dayton loosed another shaking breath. My hands trembled, and I tried to steady them. "Dante found me and proposed a deal—if you can call it that. He told me I had to kill Luka, or he would kill my family. I didn't believe him, but he had a lock of my mother's hair as proof of his closeness to them. He was going to kill my family if I didn't kill Luka, and Dante knew I could get close enough because of how much Luka trusted me."

Dayton pressed his head against the cave wall and dragged a hand down his face. When his hand fell beside me, instinctually, I grabbed it. My skin felt scorched with electricity from where our skin touched, and I shuffled closer to Dayton. He glanced down at our interlocked hands but didn't pull away.

"I felt blinded by fear and torment. If I made one wrong move, it would all go to shit again. I had to lose the rest of my family, whom I still loved fiercely, or lose Luka, to whom I owed everything I became. I felt sick, even sicker for the fact I considered following through with it. I just kept thinking of Daniel, and that if things had been different, he would never have died. Daniel would have been ashamed of me for letting our family die, so I devised a plan to kill Luka and hated myself every second for it. I felt cornered. Terrified. I planned to bring him out under the ruse of a routine patrol and just shoot him. Quick, easy, and painless."

I would have been sick with indecision, too, if faced with such a choice. It obviously hadn't been an easy choice for him to make, yet there could have been another way. He could have come clean to Luka about Dante, devised a plan—something else.

"Hindsight's twenty-twenty, Mare," said Dayton, watching me sadly. "Of course, I know now I should've gone to Luka. He would've helped me without a doubt. But I was foolish, and Luka was a powerful Alpha. He was more perceptive than I gave him credit for. He knew what I was up to. When it came down to me pulling the trigger, I faltered. Luka stood there and asked me why, and then Fenrir ambushed him. Dante sent them as insurance in case I couldn't pull the trigger. I couldn't. Then, it was all happening again, just like with Daniel. I wanted to help Luka fight them; I didn't want him to die. But before I could, I was taken."

A chill ran through the cave, and I shivered. Dayton squeezed my hand and swallowed hard.

"Dante took me back to Lycan—back home. By the time I reached consciousness, I was too late to save them. Blood spilled in buckets. My mother was mutilated beyond recognition, her head nearly severed from her body. My father was alive, but only just, and Dante tortured me slowly in front of him until I admitted aloud to him that I killed Daniel. Once I did, he made me watch as he killed my father slowly. I can still hear his screams," Dayton whispered.

I took a deep breath as he continued.

"I regret not killing Dante then and there, but he got away, and I didn't stop him. Of all the people to find me, it was Luka. I don't even know what I felt when seeing him alive. Shocked? Relieved? Scared? He got me out of the house and brought me to the Court. He asked me one question: "Why?" I had no answer for him then, but Luka showed me mercy under the promise I would stay out of his life for good. I still screwed that up."

Dayton looked away from me then and inhaled sharply.

"When something truly traumatic happens to you, your mind doesn't let you process it until you're safe again. Honestly, the weeks after it happened are still a blur. My mind refused to process it, and it took me weeks of solitude until I could think through everything that happened to me. Everything was chaos. Dante was dead, I was traumatized, and the Council was on the brink of breaking. Once things settled down, I went before them. They wanted me to take on the title of Lord and join the Council. They told me I had enough of a political standing because of my family, and no one would rebuke me after what happened. I refused; I caused quite a scene and stripped myself of my title. I all but forced them to banish me into exile to the Temple." He laughed. "Julian insisted on going with me and refused to let me be alone. After two years of not seeing him, it was like no time was lost between us. Well, you know how Julian is. The Council was glad to be rid of him. Truthfully, if Julian hadn't been with me in those initial days, I think I would have killed myself a long time ago."

Dayton was clearly still tormented as he relived his worst days. He stared at our interlocked fingers then jerked his hand away. I clasped his hand again, but he didn't move away this time. He glared down at me, and I steadily held his gaze. The wound at his side no longer bled—a good sign, yet it was still open.

"Dayton," I said, voice sounding distant to my ears. "God, I'm sorry."

"Sorry?" he repeated. "I didn't deserve Luka's mercy. He should've killed me when he had the chance. My family is dead because of me. It's my fault, and their blood is on my hands."

I noted the visible lines of exhaustion across his face just before he turned his face. "Can I ask you something, Dayton?"

He peered up at me then. "Considering you're going to ask regardless, I don't see why not."

"Did you ever tell Luka the truth?"

"Weeks after everything happened, I found Luka. He knows a version of a story I told him," Dayton said. "A story based on truth, but mostly lies. I told Luka I always planned to kill him when the time was right, and I'd used him to grow more powerful. I told him Dante wanted me in his ranks, but only if I could kill Luka. I said that it was like killing two birds with one stone. I needed Luka to believe the lie to make me look like the bad guy. I needed him to never forgive me or trust me again."

"Why?" I asked.

"Because despite how fucking terrifying Luka can be, he's a good fucking person," spat Dayton. "If I told him the truth, he would have found a way to forgive me. I needed him to hate me. I didn't want his forgiveness; I didn't deserve it—I *still* don't deserve it. Everything that happened—Daniel, my parents, and Luka? All of it was my fault."

The haunted torment in Dayton's eyes frightened me.

"You don't get to choose who you lose in this world, or when, but I lost everyone important to me all at once. The grief of that never goes away," he continued. "I had no choice but to accept what I couldn't change and find a way to move on. But I don't deserve forgiveness. I must let Luka hate me, and all I can do is try to atone for what I have done."

Repentance. Dayton had once said he sought repentance from Luka. My heart sank for Dayton, realizing how deeply his self-hatred went. He'd been dealt a shitty hand, but it wasn't his fault. Not really.

The tattoo blazed on my right arm. A bright light radiated from it, turning a fiery orange. Dayton and I exchanged a questioning look as his own tattoo flashed; it appeared to crawl over his body, curling around his bicep and up his shoulder. The wound at his side continued to bleed. I reached out to touch it.

His body convulsed and his eyes gleamed as a growl of raw agony ripped through him. My hands trembled, and Dayton snarled, shaking the cave. A burst of heat shot from me and tossed me backward. The impact had me seeing stars.

When I opened my eyes, Dayton was slumped over, his head hanging.

I jolted forward to lift his chin; his eyes were closed and his chest unmoving. I assessed his wound which was no longer there, the only evidence being the dried black goop on his skin. I listened for his heartbeat yet felt too panicked to focus. I didn't have to worry long because breath whooshed from Dayton as he shot up at once. I jumped back, clutching my heart as Dayton gasped, moving his hand to touch his wound. He stared up at me, astounded.

"What was that?"

"If you don't know then I don't know," I said, brushing my fingers over his healed, smooth skin. "That was weird."

"Weird," Dayton echoed, staring where the wound had been minutes before. He gazed back at me with wonder. "I think you saved me."

It didn't make sense; I hadn't done anything. Of course, I was grateful he was healed, but it wasn't anything I'd outright done. I couldn't quite wrap my head around it. Distantly, I wondered if it had anything to do with our bond... but if it had, Dayton would have known. Right?

"Does that make us even now?" I asked, laughing.

"You wish," he said, laughing, too. "Our bond grew."

"What does that mean?"

Dayton rose to his feet, assessing the limits of his strength. He wobbled slightly and widened his eyes as he uneasily stepped forward. He reached down and picked up his dirty shirt, pulling it over his head with a look of disgust.

"I don't know what it means," he said. "But thank you for what you did."

Our gazes met, his golden eyes slightly frenzied. We stood like that, staring at each other as if for eternity. Undiluted, he'd revealed his truth—the burden of his past, and the anger always at his surface was now put into perspective. I beheld all that he was without judgment or intimidation. He was Dayton, and he was enough.

"How do we get out of here?" I asked, my voice low.

Dayton crossed the cave, pausing only to dip his fingers into the water. Once he did, he approached the wall to trace his fingers across it. It was like he was finger painting, and wherever his fingers touched, a trail of sky blue stained the wall. Odd symbols and drawings appeared, and once completed, Dayton stepped back.

"'*The sacrifice of the Truth*'," he said, reciting the words. "'*Hidden in time by the honest folk, found only by those that walk the same path. Seeking with dishonest intent will bring you to a bitter end.*'"

Before I asked what that meant, the rocks on the wall shifted. Dayton stepped back, reaching out an arm to me. The rocks pulled apart, like metal scraping against metal. Dust collected thick in the air, and I coughed, with Dayton sputtering alongside me. Pulling me into him, he covered my face with his chest and tangled his fingers in my hair. Where he touched me, warmth spread, and I leaned into him.

I pulled away first once the dust settled and looked up at the opening that formed. Dayton nodded, and I stepped toward it, a hum vibrating through the air. The small opening in the wall was as big as a coat closet, and a silver object gleamed inside. I could see a hilt and I reached, clasping cool metal in my palm. The instant I touched it, the thrum of power ignited in me. I pulled it free and out came a long silver sword, gleaming in glory against the cave light. At the hilt was an opal stone, small and jagged, but forged into the blade to be as one.

Dayton approached, awestruck. "That's it. That's the Artifact."

I raised my eyebrows, "How do you know?"

He pointed at the opal stone. "That is a piece of the Moonstone."

Together, we balked at the sword. I don't think either of us really thought we would find it. An Infinite Artifact. Its power seemed to coil within me where I touched it, reaching within and pulling me deeper. My head felt heavy, and all I saw was the sword as everything around me blurred.

"Mare, let it go," ordered Dayton. He walked toward the wall and reached inside to pull out a sheath. "I feel that thing's power. Let it go before something bad happens."

Dayton put his hand over my own, and that touch pulled me from my hypnosis. I blinked until my senses came back and released the sword.

Dayton took it and cursed, sheathing it in its scabbard. He strapped the blade across his back—a warrior clad with the finest weaponry.

"It's time to get the hell out of here," said Dayton.

"How?"

"Look." he nodded to a spot behind me, and I whirled.

The pool of water spun upward into a glittering curtain that pulled back to reveal the same shore we stood on when meeting the Nixies. I glanced at Dayton, who offered me his hand.

I took it, and together, we ran.

Chapter 26

The entryway was another pool of water that we waded through as Dayton bobbed his head up to assess the scene. Everything looked the same, and mystical magic remained in the air. Colors of bright neon gleamed while overhanging willow trees decorated the lands with their branches and leaves. Everything felt eerily still—*too* quiet. Dayton stayed close to me and led us out of the water.

"What is it?" I asked. "Nixies?"

Stepping onto the shore, Dayton extended his hand to me. "Become attuned to your surroundings. Listen, smell, see."

"That's easy for you to say." I said, taking his hand. "You actually know what you're doing."

"Focus. The wolf is really stirring in you."

I understood what he meant. I sensed the wolf in me, too, but I couldn't understand how to utilize it to my advantage. Thinking of the wolf as a separate entity hurt my head, and I couldn't wrap my mind around it. Yet I had little trouble tapping into my heightened senses; that felt natural. My eyes automatically adjusted, my hearing picked up on things it never normally would have, and even my sense of smell improved. All parts of the wolf began to show itself in pieces until we were one.

"You say that, but it's not my fault the wolf doesn't want to come out," I muttered.

"Keep grumbling about it and see how that works out for you." He gave me a pointed look. "I saw your claws when you attacked Shetani. Your wolf is itching to break free."

Closing my eyes, I focused on relaxing my senses. I tried to hear what Dayton could, yet it heeded little results. Inhaling deeply, I was overwhelmed by the surrounding smells—a sensory overload between the murky water and the sickly-sweet flowers. My eyes flashed open, and I flared my nostrils. Blood dripped down the flowers, pooled onto the ground and smeared across the trees; it was as if someone ran out of here.

"What happened?" I gaped. No bodies littered the ground, and I desperately hoped there were no casualties, yet the blood was still alarming.

"I don't know," Dayton whispered. "We have to get out of here before the Nixies find us."

As if on cue, Dayton grabbed my shoulders and pulled me back as a trident whizzed past my head. I watched wide-eyed as it wedged into a nearby tree, nestling tight into it as it shook from impact. Dayton and I took off, running down the path we originally came from. Ducking and avoiding tree branches and vines proved difficult as they grew unnaturally fast, the vines twisting up our ankles like snakes. I jumped to avoid them. Dayton shoved me aside from incoming obstacles. He wasn't wielding the sword; he kept it in its scabbard.

"It's the Nixies' magic," he called. "They're trying to keep us here."

A burst of water exploded from beneath me, and I flew back. Water shot directly at my face, and I ingested it, flinching at the bitter taste in my mouth; it was like drinking a mouthful of hot sauce. All my senses mellowed, yet a shrill echo sounded in my ears, buoying between my eardrums. My vision blurred and my limbs sunk into the ground. I needed to move, to get up and run.

I felt pressure on my arm, and the touch snapped me from my daze. My eyes opened to find Dayton, shouting over me.

"Mare!" he called. "Mare, c'mon. Snap out of it."

I couldn't move; my body felt rooted to the floor. Dayton took me into his arms and ran. Branches and leaves nicked my skin, cutting open wounds like paper cuts across my body. It felt like we'd run for miles, yet all the trees looked like carbon copies—tall, neon glowsticks indistinguishable to one another.

Dayton grunted and sat me on the ground, and the moment he let me go, everything was like before—distant and dizzying. No amount of logic would make it make sense.

"Mare!" Dayton shouted. "Maris!"

I sat up, gasping, and clutched my chest, coughing up water. I heaved on the ground, desperate for the normal rhythm of air in my lungs. When another trident flew by, missing me by inches, I managed to jump to my feet. Dayton held onto my arm, staring at me.

"I'm fine," I insisted before he argued. "Let's get out of here before they kill us."

Screeching came from behind and I whirled to find a small army of Nixies heading towards us. They couldn't have more than a dozen or so yards away, and they launched weapons in our direction as they closed the distance. We ran until the river we first came from appeared up ahead. I recalled then the Fae stone that brought us here and reached into my pocket.

I skidded to a stop at the edge of the river and flicked my wrist back; the stone skimmed across the water's surface. It skipped just as before until a small portal formed in the water. There was no boat this time, and as the entryway formed, metal bars closed around it. Dayton glanced behind us at the approaching danger, and then at the water.

In the water, Naiads screamed, daring us to touch it. Their clawed hands appeared no bigger than a cat's claw, but it looked like it would hurt. They bared their pointed teeth and hissed.

Dayton dove for a discarded trident and attacked the water where the Naiads swam. "Mare! Go now!" he ordered.

I didn't hesitate and jumped into the water, its coolness bitter against my skin. I pumped my limbs toward the large portal as the gates slowly closed over them. A Naiad grabbed my foot and yanked me back. I screeched and swallowed water, kicking as it took me. More swam toward me.

"Dayton!" I screamed.

Dayton's head whipped up and his features paled. He hurled the trident, and the blunt end thunked the Naiad grappling with me. I felt its grip slacken and I wriggled my ankle free, tearing off like a bullet as the rest narrowed in. I made it to the portal in three strokes while Dayton battled with a Nixie.

He grabbed the Nixie by their throat and launched them back as another came at him, grappling for the sword at his back. They didn't want us to take it. Dayton struck the Nixie with the blunt end of another trident, and they fell to the ground with a thud.

I looked at the fast-closing gate now, only moments from sealing him in.

"Dayton, the gate!" I bellowed.

He dove into the water like a falling Slinky, and beneath the water, he came out the other side just as the gate stamped shut and winked out of existence. Wading through the water, Dayton heaved as he stared at where the portal had been. Now, only a Fae stone floated. Dayton plucked it up.

In the moment of calm, neither of us spoke. I gazed at the mountains and trees, grateful for the familiarity as the sunlight dwindled, reflecting against the water in orangey pink hues which bounced back around us. I glanced at Dayton, surprised to find him grinning. Dimples formed both sides of his lips, and I found the indentions on his cheeks oddly endearing. His hair caught the colors of the sun, his dark locks turning golden, and his eyes looked especially gilded in the light. His smile was truly rare, and I loved it; it transformed him. He looked younger—innocent. It filled me with warmth and a strange sense of happiness that he allowed himself a moment of unguarded emotion.

"That was fun," he panted, running a hand through his messy hair.

"I could think of a few other adjectives," I muttered.

Dayton laughed, a low gravelly sound that seemed out of practice. He threw his head back as the sound turned increasingly manic. I began to laugh, too, as we came down together from this insane high. We visited the Nixies, retrieved an Infinite Artifact, and somehow lived to tell the tale.

After what felt like forever, Dayton dared to look at me, his stare intense. Chills erupted over me; he had an uncanny way of doing that with just a look. The tattoo against my arm pulsed, pulling and beckoning me toward him. Dayton reached out and pulled at the hair tie that held my loose braid together. He had the band between his fingers, never looking away as I shook my head, allowing my hair to fall loose.

"Better?" I said, my voice rough.

Dayton raised his eyebrows and opened his mouth. His answer was swallowed by two long, piercing howls that erupted around us, and immediately, he was on the defense. Scowling, he raced toward the shore. I swam yet lagged behind. How did he manage to fly across the water? He jumped over the dock, and I took his hand as he lifted me from the water.

As my feet hit the dock, Luka stampeded toward us in wolf form. He was a blur in the distance, recognizable by his jet-black fur and blazing blue eyes. Dayton unstrapped the sword from his back and held it out for me, refusing to look in my direction. I took it and watched him walk toward Luka. My eyes widened as I realized what was about to happen, and I launched myself in front of Dayton.

"Mare, no!" he protested.

It was too late. Luka ran at us; he lunged in the air and landed in a light crouch in human form. He slowly raised his head, his eyes glowing bright. Anger practically vibrated off him the closer he got to us. I stilled, never straying from my position.

"I'm only asking this once," Luka boomed, not in rage but in power. "Where the hell have you been?"

I gulped, pulled by the force in his words. "It was my idea—"

"We went to the Nixies," Dayton interjected He grasped my shoulders and pushed me aside. "The note from Kaser. He wanted us to go there."

The full weight of Luka's gaze fell onto me. Pure Alpha. I refused to back down despite the slight tremble in my limbs. "You disobeyed a direct order."

"I took it as a suggestion." I shrugged, poking at his humor.

Luka was not amused. "You could've been killed!"

"I almost was, more than once," Dayton added unhelpfully. "While I don't recommend the experience, it was not a total flop."

"How could you let her walk in on this suicide mission?" he barked.

"Nobody really lets Maris do anything," said Dayton, matching Luka's anger. "I couldn't let her go alone. No one was seriously injured, except for your bruised ego by being one-upped and tricked by your sister."

"My ego? You were gone for two days!" Luka rumbled. He advanced toward Dayton. "I have half a mind to kill you where you stand!"

Two days? The thought of being there for such a length of time shot a wave of weariness through me. It felt like hours, not days. Two days lost, and who knows what could have happened? A bout of dizziness hit me again, and I swayed, toppling into Dayton.

Chapter 27

S harp talons caressed my mind and punctured my thoughts. I felt powerless as this unknown force snaked through me and infiltrated my senses, coiling in my mind. Each twist and turn chilled me to my core, yet there was a familiarity to its touch and a resistance. My mind felt picked apart.

An image of the sword flashed, illuminating the glistening stone on the hilt. Then it faded like a memory I couldn't unlock. The darkness pushed and pressed and pulsed. I felt its squirming—its withering. Everything moved slowly, and as it slinked past a rippling reflection, it paused. Darkness seized me as it hovered nearby, staring back at me with eyes of green pine.

I froze. I recognized the creature.

I rocketed awake, tangled in the bedsheets, while I grappled for breath. I was back in my room at the Temple. By the time my breathing settled, despite my hammering heart, I leaped out of bed. I made a beeline for the bathroom at my stomach's instant protests. As I heaved over the toilet, it was clear it had been days since I had eaten. Bile rose in my throat, hot and thick; I quaked, unable to stop the streams of tears leaking from my eyes.

I went back into the room and sat at the foot of the bed, pressing the palms of my hands against my eyes. The darkness in my mind lingered like a hovering storm cloud waiting to strike. This time, it wasn't a dream, yet the darkness remained. I would give it what it wanted if it showed itself. Anything to rid me of this sickening feeling. Being controlled by another force—something deep within—chilled my core. I tried to steady myself and tugged at my recent memories; I recalled narrowly escaping the Nixie realm and Luka confronting us.

The door burst open, and Luka clamored in, bleary-eyed. He crossed the room and sat beside me when he noticed my red-rimmed eyes. Tucking his arm around my body, he pulled me closer. The gesture was achingly familiar, and my heart swelled.

"What happened?" he asked, his voice croaky from sleep.

Anger raged inside me—not at him, but at whatever was happening to me. I didn't want to voice it aloud. There were bigger things to be worried about. Yet, I said, "I don't understand what's happening. I think it was just a nightmare."

"I can scent your fear; it's like a live wire. This isn't the first time you've had a nightmare that's sent you vomiting your guts up," he said, furrowing his eyebrows. "What's going on, Maris?"

If not for the genuine concern in his tone, I might have brushed him away. But Luka knew me better than anyone; he would see right past it. I inhaled, readying to say the words to admit how this was plaguing me.

"I don't know," I confessed. "Nightmares—scarily real nightmares—have been keeping me up at night."

"What kind of nightmares?"

Leaning my head on his shoulder, I shrugged. "Just terrors, death, blood. Being chased and forced to watch as those I care about are ripped apart."

"What about this time?"

"This time was different," I said, taking another deep breath. "I saw Derek, but not like a figment of a dream or memory. It felt like he was *in* the dream, or his essence was. I don't know, it doesn't make sense."

Luka dragged a hand down his face before bracing his elbows over his knees. He gave a hollow laugh. "Jesus Christ, what the fuck did Derek get tangled in?"

Dayton barged into the room, his eyes wide. My tattoo singed, coming alive across my body, while my own emotions relaxed at the sight of him. Dayton started toward me, but Luka sprang up, shielding me from him.

I stepped forward and grabbed Luka's wrist, who glanced stonily back at me.

"It's okay, Luka," I said.

Luka exhaled and stepped aside. Dayton was as stiff as a board until he saw me and his shoulders relaxed. A fair distance separated us yet I felt drawn to him, even from afar. Dayton furrowed his eyebrows as he took me in, his gaze hard and stoic.

"I'm okay," I told him, smiling tentatively. "It was just another nightmare."

"Again?" he asked, moving forward. His eyes bounced between me and Luka. "I don't like this. It feels dangerous."

Luka snorted. "You're worried about her being in danger? *You* put her in dangerous situations, Dayton. You're poison to everything you touch." That was the worst thing Luka could say, and he knew it.

Dayton lowered his head. He already blamed himself enough without Luka saying such things. Luka didn't know the truth to why Dayton betrayed him; if he did, he wouldn't be acting like this. It was all such a mess.

"Is everything okay in here?" asked Julian, standing bare-chested in the doorway. He wore plaid pajama pants and leaned against the frame, his arms crossed over his chest. I wondered if Kyler was with him, or if he'd left her in his bed—assuming, of course, they were together at all.

"It's fine, Jules," said Dayton, walking to the window.

"The full moon is getting closer," Julian added. "Tempers fly more easily."

"It's fair to note I haven't said a damn thing," grumbled Dayton. "I'd consider that growth."

"I can hear what you're thinking," Julian added. "You're still quite rude."

"We need to talk about that sword," Luka said as he stormed from the room.

"Sure, whatever you say, Chief," Dayton saluted Luka as he left.

I shook my head. The sword I found wasn't the only thing we had to discuss.

Dayton immediately homed in on me, stopping only inches from me. His eyes looked me up and down for injury. Julian chuckled.

"Dayton, I'm sorr—"

"Don't apologize for him," he growled. "It's true what he said."

"It is not," Julian intervened. "It wasn't true; he was being cruel."

Dayton scoffed. "Yeah, well, whatever. I don't want to talk about it."

"Julian is right," I pushed. "Besides, where I'm concerned, I know what your stance is. Without you, I would have been dead a long time ago or worse off."

"Duty calls, Mare," he said, flexing his right hand where the tattoo resided.

Julian started to cough to mask his laughter but failed miserably. "You know what I would like to know? How come a simple quick trip turned into a two days long escapade?"

"Shetani," Dayton answered. "If the bitch hadn't intervened, we wouldn't have lost as much time."

"We're back now," I said. "And we need to talk about the sword. Where is it?"

"Downstairs," said Dayton. "This is going to be an interesting conversation with Luka."

Together, the three of us exited the room and walked down the hall.

"You two didn't have to deal with him over the past few days. Let me tell you, there's not enough alcohol in the world to forget the fear of God he puts in you. He fired so many questions at me, always finding new angles to pursue," Julian said. "Nearly bit my head off multiple times. You both owe me big time."

"It warms me to know you have been on the receiving end of his anger," Dayton replied.

"Of course. Rage and violence warms your ice-cold heart."

"Always consistent," I chimed in, and Julian laughed.

We walked in silence the rest of the way; the flickering silver flames from the wolf head torches appeared more muted than usual, dimly lighting the halls. The pictures on the walls of the past werewolves were particularly eerie today, as if the eyes on the portraits followed my every move. I felt the bone-deep exhaustion as we walked. Each step made me feel dizzy like I was walking over a swinging bridge. We gathered in the living room.

Luka stood by the large windows, the early morning light pooling in. The sword was set on the long coffee table, gleaming beneath the sun. The dark black of it was stunning from the hilt to the blade, and the opal glistened, its shine reflected across the room. A part of me longed to use a weapon this gorgeous. The honest part of me knew I was nowhere near ready for that.

I sunk into the plush couch cushions.

"Coffee, anyone?" a soft voice called.

Kyler wore sweats and an oversized deep green shirt. She looked freshly styled, her black curls clinging close to her shoulders and bouncing as she entered the room, carrying a tray of coffee and mugs. She placed it down and sat beside me, her petite frame barely denting the cushions.

I grasped a mug, not hesitating to pour the coffee into it. "Thank you," I said to her, smiling.

"I know you've all had a rough few days," she replied. "Plus, I feel pretty useless around here."

"You're not useless," said Julian, stepping forward and grabbing a mug. "You've been keeping me company."

Kyler rolled her eyes good-naturedly. "I'm surprised you even remember talking to me."

Julian smiled crookedly as he winked. "You know I always remember a pretty face." His tone was light as he stared into his steaming mug. "I should make this Irish."

"Jules, it's like four in the morning." Dayton suppressed a yawn. "Give it a rest."

"It's a new day," Julian said. "Five o'clock, somewhere, right?" He started to sway around Dayton, grinning.

"You and that damn song," Dayton scowled, turning from his friend.

From the stairwell, Neville poked his head out. His dark curls looked fluffy this morning, as if freshly washed. The bandages on his chest were gone, and he wore a V-neck T-shirt that showed four brown lines where his wounds had been. I was glad to see he was alright. He entered the room and accepted a cup of coffee from Kyler, then eyed the sword with suspicion.

Kyler glanced over at me, looking me up and down. "There's something different about you. Your aura is darker."

"You can tell?" I asked.

"Of course, I can tell." She shrugged. "Your glow is more gilded than before. You did something that shouldn't have been possible."

Luka peeled from the window, glancing suspiciously between Dayton and me. Dayton appeared to find the ground utterly fascinating and made no comments about Kyler's observation. I suspected she referred to how I unexplainably healed Dayton from death. Even I didn't understand how I managed it. I felt him, and it was as if my fear somehow saved him.

"What did you do?" asked Luka, taking a seat in one of the tall lounge chairs.

"In the Nixie realm, Shetani was there; she poisoned Dayton with wolfsbane," I said. My eyes darted to find Dayton, who sulked in the shadows.

"Wolfsbane?" Luka quizzed, whirling to look at Dayton. "Did you stop taking it in your coffee to build immunity?"

"It was disgusting. It was like drinking acid every day." Dayton shuddered. "The point is, Maris somehow healed me, and it was remarkable."

Luka glanced between us, astounded.

"Don't say I should have let him die," I warned.

Luka raised his hands, a coy smile playing on his lips. "I would never wish death on anyone. Suffering slowly, perhaps."

"It's an inch," Julian muttered.

"How did you save him?" asked Neville.

"I didn't," I said, backtracking. "I mean, I did, but I don't know how. The dagger was propelling toward him, and I don't know, I moved fast. A weird light came out of nowhere and then the dagger hit his side, not his heart."

Neville raised his eyebrows, sharing a look with Luka. Neither of them commented further.

Stepping from the shadows, Dayton moved to sit directly across from Luka. He swallowed slowly, then gestured to the sword. "You want to offer your two cents first on this?"

"Where the fuck did you get it?" asked Luka.

"I take it you know what it is," I said.

"That's an Infinite Artifact."

"You found one?" Kyler balked. "How do you know it is one?"

Dayton and I glanced at each other, but it was Luka who answered.

"The opal," he said. "That's a part of the Moonstone."

"How do you know that?" Kyler asked. "Or are we just all going along with everything you say because you're the Bestial?"

"I know that because I can read," Luka chimed, motioning to the open book on the coffee table. "I never claimed to be a powerhouse of infinite knowledge, but I was researching earlier. There's no way to know for sure, but I think it's fair to assume that is one of the Infinite Artifacts."

"Besides, Kaser wouldn't have wanted us to go to the Nixie realm if it wouldn't benefit him," said Dayton.

"Well, he wanted the Artifact, and now we have it," said Neville. "Aren't we lucky?"

"And if Kaser's ominous note is anything to go by, it's safe to say Derek still suffers until he gets this Artifact," Julian added grimly.

I thought back to the note about Derek's suffering in the interim. Kaser wanted this sword, and in exchange, he would give us Derek. It was a no brainer: give Kaser what he wants, get Derek back, and damn the rest. Yet Luka had initially disagreed; he didn't want to find the Artifact, even if it meant Derek suffered. He would no doubt continue to be stubborn about it and take the same stance.

"The real question is: what do we do with it?" I glanced at Luka, who wouldn't meet my gaze.

"Let's test this thing out," said Julian, prowling toward it.

"Careful," Dayton warned. "It has power to it."

Julian unsheathed the sword, and as his hand grasped the hilt, his back immediately straightened. His green eyes widened, darting around the room. He held out the sword in admiration, the darkness contrasting with his pale complexion. It was strange to see Julian, who was so purposely unkempt, appearing like a soldier ready for war. His lip curled in a snarl as recognition rippled over his features. He sheathed it.

"What is it?" Kyler asked, raising her eyebrows.

"There's magic in that thing," said Julian. "I know that magic. We need to turn this into the Council. *Now.*"

"Wait a minute, everyone," Luka said, standing. "Let's get everything straight first before we make any decisions."

"The magic in the sword—the stone? It's the same magic I have," Julian announced, manically tapping his head with both hands. "It's dark, its volatile, and if it gets put in Kaser's hands, it's fucking dangerous."

Luka raised his hands in a show of good faith, and Kyler stepped between them. "Okay, Julian. I'm on your side here. Kaser shouldn't have the sword, but if we release it to the Council, we have no jurisdiction over it. As long as it's in our possession, we control who knows about it and how to keep it hidden."

"We shouldn't have anything to do with it, point blank," argued Julian. "This is out of our league; we need to give up while we're ahead."

I was surprised by Julian's firm stand; something about the magic had clearly struck a nerve. He wasn't thinking rationally but was acting on emotion.

"Luka is right, Jules," Dayton said, looking to Luka. "You're just triggered right now. Why don't you go put it somewhere safe, like the vault in the basement?"

Julian stepped forward and eyed the sword with rising suspicion. "Fine, but if I spontaneously combust, I will come back and haunt all of your asses."

Luka sat back down, exhaling as Julian left. "Let's start with what we know and go from there."

"Agreed," chimed Dayton.

"Kaser sends a note to Maris. In that note, he alludes to having Derek and wanting the Artifact," Luka said. "Now, we're in possession of the Artifact and we know it has part of the Moonstone. Kaser wants the Artifact, assuming for the Moonstone, and wants as little people as possible to know about it."

"That pretty much covers it," I said.

"I say we just find the bastard and end this then," said Dayton as if it were obvious.

"Ah, a real scholarly plan," snapped Kyler, moving to sit on the couch again.

"A notable observation in all of this is Kaser's absence," Neville said, sitting up. "Letting others do the work for him."

"Has anyone ever actually seen him?" Kyler asked. "Like seriously, he was Dante's kid, but I don't even know what the guy looks like."

"It makes you wonder," Luka muttered.

"Wonder what?" asked Dayton.

Luka shook his head, as if lost in thought. "Nothing. Never mind. We need to focus on the bigger picture. What are his motivations? His end goal? Dante wanted more werewolves, but he never had the means to execute it on a larger scale. All Dante had was the ability to persuade and take over a government before he was killed."

"Before you killed him," Dayton corrected.

Luka nodded. "Kaser knows the Bestial killed his father, and now he knows the Bestial is me."

It felt like years ago now since Zayne kidnapped me and trapped me in the basement with Dayton and Derek. Zayne had asked the right questions, putting the pieces together that Luka was the Bestial. He must have told Kaser before he died.

"Things changed once he knew it was you," I said. "After he knew it was you, he could associate the Bestial with something personal: taking Derek, involving me, luring you out. It makes sense."

"Kaser seems to hold a mighty grudge against you for killing Dante," said Neville. "Perhaps he wants retribution for his father."

"It's more than retribution," said Julian, walking back into the room. He seemed less perturbed and more like his usual self as he sat down beside Kyler. "Revenge is petty and easier to get on a smaller scale. With the Artifacts in play, there's something bigger happening."

"You say that because of your magic," Kyler said, looking at him.

"Yes," he agreed. "My magic is a curse, not a gift. Dante forced magic in me years ago, and I'm not going to get into it, but I never knew how he did it. It's a dark magic which I can only control enough to keep at bay."

"What are you saying, Jules?" Dayton asked.

Julian looked at Luka before saying, "Dante had a piece of the Moonstone the entire time. That's why I recognized the magic. In fragments, it can be wielded on a small scale—I'm proof of that because of my own magic. I think it's safe to assume that, in turn, Kaser now has that Moonstone."

"If he already has part of the Moonstone, why did he send us for more?" I asked. "What's the point of all this? What is his end goal?"

"Maybe it shouldn't be up to us to figure out," suggested Kyler. "What if we go to the Council with all this?"

It seemed far too simple a request. Yet, when Julian initially mentioned the idea of Kaser's return to Claire, she dismissed him from the room. They wanted proof, and now the only proof we had was the sword, but that wasn't concrete evidence that Kaser had returned. If Luka hadn't burned the note, we would have had that, but even so, it wasn't as easy as letting the Council involve themselves. It was personal, and Kaser was betting on that to keep us going.

"No, they won't believe us," said Dayton. "Besides, Luka evades the law like it's his job. The Council would happily arrest him and keep their heads buried in the sand about Kaser. No one will want to hear he is back to wreaking havoc."

"They'd listen to the Bestial," said Julian.

All eyes flicked to Luka, who straightened. His own gaze darkened as he stood, slowly shook his head, and began to pace. The Bestial was an aspect of Luka he kept hidden from the world; I knew him, and he wouldn't give up his secret.

"I know what you're insinuating, Julian, but the answer is no," said Luka. "That part of me needs to stay anonymous. If I reveal my hand, it'll only draw out more enemies and bring forward more danger. The Council would hunt me down, for starters, and I don't doubt that they hate me enough to unleash the Wolf Riders on me."

Julian didn't seem convinced. "You're being paranoid."

I wondered what the Wolf Riders were but didn't think much of it.

"Leave it Jules," Dayton cut in, glancing between them. Luka's face had began to twist, adopting a more Alpha-like expression. "The situation isn't dire enough to play that hand."

"Look," said Luka, attempting to speak calmly. "I need to figure out all the pieces of Kaser's game before I can even consider finding him."

"What about Derek?" I asked; Derek always seemed to be brushed aside during our discussions.

Luka turned to me, perplexed, gripping the back of the couch. "What about him?"

The coldness in his tone surprised me. Luka didn't prioritize Derek the same way I did, but he could at least show some concern given they were friends, too, and Derek was his Beta.

"Kaser still has Derek," I said tightly.

"Derek got caught. It's a part of this life; he knew what he signed up for," said Luka. "He knows the risks of this world and he put his neck on the line, poking around the wrong crowd for information about his family."

"That means we abandon him?" I asked. If it were up to me, I'd be halfway to whatever hell he was stuck in.

Luka's nostrils flared. "You wouldn't understand. Derek wouldn't want us to go after him, not like this anyway."

"He's right," said Kyler, looking at me. "It may not be what you want to hear, but there's a chance he may not come back from this."

Kyler's ominous words didn't sit well with me. "You don't even know him," I snapped. "I can't sit back and do nothing. It's Derek."

"If it were me who got kidnapped, I wouldn't want you to come looking for me," Luka replied. "It's a part of this life, and it must be accepted."

"Would you accept it if I were kidnapped?" I asked him angrily.

Luka's fist came down hard against the back of the couch and the fabric ripped.

"Not the couch," Julian moaned.

"You're different," Luka argued.

Before I retorted, Dayton did. "He's right, Mare. You're different because you were never supposed to be in this world. You were supposed to be safe. You were supposed to be human. All of us know the risks and we accept the consequences."

"Exactly," Luka conceded. "I won't make you any promises, but I also won't take anything off the table."

My gaze bounced between them, disbelieving. Of course, the one time they agree with each other, it's on this.

"Meaning what?" I asked.

"That I'm not going to execute a rescue mission," said Luka, "but *if* there's an opportunity to get Derek back that aligns with whatever else we're in for, then I won't abandon him."

I still didn't like it. Knowing how desperately Derek searched for answers about his dead brother and father, I knew if the roles were reversed, Derek wouldn't hesitate to find me. "Okay, fine."

"The full moon is tomorrow, Chief," said Dayton.

"That could play a part in all of this," said Neville.

"Tomorrow?" I asked, swallowing hard. If the full moon were tomorrow, that meant I would turn for the first time. I wiped the sweat from my palms. "What does that mean?"

Dayton's gaze softened. "You don't need to be nervous. You're not alone; we're all here to help. I'm here to help."

Slowly, I nodded. I wanted to talk with Dayton, but not with everyone around us.

"The aftermath of the full moon is what we should be concerned about," said Luka. "For now, I think we put a pin in further plans and reconvene after the full moon."

"Good idea," Dayton said. "In the meantime, I'll check the wards and I'll write a bullshit letter to the Council before they show up here poking around about Maris."

Luka slunk into a chair and leaned back, pressing his palms against his eyes. "Throw me a bone and tell them you followed my trail to Antarctica and that's where I'm permanently holed up."

Dayton chortled as he left the room.

Clapping his hands together, Julian approached Neville. "Are you staying here or going back to your home now that you're healed?"

"The Temple of Loup-Garou is a sanctuary for werewolves in distress," Neville huffed. "I've far since surpassed that level of emotional turmoil for the week."

"Werewolves in distress are welcomed. Why don't I show you to a room?" Julian said with a hesitant smile.

Chapter 28

With only a day until the full moon, tensions were running high. To pass the time, I ran alone. My training attire clung to my skin as I made a third round around the path. Rain drizzled like a mist, inviting humid moisture into the air. I longed for the beating sun, entrapping me in warmth. The ambiance felt off, as if a storm cloud was looming over me, and as I waded through mud and rain puddles, the noise of doing so grated at my ears. My senses felt completely open, and I couldn't control it.

A force within me stirred, sensing the wolf inside me. It wasn't ready to make its appearance yet, and the thought of turning into a wolf was hard to wrap my head around. In smaller ways, the wolf showed itself with its extended fangs and protruding claws, but beyond that, my emotions felt out of whack. I felt in my bones its anticipation to break free. I'd watched Dayton shed his skin into a wolf without batting an eye, and Luka, too, harnessed the beast inside of him. I wouldn't know until I did it, ripping off the Band-Aid.

I jumped over a large rock in the path while my mind pondered the ever-growing list of horrible things awaiting us. How had my life changed this drastically in a matter of weeks? How had I been so blind to what was in front of me this whole time? Attending college was once my biggest woe, and now it was a sociopathic man threatening me and those I cared about. I didn't want to be afraid, but what else was there to feel?

I made my way inside, hit by a wave of exhaustion. I should sleep, but the prospect of another nightmare stopped me. I ran up the Temple steps toward the decking, the wood squeaking beneath me. The torches lining the back wall of the Temple had dimmed, extinguished from the rain. The normal aroma of fresh air and earth was overpowered by a pungent stench that made me gag. I ran inside.

I peered around the empty kitchen, glad to find no one else. A silver pot of coffee sat on the black marble countertop, and I poured the lukewarm liquid into a clean mug. It tasted revolting, but at least it would chase away the exhaustion.

I turned to find Dayton looming in the doorway. It startled me to see him, but I tried not to let it show. His golden gaze studied me beneath the locks of his dripping wet hair. Mud covered his clothes and weapons, and his stiff posture made me uneasy of his mood.

"You've been gone awhile," I noted. The day was nearly over as it creeped closer to the evening. "Did you write your letter to the Council?"

"Yes."

I bit my lip before daring to ask, "Are you alright?"

Dayton, I knew, hated that question, and he always evaded answering by hitting me with a sarcastic remark. I sensed I might be able to ask, and that he might be inclined to answer me honestly.

"I'm wonderful, thank you so much for asking," said Dayton. His expression then shifted from its usual venom to somber. "Look, we haven't had a chance to speak, so I haven't got the chance to clarify what happened in the cave."

I met his defensive glare. Dayton had been open, honest, and vulnerable with me. I knew he hated being any of those things, especially all at once, but there was a shift I felt between us, and I knew he did, too. Our bond felt like a string tethered to each of us, slowly tying together at opposite ends. I yearned to be closer to him, and that confused me; it was dangerous to care about Dayton. I knew Dayton enough to know he was in his head about his own feelings, too, and I was afraid to hear what he had to say.

"What do you mean?"

"The water from the Nixie realm has drug-like properties in it. Ingesting it makes one delirious," he explained. "Whatever I told you in that cave resulted from some drugged-up high I was in. Keep what you heard to yourself, but don't think you are special because I told you."

The words were a needle in my balloon, and I deflated immediately. My shoulders fell as I looked to Dayton, who turned from me.

"Your cruelty has no bounds," I said to him. "Honestly, I don't buy it."

Dayton didn't speak as he left. I watched him go, then I stormed from the kitchen, prowling the halls. I pushed open the door to another room—one I had not yet ventured in. The library. Tall stacks of books lined the walls; rows upon rows of bookcases stretching endlessly across the room. Sliding ladders propped against the shelves for easier navigation across the rows.

I meandered over to a stack of open books; Luka had fallen asleep on the table, his arms propped over the surface while he rested his head against his bicep. I studied him. I hated how he neglected his own well-being for others. At his side, a wicked, long blade sat between his fingers. It was strange to think he had always been in the middle of all this: werewolves, the Council, a life of constant caution.

I skimmed the pages of the books around him. *The Legend of the Infinite Artifacts* was open on the table, and I flipped through the pages, not sure what I was looking for. My eyelids were too heavy, and no amount of coffee seemed to help. In fact, it had my heart pitter-pattering in my chest and every noise had me jumping out of my skin. A page had been ripped out, but not entirely, yet I could decipher one word clearly.

"Regeneration."

The other words were easy to guess, but I couldn't know for sure without looking at the entire page. An uneasy feeling washed over me that I tried to shake off.

I left the library, leaving Luka to sleep as I suppressed my own yawn. When I walked into my bedroom, something immediately caught my attention on the bed. A dreamcatcher, small and willowy, fixed onto the headboard. Dark purple feathers cascaded down it, the woven strings an array of colors. I reached to touch it, admiring the lilac lattice work while wondering where it came from.

Raised voices echoed through my ears, and I cringed from the intensity. Two voices—two familiar voices—shot back and forth. I could hear it clearly, as if I were in the same room as them. I chalked it up to the full moon cranking up my senses.

"God, why are you like this?" Julian asked with an air of exasperation.

"Like what?" snapped Dayton.

"You're starting to feel something. Don't lie," said Julian. "I can hear you, remember? What I don't get is why are you regressing?"

I gulped and instinctually moved closer to the wall. I suspected they were talking about me, but I needed to hear more to be sure.

"I'm not," Dayton growled.

"Something in you is stirring, and you can't fight it any longer. You've built up your walls, Dayton, but I can see through you."

"I let my guard down, yes, but I now see that was a mistake!" Dayton thundered. "I shouldn't have let her in. I don't *let* people in."

My heart pounded in my chest, and I fisted my hands at my side.

"Why is it hard for you to let yourself be cared for?" asked Julian.

"Because I don't deserve it! God, is that not obvious?" I imagined Dayton prowling the room like a caged animal. "I'm toxic to everything I touch."

Hearing the pain cracking in Dayton's voice had my heart in my stomach. I knew why he thought so lowly of himself, forever haunted by the death of his family. It killed me to hear how he continued to blame himself.

"It doesn't have to be that way, Dayton. Don't you see that?" Julian pressed. "I know the demons running rampant in your head, but you're one of the strongest people I've ever met."

"I'm only strong because I have to be."

I heard a rustle of movement from inside and a low tirade of bickering. I walked toward the door and peered down the hall as a different door swung open, and Julian stepped into the corridor. His flask was perched between his lips, and as his eyes met mine, he grinned.

"Maris, always a pleasure," he said. "I was just about to look for you. Please come in."

Skeptically, I started toward him. He stepped aside and allowed me into his room. I peered around. Dayton had been in here moments ago. Where was he now?

Julian's room was chaotic, littered with empty bottles of various alcohols on every available surface. The bedsheets sat in a giant heap, and I noticed claw marks against the bedframe. Clothes scattered in piles across the ground, and bottles of various colored pomades sat on the dresser. I noticed an open window, the long red curtains billowing in the breeze.

"Don't mind the mess. I forget to tidy this place up," said Julian, leaning against the wall. He raised the flask to his lips. "It's not usually this bad, but I start to clean one thing and then I get distracted and end up somehow cleaning the grout in the kitchen tiles."

Julian's hair was void of any color for once; today, it was a simple moon-white, stark against his pale skin. He wore only black—shorts and a tank top—and the piercings adorning his face were gone, save for the black hoop in his nostril. He bounced on the balls of his heels, his green eyes chasing unseen figures around us.

"Are you alright?" I asked.

Julian cleared his throat and beamed. "I'm fine."

I gave him a pointed look, trying to pinpoint his unease, but he looked up at the ceiling. I wished I could read his mind. "I don't think anyone who says that is telling the truth." I said.

"Well, I'm clearly terrible about hiding how I feel. There are many voices in my head now." He rubbed the back of his neck and closed his eyes. "Repressing my abilities affects me when a full moon nears. Yes, cigarettes and booze can help, but depleting the total use of my powers is not always wise if I want to stay in control. Not that I ever learn."

"Is not hearing voices that vital?" I asked curiously.

Julian's eyes narrowed on me in reserved judgment. "It's a complex matter to deal with. It's hard to explain without spiraling into my own demise," he said. "After the full moon, I will be fine again until the next."

I stared up at the storm clouds, growing darker with every passing moment. Through the clouds, I could decipher a sliver of the moon in the sky. "What happens on a full moon?"

"The wolf inside you gets a free pass to stay out all night."

"Is that a bad thing?"

"Yes and no. Personally, I have bad experiences with the moon," he said, like it was no big deal. I felt him side eyeing me and anticipated his next words. "I know you could hear us before."

I suspected as much. "I didn't mean to overhear."

A mischievous smile played on his lips. "Dayton carries the weight of himself like a burden; he feels worthless."

I mulled over Dayton's last words to me, then thought of us in the caves when he opened up about his past. He thought he was dying, but because he survived, a new trust now existed between us, and while I felt closer to him, maybe he didn't feel the same. I couldn't make him feel that way about me.

"I don't get him," I admitted.

Julian brought the flask to his lips. "If it helps, neither do I, and I hear all the demons in his head." He took a swig. "It's not easy to care for him; he backs himself into a corner whenever he's on the brink of a breakthrough. In all the time I've known him, I've never seen him this highly-strung."

"How did you meet him?" I asked.

Julian grabbed a cigarette, seemed to realize he was inside, and placed it behind his ear. "I was thirteen and placed in the custody of the Wolf Council," he said. "We grew up in the Moon Court together. I never had a family of my own until Dayton. Now he's all I have."

"Do you know what happened to your parents?" I asked.

Julian's face turned colder than I'd ever seen it. I was startled, yet his casual manner hinted at no ill feelings. "I never really cared to investigate the people that sold me to Dante. They left me in his care, and I endured his torture until I was found. I never knew it was him until his death when more allegations and truths were uncovered."

I was stunned by both the revelation and how he spoke of it like it wasn't a big deal. "They sold you to Dante?" I gasped. "To be tortured?"

"I've always found it funny when people repeat what you just said," Julian commented. "I don't talk about what I endured, but I bear it every day. I never ran from it. Maybe my lungs and liver will pay for how I cope, but until that day comes, I will carry on."

All of Julian's behaviors suddenly made sense. The outlandish clothes, the arrays of hair colors, the piercings and tattoos...he had no control of his life then, and now he does. Even his powers were forced on him, a burden he didn't ask for. Drinking and smoking helped him to forget. I wondered if the part about it helping control his magic was true. Dayton and Julian alone suffered enough nightmares for ten people, let alone two.

A comfortable silence followed given the tone of our conversation. A million thoughts raced through my head—a lot being thoughts I hadn't wished to entertain about Dayton. He was complex and obstinate, and I thought nobody deserved to suffer as freely as he did, but perhaps I was foolish for that.

"Hey, Maris?" I looked up at Julian, whose gaze turned somber. "Something about you makes him feel, and that's scary to him."

Unsure of how to answer, I said, "I didn't do anything. I'm not special."

"That is exactly it," Julian said, a grin breaking across his features. "Dayton lives in a world of darkness. He doesn't care about anything, least of all himself. By his own design, Dayton pushes everyone he meets away, but you've fixed yourself as a permanent figure in his life and he can't push you away. You and all your fierceness made him wake up and care about something again."

Julian's words stunned me.

"I'm just who I am. I didn't do anything."

"Come here." Julian gestured me over with a jerk of his head, and I joined him by the window, the view of the forest clear as day. "Look at him."

I peered out to see Dayton in the distance, positioned in front of his training line of targets. Despite the impending darkness, he seemed set on practicing his flawless aim. Yet he continued missing the targets, a scowl apparent on his face.

"Dayton doesn't miss," I said, looking at Julian.

"He's distracted," said Julian. "I've known Dayton for years. He has always—I mean *always*—been perfectly in line. He never thinks twice; he never looks back, and he never loses focus."

I shook my head. "I don't see why you're telling me any of this."

"I'm not stupid; you're not stupid," said Julian, giving me a pointed look. "Don't make me spell it out."

"Stop playing matchmaker," I told him, crossing my arms over my chest.

"Hey now." Julian raised his hands. "You're the one that said matchmaker, not me."

I scowled and turned to watch Dayton once more. His knives continued to miss the targets. He glowered and held back another blade, waiting a second longer than usual before relinquishing it. It missed again.

I turned on my heel and frowned, hating the pull I felt toward him. Without another word, I walked out of Julian's room and shut the door behind me.

Chapter 29

I marched down the halls until I reached the back door and yanked it open. Outside, the chilly air immediately encapsulated me. At least it had stopped raining. I tucked my arms close to my body and started toward Dayton. He was farther out than I thought. Trekking across the mud strewn grounds felt like an error in judgment on my part, yet my bristling anger at Dayton lingered at the sight of him. I paused my prowl.

His shoes were caked in mud and weapons hung around his waist. His hair looked like he'd ran his fingers through it more than once, and his scent in the breeze was soap and pine intertwined with the outside air. His shirt clung to him, a mixture of rain and sweat, and as he drew his arm back, his toned muscles worked with the movements. He relinquished the knife, and it soared, landing far from the intended target. He cursed and ran a hand through his messy hair.

"Mare, I know you're watching me." he said without turning to look. It was easy to forget how perceptive he was.

I stepped closer to him, keeping my arms crossed. "Why are you distracted?"

"I'm not distracted." His mouth was set into a thin line as he threw the knife hard and watched it sail. It nestled into a tree, another fair distance away from the bullseye. He muttered a string of curses, his face tight with restrained anger. A punching bag might have been better for his mood, but I made no comment. "Fine, I'm distracted."

"Is everything okay?"

"If I told you the truth to that question, you'd run for the hills," he said. He flicked his hand and allowed the knives to soar toward him. "Ever since going to the Nixies, I've been on edge. All this talk about Kaser and all the strange happenings has sent me into overdrive. I must be better; I have to be ready."

"Why?" I asked. "There's no present danger."

"If Kaser wants Luka, he'll go after you again to get to him." Dayton threw a knife and scowled. "As your Consort—your sworn protector—I have to be ready to protect you. I'm also not convinced that you don't want to go after your friend."

I rolled my eyes. "I won't go looking for trouble, but if there's something I can do to help those I care about, it's not a question of what I would do."

Dayton's arrogant smile twisted into a smirk. "Believe me, I know."

"I like to think of myself as proactive instead of reactive."

Dayton hesitated to throw the next knife. Slowly, he lowered his hand. "If a fallacy like that helps you sleep at night, then far be it from me to judge."

He turned on me suddenly, storming toward me until I backed away, pressed up against a tree. He stood inches away from me; his eyes rippled into molten gold, and lingering rain dripped down the ends of his hair.

"Why are you not running from me?"

"Why are you determined to make me run from you?" I shot back. "I overheard what you said to Julian. I know you're afraid that you might be feeling something."

If Dayton weren't so close, I would have missed the crease of his eyes; otherwise, he showed no sign of surprise. He'd keep the mask on. He refused to give an inch when it mattered most.

"I'm not afraid!" he thundered. His hands unclenched and his claws protruded as he tilted his head back. "I'm not afraid of feeling something, but the consequences are too risky."

He was a mere breath from me now as he braced his hands against the tree trunk and closed his eyes. I brushed the hair from his face and forced him to look at me. His eyes were dark and empty, and beneath his shirt's collar, his tattoo peeked out, the sharp lines decorating the planes of his neck. My tattoo had also grown and mirrored Dayton's, and as the tattoo grew, I felt like we did, too. My heart hammered in my chest, our shared breaths the only sound.

"The tattoo is growing," I rasped. "Why?"

"I don't know," he practically seethed. "I don't fucking know."

"Dayton," I said lowly, not backing down from his anger.

"I can't allow myself to indulge in my wants," he said, closing his eyes again. "I don't deserve it, not in any capacity."

"What do you want, Dayton?" I said on impulse. This close, his breath warmed my neck like a gentle caress against my skin. I felt that warmth all the way into my core like a dull tingle. I desperately wanted to reach for him.

Dayton's eyes flicked open in silent answer.

"What if I hurt you? You should be running from me, not getting closer."

"You'd never hurt me."

"You should be scared of me. *Scared of this,*" he hissed.

Dayton stepped impossibly closer, and I leaned in; we were like two magnets drawn together, and if we moved any closer, our bodies would touch, breaking the invisible barrier kept between us. If I touched Dayton right now, it would be extremely hard to let him go. Neither of us dared to move.

"Dayton," I said slowly. "Don't ask me to feel scared. I'm not."

"Oh, Mare," he exhaled. He stepped back, a rumble of laughter tearing from him. He placed both hands behind his head and looked up at the sky with deep longing. "You light me up: my darkest moods and vilest thoughts—my most cynical actions. Like damn starlight."

All breath extinguished from me, and I clutched the bark to keep me steady and to keep from throwing myself at him. I waited for the other shoe to drop, expecting him to try and mess this up.

I steadied my breath and kept my voice even. "You deserve more than the hell you put yourself through."

"*Ad astra per aspera*," he said, voice rough. "'To the stars through difficulties.' My mother told me that. She always hated how I tormented myself, and she would loathe me if she could see me now. All I can think is, where do the stars go from here?"

"*Dayton*."

He circled me, watching me intently. Sweat dripped between his scrunched brows, his angry expression contrasting his words. Between one blink and the next, he closed the distance between us once again, his hand catching a wisp of my hair. He inched closer, bringing the strand to his nose, and I studied the innocence in his expression, marred with self-loathing.

"*Mare*." He uttered my name like a curse he couldn't shake.

My heart hammered in my chest, and a million thoughts raced through my mind. Dayton flicked his eyes open, revealing the livid fire playing within them. He reached down and grabbed my hand, bringing it up to his lips to place a light kiss on the top of my palm. Heat rushed through me, spiraled down my spine at the simple gesture. The feel of his rough, callused hands against my soft skin tickled me. Gently, he released my hand and walked backward, never straying his eyes from mine.

"Maris."

It took me a minute to realize it wasn't Dayton who spoke. I spun, surprised to see Luka watching me. I felt his judgment thick in the atmosphere, even from this distance. Luka jerked his head towards the house and walked away, expecting me to follow. I walked toward my brother, dreading the conversation soon to ensue.

I stood on the porch step and turned to get one last glance at Dayton. He let a knife soar through the air one final time, and I watched it nestled right on the bullseye. I couldn't help but grin.

Chapter 30

Luka swung the back door open with such force it clattered against the wall. Anger bristled in me. Luka had nothing to be mad about in the grand scheme of things. While he had his own issues with Dayton, that had nothing to do with me.

Luka halted in the kitchen and leaned against the fridge. I took a seat at the barstool, refused to meet his eye.

"You think I'm angry with you," he said plainly. Evenly. His calm demeanor didn't fool me; he was always calm before the raging storm.

I twisted my fingers before saying, "Considering I've met you, yes."

"I'm not angry with you."

I peered up at his sapphire gaze, noting the worn, dark circles smeared beneath. His jaw was shadowed with stubble, and I knew him well enough to recognize this as true exhaustion; he was usually meticulous about staying clean shaven. "You're not selling it to me," I said.

He started to grin and clasped his hands together. "I'm not angry with you. Him, on the other hand..."

"I'm not discussing Dayton with you," I said, raising my hand.

"Why?" he asked, yet I sensed the anger brewing beneath his tone.

"Because you know as well as I do that nine times out of ten, you let your anger cloud your judgment," I said, trying to keep my temper from rising.

"Nine out of ten, huh?" Luka mused. "What took me down a peg?"

"Being sarcastic to evade your response doesn't work on me."

Luka conceded. "I know I'm quick to anger—and quicker to react—but this is a judgment call I get to make. I've seen what he's capable of. I know where his loyalties lie. He's selfish and arrogant, and he wouldn't bat an eye if you were in danger. Helping you was for his own gain."

"That's not true," I fumed. "Without Dayton, I would have been lost in this world and probably dead."

"I would've never let that happen!" Luka argued. "I would've protected you."

"You weren't there, Luka! He was. I'm basing my judgment on what I know and what I see. You can't see past the boy you knew years ago, and maybe that's your problem."

"People don't change! He won't change!" Luka bellowed, setting his mouth into a thin line. "This is why I never wanted this life for you."

"It's too late for that now. Things are different, and we must accept that." I crossed my arms and glared at him. "I know you still see me as the same little girl you had to protect, but I'm not that little girl anymore."

"I will always, *always*, do anything and everything in my power to keep you safe," Luka said, leaving no room for doubt. "Including keeping you safe from Dayton."

"I won't waste my breath trying to convince you otherwise," I said. "But know that I truly believe you'd be better off working together than against each other. Especially with all this shit with Kaser."

Luka cracked his knuckles. "The day I work with anyone other than myself is a cry for help."

"God forbid," I said, meeting his gaze. "You might be a badass Alpha, but you're not going to be anything if you keep isolating yourself."

"Agree with my methods or don't. I understand how to get shit done."

"Do you trust me?" I asked blatantly.

Luka's face faltered as he let the question linger before responding. "As my sister, I trust you with my life. As a werewolf, whose judgment is mine to behold, I don't. Maybe if you didn't moronically continue to disobey me, I would trust you more."

"Because I'm tired of being in the dark," I fired at him. "Maybe if you were honest about things, I wouldn't run off!"

"On the contrary, little sister, you would." He shook his dark head. "Because like it or not, you're just like me."

Before I could answer, a sound came from his pocket, and I cringed at the shrill ringtone. Luka dug through his jeans until his cell phone appeared. Rolling his eyes, he brought the device to his ear.

"Randall, this ought to be worth the breath I waste talking to you." Luka's voice was a scary whisper as he stepped outside.

My head pounded. Maybe it was the effects of the coming full moon. Between a full moon, and Luka, Dayton, and Kaser to worry about, I wanted to scream. When Dayton revealed the truth of his past with Luka, I could easily see how well they would have worked together as Alpha and Beta. The unwillingness to hear each other out built a strong animosity between them, yet I knew they'd work well together if they'd allow themselves to.

I wanted them to work past their differences so I didn't feel torn in my feelings. It would be easier to think through my thoughts about

Dayton without worrying about Luka's feelings. I didn't know how I felt about him, and sometimes I wondered how I cared about someone so remorseless. It seemed like a recipe for disaster. Dayton talked about himself like he was a ticking time bomb. He wanted me to see that in him, but I didn't. Dayton might not be perfect, but he's tried to be better. That means something.

Luka entered the room again and slunk down next to me, resting his head in his hands. Tension coiled his muscles, straining against his shirt. His breath flowed evenly, but with effort, and a low hallow laugh erupted from him as he lifted his head and shook it slowly.

"Who was on the phone?" I asked.

"Randall. He's my informant—a part of my extensive network of spies," Luka said, dragging a hand down his face. "He's an easily forgettable man who knows much more than he lets on."

"He helps you then because you threaten him?" I asked, remembering his harsh words the moment he answered the phone.

Luka grinned. "You didn't like seeing me as the Bestial?"

I rolled my eyes but felt the tension flit away. "Oh, please, I remember the days when you ate dirt."

"Hey, it wasn't so bad. Don't knock it until you try it." He nudged me.

I laughed and shook my head. "You're gross."

Luka chuckled, then sighed. "When you saved Dayton in the Nixie realm, did anything else happen?"

"What do you mean?"

"I don't know... did anything unexplainable happen? Odd?"

"Not really," I said. I had moved fast when I saw the dagger aimed at Dayton, but that could be chalked up to adrenaline and my werewolf senses. Shetani disappearing was strange, but again, she must have left the way she came. "Why do you ask?"

"No reason. I'm just thinking."

"Do you mean scheming?" I asked sarcastically.

Luka smirked. "We'll worry more about everything after tomorrow. The full moon is our top priority. It's your first one."

"Ugh, don't remind me," I groaned.

The wolf had begun to show itself through my heightened senses, yes, but I also felt it. Beneath my skin it rippled in wait, wrapping around my very essence. It felt wrong and twisted, and it made me uneasy. The human part of me feared this transition, but I was ready. I had to be.

"What, you aren't excited to meet your wolf?" he asked.

"You talk as if the wolf and I aren't one and the same," I observed. "I don't get it."

"Think of us like a vessel for the wolf," Luka explained. "Yes, we're one and the same; however, the wolf has its own way of thinking. It acts on its instincts. The full moon brings out the wolf. When we phase on free will, we hold control."

I let what he said settle over me before I commented. It made sense, but the idea of being out of control only added to my unease. "The full moon forces us to change. Therefore, the wolf is in control?"

Luka nodded. "Exactly, see, you're starting to get it. Alphas like me are the only ones who can grapple the wolf fully."

"Alphas can control us on full moons and keep us from doing anything rash?" I guessed.

"That's pretty much the gist of it."

"Is the first time you turn terrifying?" I asked. I valued his input; after all, I was terrified, and I knew he could sympathize with that.

"For me, it was, but mostly because I had no idea what was happening to me." He laughed. "Terrifying didn't even cover what I felt. At least you know what you are."

I thought of what it must have been like for a younger Luka learning all this alone. I had many people around me, willing to help and protect me through this. I don't know what I might have done otherwise. Despite Luka's age when he turned, he was never young and innocent like I'd been. Luka's life had always been chaotic, and I now understood more clearly that his becoming a werewolf—becoming both a feared and respected Alpha—fully allowed him to stop being our father's son, and it gave him the freedom to be who he needed to be.

"I'm glad you're here." I told him.

"I'll always be here for you, Maris," he told me, smiling.

Chapter 31

The next day came and went as seamlessly as it could in a house full of werewolves before a full moon. Dayton verbally ripped apart anyone who annoyed him, which wasn't hard to do. As the full moon lingered over us, it cranked up the animosity to new levels, and with everyone at each other's throats, there was little time to tread over the more significant threat: Kaser.

I felt the stir in me, a teasing broil. When the time came for my first full moon, I thought I'd be ready, yet as the moon rose into the night, it seemed jarringly obvious that I wasn't. No matter what angle I looked at it, the idea of turning into a wolf sickened me. If I had eaten anything today, other than a meager slice of toast, I doubted I'd keep it down.

Once again, sleep plagued me, waking me throughout the night. But I didn't run to the bathroom to vomit, which felt like a small bonus—if you could call it that. Either way, my small win did not aid my deep-seated exhaustion. Ingesting copious amounts of coffee helped a little, though, as futile as it seemed.

Otherwise, everything seemed eerily calm aside from no one being able to get along. To Dayton's apparent dismay, there was nothing to report, and no one to fight or kill. I was half-finished braiding my hair when a knock came at the door. My tattoo burned.

"There's no point in doing that. With the amount of pain you'll be in, it will dishevel your appearance beyond recognition," Dayton's charming voice assured me.

He propped one arm over his head against the door and watched me. He seemed far too casual from his usual disposition of pouncing at anyone who looked at him funny. His gaze softened as he beheld me.

"You really know how to make me feel better," I said. I rolled my eyes and unplaited the braid. "Better? Will I survive this nightmare now my hair is down?"

Dayton smirked and shook his head, his eyes studying my unbound locks. "It won't be as bad as you think, nor as bad as I say it will be."

"That doesn't make me feel much better," I said, crossing my arms.

"It shouldn't. The first time you shift is going to be shit. It's painful, it's unfamiliar, and it feels like it lasts for days. Over time, your body will morph itself to fit the larger needs of the beast beneath the skin."

I tried to envision myself shifting into a wolf, yet I still had a tough time with it. An animal appearing from within me felt too unnatural—unimaginable. Even watching it with my own eyes didn't help. Whenever I thought about the pain, my blood ran cold.

"I doubt you were affected by it," I said. "Nothing hurts you."

"Hey, you said it, not me." He shrugged. "C'mon. Let's go before things get too out of control."

Without another word, Dayton left the room, and I followed. He led us through the Temple down the usual halls but made a detour at the bottom stairs to a new hallway. The temperature dropped significantly. The long hall was dark, and no light fixtures adorned the walls. At the end, an arched chestnut oak door stood, and on the wall beside it hung a pair of keys. Dayton plucked them up and unlocked the door. A staircase appeared beyond it. I heard muffled voices in the distance that became clearer the closer we approached.

Carefully, I followed Dayton down the narrow stone stairs, and an instant chill washed over me when we reached the bottom. I wrapped my arms around myself. Dark stone made up the walls and floors, with tiny windows high against the ceiling. The small space felt less cramped with its circular shape and lofty ceilings. A short hallway spilled into the outside gardens, allowing fresh air to course through the room. The room itself felt tense and coiled with anxiety.

Julian sat away from everyone else, almost unrecognizable; his hair was void of any color and he had removed all piercings on his face. Kyler's wrists were bound in handcuffs, chained to the walls behind her. When she looked up at us, her eyes glowed. Luka and Neville were nowhere to be seen.

"What's this?" I asked.

"A cellar of sorts," explained Dayton, crossing the room. He rummaged in a bucket. "A safe space to allow the shift to occur before releasing the wolf inside and allowing it to run free."

Dayton came up to me, holding out a pair of chains. The clinking of the chains made me recoil, clanging against my eardrum and tickling my brain. I didn't realize I'd have to be restrained; the thought of being chained up reminded me of when Zayne kidnapped me. I recalled the feeling of being unable to move or escape.

"Don't get too freaky on me," Dayton joked.

"You're gross," I snapped, grabbing the chains from him. My neck twitched at the noise, but I tried my best to ignore it. "What are these for?"

"To hold you back as long as possible before the wolf comes out," said Dayton. "When the wolf is in control, there's no saying what you might do, especially as a newborn. Once you get to the point of freely changing between your wolf and human form, you won't need these."

I glanced at Kyler, also chained up, and she noticed. "Don't look at me with those judgy eyes," she huffed. "I wasn't born into this life. The change sucks for me, too."

Before I asked another question, a big black wolf stalked in, and I leaped back into Dayton, who steadied me without a word. The giant wolf let out a deep growl, and something in me stirred. I bowed my head in submission, and in my periphery, I saw Dayton trying to suppress the gesture yet failing. Luka materialized from where the wolf had been seconds before, grinning.

"Sorry about that. My wolf tends to be dramatic this close to the moon," said Luka, glancing at everyone.

"Are you sure it's exclusive to the full moon?" Neville piped up, cracking his neck as he entered the space.

Kyler huffed a laugh. "You noticed that as well?"

Luka ignored them. "Enough. We need to focus on tonight."

"Anything out there that goes bump in the night, Chief?" asked Dayton.

"Hard to tell. The wards are flaky in spots," he said.

I smelled the sweat and dirt on my brother, his potent aroma like an assault on my senses. Luka dropped a bright white backpack from his shoulders and crouched to dig through it. The thud of the fabric on the ground sounded cleanly in my ears with a whoosh. Overstimulated, I stepped back to lean against the wall.

"The full moon is the main source of power for them. It'll recharge the wards to full capacity. Therefore, the days before can slowly deplete its power. Normally, we're fine, but with how things have been lately..." Dayton scowled, dragging a hand down his face. "I really fucking hate full moons."

Luka made a disgruntled noise as if in agreement. "Although we are not a Cadre, tonight I will treat you as such. Anything that might be out there, I'll protect you from it."

"Thank you," Kyler said through gritted teeth; her body shuddered.

I recalled what Luka explained to me yesterday, though it felt like eons ago. One night every month, the wolf inside us got a free pass. It felt as unsettling as it sounded. I couldn't suppress the shudder rippling through me as I thought about being a wolf, out of control.

"What about your actual Cadre?" Dayton asked. "You're gone; Derek is gone. Your Beta is the stand in when the Alpha is gone, so who is with them?"

"Renetta can manage them," said Luka. "But I need to go back to them soon. Over the past few weeks, I've neglected my duties as an Alpha, and I don't like being that way with them."

It was strange to think the people I worked with on the daily had been werewolves, forming a part of Luka's Cadre. I'd spent many grueling hours with each of them—hell, I thought I knew them. But I'd learned that time didn't discern how well you knew someone. While I knew all of them much longer than I'd known Dayton, I knew him better than any of them.

"It isn't as if you don't have your hands full here," grumbled Dayton.

"You remember how Rico is," Luka remarked. "He gets antsy."

Before more could be said, Julian cried out. He fell, his kneecaps crashing onto the concrete. The sound of shattering bones echoed across the space, and Julian whimpered, curling in on himself. My eyes widened, and I started toward him, but Dayton pushed me back. Julian's bellow of pain rattled along the walls. Dayton didn't seem the least bit fazed.

"What's wrong with him?" I asked, alarmed.

"He's okay. It's the full moon. Julian is shifting," explained Dayton, his lips pursed.

It was terrifying to watch the transition firsthand, especially as Julian had been a werewolf much longer than I had, yet it sounded like a meat grinder pulverized his flesh and bones, then spat him out. I glanced out the window, seeing a sliver of light from the moon. My whole body reacted in a spasm, and in my mind's eye, an outline of a wolf appeared. I yelped and stepped back into the wall.

"What's his problem?" demanded Luka.

Dayton scowled and in two strides was across the room beside Julian, who released another pained howl. Dayton hovered, resting a hand on his shoulder.

"Jules?" he whispered. If not for my sensitive hearing, I wouldn't have heard him. "Jules, are you alright?"

Julian's head flew up. "*Get back.*"

His pine-green irises rippled into a pulsing glow, and a familiarity struck me, having glimpsed him without the rainbow hair and piercings. I couldn't place it, and it was gone as quickly as it came. Julian cried out again and lurched forward. Dayton caught him by the shoulders, attempting to push him back as he thrashed against the chains, yet Dayton struggled to control him, and dug his heels into the ground with a curse. Frantically, I looked around; Luka was halfway to Julian.

Julian broke free of his chains, leaving behind two gaping holes in the wall. Raging forward, Julian tossed Dayton aside like he weighed no more than paper, and I gasped as Julian locked eyes with me. Not daring to move, I simply watched as he prowled closer. He looked inhumane—feral—and I stood frozen, rooted in place. Luka interjected at once, his eyes a bright blue, but Julian was surprisingly quick and backhanded him. Luka stumbled backward, eyes wide in shock.

Julian roared and fell to his knees, bellowing at the sky. His spine sprang up like an angry cat, each movement followed by the snap of bones. I felt like I shouldn't watch yet was unable to look away as he cried out again. I started to walk toward him but stopped when he crumpled to the ground. He howled, flinging his hand backward as the bones in his fingers shattered. His canines lengthened as claws twisted free from his fingernails. Julian doubled in size, fur spurting from every pore of his body. A long snout stretched across his face as he released an angry cry.

Where Julian had writhed in pain mere moments before, a wolf now stood. His pale white fur glistened like a dusting of starlight, stark against the somber cave, and his head turned, preternaturally still. His green eyes were unrecognizably feral, dark, and searching.

Dayton dared to stand before him, his hands raised defensively, with his own eyes aglow. Julian's tongue flicked from his mouth as he advanced toward Dayton.

"Jesus, boy, stand down," Neville chimed in, seeming shocked yet still in tune with the situation. "I've never seen a wolf so desperate or angry to come out."

"When the fuck were you going to mention that he's a rogue wolf?" spat Luka, standing in an equally defensive position beside Dayton. I wanted to move to help, but what help could I offer?

"You're the one who taught me the element of surprise," said Dayton out of the side of his mouth. "Surprise."

Rogue wolf? I'd never heard the term before.

Julian lurched forward at Dayton, who leaped out of the way, backing up until he was cornered against the wall. Luka moved wickedly fast and shed his human skin, emitting a growl that reverberated across the walls. I was shocked this little room didn't crumble in on itself.

Nothing but absolute rage and authority rippled in Luka's gaze. I felt pulled by his authority as it reigned over all of us, dampening the mood and noise to near silence. Next to Luka, Julian looked like a boulder for size. Luka stood taller, lifting his chest as he curled his lips back. Luka's ebony fur rose against his hackles and he stood over Julian, who whimpered, beginning to back down. He never took his eyes from Luka.

"Luka, wait, you don't understand!" Dayton bellowed, rushing forward.

Julian hurtled forward, aiming for Luka's exposed throat. Luka batted Julian aside like a ragdoll, who landed in front of me. My vocal cords strained as I dropped the chains and scrambled back. Jumping up, Julian peered around until spotting the exit. He bolted.

"*Jules, no!*" Dayton tore off toward the exit, but Luka jumped in front of him. "Get out of my way!"

Luka growled, and I instantly fell to my knees against my will, the pull to submit too strong. Luka's nostrils flared as he circled Dayton, who fought against the submission. His claws were out, and his eyes aglow. I felt the moment he released his claim as his gaze tore from Dayton. Luka was himself again.

"What the hell just happened?" demanded Luka in Dayton's face.

Dayton roared, shoving Luka back. "I told you I'd handle Julian!" he growled. "I told you that you had no business dominating us."

Luka scowled and turned from Dayton. "It's not a switch that can be turned off. It's instinct to help a wolf in distress. Maybe that's why you can't understand it."

Dayton swung, but I moved fast, catching his fist before it connected with Luka. Dayton jerked back and spun just as quick, his glowing eyes bearing down on me. A low rumble rippled from his chest. I stubbornly held his glare despite straining my neck to look up at him.

"I'm going after Jules. No one follow me," he said, breaking from my grip.

Allowing no room for argument, Dayton moved fast, a massive, burly wolf materialized with dark fur resembling dark chocolate. His unruly fur stuck up in all directions, as wild as the boy beneath. An ingrained, no-nonsense power oozed from him as he lowered to the ground, his ears flattening as he drew back and howled at the moon. Dayton took off into the night.

"Can anyone explain what just happened?" I looked to my brother, who looked as puzzled as I did.

Neville smiled mischievously. "The boy's wolf is rogue. He is not."

"It's an anomaly." Luka shook his head, beginning to pace. "I've never, ever, seen that before."

"What does that mean?" I asked.

"When you turn into the wolf, you still have a sense of your own self. You can still think and react with your free will and judgment. A rogue means you are *only* the wolf; there is no human left inside. Julian is Julian, but his wolf is a separate entity. There's no Julian when he is the wolf," Luka explained. "It's nearly unheard of."

"What makes it rare?"

Neville answered this time. "Becoming a rogue results from suppressing the wolf for a long stretch of time, refusing to let it out. It's natural for your wolf to come out once every full moon, but if you're forced away from the moon and you don't shift, then you run that risk."

I considered how Julian seemed to be in an abnormal amount of pain during the transition. I had never seen Julian shift prior to that, despite Dayton shifting into his wolf whenever it suited. It made sense that if Julian couldn't control his wolf, he'd refuse to turn at will, but how had it gotten to that point?

"Julian is dangerously powerful beyond any limitations we can see," said Luka.

"Julian can do many things that makes one wonder," Kyler cooed. "Lord only knows what he endured in those years Dante had him."

Julian only mentioned his past to me once and refused to go into detail; yet whatever happened to him had been terrible, and he bore what Dante did to him every day. I wondered if this—being rogue—formed a part of that.

"Julian has the power of mental manipulation, yet he only understands it at a surface level. If he could control it..." Luka shook his head and crossed the room, his footfalls like splashing through water puddles. It was deafening. "I don't know, I think he could be really damn powerful if he dared."

"Not everyone cares about power and glory," Kyler huffed. "Julian hates what he is. Powers should have limitations."

Luka shrugged. "We don't have time to debate. They're gone now. I cannot protect those who don't want it."

Gently, he grabbed my arm and pulled me away from the others. He gestured for my hands, and I held them out without forethought. He fixed the cuff over my wrists, the metal cool against my skin, then he stood and tied the chain to a sturdy-looking post. He quickly fixed them like this were a common practice, and my hands trembled as an unfamiliar sensation seized me. Kyler must have been moving because the scrape of her shoe against the ground blasted in my ear.

"What's the point of the chains again?" I said through clenched teeth.

"Letting your wolf run rampant is inevitable. This will simply delay the inevitable. Think of it as damage control," explained Luka. "Here."

I glanced up at my brother and watched as he tossed something at me. I caught it without even thinking. A Hershey's milk chocolate bar. I tilted my head at Luka.

"Aren't dogs allergic to chocolate or something?"

Luka slunk down beside me, chuckling. "We're not dogs. We're wolves. Besides, I've found that chocolate helps ease the nerves during a full moon."

"Chocolate can help with anything." I unwrapped the candy, smiling as I plopped a piece into my mouth. Its sweetness felt euphoric as I chewed. I jerked as pain ripped through me; I clenched my fists and cursed. "Why does this hurt?"

"You're not attuned with your wolf fully. The less you let it out, the less connection you have, then resentment forms, like what you saw with Julian," he explained. "The more you change and understand the wolf, the easier it becomes."

Trying to ignore the pain wrapping around my spine, I said, "Do I have to shift?"

"Nonnegotiable," said Luka. "But you're lucky enough to know a pretty powerful Alpha who will help you every step of the way."

A wave of nausea melted over my body. "It doesn't seem fair that you're not affected by this."

Luka snorted. "Hardly. The pain just doesn't bother me anymore. It used to be hell, especially in the beginning, and hiding the shift from you was torture."

"How did you do it?" I asked. I welcomed the distraction of talking while trying to ignore the pain.

"Mind over matter. I taught myself that pain was just a mental discomfort," he said casually. "It wasn't an easy feat, and I still have to remind myself sometimes."

I bounced my legs as pinpricks of pain trickled across them. A hot ripple of agony exploded in my mind like the world's worse migraine. I shoved my head between my knees and rocked back and forth, moaning.

Mind over matter, my ass.

"You really did this by yourself?" I managed to ask once the pain dulled.

Luka was quiet for a long moment before shuffling beside me. "In the beginning, I had no one, not a Cadre or a friend to help. That was until I met Finley."

"Whose Finley?" I asked.

Luka inhaled slowly, and I could see he was working up the nerve to tell me something. "Finley was my boyfriend."

His revelation froze the nausea roiling within me. Somehow, learning my brother had a secret boyfriend felt more shocking than knowing he hid a whole other life as a werewolf from me. Luka was never the type to date or have friends. Allowing others into his circle was never his thing.

"You had a boyfriend?" I asked, the pain reigniting once more. "How? When? What happened?"

"I was a kid when I met him; well, it's not like I ever really was a kid. When you're young, you think anything is possible." Luka dragged a hand down his face. "Finley, well... something bad happened, and it was my fault."

Luka didn't sound pained, but he stated it as fact. I watched his carefully blank expression as he refused to reveal his true feelings. Despite how well he hid his pain, Luka having romantic feelings toward someone was no small feat. He wasn't exactly warm and fuzzy.

"Whatever happened, it wasn't your fault," I said.

He laughed meekly, throwing a rock across the room. "I wasn't there to protect him. It is my fault."

Waves of pain knocked me aside. I dug my fingers into my palms as shrouds of agony erupted, centering the fear inside me. My heart rate spiked, and a soft gurgle of pain oozed from me. I looked over at Kyler, whose head was planted between her knees; she shot up, her eyes blazing. At that, Luka's attention shifted, and he prowled the room. Neville heaved her back, but Kyler was strong. Like a blur, she tore free of her chains and screamed, yet a piercing howl outside shifted Luka's attention. Kyler tore free in wolf form and, faster than a streak of light, she escaped into the night. Luka swore and ran to the cave's entrance, eyes bright with anger.

Another howl resounded.

"Lukas, something is out there," warned Neville, his eyes a dull orange.

Luka looked at me and then outside, fisting his hands by his sides. "I don't like this."

Neville grunted and fell to his knees. "Once a month I endure this bullshit. Lord, help me."

It happened quickly without the added dramatics. Neville's body rippled as it grew, and a large gray wolf shook free. With a quick howl, Neville disappeared, too. He'd transformed faster than I thought possible, but before I could process it, Luka turned on me, his eyes bright. He must have done something as an Alpha as all the pain left my body.

I took a deep breath through my nose and out through my mouth as the tension eased in my body. Another round of howls cut through me, yet they sounded far away—desperate. Yet the wolf inside me felt drawn to it, and suddenly, I jolted forward on my hands and knees, pain erupting through every nerve ending in my body. I wanted to cry out, only no sound escaped. I clawed in agony against the ground as blood spurted from my fingers.

Another howl pierced the night, and my tattoo pulsed like an aching reminder of who wasn't here. I missed Dayton; I had expected him to be here for this, but he wasn't. He'd been with me through all the parts of this life; he'd become a permanent fixture in a way, but it was silly to expect such things. I couldn't shake the disappointment.

Two more howls exploded in the night, and Luka cursed, glancing between me and the outside again. He paced like a caged animal, readying to pounce, yet the howls only drew closer. It was hard to think clearly through my discomfort, but I knew he should be out there.

Then, bustling through the cave entrance, was Dayton. He was sweat-soaked and bloody, panting hard. He glanced to me and released an audible breath of relief. Luka nearly knocked him over when he didn't speak right away.

"Fenrir," Dayton managed to say. "They shattered the wards—they're here. I couldn't keep fighting them because—because—Shetani."

"—Breathe, Dayton," ordered Luka.

"Kaser sent his Fenrir here to find the Artifact," Dayton gasped. "I assume, I don't know what else they'd want; Shetani is here, and it's a mess. Neville is running point around the Temple; Kyler is actively fighting with Fenrir. Julian—I lost him."

Luka bellowed with rage, glancing between me and outside. I could barely keep up with what was being said, blinded by the pain pounding through my body as each bone vibrated with agony.

"Go," Dayton told him firmly. "They need you. I can stay."

Luka looked utterly torn.

"Go, Luka!" Dayton shouted. "I'll stay with Maris; I can protect her."

Luka loosed a breath then took off like a shot into the dark night.

My eyes flashed open, and I ran forward at full speed, violently jerked back by the chains that bound me. I huffed and yanked at them once more, the pain around my wrists throbbed and my bones felt bigger than my body.

Dayton prowled toward me, his golden eyes aglow. "Mare," he whispered. "I'm here; I'm with you."

"It hurts," I choked.

"It's going to hurt like a bitch," he agreed. "Once it happens, I'll be here. I'll keep you safe."

"What about you?"

"I'm strong," Dayton said. "I have a strong hold on my wolf; I can easily shift between skins on full moons."

Something inside me stopped stirring and finally exploded. Blinding pain snaked up every nerve ending in my body, and I felt the strain in my throat, my body protesting at the beast thrashing inside of me. A howl pierced the void outside, and I tunneled deeper into the pain. Blinded, the agony numbed me to all else, and the cracking and snapping of my bones had me writhing on the ground. With each step further into the pain, I finally crossed the barrier I had feared.

Distantly, I heard Dayton, but he sounded a million miles away.

A roar tore through me, burying the pain in the darkness. My body sang in harmony to the shift as I rose higher and higher, standing tall. Euphoria, clear and unabridged, danced through me as I connected with the wolf and its desire to be free. Pulling from the chains was no longer challenging, and as I barreled out of the cellar, my instincts kicked in.

Beside me, Dayton ran, staying close by and guiding me along. I ran, pursuing the instincts I didn't know I had, and with each step, I gained speed, the power building inside of me. The ability to do anything and be anything was possible. My limbs felt stiff and I stretched. A howl escaped me, and a high of joy accompanied it.

I halted—or the wolf did. I felt like a passenger, the wolf being the driver. I stood at the edge of a cliff overlooking the clear night sky. The full moon illuminated the night like a blazing ball of light, and I felt entranced by the sight of it. The depthless expanse of night struck me, and I loosed a long howl.

At my side, Dayton harmonized with me.

I ran again, faster than ever before. Everything blurred. I saw without looking, heard without listening, smelt without seeing. Dayton, as his wolf, ran along with me. The hoot of an owl sounded clear in my ears, and my sight automatically tracked its location in a nearby tree. If I was a hunter, it would be easy to find my prey like this. I felt the motion of the earth upturn wherever I ran; it was like I never had to worry about fumbling or falling again. There was no hesitation in my gait. I hurtled over an edge to the expanse of land that dwelled on the other side. The landing was seamless without so much as a stumble to slow me.

Dayton leaped in front of me, seeing the threat I had not. A wolf rammed into his side, knocking him over as they engaged in a brawl. I didn't recognize the wolf; it looked miniscule beside Dayton, with ashy-colored fur. My instincts roared at me to intervene, to help him, but another wolf bombarded hard into my side and swept the breath clean from me.

My paws dug into the earth, kicking up dirt as I tried to steady myself. I spun around at once and cowered. A wolf twice my size stood above me, their glowing red eyes shooting panic through my body. The wolf advanced and licked its lips. Blood streaked its maw—fresh and old. I could tell from the tackiness of its fur.

My hair stood along my back and I lowered my tail, dropping to the ground. Snarling, I backed up, never taking my eyes off the wolf. A growl rumbled through me, and the wolf lunged. Something jerked me back by the scruff of my neck; I yowled and bucked, yet nothing lessened the wolf's grip. It released me suddenly, and I could compose myself. My eyes rested on a familiar face, no longer holding back my snarl of disgust.

"My, my, Maris. You made it easy to find you. Good thing you still reek of newborn," spoke a deep male voice in human form.

A growl followed my stunned silence as Dayton shed his wolf fur, changing back into himself as easily as changing clothes. He approached the male in two strides, fiery rage oozing in his golden gaze.

"You should be dead," Dayton yelled, punching the man in the face.

When the man flew backward, the moonlight illuminated his face and confirmed my suspicions. It felt like eons since I last saw him. Dayton was right; he should be dead. Yet Zayne grinned up savagely at us, still very much alive. He stood fast, and I sensed something off about him, like a chip of wildness wrangled within him. Before Dayton reacted, Zayne returned the blow, knocking Dayton back.

I jolted toward him, panicked, but I was stopped by a white wolf with bloodstained fur, lips curled back in a savage sneer. Before the wolf even transitioned, I knew who it was. Shetani.

"Well, well, well," Shetani said slowly, shaking free her wild curls. "Finding you wasn't nearly as hard as we anticipated."

Dayton attempted to stand but Zayne moved toward him, pushing him down with a booted foot. He kicked Dayton's spine, and his body went limp. Blood trickled from his mouth. A whine escaped my throat upon watching Dayton taken down so easily. Dayton had gone toe to toe with Luka, faced multiple Fenrir, and even attempted to ward off an army of Nixies. If Zayne could overwhelm him, I was defenseless.

Zayne rolled his eyes. "Your precious Consort will be fine. His spine will heal, and once he regains the ability to move, I'll snap it again."

Shetani tsked. "Dayton, a viper with words and combat, yet refuses to join the darkness." she taunted, sauntering closer. With each step, she grew bigger. "Lukas would not admit it, but I know he likes the darkness, too. No one is as ruthless or as mercilessly as him. He enjoys the kill."

"Enough talk, Shetani. You can't play the long game," Zayne seethed. "We need Maris."

Dayton was unmoving on the ground, yet his eyes were open, urging me to run like the wind and not look back. I wouldn't—I *couldn't* abandon him. If I ran, they would only use Dayton to lure me back like they did Derek. Slowly, I backed up, watching Zayne and Shetani.

"We need Maris to come to us willingly," Shetani corrected. "Kaser's plans are nothing if she is an unwilling participant, but we have ways of gaining her compliance."

Shetani charged, turning into her wolf form. I jumped over her without thinking, and she tumbled back. I bit the scruff of her neck, tearing off a chunk of flesh and fur, the blood between my teeth. Pure nerve launched me at her, and I swiped my paw across her face. She retaliated at once, but Zayne's growl stopped all commotion.

"Maris, stand down, or your Consort's blood is on your hands," warned Zayne. "Enough blood has been spilled tonight."

I stopped all movement as Zayne crouched, holding a blade at Dayton's throat. Dayton's eyes locked with mine, begging me silently to escape, yet if anyone could understand why I had to stay, it would be Dayton. I just hoped he would.

I yelped as a large black wolf soared from above, yet one look at its eyes sent relief washing over me. Luka—the Bestial—was pure Alpha, effortlessly domineering over them. Zayne released Dayton and charged.

I lowered to the ground, my ears drawn back in fear. Battle erupted in an explosion of blood, teeth, and lethal claws. Both Shetani and Zayne aimed for Luka in their respective wolf forms, and for a millisecond, I considered coming to his aid, yet quickly realized it wasn't needed. He moved faster than both combined as the rage billowed off him and fueled his movements. Watching Luka now, I understood the rumors that made him a legend. This was the Bestial in his full form, and I would not get in his way.

I focused on Dayton, who lay in a heap on the ground. I gunned toward him while the others were distracted, yet as I lunged, the potent scent of rotted eggs invaded my senses. My back arched at once as I beheld a towering Fenrir standing above me. Facing them now, we were the same height. They appeared less terrifying than before, yet still disgusting to look at: half wolf, half human. Their snouts appeared partially formed, and their tall, gangly bodies were skin and bones, with claws where fingertips had been. Patches of fur sprouted sporadically over their skin, and their eyes moved between me and the battle as if unsure of what to do. I took the opportunity to ram my whole body weight into it, striking it down.

Its claws struck down my back, spilling blood down my fur. I yelped. The Fenrir had brute strength, and it tossed me into a tree. My side took the brunt of it, and I heard my ribs snap. Before I could run at it again, Dayton tore free from his paralyzed state, gunning for the Fenrir, who stood with only his claws out as a defense.

My relief only lasted moments before I was again pulled down. Shetani yanked at my nape, and I flailed like a fish out of water to get her off me. Yanking hard enough on my fur, she launched me back until it was only the two of us tumbling awkwardly down a hill as we spit and bit and clawed at each other's throats. We thudded against the ground and finally came to a standstill. Amusement glinted in her eyes as she brought her head down close to mine, her sharp teeth bared. I kicked at her.

"*Shetani,*" Dayton's voice growled.

Shetani's weight over me lessened as she melted into human form, just as Dayton yanked her back by her neck and dragged her away.

"Get off me, you filthy mutt!" Shetani screamed as Dayton sliced at her arm with his claws.

"Touch her again and see what happens," Dayton snarled with a crazed look in his eyes. The blade of his knife kissed her throat, and trickles of blood spurted free.

"Kill me, boy. She is dead either way," Shetani said, laughing.

"Enough, Shetani!" Zayne's voice cried from behind.

Luka prowled toward me, and I sank to the ground beside him, lowering my head. Between the chaos of battle, I hadn't noticed our group had grown. In their wolf forms, Kyler and Neville stood, both bloodied and disheveled, but otherwise unharmed. They each flanked Luka, forming a barrier around me. I was the one they wanted to take.

"Your girl is dead," Shetani snarled at Dayton. "Kaser has plans, you see. Plans that highly involve your precious girl."

Dayton roared and threw Shetani hard against the tree, which collapsed backward in a mighty thud. I gaped as Luka sprang from his wolf skin to himself and yanked Dayton back with effort. He leaned in and whispered something into Dayton's ear. I couldn't hear it. Dayton's nostrils flared in response as he stared at Shetani. In answer, she winked, then ran off like the devil was snapping at her heels. Luka let her go; he must have known something. He pushed Dayton back toward our group.

Kyler and Neville both moved aside simultaneously, allowing Dayton to see me. My ears perked up, and I lifted my head to nuzzle his hand. Relief flooded Dayton's eyes, but his rough stance conveyed little else as he stood guard in front of me, tense as a bowstring.

"I don't know how the hell you are alive, but answer me this," growled Luka, prowling closer to Zayne. "What the fuck is Kaser planning?"

Zayne quivered, backing up. "You're an intelligent male, Lukas. You have it figured out already. Kaser is growing impatient. The quality of life is fleeting for your Beta."

A whine escaped me at the mention of Derek. For weeks he had been trapped by Kaser, enduring who knew what. Yet my fear for him was overpowered by my desperation to get to him—to save him.

"What does he want?" Luka asked again. "Me? He can fucking have me if it ends all this."

"You know he won't do that," said Zayne. His voice dropped an octave as he looked at me. "He wants your sister, but he needs her to come to him willingly."

"No!" Luka bellowed. He launched himself at Zayne, punching him so hard he flew back against the tree.

Zayne laughed at the sky, wiping blood from his mouth with the back of his hand. He grinned like a madman as he honed his gaze on me.

"You know what he wants, Lukas. I'm proof of that," Zayne sneered. "Just piece the puzzle together. Kaser needs her because he believes she's special. *Different.* He wants her, and he will get her, but she must be willing to go to him."

It didn't make sense. Why would I need to be willing? It was unlikely I'd ever be willing to face him. A dark thought loomed over me: they had one thing to use against me if they wished—something that would motivate me. Derek.

Zayne reached into his pocket and pulled out something small. The smell emanating from it was revolting, and when Zayne tossed it to the ground, I nearly vomited. A finger that seemed freshly severed lay on the ground with a silver ring adorning it. I recognized the ring. It was Derek's ring. That was Derek's severed finger.

"Kaser is growing impatient," Zayne sneered, looking right at me as he spoke. "Now, it's a finger. Tomorrow, it might be an eye or his tongue. There are many parts that can be carved from him to still keep him alive. Just know this. If you fight and delay, he will still come for you, Maris."

Luka ran at him, his claws extended, and before anyone could react, he reached Zayne. No sound came from him as Luka tore his throat open. No blood spilled. He didn't clutch for his throat or gargle for mercy; he simply thudded to the ground and dissolved into dust, his ashes scattering on the wind. I didn't fully understand what I had witnessed, but as I glanced at the others' expressions, I knew it wasn't normal.

Luka staggered backward and reached down to pick up the severed finger. He turned to face us then stared up at the sky.

"Kaser wants to play?" Luka laughed darkly. "Fine. I'll fucking play."

Chapter 32

R estless energy brewed inside of me, and no matter what, it wouldn't settle. Not after last night. After everything that happened with Shetani and Zayne, the night continued as it was meant to on a full moon, with us staying in our wolf forms and running through the night. It was pure euphoria, and relinquishing the wolf in me aligned two parts of myself I never realized were astray. Aside from my run-in with danger, the pure high of being utterly free had not faded. I appreciated the feeling and now understood the wolf's need to be free. I wanted to learn more about it, lean, and tap into it. Mostly, I wanted to be able to control it and understand the shift.

That high simmered quickly as realization dawned. We had bigger, more pressing matters on our hands. Kaser made his move, and we could no longer be sitting ducks. The opportunity to face him was now before us.

Luka left the moment the sun peaked over the horizon, the full moon gone until the next. He didn't share his plans or motives, but I suspected he knew what he was doing. When Zayne showed up, alive, Luka didn't seem shocked; in fact, he acted like Zayne's appearance was inevitable. But Zayne had died; Dayton watched Luka behead him on the night I was taken, and while I didn't know how that was possible, I suspected Luka did.

My mind remained stuck on Derek and the sight of his severed finger tossed to the ground like it was nothing more than extra change. Kaser viewed Derek's life with little worth, and it made me furious. What's more, it made me sad. It was the final straw. I had to do something, even if no one else would. I didn't know what Luka was scheming, but he'd made his feelings about Derek clear, and so had Kaser. He wanted me, and he could have me. I'd figure out a way to save us both, but to get to Derek, I'd need to get to Kaser.

My half-crazed mind brought me to the weapons room in the early hours of the morning. There was a small window of chance with Luka gone and Dayton searching the grounds for Julian. I wasn't going to run away, but I hoped to plead my case to Dayton. I'd come prepared after packing an array of knives and daggers into a duffle bag to carry some defense. A part of me knew it was silly. I couldn't use any of these weapons, but at least I'd have something.

I stepped out of the bathroom, the steam escaping with it. I glanced toward the bed and where the duffle was kept beneath it. Breathing deeply, I rummaged through the closet with shaking hands and grabbed jeans, a tight black T-shirt, and a leather jacket. I considered wearing fighting leathers similar to what Dayton always wore but the millions of zippers and buckles overcomplicated matters. I combed my wet hair to let it rest over my shoulders for a moment, recalling when Dayton picked up a piece of my hair and held it ever so delicately between his fingers. That felt long ago now. I wrapped it into a bun.

I picked up the duffle from beneath the bed and rushed out of the door. I had to be careful sneaking around in case I ran into Luka, though

I didn't think he'd returned yet; he was stealthy—smart. He'd be able to sniff out my intentions. I stayed close to the walls as I moved. The silver light of the wolf head torches was dull enough to hide me in the shadows, but I remained vigilant, peeking around the corner of the stairwell where natural light spilled through. I scampered down the steps without a sound; Dayton ought to be impressed.

Two voices sounded, and my body seized. I darted to hide behind one of the marble pillars beside the front door, concealing me from sight. The front door stood inches away; I might be able to open and close it with enough stealth to be unnoticed, but the two voices were discernible now and captured my attention. I flattened against the door, extending a hand until I gripped the cold doorknob.

"Stop it, Jules, I don't want to hear it," Dayton spat.

"Ah, good. Progress. You're at least admitting there is some truth in what I said, even if you don't want to hear it," chimed Julian. "My, have you changed."

I exhaled and slowly peered around the corner. Both of their backs were turned to me. Dumb luck, really. Dayton stood by the ceiling length windows in the living room, one arm braced above his head as he brooded, while Julian braced his hands on the couch, watching Dayton with challenge.

"Jules," Dayton warned. I noticed the swords at his sides and the barrel of a gun poking from his belt. The extra weaponry was no coincidence. No doubt our run-ins with danger had put a bad taste in his mouth, and he chose to be extra cautious.

Of course, Julian went on. "I knew you then, and I know you now. When everything happened with your family, it was like a part of you died with them. I saw that light leave you. The feral look in your eyes never wavered." He paused, assessing Dayton to test the merit of his delivery. "Except around her, it's different. You're allowing yourself something you didn't have before."

"I screwed up," Dayton rumbled. "Maris is a mistake. She understands me, and I can't keep poisoning her with the association she has with me. Hell, why am I even talking to you about this? It's bullshit."

My heart stopped, and I almost bolted then and there. This conversation was not for me to overhear, and I didn't want to know what Dayton might say next. Recently, the two of us had grown close, and while I wasn't sure what that meant, I knew I liked it. Foolishly, I thought he felt the same.

"Because it matters." Julian pressed.

Dayton roared, and before I realized what happened, glass shattered. Dayton beat his fist repeatedly through the broken window, glass cutting his skin. Julian had to physically restrain him, catching his arm and yanking him back. Dayton jerked away and turned on Julian, and for a moment, I thought he might attack him. Yet Julian seemed entirely unfazed, and slowly, Dayton backed away, storming out of the room and toward the kitchen.

I let go of the doorknob and started to follow Dayton without a forethought. I paused to look at Julian, who smirked like a Cheshire cat upon seeing me. To his credit, he didn't say anything about the duffle over my shoulder, nor did yesterday's debacle show on his face; in fact, he appeared completely ordinary despite no piercings or glittering clothes.

"Don't go after him unless you're prepared to face him," Julian's voice filled my head, and he shot me a pointed look.

With a huff, I continued toward the kitchen. Dayton sat on a barstool, a pocketknife beside him on the counter and a small vial in his hand. He poured out a fine silver powder onto his wounded hand, and he didn't look up when I entered. He began slicing the top of his hand with a wince.

"What do you think you're doing?" I gasped, dropping my duffle and walking toward him. "Is that silver powder? That could kill you."

Dayton jumped, surprised to see me. Dark smudges of exhaustion lined his eyes, and his hair was messy; I doubted he had slept at all in the last twenty-four hours. It looked like he had run a hand through his hair countless times.

"If this kills me, you're lucky," he said darkly. "Silver powder will keep the wound from closing right away. I need to get the glass out from under my skin."

I almost told him he shouldn't have punched a window but caught myself. Instead, I sat beside him and pulled his wrist toward me while moving the pocketknife away. I beheld his bloodied hand that looked like he had committed a small massacre on his palm. Dayton glowered and began to pull away, but when I glared at him, he conceded.

"Don't play tough guy. You have nothing to prove," I scolded.

He blinked at me slowly. "Fine. Whatever you say, Mare."

I rolled my eyes, then picked up the knife. "Hold still," I ordered. He stared at the wall. "What'd you do?"

"I had the bright idea to put my fist through a window," Dayton confessed. "Not my worst idea, but I've had better."

I gripped his wrist and assessed how best to get the glass out. The powder worked just as Dayton said and kept the wound open. There wasn't so much embedded in his skin, but too much for a pocketknife to remove.

"Do you have tweezers or something?"

"No."

I sighed. This was not how I saw my morning going. "This is going to hurt."

I don't know how much time passed as I homed in with complete focus on the task at hand. It was like a glass grenade had exploded in his palm and knuckles. I used the knife to get out the pieces, its sharp tip cutting over his knuckle where a stubborn piece was jammed. It cut deep enough that I saw his finger bone, though it didn't bother me like I thought it might. I continued while Dayton didn't complain or speak; he didn't look pained, but merely uncomfortable. His only true tell was the occasional tightening of his jaw.

When I finally finished, I set the makeshift surgical instrument aside and watched as his hand healed as it should. Glass free.

Dayton pulled his hand back, wriggled his fingers, and made a fist. "Thank you," he said quietly, standing.

Afraid he might leave, I quickly said, "Are you alright?"

Dayton tensed. "Everyone keeps fucking asking that damn question," he said, starting for the door. "I'm fine. I'm always fine."

"Dayton." I started, then stopped. I didn't know what to say or how to convey to him... A cold sweat broke across my skin. "I'm worried about you."

He gave a hollow laugh, his hand halfway to the door. "If you're going to feel something, let it be something better than worrying for me."

I should have walked out the front door and forgot all about him. Getting Derek back was more important than this, but I stayed. A part of me thought maybe, just maybe, I could have a real conversation without Dayton's usual unpleasantness. Once again, I was a fool playing this game with him.

"Why are you being like this?" I pressed with more conviction. I had no issue challenging him when he acted like a dickhead.

"Like what?" he spat. "An asshole? I don't know, maybe because I am, but you don't want to see it."

"You know that's not what I meant," I said, both confused and frustrated.

"I don't care to have this conversation." He started again for the door. "Especially not with you."

"I'm going after Derek." I ensnared him with the words I knew would make him stay.

I thought I had wanted him to know, but as I said it, I realized I *needed* him to know. I wouldn't have felt right walking away from him and into danger. I respected our bond enough to recognize that.

"*What?*"

I set my jaw and met his gaze. "Kaser wants me for Derek. He can have me. I'm going to give myself up to him."

"You've made some questionable judgment calls, but even you're not this stupid," Dayton countered. "And the fact you think I'd allow you to go off like this!"

"I'm not asking for your permission, Dayton." I huffed, turning toward the duffle bag on the ground. "I've already made up my mind. I'm leaving."

Dayton took notice of the duffle and jumped for it before I reached it. I attempted to intercept him, but it was silly to think I could. I clawed for it as he snatched it up, dangling it above my head. I didn't bother trying to get it back; I just glared at him as he dropped the bag on the counter and yanked the zipper open. He examined the weapons I packed.

"You think this is enough to protect yourself?" He balked, then tossed the bag aside. "Are you out of your mind?"

I shook my head and began to pace, but Dayton stood before me, forcing me to still. "Probably, yes, but I'm not going to sit by any longer, not when while Derek's life is on the line."

"Okay, fine. Enlighten me on your stellar plan then, huh?" he said, raising an eyebrow in question. I stayed silent. "Oh, you don't have one? Is that maybe because you didn't think this through?"

"No, I didn't," I admitted, matching his rising temper. "Because the thought of something happening to Derek is consuming me and I can't just stand around while he's in danger!"

"I can't let you go, Mare. Don't you get that?"

"Why not, Dayton?!" I shouted.

"Because you're everything to me!" he bellowed.

Both of our breaths caught at his unplanned admission, yet the shock quickly faded. I felt terrified; never in my wildest dreams did I expect Dayton to admit such a thing. I could have chalked up his reaction to the Consort bond blurring the lines of our friendship, but instinctually, I knew that wasn't the case. Dayton cared, not just about my safety, but about *me*.

Dayton stepped closer to me, his golden eyes wide. He reached down and cupped my face in his hands, and I relaxed into his touch, enjoying the chills skittering across my body. He held me like delicate china, and I knew by the desperate look in his eyes that he wanted to help me, but he didn't see how he could.

"Please, Mare." His voice cracked. "Don't go; don't leave me."

I wrapped my arms around him, holding him tightly to me. He froze, momentarily unsure, until he gathered me into his arms. I buried my head in his shoulder and sighed deeply as I pushed down the well of emotions begging to claw out of me. Dayton made a soft shushing noise and rubbed his hands up and down my spine. My shoulders trembled as he held me tighter to him.

"What do I do, Dayton?" I asked, pulling back. If he could fix everything, if he could make it all perfect, he would do it for me.

"You can't run away," he said. "But we'll figure this out. Together."

I opened my mouth, but a deep angry voice drowned my next words. "*Dayton.*"

Dayton sprang away from me like I was a live wire, and the moment we pulled apart, I felt the ghost of his touch. Luka stood in the entryway, staring straight at Dayton. The blankness on Luka's face made me blanch and my body stiffened, recognizing Luka's rising fury.

"Chief." Dayton nodded.

Luka narrowed his dark gaze on Dayton, and I wondered when he had returned.

"You and I need to talk." Luka prowled toward Dayton. "Alone."

Dayton glared at him but bit back any sneering remarks. "Fine."

Luka turned to look at me then, his eyes bright blue. I stepped back. "You're staying here. If you so much as step a toe out of line, I'll know." His words took on that familiar Alpha, no-nonsense tone. "Let go of the fallacy of giving yourself up to Kaser. You're insane."

I looked at Dayton, who nodded.

"Julian is shadowing you. Where you go, he goes. If you move, he moves," Luka announced.

As if on cue, Julian appeared beside me. Traces of smoke lingered freshly on him, a grin stretching across his features. When he looked at me, his smile turned slightly mischievous.

"Sorry, Maris," Julian said. He jerked his head back through the hall-way, and with one last glance back at Dayton, I followed Julian out.

CHAPTER 33

"A re you nervous?" Julian asked, leading me toward the living room. He'd stopped and rummaged in a closet to take out a dustpan and broom. It was strange to see something as mundane as cleaning supplies in the Temple.

"That's a pretty open-ended question," I quipped as we turned the corner into the living room.

Sunlight poured in, glowing against the dark floors and maroon couches. I squinted and sunk into the deep cushions. If I didn't know any better, I could pretend I was sitting on Derek's red couch in his garage, talking to him. But Derek was gone, and I was conflicted on what to do next.

Julian walked toward the broken window and began sweeping up the glass. "I do suppose there are several things weighing on your mind," said Julian. "I'm referring specifically about your brother's chat with my dear friend Dayton."

"Why would I be nervous?" I asked.

Julian gave me a knowing look.

Dayton and Luka's bad blood was nothing I should worry about, yet part of me was. I was not naïve enough to believe I'd be the reason to change anything between them. Luka felt betrayed by Dayton, and

Dayton was too stubborn to admit the truth. If Luka knew the truth, he'd be more willing to reconsider his judgment call.

"Whatever happens between them is between them," I said. "I can't put myself in the middle. Besides, I've got more pressing issues to worry about."

Derek. I had not been able to think about anything except returning him to safety. I thought through all that I knew and racked my brain. Kaser wanted the Artifacts because of the Moonstones embedded in them, though I didn't understand why he wanted me other than to torment Luka for killing Dante. There were too many missing pieces. While I knew my brother well enough to know he had more weapons in his arsenal, I wished he would let me in on his secrets.

"Luka has been doing this type of thing most of his life," Julian said, pulling his flask from his pocket. He threw his head back. "I understand your frustration, but trust your brother to know what he's doing."

"I didn't realize you knew him that well," I commented.

Julian snorted. "Hardly. He has just made quite the name for himself."

"What did Luka want from you?" I asked Julian. It didn't go unnoticed by me that Luka trusted Julian to shadow me, which made me assume he wanted something more from Julian.

Julian pocketed his flask and continued sweeping. "I'm that transparent, huh?"

This time, I gave him a knowing look.

Julian conceded and rested the broom against the window. He sat beside me on the couch. It was still slightly strange to see Julian without his armor, barefaced and in plain clothes. "Luka asked me about my magic."

"What about it?"

"He wanted to know more about it. He wanted to know if he could utilize it," Julian explained, his face darkening. "It's hard to explain what he wants when you don't understand what he wants. Luka knows more than any of us, that I have no doubt. My abilities, well—"

Julian searched for the right words.

"You hate your magic," I offered.

"To some degree, yeah," he said, rubbing the back of his neck. "Honestly, I can't be that much help to him because I've repressed my magic for so many years. I'm not practiced with it, and I can't control it. You saw me last night; I can barely control my wolf."

"Do you have abilities beyond just reading minds and speaking telepathically?"

Julian's withering glance confirmed the answer.

"Believe it or not, I want to help him. I feel bad about his Beta—your friend, Derek. Beyond that, I'm itching to find Kaser and take the sorry bastard down."

Broaching a subject change, I said, "What do you think Kaser's end goal is in all of this?"

"Kaser is a bravado guy; he enjoys the show," said Julian. He sat up from where he lounged along the couch. "It does make me think, though."

"Has Luka revealed anything useful?" I asked, tapping my head in implication.

"One, it's rude to pry and gossip about the innermost thoughts of my fellow wolves," Julian chided. "And two, you think someone as powerful as Luka doesn't have protections against folk like me? His mind is like Fort Knox."

"Regeneration," a small, quiet voice whispered in the doorway.

I whipped my head around to find Kyler. The petite female entered the living room, clad in mundane jeans and a cream-colored sweater. Her hair was pulled upward into a bun that rested atop her head. The word struck me as familiar, as something I read, not heard. A book, a book Luka had been reading.

"Luka was researching that," I said, straightening. "What does it mean?"

"I heard your brother mention it alongside Kaser's name in a hushed conversation over the phone," admitted Kyler.

"You slick little eavesdropper," Julian remarked with a crooked smile.

"It was odd enough that I remembered it, but I'm not sure what it is." Kyler moved to sit across the couch from us. "It sounds like a rebuilding of something. I've never heard of it used in a magical context."

Before I pondered it further, another voice sounded from the doorway.

"Regeneration is magic older than history itself. A loose translation from the old language depicts that when creatures die, they do not always stay dead." Neville slowly entered the room; he grimaced with disapproval. "If we are correct in assuming Kaser is messing with this, then we must ask: is the life of one wolf worth it?"

"Are you suggesting I let Derek die?" I growled, surprising myself.

"Kaser is messing with dark magic; he uses the power of your humanity to lure you into it. You should be terrified at this prospect, not running headfirst into it," Neville said. "I sympathize with you deeply—truly—but one wolf's life against a whole race is not feasible to question."

"Neville's right. *If* Kaser is messing with dark magic, then the risk of one life is small in the grand scheme of things," said Kyler.

"Can any of you honestly say that you'd be okay to abandon your family for the supposed greater good?" I questioned as my anger neared breaking point.

"Are you prepared to die for this boy?" Neville asked, matching my fury.

"I'd gladly do it! Twice!" I shouted, jumping to my feet. "No one messes with my family and gets away with it. I will pay the price for my choice, but it is *my* choice."

Julian, who had silently sipped from his flask as we argued, finally spoke up. "It's fair to note we still don't know Kaser's plans. We only have guesses and pieces."

"Luka knows," I said icily.

I started toward the front door in a tizzy of anger, wanting to find and confront Luka about his secret knowledge. A million emotions raced through me: anger, confusion—outright terror—they all overlapped and begged to be felt. My tattoo blazed as if it were on fire, and as I reached for the front door, a jolt went through me like electricity.

I gasped, and my eyes widened. Suddenly, I was looking at Luka, who stood near a cliff, his posture stiff and head held high. He crouched, resting his palm flat against the ground, inhaling deeply. Luka looked at me then, his blue eyes hard and narrowed. Confusion bristled through me; I couldn't understand what was happening or what I was seeing.

"*What's up, Chief?*" Dayton asked, and with a start, I realized I was seeing through Dayton's eyes, as if I was in his head.

Dayton shrank slightly from the weight of Luka's gaze.

"*Judgment is a straightforward thing for me to bestow,*" said Luka. "*I still reserve my judgment on you, Dayton.*"

Dayton's eyes locked with his. "*Judge me for who I am, not who you knew.*"

I didn't understand what was happening or how this was possible. It didn't make sense; I shouldn't be able to see through Dayton's eyes, yet I couldn't stop it.

Luka smiled, oozing power and confidence. I sensed Dayton's unease. "*You were always defensive and untrusting. That much hasn't changed. However, I didn't bring you here to pick a fight. I wanted to thank you.*"

Dayton's eyes widened. "*For what?*"

Looking down at the ground, Luka inhaled. "*When you fought Shetani last night, you stopped her from hurting Maris, and I realized then how deeply you care for her.*" Luka's words were calm, but I knew it killed him to admit it. "*You're not the boy I knew.*"

Dayton squirmed inwardly, unable to skirt around the topic. "*I'm not who I was,*" he reaffirmed.

"*For that, I'm grateful. I'm not perfect, and I've made mistakes. Maris is my responsibility; she always has been, and I never wanted her to come into this world. Yet she's headstrong and she ran headfirst into all of this, yet I know now that without you, she would be—*" Luka paused. "*I would rather not think of what would have happened.*"

I couldn't hear Dayton's thoughts, yet I gathered a general sense of his feelings. "*She's still headstrong,*" he said fondly.

"*That she is.*" Luka chuckled. He sobered as he lifted his gaze. "*Why did you do it?*"

I knew exactly what Luka was asking, and so did Dayton. "*Dante was threatened by you and too cowardly to kill you himself,*" he said. "*He knew I could do it and threatened my family for my cooperation.*"

"*You could have come to me,*" Luka said. "*I would've helped you.*"

"*I was afraid.*" It killed Dayton to admit it, yet he continued. "*And by trying to save my family, I lost everything.*"

"*Can I offer you insight?*"

Dayton bristled but nodded.

"*Losing everything all at once is a feeling I know too well, and I'm sorry I was a part of that loss for you. Know there will be a day when you find someone willing to share your burdens, and make sure you let them. You don't realize how tightly you hold on to them until you let go, and letting go is where you will find the strength within you.*"

Dayton swallowed hard, lost for words. I knew what he was likely thinking; letting go of the pain would insult his family's memory and opened a door for forgiveness that he didn't think he deserved. "*You never changed in the merit of your delivery.*"

Luka chuckled low. "*Kaser wants to bring Dante back to life.*"

I felt more shocked than Dayton had. "*Are you planning to stop him?*"

"*Killing Kaser takes precedent over all else,*" said Luka, staring hard at Dayton. "*Plus, I still want to get my Beta back, despite what Maris thinks.*"

"*You need me to stay with Maris?*"

"*I need you for backup, Dayton,*" Luka said, meeting his gaze with steely sureness.

Something whistled, and Dayton whirled, jumping in front of Luka. His eyes widened as a bullet whizzed through the air, nestling into his shoulder—inches from his heart. He stumbled backward and fell to the ground. Luka stood over him, lip curled and canines bared. Two more bullets soared, and Luka caught each one with his brute strength. Fenrir appeared out of thin air, and Dayton's blood ran cold. There had to be at least two dozen of them, eagerly inching forward.

"*All these years later, Dayton, and you still bleed with pathetic loyalty.*" A man appeared between them, a sadistic smile on his lips. "*Attack.*"

Chapter 34

"No!" I screamed. I stumbled and clutched a hand to my shoulder where Dayton was shot, as if I, too, was struck by a phantom wound.

"Maris!"

Strong hands caught me, and I stared up at Julian. I jerked away from him, my eyes wild, my breathing heavy.

"Dayton—Luka—" I panted. "Attacked."

"What?" Kyler asked, stepping closer.

"How do you know?" asked Neville. "You didn't leave the room."

Julian watched me, his face twisted in concentration. His eyes widened. "How?"

Usually, it was me asking all the questions, and now I understood why it annoyed Dayton so much. I didn't have the answers. Somehow, I'd been in Dayton's head and he wasn't aware of it, but it felt like I could see through his eyes. It didn't make sense, but that didn't matter right now.

"We have to go. Right now," I said, mustering the scary calm Luka adopted in dire situations. "Kaser is—"

The windows imploded and glass shattered, raining down like confetti. I shielded my eyes, and my scream tore through the room as shards ricocheted off me. The air reeked of rot, and the hairs on the back of my neck stood up. My claws protruded.

Fenrir swarmed the room, jumping through the windows with the grace and awkwardness of a stumbling baby deer. Grabbing my arm, Julian pulled me into the kitchen where the others had run off. We stumbled in, and Kyler kicked the kitchen table into the entryway and ducked beside Neville.

"What the hell is happening?" she asked.

"Wards are down," said Julian. "We need help—more help than anyone here can offer. The Council needs to know what's happening. *Now.*"

It was the sincerest tone I'd ever heard Julian use.

I glanced at Kyler and Neville, the two who unwittingly got dragged into all this. "Kyler and Neville, can you manage to get to the portal together and warn the Council?"

Julian nodded his agreement at my suggestion, while Kyler balked at Neville's determined face.

"No," she said. "I didn't ask for any of this. I didn't want to be *involved* in any of this."

"And you think we all just volunteered for this stuff to happen?" I remarked. Kyler looked at me with raised brows, and I pressed on. "I don't care what you do or don't do. I'm just not going to sit back and do nothing."

Kyler looked at Neville, then to Julian and rolled her eyes. "Fine. I'll go tell the Council. But I'm telling them everything."

"I'm sorry to involve you, Ky," said Julian. He rummaged through a cabinet and pulled out a drinking glass. Grabbing a kitchen knife, he sliced his palm open and let blood drip into the glass, then handed it to Kyler, who took it with a word. "You need to use it to open the portal gates."

"What about you?" Neville asked, standing up.

Julian opened the oven and retrieved a frying pan. "I'll hold them off."

Neville laughed, grabbing Kyler by her arm and leading her to the back door. She glanced back at Julian once, who grinned manically back. The two of them took off, leaving only Julian and me behind. A loud crash sounded, and Julian looked at me.

"You need to go," he said. "Dayton will kill me if I let you stay with the Fenrir here."

"I can't leave you," I protested.

Julian's face screwed up in fury as Fenrir kicked the kitchen table into the back door and shattered the glass. Julian swung his frying pan like a baton, then nodded to me. I didn't want to leave him; he couldn't face them alone.

"*Save your friend, please,*" Julian's voice echoed; he ran at the first Fenrir, smacking the pan across its face with a clang. "*The door. Go! Now!*"

I whirled, running out the shattered back door as two Fenrir rushed through the entrance. I squeaked and barreled through them like a madwoman, feeling the prickles of their fur brush my arm. As I ran across the back decking, I veered to the right as a swarm of them ascended the stairs. On all sides, they marched toward me, their claws extended and ready to strike. I peered over the railing and backpedaled. Screaming, I jumped up and over it, landing hard on my side. I didn't think I could stand, but I forced myself up.

Chaos ensued. Fenrir spilled over the grounds like an army unleashed onto us. I scanned the grounds, focusing my vision to see farther out and discern the approaching figures between the trees. Sharp claws gripped my arm and yanked me forward, and I lost focus. The pain subsided marginally as Fenrir began hauling me away, digging their claws into my arms. I writhed violently, ignoring the tearing flesh in my bicep. I faced the Fenrir, whose lips curled back into a snarl, then I slammed my fist square into its face, though I was sure it hurt me more.

"Ah, ah, ah," tutted a deep voice. "I would think twice if I were you; they are under my orders to hold back, but if you hit them again, I can easily unleash them."

I jerked my gaze from the Fenrir to a man shrouded entirely in shadow. Darkness formed around him like a misty storm cloud, billowing out and enveloping him like a cape. I couldn't see a structured form of a person, but in the darkness, I glimpsed a pair of dark eyes. Despite his bizarre appearance, I knew with absolute certainty who it was.

Kaser.

"I have only moments with you, my dear." His voice sounded buttery—silken. "I need you. You want your friend back, which means you need me. Come with me and let us both be happy."

My heart pounded and my mouth dried. I didn't know why he wanted me, but I knew what Kaser wanted: to bring Dante back to life. Kaser dangled a choice over me, a choice I could make. Utter chaos surrounded me; I whiffed smoke from a fire and heard cries of pain. Fear coursed in me as I thought of my friends. Julian was alone, and Kyler and Neville were no doubt amid the chaos. Luka ran headfirst into this, and Dayton had been shot, too.

"This isn't even half of my Fenrir. You must come with me and if you choose not to, it will be more than your best friend who suffers," he said as his shadows creeped closer. "Not even your famous brother or strong Consort could manage the forces I will bring down on them."

"You already shot Dayton," I snarled.

Kaser raised his eyebrows. "You know?" he asked. "I knew you shared a bond, but ah, it's not the time to speak on that. He is alive; he's fighting a good fight to try and get to you currently."

Knowing Dayton was alive and fighting should have made me feel better, but Dayton would stay fighting even if his arm fell off. He was stubborn. Headstrong. Yet somehow, I knew if anything were to happen to him, I'd know. It was like an instinct—a sixth sense to his wellbeing.

I glared at Kaser. "Why me?"

Through the smoke and darkness, a victorious grin split across his features. "You, my dear, are the essence of the story. Without you, the show cannot go on, but I cannot take you unless you say yes."

Less than a half hour ago, I was ready to find and give myself up to him. Everything had changed since then, and I had barely processed a fraction of it. If I went with Kaser, I'd be going with the knowledge he wanted me to somehow help bring his father back to life. But Kaser didn't know I knew what he planned to do. If I went with him, at least I could save my friends—save Derek.

I glanced past him to where Luka limped toward the house, blood trickling down his face. His eyes widened upon seeing me. Beside him, I recognized Dayton's wolf barreling out of the woods, pure, primal rage rippling through him as he hurtled toward me. I looked back at Kaser, torn and wild with adrenaline.

"Yes, you can take me," I said quickly.

Kaser grinned like a snake in the grass. Grasping my arm, he took me away.

Chapter 35

A sharp pain thudded in my skull, and darkness surrounded me. I couldn't see my fingers and the ground beneath me felt hard, cold, and wet. Cautiously, I dared to move my arms and feel around me; fear anchored to my every movement. I shuddered when my fingers brushed against a wall. I froze, working up the nerve to extend my arm and press against the wall to stand.

I had no idea where I was or how I had gotten here. I could only recall the panic I felt when I saw and talked to Kaser. I remembered his vague words; I was a part of some story and somewhere he used the word "essence." I certainly felt like I was in the center of all this insanity, if the past few weeks were anything to go by. I'd gladly be sidelined if only my friend's safety wasn't brought into question. Now, here I was, alone in a dungeon. How much time had passed? It felt like seconds.

Water dripped nearby, and I jumped out of my skin. Standing, my heart rate spiked as every nerve ending rose on high alert. I shut my eyes to fight back the tears and focus. I wasn't vulnerable. I wasn't defenseless. I was a werewolf—a slightly out-of-control werewolf, but still a werewolf.

I focused on tapping into my wolf. I'd only seen Dayton and Luka do it, but I needed to try. My body shook, and I forced myself to take steady breaths. I flexed my fingers and focused on the movement to distract the lingering fear. A chill washed over me, and I fought back my rising anxiety. I wouldn't be afraid in the face of danger. I could deal with the aftermath if I got through the storm. I opened my eyes, and everything was bright. I smiled at my small victory and began to move.

Dark gray stone rose from floor to ceiling, and I touched both walls with my palms. The narrow stretch of stone ventured farther back, so cautiously, I stepped deeper into the cell, eyes aloft, while searching for an entrance. I gasped at the potent scent of blood, then lurched forward. My eyes went wide, and I threw a hand over my mouth to keep from screaming.

Derek sat in a heap on the ground, his shoulders slumped forward and head hanging low. Dry and fresh blood surrounded him, and he looked unrecognizable, dirt caking his skin and wounds gaping across his body. On his right hand was a stump where his ring finger had once been. He began to lift his head, his dull green eyes hardly open. I started to kneel beside him, trembling, but someone pulled me back.

"Watch yourself, little girl," a voice snarled. "The fun has only just begun."

"Get off me," I snapped, pulling fruitlessly against them. Where had they come from? I hadn't even noticed a door, let alone sensed another presence.

I struggled against my captor, who gripped me tightly and sunk their claws into my flesh. Pain shot through me and fighting back proved difficult. They threw me backward and I crashed into the wall. I threw my hands up to claw for something to hold on to as a cry of panic tore from me, but the expected impact of the rigid wall never came, and I landed harshly on my hands and knees.

"Kato, what have I told you about being gentler with our guests?" called an eerie voice.

I looked up at a man with blood dripping down his claws. He shrugged. "That is me being gentle."

Kato's wicked smile was sadistically insincere, his face deeply scarred from a mix of claw and burn marks. His pitiless black eyes were like a shark, and his shoulder length white hair was bound into a bun, caked in dirt and blood. The cleanest things on him were his clothes, fighting leathers like the ones Dayton wore.

I recalled hearing his name said before by Julian. Kato had been a part of Dante's group of supporters, and he had a twin—Shetani. Twin flames for nefarious evil. Slowly, I backed away from him.

"Run along then. Ready the forces for what is to come," the voice commanded. I could only hear them, unable to pinpoint who or where it came from.

Without another remark, Kato left.

I scrambled up on high alert and, gritting my teeth, I glanced around, perplexed by how I managed to go from one room to the next. I no longer resided in the dark cell, and instead, I stood outside in the middle of a clearing. Fresh cut grass surrounded me, soft and plush beneath my feet. Obnoxiously tall and thick trees acted as a barricade, aligning like cell bars. I looked up, and the sky turned twilight, purple hints circling the blue. The moon hung in the sky, an almost circle covered in shadow. It felt strange. Surreal.

However, the oddest thing had to be the large rock in the middle of the chaos. Obviously, the stone was made to be admired, like a podium or stage. The harsh black of the structure contrasted well against the greenery, and the shadowed darkness made it quite picturesque. In the center of the stone was an outline of a man. My blood ran cold.

I felt the gaze on me like a moth to a flame and flicked my eyes to meet those of bright red. There was no mistaking who this was. Kaser Odessa. He jumped forward and landed lightly on the ground, whipping his head up with a grin. Stepping back at once, he drew closer. If his features were to judge, he looked young, no older than Luka. His hair was shoulder length and dark, tied back into a neat ponytail with a thick, trimmed beard framing his face and a twisted smile accentuating the sharpness of his cheekbones.

"Maris Bakar." My name from his lips made my skin crawl. "I've been waiting a long time to meet you."

"I can't say I agree," I said, hoping to back away from him. Yet he circled me like I was prey while I stilled, acutely aware of his every move, even noticing the subtle movement of his eyes. I had to remind myself I chose to come here.

"Let me introduce myself. My name is Kaser Odessa," He stopped prowling and stood directly in front of me, hand outstretched. I glared at him and refused to move despite the fear urging me to do so. "You certainly have your brother's mannerisms."

"Leave Luka out of this," I warned.

"We cannot leave out the beginning of the story," his voice belted dramatically, eyes narrowing on me as he came to a complete standstill in front of me. No more than five feet stood between us. "Lukas Bakar is a legend. Because of him, we are here today, and now finally, I meet the infamous Maris Bakar, his dear baby sister he kept hidden for years."

"Maybe because of psychos like you."

Kaser shrugged and folded his arms over his chest. "I won't argue that Lukas was smart to keep you away from all this. Had you been a piece to play with years ago? Well, I think I would have won, and there would be no round two like now."

"We aren't pieces in a game for you to play with," I snapped. He laughed dryly. "These are people's lives you're messing with."

"To your credit, you have proven stronger than I expected. Initially, I wanted Lukas, a powerful young Alpha that could have the oldest of your kind at his mercy with just a look." He raised his dark brows at me. "I wonder how powerful you'd be with the right push."

Annoyed with the theatrics, I pressed on. "What the hell do you want with me?"

I knew he wished to bring Dante back to life somehow, but I didn't understand my involvement.

Kaser pursed his lips, glancing away from me again and moving leisurely forward. "The company you keep is fairly extraordinary. Neville Quinn, a hybrid amongst your kind. Julian Fletcher, damaged goods. He has much-wasted potential, too traumatized to utilize his powers."

"No thanks to your scumbag of a father," I snarled. Kaser put on good bravado, but I glimpsed the muscle jump in his jaw at the mention of his father.

"Then, there is your own father, Maris. He's an odd character. A human man who fell in love with a young werewolf woman. After her death, he chose to be the leader of the Werewolf Hunt while raising two dormant werewolves," he said, leaning against a tree and crossing his legs at the ankles. "Yet the most interesting company you keep is someone plainly ordinary, who convinced you into etching the markings of an ancient bond on your skin. Dayton Cadman, a purely simple werewolf with nothing extraordinary about him."

I might have laughed in any other non-life or death situation, hearing Dayton described as ordinary. "Don't bring Dayton into this."

"Protective of the wolf?" A blade appeared between Kaser's palm, and he toyed with it. I noted the lack of weapons belted around his waist and wondered where he kept the knife. "You two are like fire and ice. The one person you should not desire because of your split loyalties to your brother, and yet, your heart betrays you."

"Congratulations, you've been promoted to detective," I said. "You still haven't answered my question. What the hell do you want with me? I came here like you wanted, so get to the point."

A devilish grin split his face. "I'd hoped you would be unlike your brother, but you prefer to go straight to business, much like him," said Kaser. "I need you to get back what was stolen from me."

"What was stolen?"

Kaser was suddenly inches from me, his breath hot against my neck. His eyes were manic, his pupils wide in a frenzy. His smell invaded my senses—a clean cedar odor and freshly-scented shampoo. His heartbeat was like a steady drum in his chest, and my claws lengthened on instinct. I cringed inwardly, knowing any outward display of discomfort would disadvantage me.

"My father was stolen from this world too soon, and I intend to rectify it." Kaser hissed. Though it shouldn't have come as a shock, hearing it was different than theorizing.

I had to think back to what I knew of Dante. A charming, charismatic werewolf whose political influence ran deep. He wanted to overrun the world with werewolves, to take control over them and how they were created. He preferred purebred werewolves, but they were few and far between. Dante wanted people like me, a dormant wolf, to have no choice but to have their curse triggered. In Dante's perfect world, there were no choices.

"Your father was a sadistic man who did awful things."

"You believe yourself pompous enough to go about defining good and evil," Kaser said, lurching forward. He tightly gripped my arm, and pain shot up my shoulder. "My father thought he was the wolves' salvation, but it is *me* who will execute the plan."

"If you're planning to execute what he already started, why do you need him back?" I asked, despite the pain of his grip.

Kaser's mouth upturned tightly. "You're getting ahead of yourself, dear. You must understand the whole story before skipping to the end."

"All I know is that Dante took away choice and free will," I said.

"No!" he yelled, throwing me to the ground.

I crashed down hard against the grass, which hurt like hell when used as a landing mat. I growled, angry and fed up. My claws protruded as Kaser approached me from behind, and I jumped up, raking my claws down his outstretched arm. At once, he grimaced and backed away, blood spilling down his arm.

"Touch me one more time and see where it gets you," I snarled, my eyes aglow.

Kaser clutched his injured, bleeding arm to his chest and threw his head back, laughing. "You're a feisty one."

"That's not all I am," I countered. I noticed his arm still bled, the wound fresh. Countless times I'd witnessed Dayton's wounds open and closing in as little as thirty seconds. There should be no reason he still bled if he was half as powerful as he claimed. It struck me as odd, and I breathed in his scent. I smelled no dirt, no sweat or fear. It was like he hadn't lifted a finger to physically defend himself... maybe because he couldn't.

"Are you human?"

422

CHAPTER 36

"My, my, Maris. You're more insightful than I first believed," Kaser said. He drew out each word, his lips curling in the corners. "For someone as ignorant as you were, you color me impressed."

"People have a tendency to underestimate me," I said, eyeing the distance between us. Kaser didn't move from his stance beside the tree; he flashed me a manic smile.

"My father kept me hidden from the world because of my peculiarity. I was born a human child despite being bred by two werewolves, and he tried everything to turn me into one, but alas, nothing stuck." Kaser became a blur of motion until he stood inches from me, gripping my throat. "My birth defect was never to his liking. Thus, he learned to resent me. I could never make him proud, even when I learned of ways to harness a different type of power."

"You're doing all of this because you have daddy issues?" I choked. Kaser released me with an ice-cold laugh. I touched my throat, feeling the oily taint of his touch. "If he was so terrible, why do you want him back?"

"I believe he died with crucial information—the final piece to the puzzle he started, yet he didn't understand it then."

"What are you talking about?"

"Magic. Specifically raw magic—a distinct, rare type of magic, with history stretching further than the creation of werewolves. The well of its origin has been lost to us, but its powers manifested throughout generations," explained Kaser. "My father never cared for it; he thought it an unnatural creation. Werewolves were superior against all else, he would say. Of course, that didn't stand in the way of his experiments."

"Experiments?"

"Julian Fletcher," Kaser said, shaking his head. "A waste of talent. The raw magic flowing through his veins was the strongest force I've ever seen. My stupid father wasted it away; he didn't understand."

"What are you talking about?"

Julian resented his magic, and while he alluded to harboring the magic against his will, he'd never gone into detail. Luka had been curious about it, probably suspecting there was more to the story. I thought back to the Fenrir attack when Julian told me to run. He knew he'd be able to handle them; I just hadn't realized he was so powerful.

"Julian was a test to see how well magic can be harnessed when put into another by force," said Kaser. "Raw magic is the oldest magic, and my father wanted to create a hybrid werewolf, not unlike your dear friend Neville Quinn. Only he wanted more, a creature more powerful, someone unbeatable."

"Why Julian?"

Kaser shrugged. "That, I don't know, nor did I ever care to find out. My father used him, but the magic in him wastes away the more he uses it. I must give him credit, for he is wise enough to use it sparingly." Only because Julian's excessive drinking and smoking helped him to suppress it. "Eventually, the magic could kill him. It's already turned the wolf against him, though I digress. I've figured out my father's fatal flaw and found other more conventional ways to access power."

"The Infinite Artifacts?" I guessed. "Or, I suppose, the Moonstone?"

I recalled the sword with the opal and Julian's shift in behavior when he held it. He'd felt its magic, maybe even recognized it. He said it was dangerous, something none of us should mess with.

"A channel to control the raw magic through a stone." Kaser beamed. "Power great in its own right fortified into an unstoppable force. I lured you into the Nixie realm as I suspected there was a piece there, and I hoped you might retrieve it for me. You proved useful, I'll say, but you showed your hand for an unforeseen twist."

"What are you talking about?"

"It's never wise to show your full hand, which brings us back to why we're gathered here today." Kaser gestured for me to come forward, and not in a position to object, I did. "I lured you in with the premise of your friend's safety. I replicated with him what my father did to Julian, with a few adjustments. He has only had a few weeks in my care and has risen to power much quicker than anyone expected."

Suddenly, two Fenrir appeared; they dragged in Derek, whose head dangled between his shoulders.

"Derek!" I cried. I ran toward him, but Kaser's hand flew up, and suddenly, chains were at my wrists and ankles, burning with each pull. I tugged at them, but to no avail; it was like they were cemented into the ground.

Derek glanced up at me through red-rimmed eyes brewing with dread. Blood dripped down his forehead, and angry bruises swelled across his face. His clothes were in tatters, dried with dirt, blood, and sweat. He stumbled, falling to his knees at the sight of me. One of the Fenrir kicked him, and a strangled cry barely escaped his lips, his voice too hoarse to be of aid.

"Leave him alone!" I belted, pulling at the chains.

At the sound of my voice, Derek started screaming. He clutched the sides of his head and covered his ears. "Make it stop!"

My heart hammered yet I was unable to help him. I wanted to run to him and get him out of here—anything. It wasn't right; he'd been tortured, and the sight of him felt sickening. I could only witness this atrocity while another part of me knew this wasn't even the worst of what Derek had endured.

"Enough," Kaser said with finality. Derek stopped, standing up straight and peering stony eyed at Kaser. "Derek, please step forward." Derek did as he was told, like a robot only able to respond to simple commands.

"Please, leave him alone!" I cried.

One of the Fenrir flew into action at my words, slicing my arm with their razor claws. I screamed and spat at the creature, who drew back, alert. Before it walked away, the Fenrir kicked out at my right leg. White-hot agony made my knees buckle, and my wrists stung where the silver chains pulled.

"Enough! She only needs to understand what can ensue if she doesn't cooperate," Kaser hissed. "Be gone."

The two Fenrir swiftly dispersed as I composed myself, my vision sharpened to watch Kaser in action. He moved toward Derek, grabbing him by the hair and shoving him against a tree. Derek's arms were chained to low-hanging branches, leaving him dangling from the ground. Kaser flicked out a dagger and dragged it down Derek's front until his shirt tore in two. He sliced the pointed end against Derek's bare chest, carving into his skin. They could have been symbols, but it was hard to tell by the blood dripping from the wounds and marring the meaning. Derek hung, soundless. I gritted my teeth to keep from rattling my chains.

"Now," Kaser drawled, wiping his hands together. He turned to me. "The fun can begin. I'd like you to demonstrate your powers for me."

I stumbled forward as my restraints came loose. I fell to my knees, looking at where Derek dangled in a pool of his own blood. Fear seized me, but I didn't run toward him yet, lest it be a trap.

"What powers?"

Kaser rolled his eyes. "Must I spell everything out for you? Think, my dear girl. What happened in that cave with your precious Consort?"

I gulped and racked my brain. Shetani and Dayton fought, and I intervened. I saw the dagger and I tried to stop it—it had been instinctual to stop it, to save and protect him. There had been a light that I hadn't thought twice about until now. Dayton almost dying overshadowed the details, and then once we had the sword, I never thought twice over the ordeal. Had there been more to it?

"I stopped the dagger from killing Dayton," I said aloud. "There isn't anything else to it."

"You didn't just save him," Kaser cooed. "You protected him."

"I—what?" I balked, confused.

Kaser grinned, knowing he dangled the missing piece over me. "Think back on the wild whims you executed," he said, amusement glinting across his features. "When you're told to stay back, you run headfirst into danger. You can't stay back because it's instinctual for you protect those you care about."

"What are you getting at?"

I thought back on my past actions, and one particular time stuck out to me when Fenrir first attacked the Temple. Dayton told me to stay back and to let him handle it. While Dayton handled it, the moment things turned awry, I intervened. When Kyler ran away the first day we met her, I was told to stay back, yet I still ran after her and ended up fighting Shetani.

Kaser snorted. "I suppose it is the bond you share with your dear Dayton which threw the trail off course. Quite an unforeseen turn of events. An innocent act, no doubt, but it acts as a mask to hide who you really are."

"The Consort bond?" I questioned. "Dayton protects me; that was the deal."

Kaser's eyes homed in on me, glittering. "A protected protector."

"What do you mean?"

"I only put the pieces together when you mentioned he had been shot," said Kaser. "The premise of the bond works so that whatever wounds are inflicted onto the protected are reflected on the protector. There was no way for you to know he'd been shot, save the fact you saw it."

I had witnessed it; I was in Dayton's head when it happened. How could Kaser know that?

"The closer you two grow, the more the bond deepens. Now I see the etchings of it have already shifted." Kaser eyed my neck. "A Consort bond can become stronger, but it's rare for it to grow and shift. You protected him; you saved him from death. I don't know what it made your bond exactly, but it's a force to be reckoned with."

I gulped, at a loss for words.

"Tell me Maris," Kaser cooed. "Where is he now?"

I almost screamed that I didn't know, and if I did, I never would tell him, but the sudden anger from that thought alone seemed to dreg up Dayton in my mind. I gasped and braced a hand over my chest, once again seeing through eyes that weren't my own.

Everything felt sped up, like rewinding a VHS tape at full speed. Dayton's racing thoughts recounted the last few moments—hours? I couldn't tell. Julian was alive, but any relief from that was chased away by the sinister glint in his eyes. Dayton and Luka fought side by side as shadows chased them through the woods; neither seemed put off by it. Fenrir attacked and were killed just as quick. My head pounded; I wanted to go back into own mind and out of Dayton's. An underground of sorts appeared: long corridors of cold, dark stone. It wasn't unlike the cell I had been in—

"No!" I shrieked.

Kaser grinned malevolently and called for someone to check the south entrance. I didn't know what he did or what he made me do, but whatever it had been gave up Dayton's location—possibly Luka's as well. Yet I hadn't seen him, and I had to take that as a good sign.

"What was that?" I asked, panting.

"Sorry, my dear," said Kaser. "I won't have anyone interfering with my plans, least of all your brother and dear Consort."

"What did you make me do?" I asked, mad with panic.

"Blah, blah, blah," Kaser mocked. "In time, you'll be able to control going in and out of his head. I didn't have time and you needed convincing."

Before I could ask more, a rustle in the woods had me on high alert as Kato dragged someone in, who dropped an alarming number of expletives. *No.* I didn't want anyone else dragged into this. Terror seized me, but I could do nothing to stop what was happening.

Fenrir launched Dayton forward onto the ground. He hissed and spat as he tumbled forward. He looked unharmed, save for the dried blood running the length of his forearm. I touched my right arm where the

Fenrir had scratched me. His hair and clothes were a mess, and he had been stripped of his weapons. His golden gaze fell to mine briefly, his sharp coldness unnerving.

"Just as you predicted, he is here," said Kato, his voice razor-edged. "Stripped of his weapons, too."

"Yes, I suspected it was him," said Kaser. "Only Dayton would be so crass in the face of imminent danger."

"I was tempted to cut his tongue out," Kato sneered, shoving Dayton forward. "I'm still willing to do so if you allow me the pleasure."

"All in due time, Kato, I promise you." Kaser's attention turned on Dayton, whose limbs were bound in silver chains. "How far behind is Lukas?"

Dayton snarled and spat at Kaser. "I'm not telling you shit."

"I can make it quick," Kato chimed.

"Kato, find and control Lukas," Kaser directed. "I want him unharmed. A blank canvas for me."

Kato left without a word. I tugged fruitlessly on my chains at the mention of Luka. This was much worse than I could have imagined. This was exactly what Luka had been afraid of, and I could only trust he was smart enough to know what he was doing. Yet that meant having a lot of faith in the unknown.

"I know you're pissed off that Luka killed your scumbag of a father," taunted Dayton. "I just never pegged you as an idiot. Luka can't be caught or controlled; you know that."

Kaser's eyes betrayed him for the briefest moments; he turned his chin upward, sneering down at Dayton. His glare never faltered from him. "Jeering remarks? Is that all you got?"

Kaser snapped his fingers, and Dayton was dragged backward by an invisible force. Chains appeared around his limbs, and he was strung upward beside Derek, his feet dangling above the ground. Derek kept silent, blood trickling down his chest from where the markings were carved.

"Let them go, please. You want me. You can have me!" I begged, glancing between the boys and Kaser.

Kaser turned to me with bright fury. "I already told you Derek has a role to play. However, I feel generous. I promise I will not kill him, and he will come out of this alive." Kaser looked at Derek, whose head slumped between his shoulders. "Whether or not he wants that fate is up to him."

"Don't listen to him, Mare!" Dayton barked, rattling his chains. "He's a liar. He deceives people!"

"Quite a duo you two have become, like fire and ice." Kaser closed his eyes, pressing his mouth into a thin line. "I see the fire in you, Dayton. You're an all-consuming flame, and fire leaves a promise of nothing unscathed in its path."

"Fuck off with your analogies," Dayton spat.

Kaser turned and looked at me. "You, my dear Maris, are all ice, with pure intentions. The deeper you get into this world, the colder you will become. Choices and love and betrayal will turn the goodness in your heart, and you will become bitter."

"You're wrong," I said. "We are built on the choices we make, and I choose to do the right thing."

Kaser continued to prowl the ground between us, like a cat stalking its prey.

"Lukas used to be a hero. Ask him: what do heroes win?" Kaser pressed. I forced away my annoyance at being compared to Luka again. "Your goodness will not help you when faced with an impossible choice."

"Leave her alone, you sick bastard," Dayton choked.

Kaser shook his head. "You should really learn when to keep your mouth shut."

"You know, you're not the first to suggest that and probably not the last. The message doesn't seem to bode well with me," Dayton taunted, a grin splitting across his face. "I know you want to bring your father back to life, but he's dead."

Kaser reared on Dayton, bringing a silver dagger to Dayton's face, whose grin of pure mania never faltered. I jolted forward, but Kaser threw a hand up, and I froze in place. Where the dagger rested on Dayton's face, I noticed the tattoo had climbed up the right side of his cheek.

"Be careful how you speak, boy," warned Kaser.

"Guess what, Kaser? A dead man can't do shit," Dayton slowly said each word, packing a punch.

Kaser's controlled manner burst and he grabbed Dayton by the hair, yanking his head back. He drew the dagger down Dayton's face, from the corner of his right brow and down to his jawline. I screamed soundlessly, unable to move despite the fury igniting in me. As Kaser mutilated his face, Dayton hissed and spat like a caged feral cat.

Kaser marred the part of Dayton's face where the tattoo had grown, cutting clean through it. I could feel my own heat in protest, a scream bubbling in my throat. Kaser whirled on me.

"Yes," he said gleefully. "You want to do it; you want to protect him from this."

"Leave her alone!" Dayton yelled.

Kaser ignored him and prowled toward me with a predatory glint in his eyes. He grabbed my arm and pulled me forward, shoving me at my injured friends. I looked between them at Dayton's face, marred and bloodied, and Derek's wounded chest. "Choose which one to save, then talk to me about your goodness."

Both were bloodied and beaten. This felt like a fever dream, like my life could have in no way turned so drastic this quickly. Drawing in a deep breath, I forced myself to get it together. I looked at Dayton and the long, jagged wound cut deep into his face. His right eye swelled shut, but otherwise, he seemed unharmed.

Derek looked exactly how he'd been treated, like someone who had been held hostage and tortured for weeks. The ripples of his ribcage alarmed me, alongside the yellow and purple bruised skin across his torso. Where his arms bent, I noted pinpricks, like a needle had been repeatedly placed in him to draw blood. What concerned me most about the injuries was seeing them unhealed. He looked like a stranger.

"I don't know what you expect me to do," I cried out, whirling on Kaser.

"Save one of them, or I'll kill both," Kaser threatened. "Choose. Now."

My mind raced and I walked back to Derek, whose head still hung low. I thought back on all the years we'd spent together, the coffees shared, the jokes exchanged, our easy friendship and comfortable silences. Never once did he complain about my sometimes dramatic complaining, and I understood his desperation when he rambled about his family, intent on finding the answers around their deaths.

"Mare," Dayton whispered. "It's just like what you did for me in the cave. You got this."

I don't know what I did then. Kaser knew, of course. He called me a protector, though I didn't know what any of it meant or why it was important. It made no sense to me, but I pushed the confusion aside. Before, Dayton had been dying when the poison in his system threatened to kill him. We never spoke of what I did, but I saved Dayton from death, and now Derek was unwell, I had to do the same. Yet I had no idea of the extent of Derek's injuries; I didn't know where to start. Fearing Kaser would make good on his threat, I inhaled and reached for Derek.

"Derek?" I whispered. "Derek, can you hear me?"

A low grunt was my only answer.

"Derek, you need to work with me here," I said. "I don't know what's going on, but I'm supposed to protect you or heal you—or both. I have no clue, but if this hurts, I'm really sorry."

I closed my eyes and stilled my mind. I inhaled and abandoned my immediate fears and confusion to focus on the problem. A rippling eased over me not unlike the sensation of turning into my wolf. It was like two parts of myself aligned to become whole again, and the feeling of rightness tingled my skin and warmed my bones in anticipation.

When I opened my eyes, light emanated from me, cascading around myself and Derek. The light danced across Derek's wounds, wrapping them like bandages and pulling away to reveal unmarred skin. A sense of rightness flowed through me as I glanced down at Derek, unhurt. Yet as the wounds closed, the symbols over his chest remained. His familiar green eyes flew open as he wildly jerked around. Looking upward, he bared his canines and extended his claws.

"Incredible," Kaser crooned. "Simply marvelous."

"Maris, what did you do?" Derek's voice was a whining panic. I stepped back, shocked. I thought I was doing the right thing, yet as he watched me weakly and rattled his chains, I knew I hadn't. "I was good as dead. You should've let me die!"

"Now for the real fun to begin," Kaser mused, grinning at me.

CHAPTER 37

I t was like an invisible string wrapped around my waist as Kaser pulled me to him, teleporting us to the top of the podium. A pungent stench made me gag, and I almost heaved. In the center of the stage was a glass sarcophagus, and along the sides, rubies glinted, intertwined with thorns. A placard gleamed with words that had been scratched away by claw marks, yet most disconcerting was the body floating inside it, submerged in water. The body lay dismembered in the grayness. Bits of skin peeled away from the bones that were hollowed and wrinkled. A red cloth draped the middle of the otherwise naked body, and over its chest, there was a gaping open wound where its heart should be. Dante.

Luka had been the one to kill him, thus seeing his body in such a grotesque manner made me nauseous.

I looked down at Dayton strung up against the tree, his eyes glowing golden. I could hear the vibrations of his spitting rage as he thrashed fruitlessly, unable to get to us. Derek was not beside him anymore, nor did I see where he went. I pushed that aside and focused on my current predicament.

"Marvelous, isn't it?" Kaser crooned, beaming with pride. I noticed for the first time an amulet peeked from his shirt, dull gold and patterned with strange symbols. "Come look."

Hesitantly, I walked toward Kaser and loomed over the watery casket. I had to keep myself from cringing away.

"Is this your father?" I asked, averting my eyes.

Kaser chuckled, and I flinched. "Why make it sound so sick?"

Biting back my retort, I managed to look at him. "I mean no disrespect. It's just unusual for me to see a dead body so well... preserved."

"This is the part where things get interesting," said Kaser, brushing his hands together.

Considering everything that had happened so far tonight, I dreaded to know how it could get more interesting. I glanced down at a sword on the table behind Kaser. It had a long, glittering onyx base, and at the hilt was an opal stone. I recognized the hilt; this was the Infinite Artifact from the Nixie realm, now stolen from us. Kaser's eyes focused on Dante, glazed over with joy.

"You might be asking what it is I want my father back for," Kaser said. "It's fair that I tell you, so you can understand your part more clearly. Don't be confused; I do not wish to have him back to make up for lost time. No, he is required because he knows vital information that I need."

"What information?" I asked, eyebrows raised.

"My father searched high and low for resources to build the foundations of his schemes. He wanted no flaws in his victories and sought out ways to execute them. The quest for the Moonstone was his idea, and he was successful in finding just one," Kaser said, pulling out the amulet around his neck.

I looked at it, recognizing the opal of the Moonstone, a jagged piece within the amulet.

"The magic within the Moonstone called to my human blood, begging me to use it. I enchanted this amulet with the stone to contain its power so I could use it more freely. Simple thoughts would be executed, and I don't have to lift a finger," he explained. "But the magic depletes me and weakens me. My father knew how to fix this but before he could tell me—"

"Luka killed him," I interrupted. "And he died with that knowledge."

"Yes," Kaser confirmed. "Lukas killed him, so I never found out. I've tried to figure it out, believe me, but my efforts are unsuccessful. Years it took my father to uncover it while using Julian as his punching bag, but all of it was for nothing."

"Why do you need me?" I asked. "Why not take me sooner?"

"I'm a patient man and I'm willing to play the long game. If I took you too soon before you understood the full scope of this world, it would have traumatized you. It would have been too much for anyone to handle, and I feared your mind might break, thus rendering you useless to me." He shrugged, leaning on the table and blocking my view of the sword.

"Why not take me and just manipulate me to your side?"

"That would be because of your big brother. He would have found you, and your loyalty to him would have overridden all else. Plus, it was more fun to take his Beta and watch you fall for the one person Lukas might hate more than myself," Kaser said, bemused.

I felt my face flush and glanced automatically at Dayton, still bound to the tree and angry as a bull. If the situation weren't so dire, I might have laughed at his reaction.

"As for why I need you, well," Kaser said, "I plan to perform a ceremony that will raise his spirit and reconnect his body and soul. It requires opening the doors to the other side, and in doing so, letting loose spirits of those passed. Vengeful spirits will snake through and try to attach to the dead, and I need you to stop that."

"What do you mean?"

"I've attempted the ceremony once already, on my lackey Zayne." Kaser tutted. "It went horribly wrong; he was alive but not human. He had no soul; he could not be controlled. It's better now he is dead."

That put Zayne's behavior into perspective, like when he broke Dayton's spine. He hadn't been fighting a fair game but fought dirty. Yet he'd been willing to talk to Luka and supply him information, until Luka killed him. Looking back, it was almost like he wanted to be killed, to be freed from whatever Kaser had done.

"What can I do to stop that?"

"I need you to protect him," Kaser said, as if it were obvious. "While I perform the ceremony. The ceremony only works with willing participants since it dabbles with the darkest of magic."

He wants her, and he will get her, but she must be willing to go to him. Zayne's words echoed back to me. It didn't matter how unwilling I was to participate in this because I willingly came with Kaser here. Even Kaser spelled it out to me: *I cannot take you unless you say yes.* To call myself foolish now would be in vain, but I felt like a damn fool.

Kaser grabbed a jar from behind him on a table with other various jars, some steaming and others oozing liquid. Glinting in the center was the Artifact. I averted my gaze as Kaser poured a dark, ashy substance in a large circle, the scent burning my nostrils. Kaser snapped his fingers, and Derek suddenly appeared, gagged and bound, his eyes wild. The markings on his bare chest glowed, and my stomach sank.

"I guess it's time to rip the Band-Aid off and tell you that, despite your efforts, Derek is going to die tonight." Kaser grinned. "It was a valiant effort, though, I assure you. A life for a life, a soul for a soul—all that fun stuff."

My mind stilled. I tried to catch Derek's attention, but his focus jumped across the room, back and forth like he watched a ping pong match. His trauma was transparent, and it killed me knowing what he must have gone through. When Kaser turned his back to me, I glanced around, searching for something to use against him. The sword glinted on the table beside me.

Two long howls erupted in the darkness. Kaser cursed and jumped in front of me, shielding me from what was happening. He chanted under his breath, and I watched as Fenrir appeared out of thin air and charged toward the woods. He spoke lowly, then Shetani appeared. She joined him on the stage. Right away, I noticed a stark difference in her demeanor. Her eyes darted, big and round; she lacked that usual sureness, the wildness in her gone.

"We caught another one," she said lowly, bowing her head. "I assume he came to rescue the girl."

"And what of Lukas Bakar?" Kaser demanded through gritted teeth.

"We're working on dispatching him, but he is hard to catch." Shetani stared at the ground as she spoke.

"An army of Fenrir and my two most lethal assassins cannot take down one werewolf?" Kaser hissed in fury. "Do you hear how that sounds?"

"I know," Shetani agreed. "It–it's not a good look."

"Begone from my sight!" Kaser shouted. "Find me Lukas and prove yourself worthy like Kato has, you pathetic, insolent girl."

Shetani nodded and scampered off the stage. I almost felt bad for her but then remembered everything she'd done.

Two Fenrir bustled in dragging someone between them. As they drew closer, I identified the figure. Julian. My heart tugged at seeing another of my friends here. His green eyes were alert and he grinned, looking between

Kaser and the sarcophagus. His hands were bound behind him, but he forced himself to stand. Dried blood caked the edge of his face and trickled down his arms. He cut me the quickest of glances.

"*I'm getting you both out.*"

"Leave, both of you." Kaser threw a hand up, dismissing the Fenrir. "I want to speak to the intruder. Who are you?" Kaser demanded, stepping closer to Julian.

"C'mon, now." Julian bopped around with a lazy grin. "You know who I am, just imagine me now except covered in lacerations and blood."

Kaser's gaze narrowed. "Julian?"

"*Move toward the body,*" Julian said into my mind, while aloud, he said, "Past the lacerations and blood, I was always quite handsome."

Kaser cast a questioning look between Julian and Derek, then drew his dagger, pressing the tip under Julian's chin and forcing his gaze up. Kaser averted his eyes from Derek. His mind worked, piecing together information as it was presented to him. Before he said anything, Julian spoke again.

"*Showtime.*"

Julian erupted into shadows. A high-pitched ringing sound tore through the forest, and I nearly fell over from its intensity. Kaser gaped, stumbling back as he fought against an unseen force, the shadows twisting around him. I prayed my face didn't reveal my confusion.

"Raw magic!" Kaser roared.

His eyes turned a stark white as he flapped his arms. His lips parted, but the howling chaos didn't allow me to hear it. It was like being sucked into a wind tunnel, and the growing darkness that was Julian seemed to waver and blanch before a deafening silence swallowed the forest. The darkness whirled and spun, tunneling into the amulet around Kaser's neck until not an inkling was left of it. Julian manifested atop the sarcophagus, panting hard as his magic depleted. He looked at me, entirely void of his usual armor of jewelry and multi-colored hair. His green eyes glowed, and I pressed a hand to my mouth to keep from gasping.

"Nice trick, boy. I thought you were tapped out," Kaser crooned, reaching forward and yanking Julian away.

"What did you do to me?" Julian asked, clutching his chest.

I looked to the circle where Derek had been, but he was gone.

"Don't worry, it will come back. It might take a while to wholly replenish your powers," said Kaser. "Raw magic is a specialty of mine. I understand its craft and how to utilize it. I can take your magic, even if it is not my own. You haven't touched your magic in years; you can't control it. It was a sloppy attempt to face me with it."

"Can't blame a guy for trying."

With a snap of his fingers, Kaser summoned thick, silver chains to wrap around Julian, binding him to the podium. He bucked and protested, but Kaser paid him no mind as he turned back to face me. Grasping my arm, Kaser yanked me forward and forced my hand on the dead body. I flinched. Vomit churned in me from the gooey-like texture of the skin and the rubbery feel of bone beneath.

"No more distractions. This is happening *now*," Kaser snarled.

He began to chant, as if understanding the press for time. I didn't recognize the language. Cool water suddenly spun like a whirlpool around the unmoving body. He wanted me to protect the corpse, yet I had no idea where to start. Protecting someone you cared about felt worlds different than protecting a dead body. The body trembled and quaked within the water, and the sarcophagus cracked. Kaser spoke rapidly behind me while the amulet pulsed at his throat.

"I don't know what you want me to do! He's dead. I can't help him!" I screamed over the rush of water as the wind beat against us.

Kaser's eyes came alive, a fiery, burning red. Many things were still a mystery to me about this man, but he clearly had the wherewithal to overpower me with his strength. He directed his waves of fury at me and shook me by my shoulder.

"I'm not asking you to do this. I'm telling you!"

He shoved me closer to the sarcophagus, and I nearly fell into it. Dayton bellowed distantly, and my heart squeezed at the ache in his voice. A ripple of power echoed through my body, and I shuddered as my wolf's protective nature poked its head out while a less familiar power stirred within. Heat shot down my arms and plummeted from my hands. My shock wavered when the casket ceased shaking.

"Derek!" Kaser yelled. "Come fourth and offer your magic as a sacrifice!"

Several moments passed before Kaser turned back to where Derek should be. All sounds stopped; the wind ceased. Kaser roared, moving to the circle; he was met with a grinning Julian, whose bare chest had none of the symbols Derek's had. Instead, carved on his chest was a neat and simple inscription.

Fuck you.

A pile of bloodied chains lay beside Julian, and in any other circumstance, I might have laughed. Kaser circled Julian, furious, and tried to kick him. Julian lurched and narrowly avoided the hit, grinning as he backed up, angling himself in front of me.

"You didn't pay attention to what I did," Julian said, boastfully. "I may have a shaky control over my magic, but I know how to use it. Dante ensured that."

"Where is Derek?" Kaser demanded, stepping closer to him.

"Safe and away from you," Julian said. "It was easy to show my hand with my magic and let you take it. Using the raw magic he bore was an integral part of the spell to open the threshold between worlds. That's what that inscription was on his chest. So, letting you deplete me of my magic after I got him out was easy."

"Why do you care about the boy?" Kaser asked, seeming genuinely curious.

"Because Derek is my brother."

I gasped, yet I had no time to dwell on it as Kaser's hand moved toward the sword. Instincts lurched me forward and I grappled at Kaser's neck, fingers clasping over his amulet. The blade twisted sloppily in his grip as I yanked the amulet free from his throat. Julian caught it, holding it tightly, and I threw myself off Kaser and stood beside Julian.

Kaser froze, the sword clattering to the ground. No one dared to move for it, but Kaser held my gaze, unwavering.

"Protector or not, you are Lukas Bakar's little sister through and through." Kaser spat.

The wolf came alive inside of me as I stood before this human man; my anger raged at all he'd done to torture me and my friends, all leading to this moment. I fell forward onto all fours, feeling my body writhe and grow in size.

Looking Kaser dead in the eyes, I spoke with relentless fury. "My name is Maris Bakar. I'm a werewolf, and I'm more than my brother's sister."

Chapter 38

The ground shook, and the podium cracked beneath us. I fell forward, my massive paws splaying out to steady me. I had shifted into my wolf's form as if on pure nerve alone. Everything happened quickly, yet I knew what needed to be done.

Kaser bolted for the sarcophagus like he wanted to cocoon it with power before realizing he'd lost his amulet.

Julian held it up, then nodded at me. Together, we jumped. My hind legs pressed against the rock's surface as it tumbled, yet I leapt off it. My landing was far from graceful; I rolled along the ground before gathering my footing. For the first time, I truly felt like a werewolf.

Kaser stared at me, eyes furious. The sarcophagus crashed to the ground and shattered, the water from it billowing out in a flood. The body broke into pieces from the impact, and my stomach lurched at the dismembered limbs floating away on the stream. Kaser bellowed at the sight, and I almost felt bad for him; complicated relationship or not, it was his father.

But here I was, and here Kaser was, no magic and no defenses. I should kill him, I knew. It would be easy. One quick, well-placed blow to save everyone a lot of grief. It's what Luka would do, and Dayton. Neither would question it. As Kaser looked at me, he gave a hollow laugh, reading my hesitation.

"Give me the amulet," Kaser demanded.

Julian snorted. "A stellar idea."

Withdrawing a knife from his side, Kaser darted to where Dayton hung in the tree. Without warning, he stabbed Dayton's shoulder. At Dayton's scream, I lurched forward with a growl, but Kaser whirled, positioning the knife at Dayton's throat. I whined, leaning back on my haunches and readying to lunge. A stirring gathered inside me, desperate to reach for Dayton, yet death lingered so close to him. I couldn't intervene. Not yet.

"Don't give it to him," Dayton said, his voice hoarse.

Julian stepped forward, holding the amulet out in a gesture of goodwill.

"Let him loose, and you can have the amulet," he said, raising his other hand.

I growled my protest, my lips curled. I waited for an opening to lunge. Dayton's eyes were wide and desperate, fixed on Julian in a silent plea.

"The amulet first," Kaser countered.

"Dayton is more willing to die than you realize," Julian said. "If you kill him, and the amulet stays away from you, it will protect Maris. He is oath bound to protect her."

"He will kill me the moment he's freed," Kaser said.

"Then I guess we'd all be lucky," Dayton grumbled.

Beyond the forest, the trees began to quake. Red eyes littered in the distance, and I immediately whiffed the stench of rotten eggs. The hairs on my nape stood up as the distance figures appeared, forming a synchronized march of Fenrir spilling from the woods. At first, it seemed like no more than a dozen, but the trickle of them began flooding the grounds. An army of Fenrir charged toward us, yet leading them was a familiar blue-eyed wolf with onyx fur as dark as night. Luka materialized as the army drew closer. Kaser blanched.

Blood covered Luka, dripping down his temples and chin. He looked crazed and grinned savagely at Kaser. "It seems there has been a shift in allegiance with your Fenrir."

"What did you do?" Kaser hissed, scrambling away from Dayton while frantically looking at his Fenrir.

Luka took a clawed hand and cut Dayton's bindings, who hit the ground with a thud, immediately shifting into his wolf skin. I whimpered, desperate to get closer to him, to be assured he was okay. Dayton stayed behind Luka, waiting to attack. Dozens of Fenrir all stood, awaiting orders.

"Game over, Kaser," Luka taunted. "You lose."

"*No!*"

Kaser threw his dagger at Luka, who swatted it away like it was no more than an annoying fly. Then chaos erupted. Kaser ran full speed at Julian, yet I lost sight of them as Fenrir descended on us. Dayton gunned for me until a Fenrir tackled him to the ground. Half of the Fenrir seemed poised to strike Kaser, the other half going after us or each other.

Their behavior was strange, and while Luka might have been able to control them, it seemed they were too wild to truly be tamed. If Luka gave an order, they followed it without any notions as to who specifically they must execute.

I tried to fight my way toward Dayton. It was easier to navigate as a wolf; I automatically knew where to move, jumping and ducking to avoid blows. Luka shouted orders, trying to regain semblance amidst this nonsense. I searched for Kaser in the crowd, but it was like looking for a needle in a haystack. I didn't want to turn and run, I wanted to help and fight, but there seemed no way to.

I turned around to be faced with a white wolf that, despite its jaunty strut of arrogance, appeared afraid. Shetani and I stared at one another for a long moment. I glanced at the growing battle and back to where safety awaited. Her eyes were large and pleading, as if begging me to let her go. Let her go and risk her doing more terrible things in Kaser's name? For Kaser's cause? Or kill her, and carry that weight with me? I backed away; there was no right answer, and as she took off, I wondered if I just dodged a bullet or screwed us all in the long run.

When I turned again, I was met with a Fenrir, bigger than myself. It snarled, blood glistening between its teeth. It moved at unnatural speeds, ripping out a good chunk of my fur. I roared and kicked out at it, but a blow to my head had me spinning and seeing stars. I tried to keep moving.

A wolf charged at me with dark fur and glowing golden eyes. Dayton. He took on the Fenrir without hesitation, each strike poised to kill. When the Fenrir was dead, he turned to face me.

I felt myself shifting back into my human skin in Dayton's comforting presence. He turned back into himself, too, despite the rage that consumed him. His right eye had swelled to twice its normal size, and the cut on his face was raised and puffy. Worry stirred in me that I ignored, for now.

"What's going on with the Fenrir?" I questioned.

"They only respond to simple commands. Luka can order them to attack, and they attack, but they can't differentiate between who is good and evil. Luka wanted them killed anyway, so here we are," Dayton explained.

He struck out with a clawed hand, neatly cutting the throat of an approaching Fenrir.

"There's an amulet Kaser uses to control his magic," I told him. "Julian has it, but we must keep it away from Kaser. He's powerless without it."

Dayton nodded. "Stay behind me and let's get to Julian."

Dayton and I moved in sync, back-to-back through the Fenrir. I struck, never missing a beat, while Dayton delivered death blow after death blow. Unmatched strength and precision sang through my veins as I finally understood the dance of battle. They came at us in solid forces, but somehow, we were stronger. Fighting with Dayton felt as natural as breathing, and I wondered why I hadn't done this the whole time.

"*Enough,*" Luka's thunderous voice called.

Everything stopped, and the remaining Fenrir fell back. Laying on the ground yards away, unmoving, was Julian. Kaser sat panting atop him, amulet in hand. Luka charged, but Kaser only grinned, tossing the amulet in the air. Rage crossed Luka's face as he turned back to catch it, yet I understood Kaser's intent as a sword now glittered in his hand. Not just a sword: the Infinite Artifact.

In a blur of motion, Kaser charged toward Luka sword in hand. Luka didn't see it coming, too focused on the amulet. I yelled out, rushing to stand between them, but from behind, I heard Dayton's roar of warning.

"Mare, no!"

Dayton was faster and threw himself between them, crashing into Kaser onto the ground. They both leapt up, Kaser snarling and jolting backward. His eyes narrowed on Dayton, sword still clutched in his hand. Dayton roared as the sword headed directly for his chest and a guttural scream tore free from my throat. I ran forward as the swords tip touched Dayton's chest and parried Kaser backwards with a blast of white light.

Dayton flew backward as well, and he reached for my hand, and when he touched me, a jolt like electricity shot through me. I flicked my gaze to meet his own and the tattoo brandishing the bond between us pulsed to life, white light blasting from us. Everything came to an aching still of deafening silence as I beheld Dayton. My soul stirred, calling to him and careening me closer. I didn't understand why, but it all made sense. My tattoo heated, intertwining with his, and I watched the patterns seamlessly twist and shift. Heat brandished my back and leg, crawling up my neck and face. My mouth parted slightly, not understanding, but I turned at Dayton's wide-eye expression.

The light simmered and we were both on our knees, staring at one another. Dayton slumped forward, and I nestled his head in the crook of my shoulder, grasping his trembling body. He gasped for breath while I knotted my fingers in his hair to hold him. I needed to hold him. When he glanced up at me it was with a bloodstained and shocked face.

"Mare," he rasped. "What just happened?"

"You were almost stabbed," I sobbed.

Dayton gulped. He appeared ashen, though I suspected it had more to do with being strung up and tortured by Kaser than his near-death experience. "You scared me. I thought he was going to kill you or Luka."

Before I could say more, Kaser stirred and rose to stand. Luka homed in on Kaser, who clutched the amulet. Ashy red smoke settled over the ground where he stood. He gripped the sword with the Moonstone glittering at its hilt. He chanted under his breath and smoke swirled around him, billowing like ships in the harbor.

"He's getting away!" Luka rasped as shadows swallowed Kaser's feet.

His eyes narrowed, and his lips tilted upward as the smoke and shadows rose above him. A low rumbling chuckle came from his throat. I started toward him.

"Until we meet again, *Maris.*"

And with a snap of his fingers, Kaser disappeared.

I dropped to my knees, and Luka caught me.

"We have to leave! Now!" he yelled. "This place is fabricated by Kaser's magic and won't hold without him. We'll be stuck in limbo forever!"

My mind started to shut down, and my limbs felt heavy, as if my body were drained from all motor functions. Maybe it was the magic, but I couldn't think straight.

Falling into Luka, he scooped me up and ran. I stared up into the starry night as my eyelids grew heavy. Something Dayton told me came back to me, and I smiled. *Ad astra per aspera.*

To the stars through difficulties.

Epilogue

Three days passed since everything went down with Kaser. I awoke yesterday evening and hadn't slept since. Most of my time with Kaser was a blur, unprocessed as I slowly sifted through it all. I was still at a loss for most of it. Derek was back, and it was what I always wanted, yet I couldn't shake the feeling of dread.

He'd been out of it since we got back. He remained in the infirmary in a mostly sleeping state, moving every so often and muttering incoherently beneath his breath. His body was thin, and while his wounds had mostly healed, scars traced all of him. Some looked no bigger than a cat scratch, while others were long and gruesome and jagged. Luka affirmed that while physically Derek was okay, his mind was not; it was like his mind had voluntarily shut down to process his trauma.

Julian, who sustained injuries that had since healed, only checked in on Derek once. That may have been the wildest thing to come of all this, that Julian was Derek's long-lost brother. In hindsight, it was obvious from their similarities alone. While Julian usually had various colors in his hair and multiple face piercings, they could have been twins when you stripped all of that away: the white, blonde hair, pine green eyes, and ghostly complexions. Even beyond their outward appearances, they both had an uncanny way of making you feel at ease amidst the worst scenarios;

they were both easy people to get along with. I asked Julian if he knew who Derek was to him the whole time we'd met. He said he suspected it the first night he saw Derek all those weeks ago at the Temple, yet he had never wanted to know more about him, and his short, clipped answers made me drop the subject.

Evening air blew through the open window of the infirmary. I shivered but made no move to get up. I tucked my knees to my chest and clutched Derek's hand. Since I'd woken up, I hadn't left his side. Luka understood; he chose to sit next to me in silence. It was a strange sort of comfort to have him here. He brought food and coffee, but I only touched the coffee. I couldn't stomach much, but I craved the buzz of caffeine. Every time I closed my eyes, I saw the horrors of what I endured.

Suddenly, I stood and crossed the room, slamming the window shut. I paced and ignored my rapidly increasing heartbeat thumping against my breastbone. I moved back to the chair and forced myself still, yet I continued bouncing my leg. Tilting my head up, I stared into the lamp light until it hurt.

I almost stood again when Derek's hand shot out to catch my own. A calm washed over me, my anxiety lessening as I peered down at Derek, who lay on the bed, his eyes closed. He fiercely grasped my hand and, too afraid to move, I simply watched him. I jumped as a hand rested on my shoulder, and I looked up to find Luka, watching Derek intensely. He shot upward, and I stumbled back into my brother. Luka steadied me, then stepped around me. Derek's eyes were wild for a second before they focused on Luka. He moaned, pinching the bridge of his nose.

"Jesus, fuck," Derek grumbled. "You're feeling a variety of things, Luka."

"Derek," Luka said, adopting the tone of his Alpha. "Are you okay?"

"Where am I?" Derek pressed his hands to his ears and brought his knees to his chest. "Ah, fuck me!"

"Derek, you are at the Temp—" I began, but Derek's wild eye gaze struck me.

"—The dreams, the dreams, I was sending them." Derek said, shaking. "He was making me; I didn't have a choice. I know they were torturing you, and it was all my fault. I don't understand this magic."

I blinked slowly, stunned into silence. I hadn't given much thought about the dreams until now, yet "sending" them felt like an odd way to describe it.

Before I could dwell on it further, the door flew open and Julian clamored in. His hair was void of color, and his pine green eyes were furious. He gripped a bottle of vodka in one hand and a pack of menthol cigarettes in the other. He tossed them at Derek. Luka moved from the bedside while Julian loomed over him. Looking up, Derek's eyes were large and confused as he took in the sight of his brother.

"Drink this. It helps," said Julian bitterly. "The taste takes some getting used to; I won't lie to you."

Derek held the bottle in his hand, and it shook. His eyes met Julian's as understanding flowed through him. "Julian?"

Julian flinched and pursed his lips. "Don't say my name with so much hope. You're never going to see me again, understand?"

Derek flinched; it was the worst thing Julian could have said. Maybe he knew that, hence why he said it with such conviction. As long as I'd known Derek, he wanted to find out what happened to his father and brother. While I had no idea about his father, here was Derek's brother who wanted nothing to do with him. It made no sense. Julian said his family abandoned him to Dante, yet Derek was too young to have done that. I didn't know what to think.

"I found you. That first night I came here, I was looking for you." Derek gaped. "And you saved me from being sacrificed by Kaser."

"I don't want you dead, but I don't want you in my life." Julian started toward the door and paused. "Just do us both a favor and forget about me."

He left without another word. I glanced at Luka, who shrugged. Derek launched the bottle, which shattered against the wall. Leaping from the bed, he started toward the door, but Luka restrained him.

"Let him go, Derek," Luka said. "Give it time."

"I've searched for him for years!" Derek protested. "I can't just forget about him!"

My heart sank, but he wasn't thinking clearly. Derek clutched his head as if something struck him; he cried out, his knees buckling and knocking him to the ground. Luka pulled him up and onto the bed despite his thrashing.

"What's happening to him?" I asked.

"Hold his arms down!" Luka growled, struggling to restrain him.

I did as he said and pushed against Derek. He was strong as a bull, and my efforts felt fruitless against his strength. Luka leaned over him and yanked Derek's head up to expose his neck. Luka loosed his claws and grabbed the back of Derek's neck, and instantly, he relaxed.

"It's whatever Kaser did to him," panted Luka. "The magic is overwhelming him and he can't control it."

"Is he okay?" I asked, yet the question joined the void of silence. Of course he wasn't okay; Derek was far from it. He looked almost peaceful now, and I shut my eyes, laying down against the bed.

Luka dragged a hand down his face and rocked back on his heels. "I can't answer that, Maris. Derek carries mental scars that neither one of us can begin to understand."

Kaser's words spoke to me in a haunting whisper. *He will come out of this alive, whether or not he wants that fate is up to him.*

Luka saw my face and shook his head, moving toward me and steering me from the infirmary. Too stunned to protest, I moved robotically with him.

"We can find a way to help him," Luka said. "I—I'll ask Julian about it or Dayton. Hell, if Julian won't talk, I'll break into the Council's Archives and steal his file to see how they dealt with him."

My mind still raced and I asked, "What Derek said about the dreams, do you know what he meant?"

"It's the raw magic. I don't understand it, really, only at a surface level. If anyone knows about it, it might be Julian, but he hasn't been forthcoming. I can let it go for the time being, but he needs to talk eventually."

I felt a headache forming. I inhaled and readied myself for the next words. "Kaser told me I was a protector," I said.

"I knew," Luka admitted, and at my stunned expression, he went on. "I had my suspicions, I mean. I should have told you that. I thought not telling you would protect you, but I can see that was wrong."

"Do you know what it means?"

Luka paused, considering his words. He pinched the bridge of his nose. "Yes. I don't want to get into it yet. I want to tell you and explain it to you, but not yet."

"Okay, fine. That's fair."

Luka glanced down at me, studying my arm. "Your tattoo has grown."

I examined the tattoo, thinking it was strange to see the tattoo had shifted on its own accord. Not only had it grown, but the pattern had changed. "Do you know why?"

Luka glanced away, appearing somber. "I don't know much of the Consort bond, but I know its force brought you and Dayton unnaturally close to one another."

I stiffened upon hearing Dayton's name. I hadn't seen him since all hell broke loose. After Kyler and Neville reported what happened to the Council, he was forced into an emergency meeting and hasn't returned since. I was confused and wanted to speak to him, to try to understand what was going on between us. What confused me most was when I saw through Dayton's eyes, trapped in his mind. I couldn't wrap my head around why or how that was possible, and I was afraid of what it meant.

"I don't understand it either," I admitted. "It scares me."

Before Luka responded, Derek shouted for him.

"Stay back," Luka said, his gaze and tone all Alpha.

Luka moved like shadows between spaces as I watched him return to the infirmary with a lump of anxiety in my throat. Derek screamed behind the door, unhinged bellows of pure agony. I moved down the hallway, not paying attention to where I went. I stumbled up the stairs and nearly tripped, catching myself before plummeting. I needed fresh air, if only momentarily.

"Leaving so soon?" asked a familiar voice.

I turned to face Neville, who lay sprawled across the red couch in the living room. Neville had aided Kyler in reporting Kaser's return to the Council. Somehow, he never seemed involved in the action. Neville knew much yet revealed very little.

"When did you get back?" I asked.

"Just now. Truthfully, I didn't want to come back. The meetings with the Council were a bitch; I can't imagine Dayton had a good time, either," Neville grumbled. "Well, Lukas asked me to come back, and here I am, offering my company to anyone who seeks it."

"Dayton's back?" I asked, hopeful.

"Of course that'd be what you got out of what I said." Neville narrowed his gaze. "He's just getting back, probably checking his crappy wards."

I turned to leave, but Neville called out again.

"Maris, wait."

I stopped and turned back to face him. "Yes?"

"You did well against Kaser," Neville said. "But it isn't the end. This is all the beginning of something bigger."

With that, he left the room, and I stared after him, bewildered and half wondering if I had hallucinated our whole encounter. I shook my head and started toward the front door.

"Mare?"

My shoulders sagged in relief as Dayton approached me from behind. Sensing his nearness stirred a calm in me, and my breathing slowed as the lump of emotions relaxed my heart. His hand clutched my shoulder, and he gave it a small squeeze.

I let out a pent-up breath, tilting my head to look into the light. "Dayton."

Derek wailed, and it rang through the Temple. I stiffened at Dayton's grunt of disapproval. He reached in front of me and propped open the front door. Placing a hand on the small of my back, he gently guided me out, leading me down the staircase. We didn't walk far before he halted and released me. I turned to look at him, but his back was to me.

"Do they know what is wrong with him?" Dayton asked.

I blinked a few times to process what he had said. "I don't know what Kaser did to Derek, but whatever it is, it involves raw magic."

"I hope it isn't like what Julian went through or else I fear he may never recover," Dayton said. "I don't mean to sound crass."

I laughed aloud. "When have you ever cared about having a filter?"

"You don't miss much, do you?" Dayton chuckled dryly.

I watched the tightness in his shoulders and how his shirt clung to him with sweat. He wore all fighting leathers, his weapons belt clipped around his waist. This was the first we had talked since we argued about me giving myself up to Kaser. It felt like a lifetime ago, but I still remembered what he said and how it made me feel.

You mean everything to me.

"Dayton, are you alright?" I asked, recalling Kaser's torture.

He tensed at the question, his shoulders drawn back. "That's a loaded question."

"Don't wiggle around it. We're past that."

Dayton didn't say anything yet stood still. I stepped closer to him, watching the steady rise and fall of his chest. Leaves crunched beneath me as I drew closer to him. His arms were crossed over his chest, and his usual scowl was ever-present. He looked away from me, and I knew why. Cautiously, I placed my hand on his arm, and he tensed, glancing at my hand and then me.

My heart swelled in anger, rising within me. A long-jagged scar ran the length of Dayton's face, raised and puffy, as it was too fresh to have faded. The anger in Dayton's eyes mirrored my own, and I pressed my mouth into a thin line, feeling the rise of heat beneath my palm. He closed his eyes and let me rest my palm over his face. Slowly, he shook his head.

"It won't heal." His voice was rough. "The silver infected it. The Council held me in a holding cell before the meeting, and by the time I got to an infirmary, the scar already set."

I blinked up at him. "I'm sorry. I should've done more for you."

He gritted his teeth. "Don't be sorry. It's not anyone's fault except my own." When he looked at me, his eyes were dark. "I'm not ashamed that I have a scar. I'm more ashamed of the fact that I failed you, that I allowed you to be in such a dangerous position."

"You didn't, Dayton. I was the one who willingly went with Kaser." I felt a fight brewing between us.

"It's my job to protect you, Mare!" he bellowed, eyes wild. "Instead, you were hurt, and I let myself become weak."

"How?"

"I let myself feel things for you that I shouldn't," he admitted. "When it comes to you, I let my emotions cloud my judgment. You'd think it would come hand and hand, protecting you and caring for you, but somehow, I struggle to see past the caring."

Heat rushed to my face in realization. Dayton was a dangerous person to care about, a ticking timebomb, and no one knew when he would explode, yet a part of me yearned to cross that line with him.

"Dayton, I—"

"Wait, before you say anything," Dayton said, reading my expression. "I won't jeopardize the oath I swore to you because of my feelings. My feelings are a direct result of my recklessness, and I won't let it compromise your safety anymore."

Startled by his words, I blinked, taking a minute to compose myself. "Wait, what?"

"I told you I'd be your Consort, but I let it go past that. You no longer need to worry about me being more than just that."

"What about what I want? What I feel?" I asked. "Do I get any say? Or did you already make up your mind?"

"What do you want?"

"You, Dayton," I admitted, gulping as his expression turned sour. Admitting it freely without regret was like a lifted weight from my shoulders. I exhaled, watching a muscle jump in his jaw.

"You're lying," he insisted. "You're too good for that."

"Is that what this is really about?" I asked him sadly. Dayton was harder on himself than most, but for him to think he wasn't good enough for me hurt me more than I could put into words.

"*Mare*," he hissed, pulling at his hair. "I'm trying to protect you from me. I'm toxic to everything I touch. If I let this—*us*—go further than it already has, I'll end up pushing you away, and you'll tire of me and you'll walk away yourself. It would jeopardize the oath I swore to protect to you, and I can't allow that. Can't you see?"

Before I could answer, a loud horn echoed around us. Dayton was on instant alert, leaping in front of me. He didn't have his weapons drawn, but the tension in his stance had me on edge. The horn sounded again, and Dayton whipped around, his golden eyes aglow.

"What is it?" I asked, feeling my own defenses rise.

"The Council voted." Dayton shook his head.

"Voted?" I questioned. "What do you mean?"

"They sent me back so they could cast their vote on the situation." Dayton scowled as another horn sounded. "I couldn't leave Luka out of the involvement this time—the Bestial really. They wanted someone to blame for everything that happened."

"What do you mean?" I asked, not following.

"Luka needs to get out of here," said Dayton, starting toward the Temple.

"Why?"

"The Bestial is still the most wanted criminal amongst our kind, remember?"

"They're here to arrest him?" I questioned. Another horn sounded; this time, it was much nearer.

"No, Mare," Dayton said flatly, turning to look back at me. "They're here to kill him."

Acknowledgments

I'd like to first thank Missy, one of my earliest beta readers who read an unpolished, rough version of this book, and was still very kind about it. You truly helped shape this book into a version that I was finally able to have the confidence to share with the world. Though that draft of the book is a distant memory, the final version wouldn't be here if there hadn't been you.

I'd like to extend this gratitude to the rest of my lovely beta readers, Christyn and Lydia, whose blunt honesty and constructive feedback helped make this once manuscript a book I'm truly proud of.

Eden, my editor who took this book apart and stitched it back together—I cannot thank you enough. You understood my characters from the start and helped reshape them into the best versions of themselves. Your help in making this book what it is now was without a doubt the best choice I've ever made. Thank you, thank you, thank you.

Megan, your fine-combed attention to detail truly leveled this book—your eagle eye for proofreading instilled much confidence in me, and I cannot wait to be able to work with you again. Thank you for also crafting a lovely and concise blurb for this book—many writers would probably agree that writing a blurb is one of the hardest parts so your efforts and help in creating it do not go unnoticed.

Mariska—thank you for bringing my characters to life in the form of the cover. I truly am forever obsessed and love it. Kayla, you as well get a nod of acknowledgment. Thank you for reaching out and creating character art for one of my favorite scenes in this book. Seeing it brought to life has given me insurmountable joy.

Brittany, thank you for creating the formatting of this book—your work is incredible and invaluable to making a book a book.

To my cat Jasmine, who has long since passed, thank you for keeping me company in the earliest days of this books creation—that manuscript will never see the light of day, but I'll forever hold the immaculate light of joy that you gave me from the comfort of your presence.

To all the lovely readers I have found, and will continue to find—this story is no longer mine to have so I've entrusted it to you. If reading it gave you even an ounce of joy, or brought a smile to your face, all of the years spent writing it were worth it. Thank you for taking a chance, and thank you for reading.

9 798990 390201